ASSIGNMENT: CASABLANCA

A WWII Naval Intelligence Novel
Tony Romella USN WWII Series, Book 4

Peter J. Azzole

ISBN: 9781694696069

ALSO BY PETER J. AZZOLE

HELL TO PAY
A Korean Conflict Novel
A Navy Pilot's Life-changing Adventure

ASSIGNMENT: BLETCHLEY
A WWII Novel of Navy Intelligence, Spies
(Tony Romella, USN, WWII Assignments series Book 1)

ASSIGNMENT: LONDON
A WWII Novel of Naval Intelligence and Spies
(Tony Romella, USN, WWII Assignments series Book 2)

ASSIGNMENT: NORWAY
A WWII Novel of Naval Intelligence and Spies
(Tony Romella, USN, WWII Assignments series Book 3)

ASSIGNMENT: CASABLANCA

DEDICATION

To Gramps, Peter Joseph Romella (1889-1976)

ACKNOWLEDGEMENTS

I am sincerely indebted to Nancy Azzole, Sharon Friedheim, James Green, Kathy Morrison, and Shirley Wang for their detailed editorial reviews and insightful critiques of the draft manuscript.

My appreciation is extended to the staff of the Office of the Historian, U.S. Department of State, for information regarding period diplomatic facilities.

Special thanks is due Gus" Gustafson, Cryptologic Command Display, Corry Station, Pensacola, FL for period information and images; and to Stuart H. Woodward, Esq., of Ticknall, England, for period information and images of Ticknall.

Front cover photo credit: Postcards of the beginning of the xxth century [Public domain] (Wikimedia Commons)

Back cover photo credit: Shigemitsu Fukao [Public domain] (Wikimedia Commons)

Table of Contents

PREFACE

The Tony Romella WWII Assignment novel series is intended to inform and entertain as it transports the reader into the hectic world of intelligence operations, within the context of historic events.

Liberty has been taken in the creation of certain events and activities.

Names, biographic information, descriptions, personalities and activities of most active characters are fictitious, and resemblance to actual persons is purely coincidental.

This is the fourth novel of a series. Reading the preceding novels of the series, in order, would give the reader greater knowledge of the characters and an understanding of pertinent events that have shaped their lives leading up to this point.

PROLOGUE

On the morning of Friday, December 25, 1942. Commander Tony Romella, USN, and his wife, First Officer Petra Romella, WRNS, were celebrating their second Christmas morning together. Breakfast was finished, gifts were exchanged, and crackers were popped. They discussed their afternoon matinee options in Piccadilly Square. Her choice was *The Little Foxes,* starring Bette Davis. They decided to occupy the wait time for the cinema matinee by getting warm and cozy in their four-poster. Just then, the phone rang.

"Damn it!" he exclaimed and went to the desk to answer it. "Commander Romella... Merry Christmas to you, too, Bill... I understand... No apology necessary... Aye, aye, sir." He hung up and turned to Petra. "That was Captain Taylor. Something urgent. He wants me in his office immediately. I'm so sorry, honey."

MINI-BIOGRAPHIES
Primary Characters Brought Forward

ANTHONY "TONY" ROMELLA
Commander, U.S. Navy
- Cryptology specialist
- Current assignment: Naval Attaché, London
- Married to First Officer Petra Romella, WRNS

PETRA ALICE GRAHAM WILKINSON ROMELLA
First Officer, WRNS (Women's Royal Navy Service)
- Current assignment: MI5, Government Liaison Branch
- Married to Commander Anthony Romella, USN

WILLIAM TAYLOR
Captain, U.S. Navy
- Cryptology specialist
- Current assignment: Defense Attaché, London

ROY HALL
Lieutenant Junior Grade, U.S. Navy
- Cryptology specialist
- Former Chief Radioman

MIKE NELSON
Civilian Employee, U.S. Government
- Current assignment: OSS Operations Chief, U.S. Embassy, London

OWEN EDWARD LANGSDALE
Civilian Employee, British Government
- Current assignment: Special Operations Executive, S02 Section Head, London

1 – Duty Calls

11:30 a.m., Friday, Christmas Day, December 25, 1942
U.S. Embassy
1 Grosvenor Square, London, England

Commander Anthony Romella, USN, Naval Attaché London, was too excited to be able to get comfortable in the Embassy sedan. His boss, Captain William Taylor, USN, Defense Attaché, sent the sedan to The Dorchester Hotel to bring him back to the Embassy. He could not help but feel anticipation building each minute while enroute. It was not normal to be urgently summoned to the office on Christmas morning, despite being on-call. *I know one thing*, Tony thought, *Bill wouldn't do this without a damn good reason. Technically, I'm still on light duty, so it can't be another covert mission. So, what the hell could it be?* It was less than 15 minutes before the Embassy sedan turned left off of Grosvenor Street onto Grosvenor Square, the corner of which was where the U.S. Embassy was located. "Thank you, Corporal," Tony said to the driver when the sedan pulled up in front of the Embassy. The driver hustled around to open Tony's door and saluted. When the door swung open, chilly air rushed in, along with the smell of a rain-soaked sidewalk. Tony got out, returned the driver's salute, and also the rifle salutes from the two Marines at the Embassy door. He avoided the elevator, as usual, and quick paced up the steps to the level of the Attaché's offices.

"I'm surprised to see you here today, Sharon," Tony said to Sharon Freedman, Taylor's civilian service Administrative Officer, when he entered the outer office of the oak-paneled Defense Attaché's suite.

"Yes indeed, Commander, I got the call as well," Sharon responded with a smile. "Go on in, he's waiting for you."

"Get your ass in here," Taylor called out good-heartedly when Tony knocked on the half-open door.

1

"Good morning, sir," Tony greeted as he approached. "Well, I hope it's a good morning."

"A matter of perspective, Tony. Come have a seat," Taylor said, motioning at the chair by his desk with his left hand that was gripping a smoldering pipe.

When Tony got closer, the sweet, spicy aroma of Taylor's special blend of tobacco became strong. "Smells great, boss. What's going on?"

"Tony, I am sorry to pull you away from your Christmas day. Pass my apologies to your bride when you get back to The Dorchester this evening. Give her a call when we're done and let her know you're going to be a while."

"You called just in time. Another 15 minutes and I would have called the Duty Officer to tell him I was on my way to Piccadilly to watch a movie."

Taylor handed Tony a two page message, stamped Top Secret in red ink at the top and bottom and said, "Read this, then we'll talk."

The message was from OP-20-G, the organization code for the Washington, DC headquarters for Navy communications intelligence operations. It contained classified orders for him. He read both pages thoroughly and looked up at Taylor, grinning, "Temporary Additional Duty in Casablanca? Oh this should be easy, pardon my sarcasm."

Taylor nodded, "Should actually be a piece of TAD cake, Tony. Easy tasks. Wraps up in a few weeks. Quick and dirty."

Tony laughed, "Compared to my little trips to France and Norway, maybe so. But Bill, are they crazy taking FDR, Churchill and just about all the top U.S. and British generals and admirals there for a meeting? Only six weeks ago, the Operation TORCH assault just overwhelmed Casablanca's Vichy French Army and Navy and ran the Germans the hell out of there. Amazingly, the truce allowed the French military units to remain in place." Tony shook his head, "It's got to be full of German and pro-Axis sleepers and Vichy sympathizers."

Taylor's blue eyes drilled into Tony's, patiently letting him vent. A long puff on the pipe was followed by, "Are we done?"

"Aye, sir, it's my Italian blood," said Tony, hoping a smile would calm the impatience in Taylor's voice.

"Good. Further discussion about all that is not useful," Taylor said sternly. "I'll just say that several people in DC balked at Casablanca, but the President was adamant. Churchill agreed with him, too. The Allies have made their first occupation and they are making a statement to Hitler. Therefore, General Patton was told to find a conference facility and to secure the place. The OSS has been weeding out the bad guys. Short version, SYMBOL is firm."

"I saw a cryptic reference to a conference codenamed SYMBOL in a message recently, but I didn't know it was referring to this war strategy meeting of Allied leaders in Morocco. OK boss, what's the story behind the orders. I'm sure there is one."

"The information they gave us lacks the detail we'd like because this came on us fast. It will be a seat of your pants thing. You'll represent OP-20-G in an advisory role to the Chief of Naval Operations during the conference. From what I could read between the lines in other messages and a phone call, 20-G put together a draft communications intelligence support appendix for each of the operation plans they intend to discuss. But they can't spare anyone to travel down there to be on hand to answer questions. Commander Webber knows you well enough to know that he can depend on you. He asked if I could spare you."

Tony grinned, "I know what your answer was, go on."

"Well sure, Tony, I couldn't see you spending too much idle time in that nice office. This seemed like a great opportunity to demonstrate your imagination and prowess."

"Pardon me, Bill, while I put some stall mucking boots on. About this other task mentioned in Webber's message, the special intelligence communications support. Do you have the skinny on that?"

"All there is for you to know right now is in the other messages in this file folder here," Taylor said while sliding the folder across the desk to Tony. "I did get some relevant Eyes Only messages, some of which I can share with you verbally. But those in your folder have some details for you to digest. You can take a quick look now. But take them back to your office and get your thoughts together."

Tony opened the folder and started a fast scan of the messages.

Taylor sat forward, puffed his pipe and said, "I truly apologize for the short fuse on this. I had no idea about any of it until the duty officer called me last evening to come to the office for a phone conference from DC. It was Commander Webber in OP-20-G. He gave me a heads up on what was heading my way. They passed on as much unclassified info on this as they could and told me some SYMBOL messages would come in later with some details. They arrived a short while ago, and they're in that folder you have." Taylor referred to penciled items on a lined pad on his desk, "The conference will begin on January 14th and is planned to conclude on the 24th. But you're going down in two days to get the special communications capability squared away."

Taylor puffed his pipe while Tony completed his speed read of the Top Secret messages in the folder. Tony closed the folder and looked up at Taylor. They sat there smiling at each other for a moment. Neither wanting to make the next comment. Taylor puffed a smoke ring.

Tony broke the silence, "Well, it will damn sure be fascinating. A lot has been left for me to figure out. Including transportation."

"Roger that. But I do have your travel arrangements," Taylor said and referred to a message in another folder on the desk. "There's an Army Air Force C-47 VIP aircraft coming out of DC, arriving at RAF Biggin Hill tomorrow evening for an overnight. They picked Biggin Hill because it's not normally used for passengers. It's a fighter station, so no press people will be lurking the gates. There's going to be a courier onboard that has a package for you. It's Top Secret crypto key lists and OP-20-G's draft COMINT appendices. There will probably be a few others onboard. You're scheduled to depart Biggin Hill Sunday morning, 0800. It will be a direct flight to Casablanca. That's about all I have for you. Let me know if there's anything you think you'll need."

"Right off the top of my head, boss, I want to take Roy Hall along. I'll need an officer to courier materials back and forth from the communications center, wherever that might be. Also, he's had experience in the Pacific with setting up a site from scratch."

"Done," said Taylor with a sharp nod. "Providing there's a seat available on the C-47."

"Roger. Next thing. Reliable and prompt special intelligence comms for this level of people will be important, and we can't afford mistakes or confusion. I want to take two of the radiomen I took to Norway, to maintain a round-the-clock watch in the comm center, 12 on, 12 off. Specifically, Chief Radioman Hector Johnson and Radioman Hamill."

Taylor laughed, "You really think those Radiomen will give up their peaceful duty life at the MI6 intercept site in sleepy Knockholt, and the pubs and the local girls? You actually expect them to belly up to your bar again? That's a laugh, especially after what you put them through in Norway?"

"I'm sure of it. You don't know them like I do. I can trust them to perform 110 percent and keep the mission and information close to the chest. Those special skills we learned in Scotland might come in handy. Hell, we don't even know how many Radiomen Naval Operating Base Casablanca has onboard. Not to mention, none will be cleared for our level."

"I have no objection, but again, depends on available seats for them. They are still technically on loan to MI6 from the Ambassador. I'll take care of that with Ambassador Winant."

"And Bill, I'll be going down to the armory to draw weapons for us. I just can't imagine it's going to be like Central Park on a bright summer Saturday down there."

"I concur with that Tony."

"Any other background tidbits for me, boss?"

"I'm not sure if this will affect you, Tony, but I got the word this morning that French Admiral Darlan, Supreme Commander of the Vichy forces, was assassinated yesterday in Algiers, right in his headquarters building."

"They get the guy?" asked Tony.

"Affirmative. A young French royalist. The French really are divided right now. Passionately so."

"Oh, crap, that's sure to create some local turmoil. There will be a lot of competition and suspicion among the personalities loyal to French General Noguès and those of the late Admiral Darlan."

Taylor nodded in agreement. "Anything else on your shopping list?"

"Not at the moment. But I would like to go visit with Mike Nelson and see if he can give me the OSS skinny on Casablanca."

"What info are you looking for?" asked Taylor

"Things like, who they have down there, where they are located, and whatever he can share about that Moroccan snake pit. God only knows who I'll have to call upon to get things done. Knowing the current political and military climate would help."

Taylor was tapping his carved tiger head pipe bowl, upside down, in his amber glass ash tray, making a pleasant rhythmic clanking, while he contemplated. When the tobacco ashes were cleared from the bowl, he said, "You absolutely cannot, I repeat, not, tell Mike exactly why you're interested in Casablanca. He just can't know about SYMBOL. Otherwise, OK." He paused to collect some thoughts. "Look Tony, you have authority to operate carte blanche on this one. But use it wisely. It doesn't come without the responsibility for your actions. Anyway, come see me if you really need my horsepower for arrangements. Otherwise, just handle it. I'll pick you up at The Dorchester Hotel, Sunday morning at 0630. We can ride to Biggin Hill together to see you off to, uh, your conference in DC. That's your cover story, by the way. You can use that story with Petra or anyone else that's curious. There's a really tight lid on SYMBOL. It will be hard enough to keep this from the Germans. Hopefully, by the time they figure out SYMBOL's personalities and location, it will be too late for them to plan a bombing run or a major espionage mission."

"Roger that," Tony said emphatically. "Something like this just can't be kept from them very long. FDR and Churchill can hide their departures fairly easily, but as soon as they arrive in Casablanca, the clock will start ticking."

"Listen, Tony, why don't you bring Petra along for the ride to Biggin Hill to say good-bye if you like. Just make sure your men know the cover story and don't spill the beans."

Tony grinned, "Great, thanks. Will do. She will appreciate that. By the way, are there unclassified orders I can carry?" asked Tony.

"Sharon is preparing your orders now. Let her know about the other people you are taking so she can cut their orders too. Your orders will be unique. You'll be able to part any seas you encounter, get you into any building and see anyone you need to see down there. That was a little dramatic, but they are high priority JCS SYMBOL orders. By the way, have you ever met Admiral King?"

"I briefed the Admiral on one of his visits to OP-20-G, just before Pearl Harbor. He was interested in the issues we had with getting good direction finding fixes on U-boats," Tony said.

"Good. I can guarantee you that he'll remember you then," said Taylor. "You'll be working with him or his aide on the COMINT appendices. OK, get out of here. You have a lot of work to do."

Tony's heart rate was up. Adrenalin was putting a little tingle in his gut, but he was smiling as he left Taylor's office.

ASSIGNMENT: CASABLANCA

That Evening
6:20 p.m., Friday, December 25, 1942
Suite 421
The Dorchester Hotel
53 Park Lane, Mayfair, London

First Officer Petra Romella, WRNS, was waiting impatiently in the big stuffed chair in the small luxury suite she and Tony now called home. She was wrapped snugly in a plush white hotel robe with tan trim, alert for sounds of Tony approaching the suite door. She was both hungry and worried about the news he might bring back. He gave her no clues on the phone. Trying to focus on the BBC news and music all day had been nearly futile. Just knowing he was on his way home was, in itself, a bit of relief to her anxiety. Hearing his key in the door lock was the best music her ears heard all day. She was in his arms for a hug as soon as he entered. "Bloody awful Christmas day for you, love," she said. "Don't tell me any bad news." She had her hands around his neck, fixing her sparkling blue eyes on his.

"It's not as bad as you probably expect," he said, smiling. "I have temporary duty orders to Washington for a few weeks. I'm working on a special study they are putting together in DC for high level briefings. I'll be working tomorrow also. Then I fly out early Sunday morning. By the way Captain Taylor said that you can ride with us to the airport, if you wish."

"Brilliant! I'd love that," she said.

"After a day of boning up and hectic paperwork, I didn't even stop for a decent lunch. I'm so hungry, I could eat a horse right now. How about you, sweet wife of mine?" He sensed the release of her tension and concern as he spoke.

"Bone up? Is that Yank for getting informed?" she asked smiling.

"Aye, spot on, as you say."

"It's not cricket to mock me or the British Empire," she said laughing.

He felt good that the cover story worked so well. He knew she would understand when the truth came out. Having a wife that works in MI5 has its pluses, mainly, understanding how things work with classified operations. "Alright honey, will it be room service, The Spanish Room down below, or out somewhere? You're choice."

"Do you think for one minute that I am keen on dressing to go out?" she asked, as she backed away from him. "You're leaving in two days and I miss you already." She opened her robe with an impish grin and displayed a new filmy pastel pink negligée from the U.S. Army PX.

He couldn't help but laugh, "OK. Going out is not an option. You order food while I get comfortable and freshen up."

"I'll have them bring it up in an hour," she said with a wink.

"After supper, we call Ticknall," he said. "I hate breaking the news to them that we can't drive up there tomorrow. It was bad enough telling them that I was on-call today. I was looking forward to spending a couple days with Ives and your folks."

"They were too, and so was I. More's the pity," she said.

The Next Morning
11:40 a.m., Saturday, December 26, 1942
Tony's Office
U.S. Embassy, London

Tony returned to his office from a meeting with the Embassy's OSS Chief, Mike Nelson, which lasted longer than expected. Nelson was able to share some very useful information about Casablanca.

When Tony entered his outer office, his Admin Chief, Alise Haydin, said, "They're all here, sir, I got them squared away in your office."

Already seated at the conference table when Tony entered his office, was Lieutenant Roy Hall, Chief Radioman Hector Johnson and Radioman Second Class Jerry Hamill.

"Good morning. As you were," Tony said when they started to stand up. "If you haven't introduced yourselves, please do so."

"Done, Commander," said Hall.

"My apologies for the delay, men. I got hung up in a meeting. I see Chief Haydin has taken care of your coffee. Congratulations on making 2nd Class, Hamill. Let's get underway. I want to thank you again, Johnson and Hamill, for volunteering for this TAD."

"Sir, we spent a long time deciding, since you couldn't tell us on the phone where we were going. Took almost, uh, maybe, two seconds. If Barr and Sampson were still with us, they'd want to go too," said Johnson. "Any news on them?"

Tony shook his head. He regretted not being able to share the highly sensitive intelligence indicating that they had been captured and executed by the Germans during their escape from Norway. "Two damn fine men. I hope they are being held somewhere and can make it through the rest of the war. I wrote letters to their folks regarding them being listed as MIA."

"I have to admit, it was mighty damn hairy getting out of there," said Hamill. "Worse than going in or even while we were there. We saw a lot of Germans."

Tony nodded, "This time, there should be better living conditions than we had in Norway."

The Radiomen laughed. "Almost anything would be better than that, sir," Johnson said grinning. "Where are we going this time?"

"Yes, that's what I want to know, too!" said Hall. "I just got back from Scotland about an hour ago, so I'm in the same boat."

"Casablanca," Tony said without hesitation, smiling. He sat back, ran a palm over his GI haircut and enjoyed the stunned silence and surprised looks on their faces.

"Where exactly is that?" asked Hamill.

"I heard they are making a movie in Casablanca. Are we going to be in it?" asked Johnson.

"I heard about that too. I'm looking forward to meeting Ingrid Bergman," said Hall.

"OK, ladies, fun time is over," Tony said. "First, they already premiered it last month in the states. Second, it wasn't even shot in Casablanca." He got up and went to the cork-backed, map board on wheels near the table. It had a map tacked on it that displayed the Atlantic Ocean and Europe. He lifted that map and folded it over the top. That revealed a map which showed only the country of Morocco, surrounded by the Atlantic Ocean and Algeria on the west and east sides, and the Mediterranean, the Strait of Gibraltar and Spain on the north. He put his finger on the northwest coastline of Morocco at a spot labeled, Casablanca. "Thar she blows." He took his seat while they all stared at the map. He spent several minutes discussing what SYMBOL was all about, to their amazement. "Don't even ask if you'll meet the President and Prime Minister." There were smiles.

"Didn't the Allies just do a landing there a couple months ago?" asked Johnson.

"Affirmative," Tony said, "Operation TORCH, mid-November. So, our mission is going to be very different from our little Norway trip. Mister Hall will be your division officer, for lack of a better word for this situation. I won't be with you very much. I have my own fish to fry. Let's talk about your task—special intelligence communications. The Seabees landed right after we seized the port there last November. Their job is to construct the facilities required for the establishment of a fully functional NOB, Naval Operating Base, at the port. It's going to be a major Allied naval port for future operations into the Mediterranean. They are building barracks, mess hall, communications, warship support facilities, the works. I don't have any idea how far they have gotten. That's where you three come in. You'll find a way to establish special intelligence comms. That's it, boiled down, but I realize it won't be that simple. We could spend a week thinking up all the possibilities and planning for them, but for what? Just figure it all out when you get there. In the meantime, let's talk about travel and what you'll be doing there, once comms are established."

They spent the next couple of hours discussing the travel arrangements, the establishment of a Top Secret special intelligence communications capability, their unique message address, and encrypted communications operations procedures. Then, last but not least, the weather. "We can expect temperatures to be in the 60s Fahrenheit during the day and 50s at night with a six to twelve mile per hour breeze during the course of the day. Rainfall chance will average about 20%. All in all, fairly nice for being winter, I'd say. You will wear your dungarees and boondockers on watch, but dress blues anytime you're outside the building. Mister Hall, you can wear your dress khaki uniform, but travel in blues."

"Oh, that's a hell of a lot nicer than Norway," said Hamill.

"Alright men, I think we have it nailed down as best we can at this point. Here is a briefing pamphlet for each of you from the War Department about Morocco. It's 50 pages long, but it covers important info about the people, customs, and so on. Take note that I penned in the current exchange rate. It's 50 francs to the dollar. By the way, I'll have some francs for you to use for food and reasonable expenses. Take the pamphlets with you and read them before we get there. Something to do on the plane. If you have no further questions, Mister Hall and I have more to discuss. You two can secure for chow and get squared away in your quarters below. I suggest you stay in the building tonight. Tomorrow will be a long day. I'll see you planeside."

The Radiomen departed. Chief Haydin brought in a carafe of fresh coffee and spam and cheese sandwiches from the Embassy mess. "My task, Roy," said Tony after swallowing his first bite. "aside from herding you three, involves you. I'm starved so let's just eat while we talk. As soon as possible after we arrive, I want you to check my room for phone taps and bugs. That hotel was being used as, quote housing for the German Armistice Commission, unquote. They had over 200 men in there. And get this, the number two man was a high ranking Gestapo officer. So, right off the bat, I'm suspicious about everything in that damn place, since they were probably all Gestapo agents."

"Wonder what they left behind?" asked Hall, shaking his head.

"Whatever it was, General Patton's troops cleaned it out. Anyway, find quarters for you and the Radiomen at NOB, if possible, so you're secure and close together. Once we get there and know what we're dealing with, we can figure out how to contact each other."

Hall thought a bit about all he heard so far, scratching his chin, "Is NOB expecting us?"

"Affirmative. I sent them a message this morning. But it doesn't matter. If they can't give us what we need, we'll find an alternative. There are decent hotels available."

"You didn't mention transportation in Casablanca," said Hall.

"I'm counting on getting a jeep out of the Army somehow. I sent General Patton's command a message requesting one. No reply yet. Otherwise, I understand bicycles are the way people get around. As for money, allegedly, there's $2,000 dollars-worth of francs for me on the plane from DC. That should cover whatever we need to get rolling."

"Roger. I should just stop thinking about stuff 'til we get there," said Hall.

"Yes, you should. Alright, one last thing. Arrive here a little earlier than the departure time tomorrow. Go down to the armory and pick up a wooden box labeled with my name and bring it to the plane. It's sidearms and ammo for us. We'll open the box when we land. You don't know what's in there, understand?"

"Affirmative. Like I said, Tony, this sounds like it's going to be a fun trip."

Fun wasn't exactly the word Tony was thinking would best describe this trip. More like diving into water with no knowledge of its depth. But he saw no need to change Hall's opinion. Ignorance can sure be bliss.

2 – Bon Voyage

Miller (Flt. Off.), Royal Air Force official photographer
RAF Biggin Hill, Kent

ASSIGNMENT: CASABLANCA

7:05 a.m., Sunday, December 27, 1942
RAF Station Biggin Hill
Main Road, Biggin Hill, Kent

The 15 mile ride from The Dorchester Hotel to the southeastern outskirts of London passed quickly. Congenial banter with Captain Taylor and Petra helped Tony keep his mind from thinking deeply about what lay ahead. But, not entirely. The unknowns were many and gnawed at his mind. His practice of having the best possible preparation wasn't achievable on this mission.

Two British Army soldiers saluted the car as it approached the gate at RAF Biggin Hill Station. One of them came forward, carefully examined everyone's ID cards, then gave the driver directions to the flight line.

http://afhra.maxwell.af.mil]

Boeing C-47 Skytrain

Aircraft servicing personnel were stirring around the only C-47 on the flight line. It was parked near a hangar, behind a line of scramble ready Spitfire fighter aircraft. The ground crew servicing the C-47 signaled to the sedan driver to wait at a safe distance until the fuel truck pulled away. The copilot was walking around the aircraft, doing preflight checks. Once they were able to pull up as close to the aircraft as permitted, the driver parked and opened the doors for his passengers. Hall, the Radiomen and three men in dark suits were standing in two groups on the concrete apron talking among themselves. The men in civilian clothes looked over at the sedan and boarded the aircraft.

Captain Taylor said, "I'll go talk with the Radiomen while you two have a few minutes here by the car."

Tony took Petra's hands in his. She looked into Tony's eyes, "Safe trip, love," she said, then whispered, "Can I get a hug here, in view of your men?"

"Absolutely," he said and took her into his arms for a long hug and kiss.

"Call me, if possible," she said as they clung to each other.

"Time difference will make it difficult. I'll call when I can, honey," Tony said. He knew how truly impossible it would be. He swallowed hard. Having to tell her a white lie, even for the sake of security, was uncomfortable.

Her eyes were beginning to tear. "I'll be working half Saturdays, other than that, oh, bloody hell, no messing about, ring me up anytime of the night. I'll be missing my crazy Yank. Know that," she said. "Losing sleep because you rang me up will be tickety-boo."

"Alright. I'll do my best. I need to go sweetheart," he said. They had one last kiss before he picked up his sea bag and attaché case, then walked to the aircraft. Hall and the Radiomen saluted.

"Good morning, sir," said Hall.

"As you were! Good morning," said Tony.

Hamill grabbed Tony's sea bag and took it to the ground crewmen that were stowing baggage in the aircraft.

"We're all squared away and ready to depart, sir. Your little wooden crate is aboard," said Hall.

Taylor shook Tony's hand, "Good luck. Have a safe trip."

"Thank you, Captain, and thanks for inviting Petra to come along," Tony said.

Taylor leaned into Tony and whispered, "As soon as I learn that the cover is blown on SYMBOL, I'll call Petra and let her know where you are."

Tony smiled and nodded at Taylor. "Alright men, let's get aboard and get this show on the road." He turned at the foot of the stairs and waved to Petra. She was blowing a kiss to him through an open car window.

The airplane was VIP configured. The exterior was painted the standard dark brown-olive and marked like all C-47 cargo and troop aircraft. The interior had a forward compartment, behind the Radio Officer and Navigator stations, that had a table by a window that sat three along its length, and two off the end by the compartment wall. Aft of that compartment, were nine comfortable brown leather seats, in three rows. Two on one side of the aisle, one window seat on the other side. They were spaced for nearly full declination for sleeping. There was a galley in the rear, plus a head, coat closet and storage locker. The three civilians were seated in the rear row of seats. Tony took the single window seat in the first row. Hall took the window seat opposite Tony. The Radiomen took the two window seats in the second row.

As the ground crew secured the door, the Captain came from the cockpit to the first row of seats in the passenger compartment and announced, "I'm Major Jim

Morris, Captain of this flight." He pointed at a female Army officer who came forward from the galley to the last row of seats. That is 1st Lieutenant Sheila Malden, Army Nurse Corps. For fuel conservation purposes, we left the two passenger service crew behind in DC. This is a long direct flight, not much fuel to spare. We'll have a tailwind most of the way. It will be close to a 1,500 mile trip. We expect a 10 hour flight at max economy cruise speed. The cabin will be heated, but not pressurized, so you may experience the effects of thin air. Lieutenant Malden will be doing double duty, performing the cabin service role and as flight nurse for your health and comfort as well. If there are no questions, we'll be taxiing as soon as our pre-taxi checklists are complete." He paused for the roar of two Spitfires taking off. "Remain in your seats with seatbelts secure until Lieutenant Malden announces it is safe to do otherwise. Smoking will be permitted at that time. Welcome aboard."

Twenty Minutes Later

"We're level at 12,000 feet gentlemen," announced Malden above the slowly pulsating drone of the two supercharged Pratt & Whitney engines. "You may move about. If we encounter any turbulence at all, take your seats and strap in. We have limited liquid refreshments available. There is water, orange juice, tonic, coke, ginger ale, gin, whiskey, bourbon, and scotch. Lunch will be served at 1100, light supper at 1530. That will give you time to eat before we begin our approach. Just raise your hand if you need anything."

While she attended to raised hands, one of the civilians walked up to visit Tony. He had two leather diplomatic pouches with him. "Commander Romella?" he asked in a very deep gravelly voice.

Tony stood, smiled briefly, "At your service, I'm Tony." They shook hands.

"Major Charles Rossi, U.S. Marine Corps. Call me Chuck. Can we go up front to the conference table and talk?" Rossi was 30 or so years old, about an inch shorter than Tony, with short black hair, clean shaven and had dark brown eyes. The strong handshake grip, width of his shoulders and trim waist, indicated to Tony that he was very much in shape.

They moved into the conference compartment and slid the curtains across the front and back doorways. Tony slid behind the table, facing the aisle. Rossi took the bulkhead seat adjacent to Tony.

"They saddled me with courier duty," Rossi said. "These two pouches and a sealed envelope are yours. Ready to sign and take them off my hands?"

"Affirmative, Chuck. Let's do it. You must be from Joysie."

"You must be from New England," Rossi said. They laughed, nodding. They had to lean close to each other to be able to talk privately, due to the engine noise. Rossi put the pouches on the table, seals facing Tony. Then he pulled two copies of a custody sheet and a brown envelope from his jacket pocket. He unfolded the sheet and laid it down next to the envelope. "Sign your life away, Tony."

Tony compared the seal numbers on the pouches and envelope to those shown on the custody sheet. Then he tore open one end of the envelope, removed the contents onto the table and counted $2,000 worth of 50 and 100 franc notes. He took a mechanical pencil from his shirt pocket, clicked the lead into view and signed both copies on the dashed lines above his typed name and dated them. "You are relieved, sir," Tony said smiling and handed one copy back to Rossi.

"I stand relieved, sir. I feel much lighter," said Rossi, grinning.

"I bet you do."

"We have a mutual friend, Tony. Mike Nelson told me to take good care of you."

Tony had done his best to keep Nelson from knowing about his actual interest in Casablanca. I should have known, Tony thought, Mike is too smart to be fooled easily. This is Chuck's way of telling me he's OSS. "Yes, indeed. Mike is a great guy. We worked a couple of uh, trips, together."

"So he said. He thinks very highly of you. Listen, while you're in Casablanca, if you should need anything, anything at all, I'm in our consulate."

"Roger that. I just might have to call on you or the Consul. I have the address," said Tony.

"Oh hell, Tony, pay us a call anyway. You're a U.S. military officer paying a courtesy call on your consulate. Earle Russell, our Consul General, would be happy to talk with you. I'll see that you get treated well."

"What can you tell me about transportation around town, Chuck?"

"Oh, if you don't have that lined up already, you'll need a bike. Gas is rationed. Bikes are everywhere. Motorcycles here and there. Cars are mainly for officials and the wealthy. Depending on how much traveling you'll be doing, bike is your best bet. Where are you staying?"

"Anfa Hotel," said Tony.

"Ohhhhhhh, you're one of those muckety-mucks going to the Anfa Camp. Roger. And you're only going to be here for a few weeks, right?" asked Rossi, with a sly grin.

"Affirmative." He's letting me know he's aware of SYMBOL, thought Tony.

"I'll have a bike delivered to you at the hotel," said Rossi.

"Chuck, I'll need two more, same time frame, but different location. Maybe you can direct me to a place to rent a couple."

"Just tell me where the other two bikes need to go, I'll have them there in one or two days," said Rossi.

"They're for Lieutenant Hall and the Radiomen. They will be at the Naval Operating Base," said Tony.

"Taken care of, Tony. Someone meeting you at the airport?"

"No, we're on our own. Figured I could cumshaw some Army transportation."

"Things aren't that organized here yet. But a consulate car will be waiting for me. I would rather you hitch a ride with me, since you have those bags and all those Francs. Where you going first?" asked Rossi.

"Sure there's room for the three of us and the other two you're traveling with?"

"My guys have their own arrangements. They are also Vice Consuls, as we all are, but, well, they are taken care of. So, yes, there's room for you three."

"Excellent. I need to get those men to NOB first, then you can get me to Anfa Hotel," said Tony.

"Roger," said Rossi.

"You solved my first worry, transportation. Much appreciated!"

"I mean it Tony, anything you need, at any time, just holler. I, we, have connections. Getting shit done here ain't easy," Rossi said, smiling. "I've been down here for almost two years, so I know a lot of people, Americans, Europeans, French, Moroccans. Besides, you might be able to scratch my back some day. I'd help almost anyone, but we Italians stick together in the thick and thin."

"Affirm," said Tony, smiling. "My dad used to quote the bible often, and he loved the phrase, as you sow, ye shall reap, or something close to that."

"Yes, that's how it is. It applies both ways too, good and bad," Rossi said, slapping Tony on the shoulder. "Have you been briefed on where to go and where not to?"

"Oh yes. Mike Nelson gave me the skinny on Casablanca, from uh, his organization's perspective. Also, one of the foreign service officers at the Embassy in London, John Hunter, was down there earlier in the year. He has kept up with things and gave me a lot of good dope on the place."

"I remember Hunter coming down. Didn't care for him much," said Rossi. He spent another 10 minutes giving Tony some insider's information about Casablanca. "Alright, Tony, I'm going back and nap 'til lunch. I was up late last night."

The Radiomen and Hall were reclined and napping when Tony returned to his seat. He stowed the diplomatic pouches under his seat. He reclined his seat back, covered himself with an Army blanket and closed his eyes. I'm not quite sure how to take Rossi, thought Tony. Dad also told me to beware of Greeks bearing gifts. I wouldn't be surprised if he asked me to help him dispose of a body some night. On the other hand, Mike Nelson likes him. For now, I appreciate the help and will take him at face value. Tony's thoughts shifted to Petra. He visualized her working at her desk in MI5 headquarters on St. James Street. He knew she would be wondering if something would come across her desk that would give her an update on whatever he was doing.

3:35 p.m., Sunday, December 27, 1942
Aboard the VIP C-47

The flight was uneventful all day, aside from two patches of very bumpy air shortly after lunch. The constant and bothersome song of the engines served to hypnotize everyone into slumber. Lunch of a ham and cheese sandwich had everyone awake and chatting for a while. Then slowly, one by one, they drifted back into a nap.

A gentle nudge on Tony's shoulder by 1st Lieutenant Malden brought him slowly out of a dream, which he was enjoying, but couldn't remember. His eyes still closed, he detected the unmistakable smell of beef and gravy. Now fully awake, he looked up and saw her standing by him, smiling.

"Commander, would you like an open-face hamburger, brown gravy, mashed potatoes and carrots?" she asked holding the tray of food out for him.

"Oh hell yes," he replied, "Thank you!" God only knows, he thought, when I'll eat my next meal. He looked at his watch.

She removed a stainless steel cover from his plate. "You have about twenty minutes, the pilot said we've had a great tailwind and are ahead of schedule. What would you like to drink with your meal, sir?" she asked.

"Ginger ale would be great, please," said Tony.

Malden was taking the last of the trays back to the galley. The pilot came through the conference compartment and stopped at the first row of seats, between Tony and Hall. "Gentlemen," Major Morris called out. Once he had everyone's attention, he continued. "I am estimating that we are about 35 minutes from landing. Thanks to a nice tailwind, we have the fuel and weather to proceed the additional 50 miles past Port Lyautey airport, which was our alternate, and land at Médiouna airport. That is about five miles southeast of the port at Casablanca. It's both convenient and free of press and other attention. Médiouna is a grass strip and I'll probably need most of the 2,200 feet of it, so be prepared for a bumpy rollout and heavy breaking." He paused for questions before returning to the cockpit.

Tony got up and looked back at Rossi to see if landing at Médiouna changed anything. Rossi gave a thumb up sign. He crossed the aisle and sat next to Hall. "Roy, I have a ride for us from the airport to NOB. It's a car from our consulate, thanks to Marine Major Rossi. That's the courier I was talking to this morning. We will open the weapons crate when we park. You and I will be armed. The 45s are for the Radiomen but will stay in the crate until you get to NOB. They will wear them in the comm center."

"Aye, sir. I'll pass the word on all that," said Hall.

"Also, you'll be taking custody of the pouch that has the documents with ECM crypto system daily settings for our mission. DC advised that NOB definitely has that system. Very first thing you'll do is find the Commanding Officer of NOB. Tell him you need T.S. storage for those crypto documents that only you or I have access to. Stow that stuff then work on quarters for the men and yourself. If you can't find secure storage, call me at the hotel."

"Roger. Will do," Hall said.

The port side window seat provided nothing but a view of clouds and Atlantic Ocean after departing Britain. Their flight plan kept them well away from known German air patrols based in France. But now, the coastline of Morocco was just barely visible ahead. He sensed the aircraft begin a gentle descent when the engines changed their drone as a result of being fed less fuel.

"Seatbelts, gentlemen, we are approaching Casablanca," announced Malden.

Walter Mittelholzer

Casablanca, Morocco (circa 1930s)

Slowly, a patch of settled land on the distant shoreline became a white patch, which then blossomed into a city of whitewashed buildings, from which it got its name. It looked simply beautiful. The whitewash gradually became tinted a pale pink as the sun sank into the equator. The pilot flew to within a mile of the shoreline and made a turn to parallel the beach. Tony heard the flaps come down. Later, wheels clunked into position. Soon the aircraft banked left and turned inland. An airport's distinctive structure was visible in the distance for a few moments until the aircraft turned left onto final approach. More flaps came down and engines growled louder. Tony watched the city scene passing by as they descended. The all brilliant white city he saw from the distance had areas significantly less than brilliant. The pilot planted the aircraft unceremoniously onto the nearest part of the runway. Dirt patches provided a dusty, rumbling and bumping rollout. The engines wailed against reverse pitched propellers then heavy breaking was applied. The aircraft slowed so rapidly that Tony strained against his seatbelt. The engines calmed down, and the breaking became negligible as they neared the opposite end of the runway. The aircraft turned and taxied to a hangar and parked in front of it.

"Casablanca, gentlemen," announced Malden when the engines went silent. "I have the coat and storage closets open. It's been a pleasure."

Everyone gave a short applause, putting a blush on Malden's face. When Malden and the ground crew opened the fuselage door, the cabin was filled with 49 degree air and unfamiliar smells.

Hall and the Radiomen waited for the civilians to exit before going aft to retrieve their belongings and the weapon crate. Tony and Hall put their shoulder holsters on, checked and loaded their 38-caliber pistols and holstered them. The Radiomen handed Hall and Tony their hats, uniform jackets and bridge coats.

Tony looked back from the doorway to be sure Hall had the diplomatic pouch. "Ingrid Bergman, here we come," Tony said, exiting. Hall and the Radiomen snickered and followed him. They walked over to the ground crew that was unloading their seabags from the cargo hold.

Major Rossi waved at Tony from beside a black four-door Renault sedan, parked close to the hangar. The other two civilians were getting into a black Chevy coupe.

The Radiomen piled all the seabags between the fore and aft seating in the back of the Renault. Tony and the others crammed themselves into the back, using the seabags as footrests. It struck Tony's curiosity that Rossi had his own car. He filed that away with the other misgivings. But he wasn't looking into a gift horse's mouth.

3 – City by the Sea

U.S. Army Map Service

Casablanca Town Plan 1942

4:55 p.m., Sunday, December 27, 1942
Mediouna Airport, Casablanca

The driver, Faraji, a French-Moroccan employee of the consulate, exited the airport and headed north toward the port, on Route de Mediouna. Tony was paying close attention to the road signs, storing it all in his memory that was blessed with high-retention. That information could possibly be useful in the days to come. Progress along the route was slow to avoid seemingly oblivious pedestrians, bicycles, and a motorcycle, car or jeep now and then.

"The Vichies had a tight hold on anything petroleum," Rossi said. "So shoes and bicycles are the primary means of getting around for most people."

"It's still going to be rationed because the Allied forces need it for war machines," said Tony.

"Any taxis available?" asked Hall.

"Parked in garages, probably. You'll be dependent on Uncle Sam for longer trips," said Rossi.

Nearly all private residences were whitewashed. Some still bright from being refreshed the previous spring. Kids playing in the yards often waved vigorously. Residential yards contained palms, date palms, orange trees, bougainvillea, and other flowers and bushes. The mild winter weather produced a lush landscape. Commercial and government buildings appeared to be mostly unpainted concrete. Palm trees lined larger streets and well-manicured medians.

"I don't think I've seen more than a handful of men in suits," said Hamill.

"Yep, those are going to mostly be the European businessmen, French and otherwise," said Rossi.

"Or spies," said Hall with a laugh.

Rossi laughed, "Oh, those come in all forms of dress."

Most Moroccans were wearing ankle length white, black or dark colored robes that also covered their heads. Most women had their heads and faces covered, showing only their eyes. French police were present for traffic control and general order at the larger intersections and were visible patrolling beats.

"How is our relationship with the police?" Tony asked.

"For the most part, I guess I'd have to say, guarded, or neutral now," replied Rossi. "I understand that the Sultan is pro-American, so that attitude will slowly seep down into those governmental organizations that weren't hard core Vichy. I think some of the French police were leaning Vichy and some were not. But there's a new sheriff in town. It's an entirely new game now. There's a lot of reassessing of loyalties going on."

The further the car moved from the outskirts of the city toward the port, the density of homes, shops, hotels and humanity increased. So did the complexity of aromas.

"This is a good market to shop, here on Rue de Strasbourg," said Faraji, passing a bustling open market with many men, women and children milling about. Vendors displayed nuts, dates, chickens, fish, fruit, vegetables, clothing, rugs, pots, pans, and so much more.

"This city is interesting, Chuck," said Tony. "It's similar to all other thriving cities I've seen overseas. I hope I'll be able to do some walking around."

"I recommend the new section, Tony, on the eastern side of the city. It's where the tourists go. Nice hotels and restaurants. Hell, there must be 20 movies with a hundred seats or more in the city. And even with the war on, they're getting some American films. There's not as many tourists since the war started. But still enough from France and elsewhere to keep the businesses and hotels alive."

"I assume there's a list of prohibited areas and places," said Hall.

"Oh yeah," said Rossi. "When you get to your destinations, they'll have a copy."

"Cruise ships still come in here?" asked Tony.

"Some. Not near as many," Rossi said. "Of course, the refugees fleeing war torn Europe try every trick in the book to get on one. They don't care where. America, South America, anywhere they can, to get away from this part of the world."

"Chuck, that sounds like a swindler's dream," said Tony.

"Exactly, Tony. They are constantly arresting people claiming to have connections with customs and the cruise ships, charging people ridiculous sums of money for passage arrangements. Of course, the money and the entrepreneur disappear after payment."

Faraji drove carefully through an open plaza which served as an intersection of several streets. He identified it as Place de la Victorie. It was full of people and bicycles all competing for rights of way. Nearby streets had a dense concentration of street vendors, shops and markets overflowing with noisy people.

Tony found it interesting that the looks on the men's faces passing by the sedan progressed from mostly friendly or neutral at the city's outskirts, to some that glared angrily, as they neared the port. Tony was expecting those who were impacted by the assault on the port by Operation TORCH forces would probably be unhappy with Americans. Certainly the Vichy French Army and Navy loyalists would be bitter. The Vichy French Army and Navy, despite the best diplomatic efforts by the Allies, refused to stand down and allow an unopposed occupation. The result was that they sustained significant casualties and damage.

As they passed through another plaza intersection, Faraji announced, "Rue de Peymirau. Not far now." Not long after that, Faraji turned left at a T-intersection onto Boulevard du Chayla, which ran along the wharves and light rail tracks of the port. There were no residences on this road, just warehouses, factories and commercial buildings. By now, the sun had sunk well below the horizon and darkness was approaching quickly.

U.S. Navy

Casablanca Harbor, Post Attack, Nov42, French Battleship Jean Bart far left

"You may not be able to make it out," said Rossi, pointing out the window as the car made the left turn, "but the French battleship *Jean Bart* is laying kinda catawampus at her berth, over there," he pointed, "on the far end of that phosphate and coal pier. You Navy guys really banged her up good. She was unable to get underway when the assault began, but she managed to get into a gun fight, while tied up mind you, with your battleship *Massachusetts* and fighter-bombers from the aircraft carrier *Ranger*. If you get a chance, come down and take a look at her. Not a pretty sight. Lots of damage. It's not a long walk from the Naval Base building."

"I'll make a point of doing that, if I can find the time," said Tony.

They proceeded west to toward the intersection with Boulevard du 4th Zouaves. Tony saw a building ahead that had a new chain-link fence with a barbed-wire top. Two Marine guards came to attention when the car pulled up to the gate in the front fence. A sign over the gate, illuminated by a small bulb mounted above it, said -- Commander, Naval Operating Base - Commander Moroccan Sea Frontier.

"Your new duty station men," Tony said, as he got out to allow the others to exit and unload their seabags more easily. "Mr. Hall, if possible, call me as soon as you get everything squared away this evening. If you can't get secure storage tonight, you have to sleep, armed, with that pouch."

"Aye, aye, sir," said Hall with a nod.

Tony reached into his jacket, removed the tan envelope and removed some franc bills. "Here's five 500s, one each for the Radiomen and three for you to use as needed. Keep track of the expenditures. I'll try and get by tomorrow and see how things are going. Good God, this breeze is coming off of something that damn sure stinks," he said, getting back into the sedan.

The men chuckled and agreed. Hall said, "It's probably the sardine packing plant we passed up the road a bit."

Tony watched Hall and the Radiomen pass through the NOB gate and said, "Take me home, James."

"We'll have you there shortly, Tony," said Rossi. "It's only about three miles."

Unable to read signs and see anything interesting in the darkness, Tony drifted off to sleep.

"Where are we?" asked Tony, waking up when the sedan hit a rough spot in the road. "How long have I been out?"

"We're on Boulevard d' Anfa, getting close to the hotel, maybe five minutes ahead," Rossi said.

"What's that, coming up on the right? I can't make it out. The lights aren't much good, but it looks odd," asked Tony.

"Racetrack," replied Rossi. "They call it the hippodrome."

Immediately after passing the racetrack, the driver made a right turn, went a short distance and stopped at a gate in a triple barb-wired fence. U.S. Army soldiers were checking everyone's ID cards. Satisfied with their credentials, the guard signaled to raise the wooden semaphore and allow the car to enter.

Periscope Film, LLC, Los Angeles, CA

Anfa Hotel (in the circle), Anfa Camp, January 1943

"This, Tony, is what's known as Anfa Camp," said Rossi. "General Patton just put this barbed wire fence down in a big perimeter around Anfa Hotel and a dozen or so villas they've commandeered. There's only two entrances and U.S. IDs are now required to get in. There's a bunch of roving patrols with guard dogs working the perimeter. Access to the hotel requires special passes. I can't even get in there now. But you know why there's all this fuss, because you're part of it."

Tony didn't know some of the details Rossi shared, but nodded affirmatively, without offering details of what he did know.

Lieutenant H. A. Mason

Anfa Hotel, Anfa Camp, January 1943

"End of the line, my friend," Rossi said when the car entered the narrow circular road around the boat-like shaped hotel. Faraji stopped at the barricaded driveway to the hotel entrance. Several U.S. Army guards protected the entranceway. "I'll have a bike here sometime tomorrow afternoon for you."

"Chuck, it would probably take over an hour to peddle my ass over to NOB, not to mention the security aspect. Based on the odometer reading, well, I don't want to sound ungrateful, but the bike isn't a reasonable answer for that trip."

"Oh, damn Tony, I didn't intend for you to travel to the port on a bike," said Rossi. "I was thinking it would be handy here in Anfa Camp. I don't know what all you'll be doing.

"I looked at my map after we talked, and the Consulate appears to be about two miles from here, as well," Tony said. "Let's just arrange for a bike for my men to use to get around the port and forget the one for me, OK? I appreciate the offer, though."

"Fair enough, Tony. Tell you what, when you check in, find out what the procedure is for getting Army VIP transportation. If you need a lift otherwise, just call us. We'll work something out." He reached into his pocket for a calling card case. "Here's my card. That's the Consulate switchboard number. Ask for me. If I'm not available, they'll connect you with someone that is taking my calls. I'll let everyone know about you and our arrangement."

Tony presented his orders to one of General Patton's Provisional Guard soldiers at the far end of the driveway to the hotel's entrance before he was permitted to proceed. The Army sergeant at the registration desk in the lobby reviewed Tony's orders and checked a typewritten list. "You're in room 210, Commander. If you need anything ring the switchboard. You should find your room all made up and spic and span. You're one of the early birds we were expecting. We just arrived four days ago ourselves. We've been working some long hours. So, the clerical and typing pools aren't up and ready to work yet, just so you know. Those are being set up in Conference Rooms B and C. They should be ready tomorrow. The VIP conference will be in Conference Room A." The sergeant handed Tony a ground floor map of the hotel.

"Roger. How about secure storage?" asked Tony.

"That, sir, has been set up in Conference Room D. It has 24 hour armed guard. You will be able to log your documents in and out of secure storage. There are safes, tables and chairs, so you can review and work on documents in there."

"Excellent. How about a list of things to do and see and places off limits?" asked Tony. "Any recommendations?"

"Ah, you'll see a little PX type thing set up near the bar. They have mainly toiletries, cigarettes, cigars, a few uniform items, and even underwear. But they have a tourist guide for 20 francs that has a map and walking tour descriptions. The list of places off limits will be provided with the guide. I'm told that places with ads in that guide are all OK for GIs. I personally haven't had a chance to see the town. Been too busy trying to get things ready."

"OK, thanks. How about meals, phone service and transportation?" asked Tony.

The sergeant retrieved the room 210 key from the keyboard behind the counter and slid it across the counter to Tony. "Meals are being prepared by U.S. Army cooks for this conference, at standard military ration fees. The chow hall is on the top floor. No room service. Army Signal Corps has taken over the telephone system. You'll be able to make local calls only. When you need transportation just call this desk, as soon in advance as you can, and we'll get you where you need to go. Same for getting back here from in town. Most places will have a phone you can use. They will probably charge you to use them." He gave Tony a card with the hotel's address and phone number on it.

Tony stowed his diplomatic pouch in Conference Room D. He put his sea bag over his shoulder and took the stairs up two flights. Room 210 was fairly spacious, with a double bed, wooden desk and chair, armoire, chest of drawers, stuffed brown leather chair, a four-lamp crystal chandelier and Persian throw rugs. The elaborate Moroccan wall décor was intriguingly designed, with geometric white lines on a blue field with gold doily-like designs mixed in. The full bath was luxuriously appointed. The desk had an information sheet laying on it that provided the meal hours, information about laundry, dry cleaning and other miscellaneous information about hotel services. He hung his jacket in the armoire and draped his shoulder holster and weapon over the back of the desk chair. He took a brief look at his sea bag and decided that could wait. He sank into the leather chair, took a deep breath and relaxed. The Germans sure picked a good place to roost, he thought. Then the realization struck him that a Gestapo officer slept in this room just six weeks ago. That gave him a chill. A subtle odor of German cigars still lingered. Tony closed his eyes and allowed random thoughts to percolate in his mind. I wonder if Petra's home from work. I'll miss our Sunday phone calls to my sister, Petra's folks and son. Petra and my sister would find this city immensely interesting…

The phone on his desk began ringing and woke Tony from an unexpected snooze. He looked at his watch – 8:25 p.m.

"Good evening, sir, it's Lieutenant Hall with an update."

"Good evening to you, Roy. How did you make out?"

"Pretty good, boss. The ship's company Radiomen were really glad to have the help. They had the same offline function for the regular Navy, ya know, that we came to do, in a room by itself. So, for security reasons, we took that whole room and those functions over, for them and us. They had two file safes in there and were only using one, so we have one to ourselves."

"Were there any messages waiting for us?"

"Negative."

"How about quarters and chow?" asked Tony.

"The SeaBees converted some nearby warehouses, easy walking distance, into enlisted and officer messing and quarters, so we're doing OK there too," Hall replied.

"Very well, Roy. Sounds good. I plan to come out there tomorrow morning to pay my respects to the CO and send a status message. Then I'll bring you back here to do a bug sweep in my room."

4 – One More Thing

8:10 a.m., Monday, December 28, 1942
Defense Attaché Office
U.S. Embassy, London

Captain Taylor quickly scanned through his incoming message board for a status message from Tony; he found none. He called his Admin Officer on the intercom, "Miss Freedman, have we heard from Commander Romella?"

"I haven't seen anything. I'll check with his office, sir," replied Freedman.

Taylor's phone rang. "Good morning Bill, this is Ed Langsdale."

"Ed, how are you? Good morning! What can I do for you?"

"Do you have 20 minutes at your office for me this morning?" asked Langsdale.

"If you can be here in the next 30 minutes, yes, otherwise, next opening I have is right after lunch," replied Taylor.

"Right. I'm in town, so I'll leave here straight away."

"Mr. Langsdale to see you sir," Freedman announced on the intercom.

"Send him in, thank you," said Taylor. He got up and walked toward his sitting area as Langsdale came through the door. "Make yourself comfortable, Ed. What's on your mind?"

"General Gubbins gave me a new project, Bill. A smidgeon unusual for my section, but my relationship with you and Commander Romella made it right."

"Before you get too far into this, Tony is out of the U.K. for about three weeks," said Taylor.

Langsdale smiled, "Quite. As background, MI5 keeps a record of all incoming and outgoing passenger and cargo manifests for ships and aircraft. They send a daily report to MI6 and others, I suppose. 1st Officer Petra Wil... pardon me, Romella, now, in her role in the Government Liaison Office, brought a report to General Gubbins that included an aircraft departure out of Biggin Hill yesterday for Casablanca. General Gubbins recalled the Commander's name and called me with a new item of interest."

Taylor laughed, "Did Mrs. Romella see that report?"

"I can't imagine that she didn't," said Langsdale.

"That mission of Tony's is Top Secret, by the way, Ed."

"Yes, SYMBOL is Most Secret for us as well. Let's get to it. General Gubbins believes the Commander's presence there may be of great use to both the Crown and the U.S., if you're agreeable." He paused, focusing on Taylor's eyes, twisting his mustache, looking for a favorable response.

Taylor grinned, "Alright, Ed, what are you proposing?"

"Right. You see, we closed our consulate there when the German High Command became irritated with the Vichy French government for allowing us to remain after we declared war on Germany. The Vichy government had no love for us for other reasons I shan't bore you with. No messing about, we have no resident officials or SOE agents that we can call upon in Casablanca at present. Whilst Commander Romella happens to be there, and he has worked with us in the past, perhaps we could call upon him for a small operation…"

That Morning
08:45 a.m., Monday, December 28, 1942
Naval Operating Base (NOB), Casablanca

"Good morning, sir," Hall said, meeting Tony at the NOB Quarterdeck.

"Good morning Roy. First, I want to see if Captain Greenwood is in his office."

"I talked with his Yeoman after the gate called about your arrival. He's down at the docks. They'll call us when he returns."

"Roger. Let's see your operating spaces."

"We're on the top floor," said Hall.

At the head of three flights of stairs was a door placarded with AUTHORIZED PERSONNEL ONLY and an electric combo lock to gain entrance. Hall pushed four buttons, causing the door lock to make a three second raspy sound as it released the lock. They walked through the small communications center, alive with Radiomen at desks, teletype equipment and radio positions. There was a room in the back that had a placard on it that read RESTRICTED AREA. Hall opened the door with a key. The smell of new paint and tile still lingered. It was a 12' x 12' room, with speckled gray linoleum tiles, and white walls and ceiling. There was one center-ceiling light, but each desk had its own gooseneck lamp. A typewriter and phone sat on Hall's desk, as well as a small clutter of paperwork. Chief Radioman Johnson was at the other desk in the room, banging away on a typewriter.

"Mornin', sir," said Johnson, standing up when Tony entered. "I'm typing up a couple incoming general service encrypted messages that we processed."

"Good morning Chief, as you were."

Also in the room were two tables with ECM (Electric Coding Machine) cryptographic devices sitting on top of them. "Commander, we have one of these set up with today's general service Navy settings and one for our special intelligence settings," explained Hall. "When the guys out front get an encrypted message, they just bang on the door. We process it and pass it back to them for delivery, if it's not to us, of course."

"Very good. This works out really fine. Good job men," Tony said.

"I'm going to the coffee mess out in the comm center. Shall I bring a mug back for you?" asked Hall.

Hall and Tony chatted over coffee for only a short while when the telephone rang with the message that the CO was back in his office.

Tony spent over an hour in the CO's office. Tony thanked him for the operational hospitality. As if fast friends, they talked about Navy tours and families. Then Captain Greenwood satisfied Tony's curiosity about the trials and tribulations of seizing and repairing buildings, displacing French personnel and converting the port to a naval base from which the Allies would springboard into the Mediterranean to attack the Axis.

Tony returned to the comm center and two anxious personnel. "We just got our first incoming. It's for you, sir," said Johnson.

Hall got up from his desk smiling, "It's already decrypted and ready for you, here on the desk, have a seat and read it."

It was a Top Secret Ultra message from Captain Taylor. It explained a side mission Tony was being assigned on behalf of MI6 and OP-20-G. Message traffic addressed to the German Intelligence headquarters in Berlin, had been intercepted and decrypted by Bletchley Park. It indicated that a B-Dienst, German Navy intelligence service, building in Casablanca was abandoned so quickly during the Allied assault last month that classified material may have been left behind. MI6 intelligence analysis about the site reported that the Germans probably had a radio intercept capability there that was targeting Allied navies. The bad news was, it had been referred to only by a German alpha-numeric designator. The address was not known. Tony's assignment was to locate and impound any and all German classified material, as well as anything else of intelligence value. Then, get the materials sent back to London.

Tony looked up at Hall, sitting on a folding chair next to his desk, "Roy, I'll need your help on this one."

Hall nodded positively, "I thought you'd never ask, boss. It sounds as though they think it's just sitting there as it was when they grabbed their hats and guns and hauled ass."

"Maybe," said Tony. "Unless the Vichies or some Axis sympathizers have gotten to it." A thought popped into his mind. "Roy, since you've been here, have you heard anything about the facilities the Germans were using in the port for U-boat repair, provisioning and refueling?"

"No, I wasn't aware of that. But I can guess where you're thinking is going with that."

"Stay put. I'm going below and ask Captain Greenwood about it."

The CO's Yeoman gave Tony the nod to enter when the Captain got off his phone.

"Jim, sorry to interrupt your day again. I just recalled something. Tell me about the German U-boat facility. Were there any U-boats in port when we attacked?"

"I wasn't here at the time," said Greenwood. "I wasn't even in the invasion force. But I understand that there were no U-boats in port at the time. The locals said that all German military in the area appeared to get the word to evacuate simultaneously, not long before the attack began. The U-boat facility was abandoned when the attack kicked off."

"What happened to it?" asked Tony.

"Oh, it took a lot damage from nearby shell and bomb blasts. The CBs refurbished and expanded it for Allied sub use," Greenwood explained.

"Did the Germans take all their stuff with them?"

"The skinny I got on it is that the Intelligence Officer from the USS *Ranger* choppered in and hauled a bunch of stuff out of there," said Greenwood.

Back in the crypto room, Tony sat down at Hall's desk, picked up the phone and dialed zero. The song, "Pennsylvania Six Five Thousand," crept into his mind and he nearly said it to the switchboard operator. "This is Commander Romella. The American Consulate, please."

"One moment, please," she said, but it was more like three minutes.

"United States Consulate, who's calling, please?"

"Commander Anthony Romella, U.S. Navy. May I speak with Major Rossi please?"

"One moment, sir. I'll see if he's in."

"You're not in jail, are you?" asked Rossi.

Tony could hear the smile in his voice, "Negative. I need to come talk with you. Have some time now?"

"Sure, Tony. Need a ride?"

"That's affirm. I'll be at the NOB gate."

The U.S. Consulate Annex
Corner of Blvd. Moulay and Blvd. de Anfa, Casablanca
Major Rossi's Office

"Have a seat, Tony. Can I get you something to drink? Tea, coffee, whiskey?"

"No, thank you, Chuck. I noticed the consulate sign out front was a makeshift one. What's the brass one under it say?"

"British Consulate, or words to that effect," replied Rossi. "They closed it back in 39 and asked us to look after it. We were swamped with requests for visas and other services but didn't have the room to lay on more people. So, we got the OK to use their building. We call it, the annex. Long answer to a short question, I know. What can I do for you, Tony?"

"Do you, by any chance, know where a German radio intercept site is in Casablanca?" asked Tony.

Rossi smiled, "Affirmative, if you mean the one on the western outskirts of the city, down by the Hank Cemetery."

"Possibly. I have information there is such a building here in Casablanca, somewhere, address unknown," said Tony.

"Well, I have several locals, French and Moroccan, that are in my, uh, network. They feed me info. Two sources have had suspicions about what the Germans were doing in a building down near the end of Avenue du Cimetiere. One of them told me it was well guarded around the clock and that he heard Morse code coming from open windows last summer. The Germans left in a hurry when the action started last month. It's unoccupied now they said. All locked up tight."

"Chuck, I have a favor to ask…"

Abandoned German Radio Intercept Site
Avenue du Cimetiere, Casablanca

Major Rossi's driver parked the big Renault in front of a graying-white, two story, flat-roofed building near a cemetery. It was located west of the city, about two miles from the port, and a block from the ocean. Tony was riding in front. Hall was in the spacious back, with several empty cardboard boxes they picked up at the Naval Base mess hall loading dock. Hall and Tony got out. The driver stayed in the car, as Rossi instructed.

Tony looked around. There was no one in sight. The villa was nearly remote, with the nearest neighboring buildings more than a city block away. It was of Mediterranean design. The whitewash was wearing through to cement in some areas on the first floor.

White paint on the 2nd floor trim was peeling. The roof was flat with a chimney poking up on one side. "First impressions, Roy?"

Hall scratched his chin as he looked the place over carefully. "Well, let's see. Recent six-foot stone wall around it, windows all have shades pulled down. Iron gate is chained and locked. It definitely doesn't look like someone was living here this month. It looks like a residence turned into a German site would look. If not, we could be in deep shit breaking in. Maybe we should do this at night."

"At night, we can expect power to be shut off in an unoccupied building," said Tony, "so we'd only have flashlights to see things. I'm concerned about booby traps. It would be easier to miss those in the dark." Tony noticed something tightly crumpled into a ball behind a dead shrub to the right of the gate. He reached in, picked up a tan and orange thick paper ball and carefully opened it. "Bingo. An empty pack for ten Weisse Garde cigars. That, plus the two whip antennas attached to each side of the chimney on the roof tells me the B-Dienst was here alright."

"I won't argue with that, boss," said Hall. He examined the lock on the gate. "Jumping the wall is not practical. I'll go talk to the driver and see if he's got a tire iron to force open the lock on the gate."

The lock was no match for the inertia of a heavy tire iron. "Stay back. I'll check out the front door," said Hall. "No use both of us taking booby trap shrapnel."

"Roger, but I doubt they had time to rig traps. I'll go around back and see what I can find," said Tony.

The patio and flower garden in the back of the villa had not been cared for in many months. It was a mess of dead vegetable plants, flower beds and weeds. Three ten-foot clothes lines still had sheets and underwear hanging on them, grayed from weathering. A wooden crate with German markings that was sitting at one side of the back door was full of wine bottles and German field ration cans. A 50 gallon drum, with a screen over an open top, was sitting several feet from the door. In the bottom were ashes of some of the papers they had time to set afire before they left. There were several incompletely burned documents at the bottom, appearing to be scorched on the outside. This put a smile on Tony's face.

The back door opened, "All clear, boss," Hall said. "They either didn't have time to set traps or didn't have them in the first place."

"Keep a sharp eye though," Tony said. "There's some unburned material in the drum there. Get a box from the car and fish them out of there. Meanwhile, I'll go see what we have inside."

The back door was attached to an unfinished one-story add-on room used for storing garden tools and a clothes washing machine. The inside door opened into the kitchen, where the sink was full of dirty dishes and utensils with dried food residue. The next room had a large dining table, on which there were several cups and glasses stained from dried contents.

"Ah, now we're getting somewhere," Tony whispered to himself when he stepped through the kitchen, through the vestibule, into what appeared to be, originally, a living room. The previous owner's rugs, wallpaper, and framed pictures on the wall remained in place, although the furniture had been removed. It was now a short-wave radio intercept room, with four operator positions. Each had a short-wave receiver, a box of blank paper sheets, pencils and headphones. One of the positions had a typewriter. A cable ran down the flue of the fireplace from a whip antenna on the roof to a crude antenna distribution device lying on a hearth. Wires ran from the device, around the walls, to each of the radio intercept positions. Tony reached into his jacket pocket, took out the Minox camera Rossi loaned him and documented the equipment in the room, including closeups of the faces of the radios.

"I stowed the box of partly burned documents in the car, boss," Hall called out.

"In here Roy." When Hall entered the radio room, Tony said, "See, Roy, we wouldn't have gotten good shots of this stuff if it was dark."

"Roger. But I won't relax until we're out of here," Hall said.

"OK, topside will be berthing, but there's two things I haven't seen yet, the Enigma and a transmitter," Tony said.

"Roger that, and the code books, if we're extremely lucky," said Hall.

"Affirmative," said Tony. "The officer in charge would have had to be damn stupid to leave crypto gear and keys. We can only hope."

The Persian runner on the stairs going up from the vestibule was worn nearly bare in the center and creaked as they walked up. There were three rooms off the hallway at the top of the stairwell. Two rooms on the left side of the hall had two, three-high, bunk beds. Half of the beds were made, the others looked like people just climbed out of them. At the end of the hallway there was a small but full bath. The only artifacts of the Germans present in the bathroom were a straight razor, a shaving soap mug with a wood-handled hairbrush in it, a used bar of soap and a couple of scruffy looking towels on a rack.

"Aha," exclaimed Tony when he entered a large room on the other side of the hallway. It had been the elegant master bedroom of the local owner, long gone to somewhere they felt would be safer than Casablanca. Now it reeked of cigar smoke and showed the mistreatment of an uncaring German squatter. "This was the quarters and office of the officer in charge, Roy."

"No Enigma here either, dammit," said Hall.

"Roger, but there's the table it probably sat on, by the transmitter and the operator's desk. From the marks on the rug, there was a file safe or heavy file cabinet here by the operator's desk. The transmission antenna runs out the window, here, and up to the other whip antenna," said Tony, as he took pictures of everything in the room. "Roy, I'm sure he kept the code books in this room somewhere. Look everywhere, just in case."

After searching every drawer, under the bed, mattress, and in the library, they came to the conclusion that the German officer left nothing of value behind. Not counting the wine and booze bottles he stowed in some of the library shelves along one wall. The displaced books were stacked on the floor in one corner of the room.

"Damn, I hate to leave with only scorched documents," Tony said. "Surely, the bastard forgot something! I'm thinking somebody may have beat us to it. It's just too clean for a hurried scramble out of here." He stood at the foot of the unmade bed, slowly scanning the room.

"This place stinks and gives me the heeby jeebies," said Hall. "I'm going down and take another good look at that operations room before we leave, which won't be soon enough."

Tony rechecked the drawers in the chest, armoire and side tables for false bottoms. Nothing. Nothing but a French romance novel, and a cigar stub with its pile of ashes in a white marble ash tray on the side table.

"Down here, quick!" Hall called up the stairs with alarm in his voice.

Tony drew the pistol from his shoulder holster and hurried down the stairs.

"Four civilians in black robes have the driver kneeling on the ground at gunpoint, looking at his papers and questioning him," said Hall, peeking around the side of the shade on the front door.

"I don't speak French. Do you know any?" asked Tony, peeking around the shade of one of the front windows.

"Not a damn thing beyond yes and no," said Hall.

"One thing for sure, they are pissed off," said Tony. "We're going to stay quiet in here and see what develops. Where the hell did they come from? There's no car, camel, horse, donkey, nothing."

They watched the leader of the band of miscreants angrily asking the driver questions and pointing at the house. The interrogator was clearly exasperated with the driver's silence and shoulder shrugs, pressed his pistol between the driver's eyes and pulled the trigger. The driver jerked backward to the ground. The leader turned and gave orders to the three men. Two of them started searching the car. The other one walked to the gate and opened it while the leader put his weapon in a pocket in his robe and repeatedly looked up and down the street.

"Roy, listen to me," said Tony as he holstered his pistol. He felt the heat and tingle of adrenalin spilling into his bloodstream. "These are not cops. They are Nazi collaborators, probably members of an SOL militia. I'll explain that later. Put your gun away, go to the dining room and peek around the corner of the doorway at the front door. Don't say anything. He'll be puzzled seeing that Navy uniform, which will give me just the second or two that I need. Do what I tell you, just trust me, and we'll be OK."

Roy swallowed hard, went to the arched entrance of the dining room and stood facing the vestibule. He watched Tony take an action-ready, semi-crouched position off the hinge side of the front door.

The man opened the door very slowly, his pistol leading the way. He saw Hall right away and moved cautiously inside, saying words that probably meant something on the order of put your hands up. Hall put them up instinctively and lost some color in his face. Tony pushed the door shut far enough to obscure the view from outside. The door made a squeak and the man turned. Tony's hand-to-hand combat training in Scotland came in handy. In a series of very quick moves, Tony disarmed the man with a powerful hand chop which caused the pistol to fly across the floor. Without hesitation, Tony snapped the neck of the unprepared scoundrel. The man dropped to the floor with his muscles twitching randomly. Tony quietly closed the door the remainder of the way.

"Holy shit, boss!" Hall blurted out softly.

"Drag his ass into the laundry room," said Tony. "Three to go." He peeled the door shade aside just enough to make a slit to see through.

A minute went by before the leader yelled something toward the house. The two men were still looking through the glove compartment and the boxes in the back.

Tony recalled a word he heard yesterday and hoped it meant simply—what? "Quel?" he yelled, with his best imitation of the pronunciation and voice he heard from the victim.

The leader repeated what he said.

"Quel?" Tony yelled back.

The leader shook his head and told one of the other two to go into the house.

"Same drill, Roy," Tony whispered.

Hall smiled. He played his role in Tony's encore performance and dragged the second victim into the laundry room.

"Roy, they're going to both come in this time. Get behind the archway into the kitchen, out of sight, with your weapon ready. When I fire, yell something and lean around and shoot at the head of the guy still standing."

"Roger," Hall said with a notable quiver in his voice. His adrenalin was overflowing.

Tony watched the leader pacing back and forth for a minute then call out again toward the house.

"Quel?" Tony hollered.

Didn't work that time, Tony said to himself. "They're coming through the gate, Roy," he whispered.

Tony was down in a one-leg kneeling position, hidden by the slowly opening door. Getting low kept him out of the primary line of sight of the men coming through the door and Hall's line of fire to the head of the intruder. The leader was right behind the man entering, taking his leader's whispered instructions. The door opened about two-thirds of the way, nearly bumping Tony. They both moved into the vestibule walking softly, pistols ready. As soon as the first man was visible, Tony fired two quick shots to his head, taking him down. Hall yelled on cue, then came part way around the archway. That confused and distracted the leader. Tony took the leader down with another fast double head shot before Hall had a chance to fire a round.

"Worked perfectly!" said Tony, smiling.

"Damn boss, where'd you learn this shit?" asked Hall.

"If I told you, I'd have to kill you," joked Tony. "I'll just say, I didn't spend time in Scotland drinking whiskey. OK, we've got to get our driver into the car and get him back to the Consulate. I'll check these two guys for papers, see if the other two have any."

"Aye, aye, sir."

Tony took mug shots of the two victims on the floor.

All wallets and documents in the pockets of the victims were collected quickly. Tony became more sorrowful for the driver with each step they took toward the car. He also hated the thought of telling Rossi, and not knowing what lay ahead for him and Hall. "Open the right side door, Roy. Let's get him in there and get the hell out of here before this gets any more complicated."

Hall grabbed the driver's feet, Tony lifted him by the shoulders. They got the driver onto the floor in between the bench seats in back and covered him with the empty boxes. Tony heard car engine noise and looked in the direction of the sound. "Damn it, Roy, here comes a French police vehicle. Kick dirt over that blood pool on the ground and make it look untouched."

"They're hauling ass too," said Hall, looking up as he covered the dark red sand.

"Get in, I'll get this thing started. Hopefully, they're going elsewhere," said Tony.

The French police, in an old two-door Citroën with a faded black paint job, came to an abrupt stop in front of the Renault. Two policemen, in navy blue uniforms with sidearms, got out and walked to each side of the Renault. Tony cranked down his window, "Good morning, sergeant," Tony greeted.

"Good morning," the sergeant said curtly. There were reports of possible gunfire in this general area. Did you hear or see anything?" asked the sergeant in well spoken English, with a strong French accent.

"We did hear something and stopped to see if something hit the car," explained Tony. Hall nodded. "We found nothing and were just returning to the American Consulate."

While the sergeant and Tony were talking, the other police officer looked carefully into the front and back seats, then circled around the car to the sergeant. The policemen exchanged a brief conversation in French.

"What were you doing out here?" asked the sergeant.

"We just arrived in Casablanca, yesterday, officer. The Consulate loaned us this vehicle to tour the local area, just sightseeing."

I hope they don't notice the dangling chain on the gate and missing pane of glass on the front door, Tony thought. These guys are very curious.

"Have you seen anyone else in this area?" asked the sergeant.

"No, we drove as far as the cemetery and turned around. That's when we heard the noises," Tony replied.

"What did these noises sound like and how many did you hear?"

"I recall hearing two, like pops, I thought maybe a stone hit the side of the car or hub cap," said Tony.

"That's what I heard also," said Hall.

"I want to see your identifications," the sergeant said coldly. Tony and Hall presented their Navy ID cards. The sergeant handed them to the other officer, who wrote down all the information on both IDs into a small notebook. The sergeant looked at both of them again and handed them back. "Where are your quarters?

"I am staying at the Anfa Hotel and Mr. Hall is staying at the Naval Operating Base."

The sergeant raised his eyebrows briefly when he heard the words Anfa Hotel. "Are you traveling together? How long will you be in Casablanca?"

"Yes, sergeant, we are traveling together and will be returning to London in about three weeks. We are both assigned to the American Embassy in London, but here on official business. I am the Naval Attaché there."

"Do you have any diplomatic credentials with you?" asked the sergeant.

Tony and Hall took their Embassy ID cards out of their wallets. Tony handed them to the Sergeant. Again, the other officer recorded all the information on the IDs. The two policemen had a conversation in French. Tony tried to pick up French words that sounded similar to English words, to no avail.

The sergeant handed back the Embassy IDs. "Gentlemen, you are free to go. Good day." They exchanged salutes.

Major Rossi's Office
U.S. Consulate Annex

"Have a seat guys," said Rossi. "What did you find?"

"Trouble," said Tony, emphatically. "Big damn trouble. You're not going to like it."

"Talk to me," Rossi said.

"Very bad news. Faraji was killed by probable SOL thugs while we were in that German intelligence uh villa. He's in the back of the Renault. I can't tell you how sorry I am."

"Oh my God, Tony. He's been with me since I got here. He's 29, lives with his two brothers." He raised his head as if scanning the ceiling and took a deep breath. He was shaken. "The bastards got away I take it?"

"There were four of them and all are dead, Chuck," Tony replied. "Two are laying in the living room and two are in a utility room at the back door. We have all their pocket contents." Tony and Hall emptied their pockets of the material they took from the SOL bodies. "I took pictures of the guy giving orders and one other. And a bunch of other pictures of their stuff in the building." Tony handed the Minox to Rossi.

"I'll get these developed and printed for you. They'll be ready in a couple days. Damn it, I wish to hell this didn't go this way. Wait here while I get somebody to take care of the car and Faraji."

"Chuck, before you go, don't let that box of documents in the back of the car get away. I need to package that stuff and send it by diplomatic pouch to the Defense Attaché in the London Embassy."

"Affirm, sailor. I'll take care it."

Rossi returned forty minutes later.

"Did Faraji have a family?" asked Tony.

Rossi sat the box of recovered documents on the floor next to Tony. "Just his two younger brothers. His parents died in a freak car accident, so Faraji raised them. One of my guys is delivering the body to the brothers and will help them with whatever arrangements they want. The Consul authorized a hefty compensation payment for the brothers."

"Are they going to be a problem?" asked Tony.

Rossi shook his head, "Not a bit. They are really, really pro-U.S. They have been giving us intel on the troublemakers and Nazi sympathizers in the city. It will just make them more eager to help us. To get even. OK, where were we?"

"Who the hell are these SOL people?" asked Hall.

Rossi's reddened face and gestures showed his disgust, "Roy, that damn SOL has a beautiful sounding name, Service d'Ordre Légionnaire," he said in a bad French accent, with emphasis, "but they are thugs, like Tony said. Rogues too pro-Hitler for even the likes of the Vichy French. But they live and breathe thanks to support from that damn Marshal Philippe Pétain. Most of those cowardly SOL assholes here in Casablanca relocated to Spanish Morocco, Spain and God knows where else. Some of the more dangerous and stubborn ones stayed behind to stir shit and give us a bad time. We've been slowly identifying and, uh, neutralizing them." Rossi began quickly sorting through the materials recovered from the SOL bodies. "Of the four, I recognize this guy's name. He's the cell leader. I knew he had a small group of militants but could never figure out where he sleeps. Good riddance. I'll have to figure out whether to remove the bodies or leave them. I'm thinking they'd be better as fish food." He took out an empty folder and put the materials into it. "I'll review this stuff more carefully later. Tell me exactly what happened and exactly what the gendarmes said."

Tony described in detail all that occurred.

"Alright. It sounds like you're probably OK, especially due to their assumption of diplomatic immunity, thanks to the car and your IDs. The Consul General isn't happy about this. If the cops decide to write up an incident report, they'll send a copy to General Patton's HQ, because U.S. military are involved and the Consul because U.S. personnel are involved, and worst of all, French General Giraud's office, the local head of government."

"Oh crap. I hope that's not the case. Dammit, this could get bad," Tony said.

"If the cops call here, the switchboard knows to route the call to me. I'll confirm everything about your story, well, the parts they ask about. If they discover those bodies before I get rid of them, they will figure out who they were, and believe me, they won't be sad about their demise. But, by the same token, they won't be happy about us being responsible. They'll probably voice their displeasure and blow a lot of hot air, but that will be the end of it."

Tony smiled. "That is an outcome I can live with."

"That's my life here, Tony. Always on the diplomatic edge. Alright, I have another car available for a while. I guess you two need rides?" asked Rossi.

"Affirmative," replied Tony. But first, I need to get these documents stowed. I won't package them until I get the photos from the Minox. Until then, I need secure storage."

"Can do, sailor," said Rossi.

"Excellent. Then we both need to get to NOB. I need to report this unplanned event and our findings at the villa. It won't take long. So, if the driver can wait for me to do that, then get me back to the hotel, that would be terrific."

"Roger, Tony, whatever you need. Driver and car will be at your service for the next three hours, then he needs to be back here," said Rossi.

5 – Twinkling Stars

3:30 p.m., Monday, December 28, 1942
Captain Taylor's Office

Captain Taylor answered his phone, "Good afternoon Ed. You've been reading your mail I take it. Good news and bad news as well, isn't it?"

"Right," said Langsdale, "bit of each. Excellent report, albeit some unwanted turmoil. But the commander will sort it. If you hear anything new through other channels, keep me in mind, if you'll be so kind. And please ring me up when the package arrives."

"Absolutely, Ed, I certainly will. As best I can tell, it hasn't departed yet."

Three hours later
The Spanish Grill
The Dorchester Hotel, London

Captain Taylor waited by the doorway to the Grill for Petra to come down from her suite. "Good evening, Petra, glad you could join me for supper."

"Good evening Bill, thank you for the invitation and for allowing me to go up and drop off my hat, coat and that wretched gas mask bag."

The maître d' showed them to a table, issued menus and signaled a waiter.

"You two pulled a good stunt at the airport, but I'm wise to you," she said with a sly grin when they were alone.

"I suspected that to be the case. Ed Langsdale told me about the manifest reports. I'm glad you were able to see it, officially. Tony hated telling that story, but it was necessary," said Taylor.

"Whilst I dislike what the war calls upon us to do, from time to time, I always say, we do our bit, yes?"

"Indeed we do, Petra, indeed we do. And what's your recommendation?" he asked, reviewing the menu.

"I shall have the consommé to start and the chicken with mushrooms," she said, without looking at the menu.

"And so shall I, they sound like excellent choices," he said.

The waiter arrived and took their wine and meal orders.

"Tony's a lucky man to have a wife who understands his rigorous schedule."

She blushed, "You need not charm me, sir."

"I suppose not, Petra. How's the family?"

Taylor thanked the waiter when their goblets of red wine were served. He raised his goblet toward Petra, "To a short war."

"Yes, a short war," she said as she raised hers. Their goblets touched with a delicate clink.

"And the family?" asked Taylor.

"Right. You mention rigors. Ives and I miss each other terribly. He just can't quite grasp what this is all about. We cry on the phone together sometimes on our Sunday evening calls. It breaks my heart. But he keeps his pecker up and sorts it. He helps mum and dad a great deal and does smashing in school. I'm most proud of him. Tony loves chin wagging with him. They have a jolly time. They've become keen for each other. I can't wait to find time for a home visit with Tony."

"We're all kept too busy to have time from work for much more than eating and sleeping. The pace seems to be quickening too," he said with a head shake.

"Quite so. But I must say, I'm a lucky bird. Busy man he is. But Tony is as fine a man as I could hope to have in my life. And I'm thrilled for him on this trip. I'm jealous. Oh, here comes our soup. How about your wife, Evelyn isn't it? And your daughters?"

The Next Day
9:10 a.m., Wednesday, December 30, 1942
Conference Room D – Classified Material Storage Room
Hotel Anfa

Tony was sitting at a table studying documents and making margin notes, concentrating deeply. Before him were the proposed Top Secret communications intelligence appendices of the various theatre operations plans to be discussed in the conference. He had been at it for over two hours, when he heard his name called out. Tony raised his hand, not wanting to be separated from the documents.

The Army corporal that called his name, part of the room's security staff, came to him. "Commander Romella?" she asked in a soft voice.

"Yes, corporal," he replied. There was a faint, unique and delightful scent of what had to be a local perfume. "May I ask corporal, what is the name of that perfume? Is it local? I'd like to buy it for my wife."

She blushed fully and smiled, "Local, yes sir, I'll write it down." She wrote the name of the perfume, the shop's name and address where she bought it, on a small note pad. She handed it to him, along with another message. "This message was called in to our front desk for you, sir."

The message was brief. Call Major Rossi. This is not a good thing, he thought. What's this day have in store?

9:45 a.m., Wednesday, December 30, 1942
The U.S. Consulate's Renault

Tony walked from the hotel to Rossi's sedan waiting at the foot of the driveway.

"Good morning, Tony, we have a 10:45 appointment," said Rossi, in his service dress uniform, as Tony got into the back seat with him. "This is Hamid, my new driver. He's OK, Tony, he also helps with operations."

"Good morning Chuck and Hamid," said Tony. "I hesitate to ask who the appointment is with."

"Ever meet General Patton? You're going to," said Rossi, smiling.

"Why are you smiling? This is about the uh, situation, right?" asked Tony.

"I think the situation is handled, but any visit with the General is going to be interesting. This is my third trip to his HQ, second with him personally. His Western Task Force HQ is in the former Shell Oil office building, on the other side of town."

"I have two questions," said Tony. "What's the status with the SOLs? And how did it go with the two sons yesterday?" asked Tony.

"The SOLs are fish food, offshore about a mile," whispered Rossi. "The rug you soiled with brains and blood has been burned. As for the brothers, it went very well. They know the risks they all took with being pro-American and helping to root out the ne're do-well sympathizers. Frankly, I think the 79 000 f in unpaid wages and death benefit went a long way in keeping their anger with us to a minimum."

"This is it," said Rossi, as the driver made a left turn off of Route de Rabat onto Boulevard de Gergovie. Tony noted a cement works on the right, just before the Shell Oil compound. They showed their IDs at the gate and parked in front of the building. A private was assigned to escort them from the lobby, up to the third floor and into the General's office suite.

A staff sergeant took their names, offered them seats and disappeared into the interior of the suite. He returned and said, "The General will be available shortly."

Several moments later, an intercom on the staff sergeant's desk barked, "Send 'em in!" The staff sergeant pointed at a polished, dark wood double-door. "Come to attention three feet in front of his desk and salute. Be very formal."

Major General George S. Patton looked up from behind a desk of impressive size and antique design. He looked intently at Tony and Rossi as they entered. Tony's eye for his surroundings registered the ornately paneled and plushly furnished office. General Patton stood at attention as they approached. There were eight shiny silver stars twinkling at Tony as the trim, 6' 2" General stood under the chandelier above the desk. Two stars on each shoulder of his green waist jacket and two on each collar of his shirt.

There it is! The pearl handled pistol I've read about, thought Tony. The pistol was pretentiously exposed in the holster on the General's right hip.

Rossi and Tony stepped in sync to the three-foot spot, saluted and announced their ranks and names in unison.

The General returned their salutes smartly and sat. He took a moment to look deep into each of their eyes. "Commander, I don't like to get negative reports from civilian police about incidents involving American military personnel." His voice had a higher pitch than Tony expected, but was sharp and rich with authority. "What the hell happened. And don't spare any damn details."

Tony gave the same story as he related to the French policemen, as Rossi had suggested on the way to the meeting.

The General's eyes bored into each of their brains again for a moment. "Major, I understand you were not part of this fiasco."

"That is correct, not directly, General," replied Rossi.

"Major, you are excused," said the General. When the door closed behind Rossi, the General said sternly, "Stand at ease Commander. Never mind the bullshit. Tell me what the hell really happened, and I mean everything."

Tony described the entire episode in detail, from receiving Top Secret message orders to investigate the German radio intercept site, through being questioned by the French police.

"You killed all four of those rotten SOL bastards by yourself?" asked the General.

"Well, no sir, not exactly. Lieutenant Hall provided a critical distraction, which put him at personal risk."

"You didn't mention anything about the disposition of the bodies," said the General.

"Major Rossi took care of them last night, General."

"Exactly how?" asked Patton.

"They are fish food, a mile offshore, General."

General Patton started to smile like a cunning cat with a mouse. He stood and walked around his desk to Tony and extended his hand. "I've said many times, Commander, it's a good day when you kill the enemy rather than die for your country. If you were an Army officer, I'd put you on my staff."

The handshake was exactly what Tony expected, powerful, long and animated. "Thank you General," said Tony, trying not to show his excitement.

General Patton went to his desk and picked up an index card. "Commander, there's information on here that my G2, my Intelligence Officer, thought you should have. Now get back to work. And if you plan on killing any more of those sons o'bitches, do it so you don't get caught. I managed to convince the French police chief not to send a report to the French General Giraud or the Sultan. I could handle the Sultan, but keeping it from Giraud cost me some fine Colorado steaks, a carton of Lucky Strikes and California champagne. It worked. This time. A word to the wise."

Tony summarized the conversation with General Patton for Rossi as they drove from the Shell Oil compound.

"I had a feeling it would go that way, you two are definitely in good shape," Rossi said. "So, sailorman, back to the hotel?"

"Yes, back to the hotel," Tony said, reaching into his jacket pocket for the index card. "But here's the dessert." He handed the card to Rossi. "I'm not sure what to do about it."

"Tony, good God, this is good stuff. You know what this really is, right?"

"Yes. It's intel from an informant on the address where that SOL squad operated from," Tony replied.

"Affirm, sailor. It's not far from the German villa either. Listen, do you have time to come to the Consulate and talk about this?" asked Rossi and handed the card back to Tony.

"Yes, what do you have in mind, Chuck?"

"We'll discuss it there, Tony. Hamid, take us back to the Consulate," said Rossi.

An Hour Later
Major Rossi's Office
U.S. Consulate Annex

"When lunch is ready, we'll go over to the Consulate and have a bite," said Rossi. "I'll introduce you to the Earle Russel, the Consul General. Meantime, make yourself comfortable. Let's talk about this."

"Sure. I was thinking on the way back…"

Rossi interrupted, "I smelled the wood burning."

"Seriously, Chuck. I had a feeling that the German site was too clean, in terms of documents and papers. No equipment manuals, unclassified correspondence, intercept logs, stuff like that, which they probably wouldn't take the time or space to remove in a hurry. There was evidence on the rug of a heavy filing cabinet."

"And you think the SOL guys did the cleaning and might have it stowed at their villa, right?" asked Rossi.

"That's a roger, Chuck. I'm thinking of sending a message back to ask if I should pursue that."

Rossi stared for a few moments at a street map of Casablanca on the wall to the right of his desk. Here and there were steel thumb tacks with heads colored by different shades of nail polish. He looked back at Tony. "Sailorman, don't take this the wrong way. But I think this one is more likely to get sticky, and frankly that's not really your cup of tea."

"Ground pounder, you have no idea," Tony said with a chuckle.

A smile formed on Rossi's face, "Mike Nelson told me you were capable and a damn scrappy guy. Yeah, you took care of four SOLs. But listen. You've already gotten snagged by the gendarmes. You can't risk getting caught again and get kicked the hell out of Casablanca. You have other important business to take care of."

"Roger that. So, what are you thinking?" asked Tony.

"Oh, by the way, Tony, your package is double wrapped and ready to go out on the next flight out that can take diplomatic pouches."

"Excellent. Let me know the date and flight details so I can send a message back."

"Will do. Back to my thoughts. You should let me, and my OSS assets, do this. It falls under my general operation guidance and I don't need to ask anybody first. I'll bring back all the junk we find, and you can go through it. Take whatever you want. Hell, I can probably get it done tonight." He looked at his watch. "Chow time, sailor, let's go meet some new faces and fill ours."

An Hour and a Half Later
Major Rossi's Office

"Well, Tony, you and Earle Russel seemed to hit it off OK. He and I get along just fine too. He doesn't ask many questions. I let him know about things he might get blown back at him. Otherwise, we operate, ya know, how we must."

"I figured he didn't ask about yesterday because of others at the table," said Tony.

"No. He knows I'll brief him on things he really needs to know. Otherwise, he's got his hands full with routine consular business. They deal with a ton of bullshit over there. So many people trying to get out of here, passports, visas, it's a mess."

Tony nodded, "About the, uh, raid. You won't really know what is valuable to me. I should go along. After you clear the decks, I can go in and figure out what I want."

Rossi grinned, "Let me put it this way, swabby. This is going to be a strictly OSS operation. I'll vacuum clean that place. Everything is coming back to the annex across the plaza that's not normal furnishings or a body. I'll have the driver pick you up at the hotel about 0900 tomorrow and bring you to the annex. You can sort through all that crap then. OK? If I don't call your room at 0830, we slip to the next day."

Tony chuckled, "OK dogface. Fair enough. I can't wait."

"Alright. Now that hurt. Truce on the nicknames!" Rossi said grinning.

6 – Warehouse Field Day

8:30 a.m., Thursday, December 31, 1942
Room 210
Anfa Hotel

Right on time, Tony's room phone began ringing. A smile formed on his face with anticipation on what Rossi's men brought back to the Consulate Annex. He answered, "Commander Romella."

"Good morning Tony, Chuck here. Listen, change of plans. Can you be in your hotel room to take a phone call between, say, nineteen and twenty-hundred hours tonight?"

"Affirm."

"Roger. I'll have an update for you by then. Adios."

The smile on Tony's face changed into a puzzled expression. Oh well, he thought, no sense wondering about it. I'll use the day to finish studying my appendices. He picked up the phone and dialed the operator. Several moments later, the phone on Hall's desk was ringing.

"Lieutenant Hall speaking."

"Good morning Roy. Anything going on?" asked Tony.

"Good morning boss. Well, two bikes were delivered about 15 minutes ago. Thank the Major when you talk with him. Aside from that, it's been quiet for us, I mean our messages. But we've been doing a lot of processing of NOB traffic."

"That will keep you out of trouble. Roy, I'm not sure I'll need you, but be at your desk tonight at 2000? If you don't hear from me by 2045, you can secure."

ASSIGNMENT: CASABLANCA

That Evening
8:50 p.m.
Major Rossi's Office

"Come in Tony, Roy, have a seat, I'll get you caught up. I've been busy," said Rossi.

"I take it you changed your mind about us being involved," Tony said smiling.

"Changed it about several things, and good thing I did. OK. So, let me boil this down. We just assumed the address the General's G2 gave you was a villa. It is actually an old warehouse, located at the end of a dirt road off Cemetery Avenue, easy walking distance and in view of the German villa you raided. You said those guys didn't have transportation when they showed up at that villa. That's why."

"Well I'll be damned," said Hall.

"Yeah!" said Rossi. "After we took a peek at the place, I thought I better have some men begin a continuous, covert surveillance of the target yesterday afternoon. Those four guys you took out were not the major part of the cell. Best I can tell, there's eight SOL members remaining in the cell, six of them are single and living in the target building. We found out where the other two are living with their families. All of them are looking and acting alarmed, scared."

"Losing four out of twelve would tend to ring a bell," said Tony, grinning. "But it also puts the remainder on general quarters, security watches and so forth."

"Affirmative. So, we needed a better plan. I have a rather unique relationship with a special branch of the French police. They are weeding out the troublemakers and German sympathizers. They have a lot of them detained in internment camps already. We scratch each other's backs. They know I'm just after the German agents and their saboteurs, so they turn their heads. And nothing I do, that they learn about, gets reported to anyone. Anyway, we're teaming up with the French special branch officers on this one. At midnight, they are going to arrest the two married men and all those in the warehouse, simultaneously. They will leave the warehouse for us until sunrise, then they will return and impound the place."

"Aha," said Tony. "That's where we come in. Strip it before sunrise."

"Roger that," said Rossi. "Me and my team will establish a perimeter when the gendarmes leave and you and Roy will haul shit out of there, into my big Renault. Make as many trips as needed until you're satisfied, then we all withdraw."

"Sounds like a plan to me," said Tony.

"Let's not get those nice dress blue uniforms dirty," said Rossi. "Come with me. I have some Army fatigues in the basement."

"I'll swallow my pride, but it's for a good cause," Tony said laughing.

"Oh, and we saved those cardboard boxes that were in the Renault, they're down there too. We'll load them in the car when we go.

That Evening
11:59 p.m.
Major Rossi's Office

"According to my watch, there's 30 seconds left in 1942, and my watch is correct," Rossi said grinning. He raised his coffee mug, "To a flawless op tonight and a happy new year to you and yours!" All three of them touched their mugs together and drank to the toast.

"I think that is the first time, since turning 21, that I've brought in the new year with anything but champagne," said Tony.

Rossi laughed, "And if we weren't going on this op tonight, I would have taken you to the Hotel Transatlantique in town. We would have brought in 1943 in style with some fine Mumm Cordon Rouge Champagne. But that will have to wait. Alright gents take your last drink of coffee and let's head out for the warehouse. By the time we arrive, the cops should be gone or damn near it."

The French police were still at the warehouse when they arrived. The last of the thugs were being loaded into the back of their truck. The only lights on this street were from headlights of police vehicles. A half-moon provided a dim glow over the area. Silhouettes were moving about. Roy and Tony, waiting in the car for the go signal, rolled down the rear windows. It was eerily quiet, except for an occasional order barked in French. The smell of decaying kelp on the beach was evident due to a slight breeze off the ocean. Rossi, M42 submachine gun over his shoulder, was having a whispered conversation with the French police officer in charge. The other three men of Rossi's team arrived separately and were standing near him, also armed with M42s. The police shut and locked the rear doors of their paddy wagon. Rossi signaled toward the Renault with a thumbs up. His men took up their perimeter security locations around the warehouse, Rossi in front.

"Here we go, Roy," said Tony. They quickly walked to the warehouse door, boxes in hand.

"Cops said they have cleared all the SOL from the warehouse," said Rossi.

"Yeah, well, we'll see," said Tony.

The wood-sided warehouse, about 30 feet long and half as wide, with a rounded corrugated metal roof, reminded Tony of an oversized Quonset hut. The front door, left open by the police, was wide enough to drive a jeep through. A normal size door was in the center of the big door. They went in and closed the big door behind them. What few lights there were inside, were all turned on, revealing an open bay with a concrete floor. An enclosed office area was located in the rear of the building. The bay was furnished crudely and sparsely. Metal cots were spaced along one side wall. Six were unmade and obviously just vacated. Thin mattresses, folded in half, were on the other cots. Two rectangular wooden tables were pushed together end-to-end in the middle of the bay. Some of the wooden chairs around it were in the disarray expected with a hasty departure. Sections of a French newspaper were scattered on the table. Along the opposite wall was a small two-burner electric stove, a small refrigerator that growled loudly now and then, a deep sink and a few open library shelving units being used as a pantry. A toilet in the far end corner, by the office, was made private by a curtain that was suspended by ropes from wooden cross-beams.

"Well Roy, there's not a damn thing out here worth grabbing, whatever they have of value to us will be in that room in back."

"Good grief, Tony, this place stinks of tobacco, their last meal, scroungy sweaty bodies, and that damn toilet," Hall exclaimed.

"There's no bathtub or shower. Just imagine seeing them taking a bath at the deep sink," Tony said with a laugh. The memory of the cabin he lived in during his mission in Norway flashed into Tony's mind. He recalled his team having to bathe in just a bucket of water, once a week. "OK, let's get serious now. If that window in the office wall isn't shaded, there's either no light in there or it's turned off. Be cautious. Seems to me that the police would have entered to clear it and left the light on. They could have missed one or more of these guys." He put his box down, drew his 38 and unclipped a flashlight from his belt. Hall did the same.

"Duck below the window and go to the other side of it," Tony whispered. "On my signal, shine in and take a gander from your angle. I'll do the same for the other half of the room." Hall nodded.

When they were up against the wall, on each side of the window, Tony nodded. Their flashlights came on simultaneously and scanned respective sides of the room.

Hall shook his head from side to side, indicating nothing seen and put his finger to his lips. They both realized their view angles left places to hide. Hall ducked down and went to the near side of the door. Tony moved to the other side of the door. Hall clipped his flashlight to his belt, turned the knob slowly and pushed the door open cautiously. The hinges gave out a supernatural squeal worthy of a Hitchcock movie. He paused, reached around the doorjamb and groped, unsuccessfully, for a light switch.

Tony signaled to wait and peeked in from his viewpoint, weapon in hand, and tossed his flashlight into the room. Getting no reaction to that, he rushed in ready to shoot. It was unoccupied. "I just couldn't chance it, Roy. We got lucky."

"Affirmative, boss. Ah, here's the light switch. I was close."

"Looks like we found some goodies. Get the boxes," said Tony, as he took a Minox camera out of his pocket.

The room had a 6'x4' office desk, a high wooden stool, and a metal five-drawer filing cabinet. A bare bulb hung above the desk on a wire from a bent nail in the ceiling. Its wire ran down the wall to a plug in the baseboard. On the desk was a German mobile battery-powered field transceiver, a hand key, a few pencils, an ash tray overflowing with cigarette butts and ashes, a notepad and a messy stack of several sheets of paper. The top sheet had hand-written groups of five-digit numbers and French paragraphs.

Hall returned with the two boxes they dropped in the bay, "Taking pinup pictures of that German radio, huh?"

"Affirm. These guys must have had a damn good relationship with those B-Dienst guys to get a transceiver out of them. I would like to know who they were talking to."

"Holy crap. What a sloppy hole in the back wall for the antenna cable," said Hall laughing. "They stuffed the cable hole with an old rag to fill the gap."

"They didn't have the same pride in workmanship as the Germans," joked Tony. "With any luck, this is the file cabinet I figured was missing from the villa. I'll start going through the file drawers. You take everything of value on and in the desk and put it into a box."

"Roger, boss. Oh, Chuck might get some use out of this Luger pistol and ammo."

"All the documents in the top drawer of this cabinet are in French," said Tony. He pulled the top drawer out of the cabinet and put it on the end of the desk. "Put everything in the drawers I put on this desk into boxes."

"Roger, boss."

Tony took a quick look at the contents of the other drawers. "All the rest of these drawers have German files and documents. Too bad neither of us know German."

"By the time I learned it, the war would be over," said Hall.

"Eureka, Roy. Crypto keys. Oh, I damn sure didn't expect that. I might not speak German, but I can see these are Enigma keys for February and March 1943. They only took the current keys with them."

"Makes it all worthwhile," said Hall.

"Yes, indeed. Sure does."

The subtle sounds of paper being shuffled and dropped into a box was broken by loud terse voices, exchanging French.

"Shit's hitting the fan, Roy. Kill the light. We'll watch through the window to see who comes through the door."

Two SOL members came through the door with their hands clasped over their heads. Rossi followed with his weapon trained on them. "Come on out here guys," Rossi called out. "Have you found anything we can use for gags and to tie their hands and feet?" asked Rossi.

"Yes, rags and small rope, like clothesline," replied Hall.

"Good. Hurry and secure them, really good. Tony, keep a weapon on them while Roy does that. Lay them face down on racks, far apart. Tie their hands behind them and connect the hand and feet bindings taught enough so they have their feet up at

90-degree angle. I don't want them to be moving around. And make it fast. We need to get out of here. There may be more. The wives of those two the French arrested must be beating the jungle drums."

Hall finished immobilizing the two captives. "Finish filling boxes?" he asked.

"Yes, there's only one drawer in the cabinet left," said Tony. "I'll watch these two while you finish and get the boxes into the car."

Hall emptied the cabinet and shuttled back and forth, stowing the boxes in the Renault.

"Last one, we're done boss," Hall said as he turned out the office light.

"Good, let's get the hell out of here," said Tony.

As they were putting the last box into the car, Tony heard an owl-like hoot from the north side of the warehouse. It was a signal from the perimeter guard of danger. Then he heard faint sounds of two or three people talking and walking quickly down Avenue du Cimetiere toward the dirt road to the warehouse.

"Roy, get inside and keep the lights out," said Rossi. "Take out any of them that get past us and come through the door. Tony, get behind the Renault and follow my lead. I'll get behind my guys' Citroën over here. With us and my two guys on the front corners of the building, it will be an unmistakable losing situation for them. We should be able to capture these guys without any blood spilled. The French can collect them all in the morning."

Tony had a combat knife in one hand and his 38 caliber pistol in the other. The foot sounds turned the corner of Avenue du Cimetiere and headed down the dirt road toward the warehouse. They slowed to a cautious walk about 30 yards away. There were three of them, whispering. Tony could see one of them pointing at the cars. They all had pistols in their hands. He ducked down.

When the three men were within ten yards of the cars, Rossi hand signaled his two men at the sides of the warehouse, popped up, pointing his M42 at them and called out, "*Lâchez vos armes!*" Rossi's men also called out the same command for them to drop their weapons. Tony popped up and aimed his weapon at them. The three men froze, looking alternately from one weapon pointed at them to another, dropped their pistols and raised their hands above their heads.

An Hour Later
Basement, Consulate Annex

The Annex basement was mainly a cement floored open area, with two enclosed rooms in one end. One was a combination toilet and storage area. The other was a small short-wave radio communications station. At the opposite end of the basement was an office desk and chair with a lit desk lamp, desktop paraphernalia and documents awaiting attention in a wire basket.

"Is that the last box?" asked Rossi, coming out of the radio room. Tony heard Morse code coming from the room when the door was open.

"Yup," said Hall, bringing the last one down the steps. "Now what?"

"You're welcome to leave all that junk until tomorrow," said Rossi. "I sent my three men home after I collected the documents they rifled from the prisoners."

Tony was tempted to get some sleep. I trust these guys, and all that, he thought. But some of this stuff would be a good find for the OSS to claim, so, the hell with sleep. "OK Roy let's consolidate this stuff into as few boxes as we can," said Tony. "Seal them and get them double wrapped for diplomatic shipment back to our Embassy."

"Alright, I'll give you guys a hand with that," said Rossi.

"Will the French cops be pissed about the captives we left for them?" asked Tony.

"My guess is, there's a good chance they won't even be there when the cops show up at sunrise. There may be more of those damn SOL scum that we don't know about. They won't want any of their merry band to be captured by the cops. We pulled that off perfectly, that is no blood spilled by us. Alright, I'll go upstairs and get some coffee for us," said Rossi. "While I'm up there, what do you guys need for supplies?"

"For starters, Chuck, packing gear," said Hall. "Wrapping paper, gummed tape, water bowl, sponge, scissors, marking materials, you know. And that coffee!"

"Going to be a wimp and use the sponge instead of licking the tape huh?" asked Rossi with a chuckle.

Hall laughed, "I couldn't muster up enough spit for all the tape it will take for this job."

Rossi laughed, "Roger. Some of the stuff you need is in my desk over there. That's my, let's call it, my covert ops desk. It's got classification stamps and ink pad, scissors and stuff like that. The rest of the things you need I'll bring down."

"Just then a man in civilian clothes came out of the radio room and whispered to Rossi, "Tangier QSL'd for your message." He handed Rossi a sheet of paper with hand-printed English five-letter code groups on it and returned to the room.

Rossi nodded acknowledgement and put the sheet in his desk basket. "That's my OSS comm center. He's a former French Army radio operator that I hired. He just sent my report of our activity tonight to my boss in Tangier. We have our own OSS communications link with Tangier, and I have my own little network of operators in this general area. They are scattered in about, oh, I guess a 20 mile radius from the port."

"Send that stuff in the clear?" asked Tony.

"Oh no, we have a strip cipher contraption we use with Tangier. We made up something simpler for the cells in my local network. Code phrases, which we change weekly. We rarely talk with my cells. It's too dangerous. If we need to get something hot to each other, we use dead drops."

"Right under the noses of the B-Dienst intercept site too. I don't know how you got away with it. They didn't have a direction finder truck?" asked Tony.

"Affirmative. That was my salvation. We have the antenna hidden inside the chimney of that fireplace we're not using, over there. Although we've seen Germans cruising certain neighborhoods and buildings, especially our buildings, looking for antennas and what not, there was nothing they could find suspicious," said Rossi smiling. "Come with me, Roy, I'll fix you up with some supplies."

7 – Meanwhile...

3:10 p.m., Friday, January 1, 1943
Owen Edward Langsdale's Office
Special Operations Executive S02 Branch,
Mansion Office Building, Greater London

L angsdale's secretary knocked on his open office door, "Captain Taylor here to
see you, sir."

"Thank you, Jayne. Tea for us please. Come through Captain." He
motioned toward his small circular conference table. "Hang that wet coat and hat and
come sit. Frosty out there as well?"

"Thank you, Ed. Yes, it is a little nippy," said Taylor and put his leather attaché
case beside his chair.

"When you called earlier, you said you had good news. What have you, Bill?"

"I thought it was time for a chat over tea, since it's been a while, and to bring some
information personally rather than send you a message."

Taylor took in a deep breath to savor the smell of the fresh British tea, just arriving,
which he had come to enjoy immensely.

Jayne sat a tray of cups, saucers and a steaming ceramic tea pot down on the table.
She poured two cups and departed, closing the door behind her. They each eagerly
took their first sips.

"I received another message report from Commander Romella today, Ed. He sent
information on a second operation they ran last night that was very successful. He's
got five boxes of material to send us from that one. You can read the full report at
your leisure." He opened his case, removed a six page Top Secret report and handed
it to Langsdale. "Summary is, he found a file cabinet that he believes came from the
B-Dienst villa. Apparently removed for safe keeping by a cell of the SOL. Should be
very interesting."

"Right. Splendid news, Bill. When can we expect those boxes?" asked Langsdale.

"At the end of the report," continued Taylor, "Tony provides flight information on their first diplomatic package of material. The five boxes from last night haven't been scheduled yet."

"Right. Briefly, what is in these five boxes?"

"He didn't analyze, or itemize the materials," explained Taylor. "But he describes the most valuable material as, and Bletchley Park will love this, Enigma keys. Plus radio intercept logs, traffic analysis reports, order of battle reports, personnel information and correspondence. As you'll read, he had quite the interesting time on this one, similar to the last, but no shooting this time."

"Brilliant! I expect you will want to photograph what you wish of the lot. But please expedite your processing of the materials for Bletchley. I'll come pick those up and deliver them to Bletchley straight away."

"We'll certainly screen it all for Bletchley interest first. But we won't dilly dally on the rest either, Ed. As we agreed, you'll get the originals."

"Commander Romella is quite the chap, is he not? Any chance we can steal him for a while, say, perhaps, the remainder of the war?" Langsdale asked smiling as he twisted his mustache.

Taylor laughed and looked alternately into Langsdale's twinkling eyes, one blue and one brown. "We have shared a lot of things, from time to time, Ed. But he is not someone I'm willing to part with."

"Blimey. Hoped you would be a bit more sporting about it," said Langsdale with a sly grin.

4:30 p.m., Washington Time, Friday, January 1, 1943
Commander Jerry Webber's Office
OP-20-GB, Main Navy Building
Washington, DC

Commander Webber kicked off the meeting promptly, "First, I hope this is a happy new year for us. With any luck, we'll survive the move to Nebraska Avenue next month."

"Yes, sir, on both," said Lieutenant Commander Paul Archer, from OP-20-G's COMINT Division. "Everyone has been working their butts off, working long hours, trying to move stuff with a minimal impact to operations. Older archives are going first."

"Very well," Webber said. "OK. Let's get underway. I have reviewed your report on the effectiveness of the direction finding networks, Paul. I thought you should come in and talk about it."

"The results of the study are very interesting," said Archer. "It was no surprise that the quality of U-boat location determinations from DF fixes have varied widely, depending on the geometry involved with our existing DF station locations. But the qualitative improvement seen when I modeled the addition of the two stations you requested, Jan Mayen Island, Norway and San Miguel Island, Azores was significant for their respective ocean areas."

"I found it interesting too, Paul," said Webber. "But I'm not thrilled with the idea of putting people up on Jan Mayen Island. That would be some extremely tough and isolated duty and would be a difficult logistic support problem."

"Commander Romella's recent report of his visit to Jan Mayen made my blood run cold," Archer said.

"We could probably get the Norwegian Government in exile to let us go in there," said Webber, shaking his head, "but it's a location with a high risk of German occupation and too difficult to support. Maybe we should just give some help, encouragement, equipment, or something, to the U.S. Coast Guard DF site that Commander Romella visited up there."

"That's a thought," said Archer. "But being a Coasty site, we would have no real control of their ops," said Archer. "Plus, if we weren't successful in getting them pulled into a DF net, with reliable communications and participation, they wouldn't be worth the trouble."

"Correct," said Webber. "But the Azores is a different story. That would be excellent duty and easily supported. Problem is, our diplomatic efforts to get us in there militarily have not been successful. Portugal wants to remain completely neutral to keep the Germans from occupying mainland Portugal. Intel says the Germans want that archipelago also. So Lisbon is balking."

Archer nodded.

Webber continued, "It may be worth discussing, at a later date. It sure is an intriguing idea, though. But for now, Azores goes on a back burner, unless or until situations change."

"I'll keep my ear to the ground," said Archer.

A fresh cup of coffee and the quiet of an empty office allowed Webber's mind to conjure up an idea. He picked up his phone and dialed a contact in the State Department.

8 – A Peach

8:40 a.m., Monday, January 4, 1943
Crypto Room
Naval Operating Base, Casablanca

It was a pleasant ride from Anfa Hotel to NOB. The sun had been up for a couple of hours, trying to burn its way through an overcast sky. The temperature was rising slowly from the low 50s. Tony had his car window down so he could enjoy the scent of bougainvillea blooms, hear the rustle of palm fronds from wind gusts, and the many sounds of bustling citizens, vendor and prayer calls. He cranked up the window when the unpleasant aromas of the port area became more dominant.

Lieutenant Hall answered the knock on the crypto room door, "Good morning, sir."

"As you were," Tony said as he entered.

"Good morning, sir," greeted Chief Johnson with a smile. Their unique operational experiences together had forged a solid bond that was evident to Hall.

"Good morning, Chief. How is Casablanca treating you?"

"12 on and 12 off, with no break is tiring," said Johnson. "Haven't seen much of Casablanca. I did take a few hours to go to the Rialto this weekend. I didn't expect to find a Rialto in Morocco, but it was a really nice movie theater."

"What did you see?" asked Tony.

"A western about General Custer, I think it was called *Died with their Boots On*. Errol Flynn and that gorgeous Olivia de Havilland."

Tony nodded, "Did Flynn play Custer?"

"Yes, sir. He made his last stand, too," Johnson said with a laugh.

"Ah, too bad," Tony said with a chuckle. "Alright Mr. Hall, what's new this morning?" asked Tony as he sat down in the chair at Hall's desk.

"That folder on the desk has some messages inside for you," said Hall. "There's only one received specifically for you since the last time you were here. I saved the intel summaries for you, as well. We are getting quite a bit of traffic for the Secret Service advance party, though. They send a guy over when I let them know something's here."

Tony opened the folder and read the top message, addressed to him. "Captain Samuel Milz. Don't know him. How about you, Roy?"

"Nope. Never heard of him," replied Hall. "I saw that the message came from CNO, N2."

"Affirmative. He's on the intel staff of the Chief of Naval Operations, Admiral King. The Admiral is arriving on the eighth, Friday, in the late afternoon," said Tony.

"I see he mentioned he has transportation arranged to the hotel and wants to have supper with you that evening. At least we don't have to arrange that. Will I be involved at all with this?" asked Hall.

"Negative, Roy. You are clear on the conference aspect of the trip. Just ride herd on Johnson and Hamill., But this means you'll start getting a lot of traffic for the Navy wheels that will start showing up shortly." Tony read the intelligence summaries in the folder. He was glad to read that the U.S. Army Air Force sent a flight of heavy bombers to the U-boat pens at Saint-Nazaire, France, the previous day. He had a special place in his mind for eliminating the U-boat threat in every way possible. "By the way, Roy, the Brits are going to be using that big Royal Navy auxiliary ship tied up out there, the HMS *Bulolo*, for comm support. You'll only have our Navy's classified traffic to deal with."

"What is that thing, anyway?" asked Johnson.

"They call it an LSH, landing ship headquarters," said Tony. "It's a command ship for amphibious landing operations. I doubt you can get a tour of it. I'm sure security is sky high on her while this conference is here."

"I wondered why there was so many British Navy gals, both officer and enlisted, going back and forth to that ship," said Hall. "You just don't see women going aboard Navy ships. They are all Radiomen and Yeomen. Some good lookers too."

"Yep. And you two be gentlemen with those gals. I don't want to hear any complaints. They are mostly the typing pool for British classified documents and their communications support. Anyway, Roy, when you get messages for our Navy's VIPs, figure out how to get them delivered. If you need help with that, just call me."

ASSIGNMENT: CASABLANCA

The Following Friday
6:40 p.m., Friday, January 8, 1943
Anfa Hotel

Tony answered his room phone.

"This is Captain Milz. I got your note at the front desk. Glad you received the message from CNO. Means I don't have to explain. Thank you for confirming supper. I'll meet you up there in about 10 minutes. I assume you'll be ready then." He hung up before Tony could reply.

The fourth floor of the hotel could be best described as an open deck restaurant, but with a roof. The large windows were usually open on the warm days, for the balmy breeze, tropical atmosphere and visibility. The side of the restaurant with a view toward the city, port and the Atlantic Ocean was breathtaking. The tan sand beach was only three quarters of a mile away. Tonight, it was too chilly for open windows, but the lights of Casablanca and the ships in port were a captivating sight, just the same.

Tony was already seated when the Captain arrived. He stood to greet him. "Good evening, Captain, Tony Romella, nice to meet you."

"Captain Samuel Milz," he said coldly.

Tony was surprised at the weak and brief handshake. Milz was bald, slightly overweight and stood perhaps five feet tall. A dark mole over his left eyebrow was a distraction. Well, thought Tony, this looks like an attitude that's going to be disappointing.

The waiter arrived with menus.

"I won't need a menu. I'm not very hungry. The flight was abominable," said Milz. "Just vegetable soup and a dinner roll, please."

"Will tomato soup do, sir?" asked the waiter.

"No vegetable soup? Alright, tomato," replied Milz.

I'm not going to make this supper last longer than necessary, thought Tony. "I'll have the same." The waiter gave a bland look, nodded and left.

"No need to do that," said Milz. "You can stay and finish whatever meal you wish."

"It's OK, been a long day for me," said Tony. That son of a gun was going to get up and leave me here when he was finished. He's going to be hard to like.

"I understand from Admiral King that you brought appendices for discussion. Where are you keeping them?" asked Milz.

"Conference Room D is set up for round-the-clock storage and protection, Captain. They have tables in there that we can use to review and discuss them," said Tony.

Milz shrugged, "I don't see the point of spending much time on them, at this point. The first conference meeting on the 14th will be solely for the establishment of an agenda. The British are coming with an agenda that we already know is very different than ours. Their idea of what operations and their sequence we should plan is not what the President and General Eisenhower have developed. Thus, you have appendices for things that may not be useful in any way. When I know the agenda, I'll determine what is worth concentrating on. But I wish to take a quick look at what you brought. Let's plan on meeting in the secure room at, say, 0600 tomorrow? I have more pressing things to attend for the remainder of the day."

The Next Morning
5:50 a.m., Saturday, January 9, 1943
Conference Room D
Anfa Hotel

Tony came down early to withdraw the appendices from storage. He had them sitting in the center of a four-foot round linen topped restaurant table that had three chairs around it. Captain Milz came to the doorway at 5:59 and seemed put out that he had to show his ID.

"You would think a Captain in uniform would be ID enough," said Milz, as he approached the table and pulled a chair out. "I thought I left bureaucracy back in DC, but I see that's not the case. What do we have, Commander?"

"Yes, sir," replied Tony, "they are following the strictest security procedures to the T. These are the eight appendices for each of the operations that OP-20-G believed could possibly be discussed."

Milz read the cover page of each of them without expression. He picked up the appendix for Operation HUSKY, the Allied invasion of Sicily. He scanned each page for about three seconds each, closed it and put it down. "I assume that they are all relatively the same, just minor differences."

"True, Sam," replied Tony. "Each operation has its unique COMINT requirements which is covered in one or two pages at the end. The rest of their needs are satisfied by our existing exploitation capabilities."

"Uh, let's keep things formal, Commander," said Milz. "Let's not use first names. High professionalism, I find, produces higher levels of effectiveness."

"Aye, aye, sir. Understood." Oh brother, Tony thought. This guy is a peach. I know just how to handle him.

Milz made a sharp nod. "Good. Frankly, I'm not sure there's a need for appendices. You OP-20-G people are going to do your secret things, behind your curtain, regardless. From what I saw in that appendix, I still don't know what you plan to grace us operations people with, nor when."

"The nature of communications intelligence..." Tony paused when Milz held his palm up.

"Stop, Commander. I've seen enough of COMINT in my three months in N2 to know how you people like to hide your esoteric sources and rarely give us anything concrete to work with. Possible this. Probable that. It's not like that for me in photo intelligence. I could never get away with that kind of imprecision. You people didn't do a very good job alerting us about the Japanese attack plan for Pearl Harbor. I doubt you'll do better in the Mediterranean and Europe."

Thoughts raced through Tony's mind. Oh, great. A guy with a PHOTINT background, and an axe to grind with COMINT, is passing judgement on these COMINT appendices. Do I tell him off? Or, just give him some rope. "Captain, I certainly respect your guidance, experience and N2 viewpoint. You certainly are correct about us continuing our maximum capabilities, sir. We will support all Naval operations fully, to the best of our ability, in any case, and in all situations."

"Excellent," said Milz. "I see no need to discuss these further, Commander. If there is a need to meet again, I'll let you know. In the meantime, put me on the access list for these appendices in event I wish to look at them later."

"Aye, aye, sir," replied Tony. Captain Milz rose and left the room.

Tony's blood was boiling. Well now, that was fun. I smell politics or funding competition in there somewhere. Probably both. I need to send a report of this conversation. He's wants to cut COMINT out of this conference and OP-20-G needs to know it.

That Afternoon
5:30 p.m., Washington Time, Saturday, January 9, 1943
Commander Jerry Webber's Office
OP-20-GB, Main Navy Building
Washington, DC

"How are the move preparations going in your area" Webber asked Lieutenant Commander Paul Archer.

"This is going to be a son of a bitch move. But, for all practical purposes, we're meeting the timelines."

"Excellent, Paul. I want you to read this message from Commander Romella," said Webber.

"Sounds like someone ate the Captain's porridge," said Archer, humorously. "Foolishly open about a bias he has developed."

"I don't like the sound of it," said Webber. "I want you to do two things for me. First, call Admiral King's aide and read that to him. The Admiral hasn't left for

Casablanca yet. Tell his aide that I want to get on the Admiral's calendar for 20 minutes on an urgent matter before he leaves for Morocco. Then call around to people you know here in 20-G and see if anyone knows Captain Milz or have any idea about why he has such a negative attitude toward COMINT."

"Aye, aye, sir. The second thing?"

"Second," Webber continued, "call the Naval Research Lab and find out if that experimental DF system, they are calling the DX, is ready for a field test. If so, find out what the installed dimensions will be, the minimum space required for it, and power requirements."

9 – Saint Michael

Three Days Later
2:15 p.m., Tuesday, January 12, 1943
Crypto Room
Naval Operating Base, Casablanca

Chief Johnson answered Tony's knock on the Crypto Room door. "Good afternoon, sir. We've been trying to track you down for a couple hours. Mr. Hall just stepped out. He went to get some donuts. He made friends with a supply officer on one of the ships in port. He'll be back shortly."

"I had some spare time, so I went into the city," said Tony. "There is a very nice shop that was recommended by a waiter. It's called, Broadway. You heard me right. Sounds very stateside, doesn't it? Go if you get a chance. It has things all women are interested in. It's on Rue Bendahan. They have some great stuff to take back as presents for your British girlfriends. Don't be afraid to negotiate. I bought some really nice French negligée for my wife."

"I'll do that. If I ever find the time between being on watch, eating and sleeping," said Johnson with a chuckle. "But I'll make time, before we leave."

"What do you have for me?" Tony asked.

Johnson motioned toward one of the crypto machines. We received a double-encrypted Eyes Only message addressed to you. You have to type the underlying groups of letters to get your message. I have the crypto rotor wheels set for the officer's key list for today. All you have to do is type the characters you see there on the sheets on this copy holder. It's a long one, so it's easy to miss a group or a line. I numbered the pages, so you don't get them out of sequence. If it starts printing garbage, let me know."

"Johnson, you're a hell of a lot better typist than me, and with that length, I'm delegating that task to you. Just don't read the tape other than confirming it's not garbled. Whatever you do happen to read, keep to yourself."

Lieutenant Hall entered the room. "I see you put the Chief to work, Commander."

"He is a slave driver, Mr. Hall," Johnson said, smiling as he typed.

Tony laughed, "We better be quiet and let him work, Mr. Hall."

Johnson quickly typed the code groups on the sheets in front of him onto the crypto machine's keyboard. Each keystroke on the keyboard resulted in a character or space being printed onto a narrow, gum-backed, endless tape. After working on it for twenty minutes, Johnson stood. "I'm done, sir. If I process the tape, I'll have to be reading it."

"I've done that part before, Johnson, you're relieved of that duty. Go back to what you were doing when I arrived," Tony said as he ejected the printer end of the tape. He searched for the other end of the tape in the pile on the floor. Using a glass dish that held a wet sponge on a nearby desk used for this purpose, he tore off sections of the tape to fit the width of blank message form sheets, pulled the back of the tape sections across the wet sponge and pasted the sections onto the forms, line after line, similar to a telegram.

"I'm done Johnson, you can reconfigure the machine," said Tony, as he took the sheets of the decrypted message to Hall's desk to read it.

"I know you're curious men, but it isn't anything that affects you," Tony said. He put the message in a folder and motioned for Hall to come to the desk. "Roy," he said in a low voice, "I'm leaving Casablanca early tomorrow morning on a Pan Am Clipper flight to the Azores. I don't know when I'm coming back, but it shouldn't be more than a week or so. I'm making a courier trip to our Consulate in San Miguel, Azores. Effective immediately, you're in charge. Take care of everything until I get back."

"Aye, aye, sir," said Hall.

"I expect to be out of communications. I can't tell you more at this point. I'm going to run some errands and stop at the Consulate on my way back to the hotel." He took the Casablanca tourist guide, bought at the hotel, out of his jacket pocket. He turned to the page he had dog-eared to locate an ad for the shop Lucienne, which was recommended to him by a female corporal at the hotel. The address on the ad was 42 Rue Clemenceau. The guide had a street lookup list with map grid references, which indicated D47. He unfolded the large map of Casablanca in the back of the guide and located D47.

"You men might take note of this store, also, if you will be shopping for girls back in London," Tony said, pointing at the location on the map. "I'm told they have a great selection of French perfume. Easy walk from here, too." He jotted down the name and address on two slips of paper for them.

The signage at Lucienne's indicated it was a *parfumerie* and sold other delights for women. The composite fragrance of many was evident as soon as he entered. A bell on the door announced his arrival. A sedate, attractive woman came through a bead door at the rear of the store. She was wearing a slim, ankle length, black dress with a natural colored floral design print.

"*Bonne jour, monsieur,*" she greeted.

"Good afternoon," he replied.

She smiled, "I speak English. Thank you for shopping here today, sir. What are you looking to buy?"

"Fragrances, for my wife."

"Something special then. For an American lady?" she asked.

"British."

"Oh. Something more subtle, but still special. Come with me to the perfume counter."

She lead him to a glass encased counter. She took out two fancy bottles and set them on the counter. "These are my two newest perfumes by a new and excellent French boutique in Bordeaux. I don't have an open sample for you. But, even without opening, you can still catch the fragrance well enough for you to choose. Go ahead."

He picked up one and smelled near the top. Then the other. "Those are both wonderful fragrances. How much for both?"

"Only 5,000 francs, for both," she replied with a smile.

It took little math power for him to realize she was asking for $50 equivalent per bottle. He had purchased fine perfume in Washington. Based on that experience, he decided to participate in the Moroccan sport of haggling. "Would you accept 3,000 francs for both? Since it is a new boutique and not in Paris?"

She struck a coy smile. "4,500 francs?"

He could tell from her facial expressions that she was enjoying this. He decided to be a little ruthless, since she was clearly asking a ridiculous price; he offered even less, "2,900."

"Oh, monsieur," she put her hand to her forehead dramatically. "4,000?"

She's a fine actress, he thought. But she is dealing with a man who took hundreds of dollars in poker winnings from men who were no slouches at the game. He proposed an even lower price without hesitation, "2,500."

She could not hold back a laugh. "Please, 2,900?" she asked. "That's a fair price, sir."

He grinned, "2,900, OK."

"I must pay my rent," she said with a grin. "I have these in original unopened boxes. Would you like me to pack them in one box for you?"

"Please. That would be wonderful," he said, as he counted out the francs.

That Afternoon
The U.S. Consulate Annex
Major Rossi's Office

"Have a seat, Tony. Where's it hurt you most?" asked Rossi, jokingly.

"Nowhere, not yet anyway. What do you know about the Azores? Is there an OSS officer there?" asked Tony.

"Is that two questions, or one in the same?" asked Rossi.

"Two," said Tony.

"OK. Let me think a minute." Rossi paused and sorted through folders in a file-safe. He pulled a document out that was marked Secret. "I received a report on the Azores from Colonel Donovan, last month. Let me read for a bit. It's restricted to OSS, but maybe there's a few things in here that I can tell you. Any particular island you're interested in?"

"San Miguel Island, primarily," said Tony.

Rossi read for a few minutes then looked up. "Alright. The Portuguese Air Force has a major air base on Terceira. They have that island locked up. We have a consulate in San Miguel. It's a very small operation. No OSS officer is assigned to the Consulate there. That's pretty much what I can tell you."

Tony nodded, "OK. Thanks, Chuck."

"Wouldn't be heading in that direction, would you?" asked Rossi.

"Why do you have a report on the Azores, Chuck?" asked Tony.

"Touché, my friend," Chuck replied with a wide smile.

Tony just grinned, "Thanks again. I appreciate the info."

The Next Morning
7:30 a.m., Wednesday, January 13, 1943
Port of Casablanca

Auckland Museum [CC BY 4.0 (https://creativecommons.org/licenses/by/4.0)]

PanAm Clipper (Boeing 314 Flying Boat)

As the Army sedan approached the wharves, Tony immediately spotted the big four-engine Boeing flying boat, in the form of a PanAm Clipper, looming large in the port. It was floating peacefully at the end of a finger pier, tied up to a floating platform that was lower than the pier, due to the tide and pier height above the waterline. The Clipper had a U.S. flag painted on the side of its nose, along with a small PanAm logo. He was surprised to see any markings on the plane at all.

Tony recalled reading a report that explained how PanAm's Pacific and European routes were severely impacted by the start of the wars in those areas. The U.S. and British Governments took advantage of the resources the Pan Am system afforded and coordinated contractual agreements with Pan Am for all of the Clippers in service and those being built. He recalled that the crews were often an amalgamation of PanAm and Army Air Force personnel.

A cool breeze, with the typically unpleasant smells of the port, tugged gently on his hat as he hurried along the pier, sea bag over his shoulder and attaché case in hand. Tony slowly and carefully walked down the gangway from the pier onto the platform alongside the Clipper. A dockworker on the platform relieved Tony of his sea bag and handed it to a steward waiting on the inclined lower wing stub that served as a flotation stabilizer and ramp to the doorway. The First Officer appeared in the doorway and said, "Come aboard, Commander." Tony stepped easily from the platform onto the wing stub and walked a few steps up to the doorway.

"Cliff Harkin, First Officer," a man in the doorway said. Tony saw his eyes shift to the discernable contour of a shoulder holster under the upper left part of Tony's uniform jacket. "Just for the sake of formality, please show me your ID."

"I'm Commander Tony Romella," he said and showed Harkin his Navy ID card.

"We're ready to go Tony. We were just waiting for enough light and you. You're the only passenger. Our cargo run out of the Belgian Congo was diverted for this leg. I've done a lot of these Congo-U.S. cargo round-robins. We've been prohibited from taking on passengers in the past, in either direction. Although we're puzzled, I won't ask."

Tony just smiled. He couldn't share the nature of his mission with Harkin. Nor could he reveal his knowledge, from intelligence briefings, that their secret Congolese cargo was uranium for the Manhattan Project. One clipper was constantly doing round-robin trips to and from the Congo, bringing to the U.S. the richest uranium ore known to exist.

Harkin nodded, "OK. I understand we're picking you up in the Azores on our way back to the Congo."

"That's my understanding as well," Tony replied.

"We'll take good care of you, Tony. Make yourself comfortable in the dining lounge in the next compartment forward or the passenger compartment, forward of that, which is just aft of the galley. We're a cargo mission, so there's only one steward. His name is Greg. He can cook fairly well, and we have plenty food onboard. Not haute cuisine, but we eat pretty good. Harold Mullen is our Captain. He said he'd visit with you once we are level at cruise altitude. Please don't wander aft of this compartment, or the upper decks. Uh, the cargo could shift."

"Roger. I understand," Tony said with a grin.

"Excellent. Flight time will be six point six hours, if the upper air winds forecast holds true. If you need a bunk to nap, just let the steward know."

"Great. I'll probably need food more than sleep," Tony said with a smile. Oh Petra, I wish you could experience this, he thought, as he began making his way forward to the passenger compartment next to the galley.

The steward looked around the galley doorway when he heard Tony taking a seat, "I'm making sure the galley is secure for takeoff. Once we're at cruise altitude, I'll check to see if I can get you something, Commander."

"Roger. I missed breakfast, so when you get the chance, coffee and whatever you have, will be great."

ASSIGNMENT: CASABLANCA

That Afternoon
2:55 p.m., (GMT-2), Wednesday, January 13, 1943
Aboard the Clipper

The slowly pulsating drone of the four engines and a full belly from a lunch of tuna and yellow cheese sandwiches, had a powerful drowse inducing effect, despite the caffeine.

He was awaking after a two hour nap. His mind wandered blissfully through thoughts and images of Petra. He became alert at the distinct sound of engines being throttled back a bit and a slight downward pitch of the aircraft. He looked at his watch. They were descending from cruise altitude, approaching San Miguel Island, Azores. The mental image of the island fresh in his mind, he moved to the window seat on the right side of the passenger compartment and peered out of the window. The sky was dull from high overcast clouds. Searching the blue open sea ahead for several minutes, a distant view of the southeast coast of San Miguel finally emerged. From the plane's height and distance, it appeared to be a green, uninhabited coast. Slowly, the entire eastern end of the long, sock-shaped island was visible. As minutes passed, settled areas became evident. Ponta Delgada, the largest city of the island, was discernable, three-fourths of the way up the southern coast.

Hansueli Krapf [File uploaded with Commonist. [CC BY-SA 3.0 (https://creativecommons.org/licenses/by-sa/3.0)]
Ponta Delgada (left foreground), San Miguel Island, Azores, Portugal (2012)

The aircraft made a turn a few miles from the shoreline, flew parallel to it and descended down to approach altitude. Fishing boats were sprinkled along the coast. Some were anchored, some had wakes trailing behind them. The port of Ponta Delgada was a few miles away, nearly directly ahead. The sound of flaps coming down, and the engines throttling up, gave evidence of the pending water landing. His mind recalled hanging from a chute over Norway, preparing to land in cold water. The port was peppered with boats of many sizes, powered and sail, many were dockside, some in anchorages, several were moving about. More flaps came down, the engines roared louder as they fought against the drag of the flaps. The aircraft slowly descended toward the ocean until the hull settled onto the water with a gentle splashing bounce, then came the thumping of small swells. The engines were powered back gently to water taxi power. After a few minutes, they had entered the calmer water of the port. The engines slacked then shut down.

The steward come into the compartment. "Commander, here's your jacket and hat. They are securing us to an anchorage buoy. Captain Mullen said a boat will be coming out to take you to the dock. Someone from the U.S. Consulate should be waiting for you there. Oh, and don't forget to set your watch back two hours. Azores is GMT-2. Stay aboard until I get your sea bag into the boat," said the steward.

"Thank you, Greg. Good food, nice ride. Appreciate the hospitality."

Tony and the steward waited at the doorway. An 18 foot skiff was making its way from the city side of the port. It was powered by a noisy, one-cylinder engine that was mounted forward of the tiller. Tony smiled as he watched the skiff coming across the open water of the port, chugging and puffing blue smoke from its vertical exhaust pipe. A Portuguese boatman navigated the skiff slowly and skillfully alongside the Clipper's lower wing stub, the lower end of which was awash. The steward took Tony's sea bag down the ramp partway, level with the boat and handed the bag to the Portuguese boatman. Given the brisk breeze causing the light chop in the open water, he pulled his hat down tight on his head and stepped through the doorway onto the wing stub. With the steadying hand of the steward, Tony transferred into the skiff and took a seat on a weather-beaten wooden cross-bench that was sprinkled with sand, or salt crystals. Glad I wore my khaki uniform, Tony thought. He kept a firm grip on the handle of his attaché case, resting on the seat beside him.

With a wave to the steward, the boatman pushed off. He wrapped several turns of starter cord around a capstan protruding from the small engine's side. With a mighty pull on the cord, the engine coughed to life. The skiff came around and headed toward the dock area on the city side of the port.

Tony looked back when he heard the Clipper's engines powering up, one at a time. He watched her water taxi clear of local boats, then make her lumbering takeoff.

About a hundred yards from the dock, and after several light sprays off the bow, Tony saw a man in a business suit waving. He waved back. That's either Daly or his driver, he thought. So far, the hastily developed travel plan was working without a snafu.

The boatman reached over and cut the skiff's engine off as they approached the dock. He steered the coasting skiff alongside a narrow landing on the side of the dock. The landing was about a foot above the waterline. The greenish-bronze color of the landing indicated that it was often below the waterline, and probably slippery from algae. The boatman motioned for Tony to debark as he held onto a rope cleat to keep the skiff snug against the landing. Tony tossed his sea bag onto the landing and stepped carefully out of the skiff, and found the landing was, as expected, slightly slippery. Tony brushed the dirt off the seat of his pants, put his bag over his shoulder and climbed the stairway up the side of the dock. A tall, lanky man, the one he saw waving to him earlier, was waiting at the top.

"Leonard Daly, Consul General. Have a good trip, Commander?" he asked. A full head of red hair blew freely with each gust of wind.

Tony dropped his bag onto the dock. "Tony Romella. My pleasure," he said as they shook hands vigorously. "I did indeed. The Clipper is one fine ship. They are everything I heard about them."

"I have had the pleasure of riding a Clipper as well, to Hawaii before the war," said Daly.

"This one was rigged for cargo, so probably not as full an experience as yours was."

"I have a car waiting, Tony. First, we have to get you cleared through the Portuguese Governor's customs and security office. The Island Governor is an Army General, who keeps a close tab on the coming and going of non-natives. Being a U.S. Navy officer, expect a good grilling. Show both your diplomatic and Navy IDs. Then we can get something to eat, if you're hungry, or we can go directly to the Consulate. That's my car," he pointed at a black, 1941 Packard coupe, at the side of the road, close by. "Let's get your bag in the trunk."

Cooper, U.S. Navy

City and Port of Ponta Delgada (1955)

An Hour Later
U.S. Consulate
Avenida Infante Dom Henrique
Ponta Delgada, San Miguel Island, Azores, Portugal

"Terrific view of the port you have, Leonard. Good choice! It must be absolutely stunning in the summer," said Tony taking a quick look out Daly's second story office window. He settled into a red leather stuffed chair across from Daly.

"That judges chair by the window is where I often sit and read. It's pretty slow here, as you might imagine."

The consulate was in a modest rented building. It was located across the street from the docks of the harbor, on a long cobblestone thoroughfare that ran the length of the port. The building was a two story apartment that had been converted into the consulate. An armed Portuguese policeman stood a leisurely guard at the brass-plated doorway. A U.S. Marine stood guard in the foyer. Clerical staff offices, kitchen and dining room were located on the bottom floor. The upper floor was the Consul General's suite, consisting of a visitor reception room, a locked room for classified material storage and the strip cipher system desk, a full bathroom, and the Consul's office. The entire consulate was conservatively decorated in a manner that created a sense of both home and business. The walls throughout displayed a combination of American and Portuguese art. Wood floors had area carpets of various designs, purchased from the local Portuguese markets.

"By the way," continued Daly, "I have an apartment that I lease for visitors, a block down the avenue. The apartments for me and the staff are a little farther away, but a reasonable walking distance. The VIP apartment has a nice view of the port from the bedroom's second floor front window. You'll find it comfortable. Our custodians, Maria and Jorge, a very nice Portuguese couple, have it spruced up for you."

"Sounds great, thank you," said Tony, smiling. "Good grief. You said to expect a good grilling at the port office. I certainly got one."

"Yes, but you did fine. You're not in jail," said Daly, laughing. "It would have gone more rigorously if you didn't have a diplomatic ID. Alright, let me give you the rundown on what we have here," said Daly. "First, I have only a handful of civilian staff and four Marines. Portuguese police provide one armed guard at the front door, around the clock. I'm the only Foreign Service Officer. State said they have another FSO to send here, but they haven't said anything more about it in weeks. If it wasn't for Portuguese in the States that have relatives here, with visiting taking place in one direction or the other, it would be dreadfully slow. So, except for having a backup, I don't really need help. Perhaps relative to your visit, however, it's begun to get busier with cables bouncing back and forth mostly among the State Department, the War Department, our Consulate in Lisbon, and the British Foreign Office. The Allies sure want Portugal to grant permission to use the Azores for air and naval forces."

"I'm aware," said Tony. "Let's just establish that our conversations are Top Secret to cover all our bases."

Daly shook his head in acknowledgement.

"That being said, before I was sent to Casablanca, I was watching all those messages flying back and forth. I can understand why the Doctor Salazar isn't too thrilled with our ideas for us having Allied bases in his Azorean archipelago. It's not unrealistic to think that the Germans would have a fit. The strategic advantage of us having airfields here might push Hitler over the edge and result in him occupying Portugal, Azores as well."

"Exactly!" said Daly, his lively blue eyes focused on Tony's for a few moments.

"Go ahead, Leonard, what are you thinking?"

"Well, if I may be direct, Tony. Why exactly are you here?"

Tony smiled. "Apparently the message you received about my arrival was, uh, less than informative. I didn't see it. State didn't info copy me."

"It merely certified your clearance level as Top Secret Special Intelligence and stated you were on a Navy fact finding mission."

"Ah. Well, in a nutshell, I am here to study the feasibility of establishing a high frequency direction finding facility on this island. It could be critical in our ability to accurately locate U-boats. As you are surely aware, they are wreaking havoc on convoys. But rest assured, your input on this idea will be invaluable."

Daly's fair, freckled face began to flush. He looked away, toward the window, and ran his fingers through his curly red hair. He returned his gaze to Tony. "That will simply not be feasible at all. Such a thing could put the existence of this Consulate in jeopardy. That would just not be something in the long term interest of the United States."

Tony sat back in the chair, crossed his leg, and relaxed a few moments. He hoped body language would defuse the bomb he just dropped. "Leonard, covert operations actually based inside of consulates and embassies is commonplace. Not just the U.S. facilities, but in those of all nations, including Portugal."

The flush did not leave Daly's face. "I'm not responsible for those other facilities, Tony. I don't know the intricacies of the politics of those countries where other diplomatic facilities are located. But I am responsible for this one and I know the politics of this island. I am telling you, if such an operation was discovered, decisive action would be taken. Since the start of the war, we've been looked at rather suspiciously by the senior military here, and thus, the police."

"Is there a bathroom up here, Leonard?" He needed a break at this point, both physiologically and strategically.

"Yes, a full bath, on the right," replied Daly.

Tony took several minutes to let Daly cool down and to develop ideas for the salvation of the concept of a covert DF operation. He returned to Daly's office.

"I apologize if I was harsh with you, Tony," said Daly, whose facial freckles no longer contrasted against red.

"Not at all, Leonard. I appreciate frankness and truth without sugar coating. I can damn sure appreciate your position. All that aside, let's explore this a bit. The term, covert, is an interesting one. It only applies to those who are not privy. If we were to get Dr. Salazar's approval of such a facility, the risk to this Consulate would be nil. However, we would keep this facility covert from the general public of this island, including any German agents or Nazi sympathizers, that might exist here." He watched Daly closely for reaction.

Daly's eyebrows lifted briefly, and he sat back in his chair. He looked over at Tony and smiled, "That's a tall order. You know how badly the talks are going in Lisbon."

"Ah, but are they not apples and oranges? You can't keep an airfield secret from anyone," Tony said. "They could not be covert, in the slightest."

"Point taken," said Daly. "This is my first Foreign Service Assignment. I have no experience in covert operations. Tell me about your intelligence background."

"The short version is that my entire Navy career has been in communications intelligence. My assignment in London expanded my horizon to other facets of the business, including counter-intelligence. I guess my point is, I personally, and the organization I am representing in this study, are uniquely and well qualified to implement a covert operation."

Daly smiled, looked at his watch, then asked, "Getting hungry? Let's go have some local wine and a langosta dinner. Familiar with langosta?"

"I only know they are in the same family as lobsters," Tony replied.

"Well, langosta look like lobsters, but don't have the large claws. They are just as delicious, though."

"That remains to be seen. I grew up in Maine, where we have real lobsters, with big fat pincers filled with delicious meat," Tony said with emphasis on the word, real. "Ours have nice big claws full of sweet meat," Tony said with a smile.

Daly laughed, "I concede that it's hard to beat a Maine lobster, but I guarantee that you'll enjoy these boys. There's a nice little restaurant in walking distance. Grab your hat."

10 – *Bom Dia*

The Next Morning
8:10 a.m., Thursday, January 14, 1943
U.S. Consulate VIP Apartment
Avenida Infante Dom Henrique

It was a great treat to have a fully furnished apartment for VIP quarters. Simply stated, the layout was very similar to the Consulate, just smaller, but the décor was the same. Nothing extraordinary or luxurious, but very comfortable. The bedroom's side-window had a view to the east, the front window had a view of the busy harbor and Atlantic Ocean. Rain was not expected, so Tony opened all the curtains and windows before going to bed. The feel of crisp on-shore breezes on exposed skin, the familiar smells of a clean seashore and warmth of the morning sun would be a pleasant way to start the next day.

The morning sun became high enough to bathe his face with direct sun light and wake him. It was a day of exceptional weather for an Azores January day. He went to the front window to take in the beginning of a new day in yet another part of the world. Sea birds were already in flight, calling, squawking and diving. Fishing boats were in motion. Foot traffic, animal drawn carts, bicycles and an occasional vehicle were plying Avenida Infante Dom Henrique. Tony wanted to sit by the window, breathe the sea air and enjoy the sights of this beautiful, vibrant harbor. But it was 8:10 and there was work to do. Staying up until 1:30 a.m. last night was for a good cause-- diplomacy. It would make his day go well, or so he hoped. Daly took Tony to his private residence after dinner, where they shared a bottle of wine, played poker and engaged in congenial non-business conversation long into the night. It was no accident that Daly won a few bucks by the time they packed up the cards.

Later, as he was getting dressed, Tony heard the sound of someone knocking briefly on the front door, then using a key to enter. His watch said 8:55. Maria, the custodian and jack of all domestic trades arrived, just as Daly had advised. She came to get coffee started and prepare Tony's breakfast.

"*Bom dia, senhor,*" Maria called up the stairs to make sure he knew she had arrived.

"*Bom dia, senhora,*" Tony called back. He walked to the front window and was mesmerized again by the panorama of activities in the port. The wind had picked up and clouds were moving in. As he shut the windows, his mind shifted to Casablanca. Damn, I was looking forward to seeing a historic event, thought Tony. Here I am in the Azores, missing the arrival of the President of the United States in Casablanca and the kickoff of the SYMBOL Conference. I wonder what I'd be doing right now, if I were there. I would like to have Petra standing here with me, enjoying these sights and sounds. I need to get an initial report off to OP-20-G. Time to get moving.

Later That Morning
Leonard Daly's Office

"Come in, make yourself comfortable, Tony. Sleep well?" asked Daly.

"Like a baby." Occasional wind gusts caused some creaking in the building for a while last night. "It's sure windy here."

"It's often windy, overcast and rainy in the winter. Nice summer though. How about some coffee?"

"No, thank you, Leonard, I've had enough for now."

"I told Maria to come to your apartment at 8. Didn't think there was need for an earlier wakeup. No sense of urgency in this part of the world. Let me know if you want to change that."

"No need for a change, thanks. This is like having a vacation. Things are quite different in London, though."

"I am sure of that. I'm sorry if you were craving bacon this morning, we ran out of it a week ago. Should be some on the next Portuguese flight from Lisbon next week, probably Monday. Our Consulate there takes care of filling my wish list for supplies and provisions. They have an arrangement with the Portuguese Air Force. A Portuguese cargo plane comes from Lisbon and stops here every couple of weeks, on their way to Terceira Island. They have an air base on the other side of the island."

"Bacon is worth staying for, at least until Monday," Tony said laughing. "Even though Maria doesn't say much, she seems to understand me. I don't know any Portuguese, beyond what you taught me last night, but I tried what little Spanish I could recall. That didn't seem to be as effective as speaking English. The strong coffee, eggs and diced potatoes she prepared were just fine. I was a bit surprised by the slight sulfur smell to the water. Glad you had plenty bottled water in the fridge, by the way."

"Although there are similarities to Spanish," explained Daly, "with some words reasonably common, there is enough uniqueness in their language and pronunciation to make Spanish less than useful. As for the water, yes. These islands have relative degrees of volcanic activity. We have hot springs here, so the water has iron, sulfur and other minerals. There was some discussion about us offering to provide a water treatment plant, but I think that idea got pushed to the back burner in Lisbon. God knows, we have plenty places to spend war bond and tax dollars."

"Roger that. Well, Leonard, I would like to work on a draft proposal for the U.S. Consulate in Lisbon to present to the Portuguese Prime Minister, Dr. Salazar. In order to do that, I need your help. First thing to figure out, is where in hell we might house this operation."

"What do you know about the size of this thing? How many people would be involved?" asked Daly.

Tony smiled internally, feeling successful in getting Daly to engage from a helpful viewpoint, rather than just watching the game from the sideline. "Frankly, as a point of reference, the layout of the apartment I'm in right now would do it. Near the water would be best, as that apartment is. There would be five or six enlisted men and a junior officer. Any ideas at this point?"

Daly shifted in his chair, in thought. "I just might. My landlord, Tiago Pinto, is a relative of the current Azorean Governor, an air force general. Pinto owns quite a bit of the residential property in the port area of Ponta Delgada. A few businesses around the city also. All that is both good and bad."

"Give me the bad part first," said Tony, smiling.

Daly took a deep breath. "I have no doubt that he tells the General everything he observes going on. With this Consulate, and the city in general. Which is why, without Salazar's blessing, you just can't pull your operation off."

"Understood," said Tony. "And the good?"

"He can get things done. He likes the U.S. and he likes U.S. dollars. He would not make trouble for you if you got an agreement from Lisbon and the OK from the governor."

"I guess that leads me to believe that leasing a place from him would be absolutely key to making it happen?" asked Tony.

"That is absolutely the case," Daly said with a grin.

"Dare you ask if he has an apartment available? Or, would you consider using the one I'm in?" asked Tony.

"I won't give up the VIP apartment. But it just so happens, he has been after me for a week or so to lease the apartment next door to us when it vacates at the end of February. It's almost exactly the same as this one. I've seen the floor plans. I was considering leasing it for expansion and my number two man's residence. I don't have a large staff, but we are cramped."

"Ah, but the additional presence of seven men would be less, shall we say, unusual, if they were, for all practical purposes, working in the expansion of the Consulate. There would be an operations security value to them being part of the expanded staff, rather than an outside organization," suggested Tony.

"That's a good point," said Daly, pinching his chin, thinking.

"How about your communications? How is that working?" asked Tony.

"Everything goes by Western Union telegram. We have a teletype link to their office in Horta, on Faial Island, about 170 miles to the northwest. They have a cable to both Lisbon and London, although it appears to our Consulate in Lisbon that all the cables they get are via London. Oh, you may be interested in this. There's a German cable company in Horta too, but their cable was cut and not getting repaired, it seems. Not sure about the details on that, though. Their office is located in the same compound as the British Consulate, so the Brits are able to keep a good eye on them. Even though their cable is cut, I'm told all the all-German staff still come to work every day."

"I would expect nothing less from the Germans. By the way, I'm curious, how you knew when to come meet me at the dock?" asked Tony.

"Pan Am has a station in Horta. They have their own direct communications with their Clippers. Your plane gave flight progress updates and final ETA to Pan Am Horta, who advised the U.S. Consulate there. The Consul in Horta sent us telegrams with their info."

"Alright, what do you have for an encryption system?" asked Tony.

"All I have is a strip cipher system. I have to do all the encrypting and decrypting. I don't have a cipher clerk, so I'm not volunteering to add more to my workload from your communications needs."

"Oh, we would take care of our own communications," Tony assured him. "There would be no impact on you at all. Hmmm. Do you think we could get away with having a radio transmitter for direct Morse communications?"

"When you say, get away with, do you mean have it but not declare it?" asked Daly.

"Affirmative. I assume it would be impossible to get it approved in writing," said Tony.

"Ah, I think you're right about it being too difficult to obtain approval. Since the war started, they put a tight rein on civilian resident ownership of radios of all kinds."

"Have you seen or heard about any radio trucks on the island, or heard of their military having an ability to detect and locate transmitters?" Tony asked.

"No, not on this island, anyway," replied Daly with a head shake. "But I know of a situation where someone got into trouble when the police or Army saw his short-wave antenna."

"How about power? Do you have any technical information about the power available to these apartments? Tony asked.

"Yes, I have a data sheet in a file with all that info. I'll make a copy for you. A State Department electrician put it together," Daly replied. "All I know about it is that it's 400 volts DC in the main trunk to this building, with 200 volts DC in the ceiling lights and receptacles. We have to plug our U.S. equipment into a device to convert it. My background is world history and political science, not engineering."

"Oh a copy of the data sheet will be just fine, thank you. My background is math, but I've picked up a lot of communications engineering knowledge in the Navy," Tony said.

"What about languages?" asked Daly.

"Just English, and the mandatory credits of Spanish in high school and at Harvard."

Daly nodded, "They sent me to a crash course in Portuguese before they sent me here."

"Changing the subject a bit, how about the presence here of German agents? Or agents from any Axis country?" asked Tony.

"I'm not aware of any Axis agent being discovered. There are German residents in the islands, mainly here and on Fayal. They have a large pineapple farm here, that has a significant export business. Also, German merchant ships stop here, now and then, for water, or passenger pickup or drop-off. The Port Captain, who is very pro-Britain and very pro-American, and very cooperative I might add, scrutinizes that activity."

"That farm is a terrific façade for agent operations and the port visits provide a means of agent transportation and communication," said Tony.

"Very true," said Daly. "I understand that the police have the German residents of the islands on their watch list. I don't know how thoroughly they pursue monitoring the people on that list. My guess is loosely. Perhaps more diligently here than on the other islands. But, even so."

"That's understandable, really," said Tony. "Ever pick up any sense of someone being genuinely suspicious?"

"In that category there is Herr Bruno Ziegler. State Department intelligence people say they recently learned that he's a retired German Army Major, served in WWI. He seems to be highly respected by the German residents, at least those on this island. Sort of their representative without portfolio, if you will."

"Just that little bit about him already raises my interest level," Tony commented.

"There's an interesting story my landlord told me about him, not from a question I raised, but just an incidental anecdote during one of our first conversations over dinner. It seems when Ziegler first arrived here, sometime in the late 30s, he built this really big home. It had a commanding view of Lagoa das Furnas, a large lake about 20 miles east of here. This alarmed the Portuguese when the Germans started occupying countries. They evicted him and ordered him to live in Ponta Delgada."

"Evicting him seems like a drastic action to take. They must have had some reason for alarm. Do you know where he's at? His address?" asked Tony.

"Oh, sure. I have a file on him. It's pretty thin, just the things I've learned, personally, but I can share it with you," replied Daly. "I have a city map in the file with his apartment location marked. It's not far from here, actually."

"Great. I'd appreciate seeing that, at some point. But what was so alarming about his house at the lake?" asked Tony.

"That's what I wondered. I wasn't here at the time, so I had to piece together bits of information I got from Tiago Pinto and the British Consul General here. I'll try to boil it down. When he built that house, Hitler had already started his thrusts into Eastern Europe which made the Portuguese military uneasy. There was no airfield on this island at the time, so they feared an amphibious troop landing or seaplane troop landing. The latter was the most likely, since most of the months in a year have wind and wave conditions making an amphibious landing problematic. Lake Furnas, being relatively calm in all wind conditions, and over a mile at its widest point, was suitable for the largest of German seaplanes. The Island Governor met with the American and British Consuls General regarding Ziegler. I don't know who initiated that meeting. The result was the eviction and the installation of defenses for Lake Furnas. For example, they floated felled trees in the lake, anchored strategically on the surface to ensure certain disaster for seaplanes that try to land. They also constructed a machine gun post with a good view of the lake area, etc."

"That is a very interesting story," said Tony. "I noted defensive positions on the most vulnerable beaches on the way in too. Most of the shoreline looked like tall, steep drops."

"Correct," said Daly, sitting back, crossing his legs. "They built defenses throughout the archipelago. Doing so has stretched their already lean military forces. As the war has progressed, the Portuguese military and government has become more concerned that an invasion may occur. As I said earlier, there are hints that there may be some senior officials that have suspicions about American and British intentions."

"That's troublesome," said Tony. This treasure trove of defensive information was particularly useful, since he was aware of American and British contingency planning for the occupation of the Azores, by force if need be. The Azores are critical to both countering U-boat operations and providing logistical support to Allied operations in eastern Africa, the Mediterranean, Sicily and onward into Europe.

"It is worrisome, for sure. If bad relations were to develop, that would affect our ability to function, perhaps even to remain here, in the worst case. But their concern about Germany is absolutely evident. They feel they are on the brink. And that's why the negotiations in Lisbon about Allied forces using the Azores is such a touchy subject. The German Armistice Commission in Portugal is watching their compliance with neutrality very carefully."

Tony ran his hand over his black crew cut hair a few times. "Do all you can to assure the locals that they need not worry. Hitler's adventure into Russia has cost him troops and resources to such an extent, much to his chagrin, that Portugal and the Azores is way down on his list of things he can do. Not to mention our entry into western Africa last November. That really got his attention, and well it should. It's the beginning of his end. But defeating his U-boats is a critical element in our success. We must ensure the unfettered flow of the massive amount of resources required to support Allied forces going into the Mediterranean."

Daly's freckled face cracked a little smile, "Which is why you're here."

Tony nodded, "Which is exactly why I'm here. We are willing to go to great extents to locate and neutralize those U-boats. Do you have a place I can sit and do some writing?" asked Tony.

"Sure, that little conference room across the hall. I'll get that data sheet on electrical power for you and have my secretary bring you a pad, some pencils and coffee."

"I'd like to review that file on Ziegler while I'm at it also, please."

Later That Morning
Leonard Daly's Office

Tony knocked on Daly's doorjamb, "May I interrupt, Leonard?"

"Of course, Tony, I was just doing some interesting reading. Have a seat."

"What are you reading?" asked Tony.

"A new book by Joseph Schumpeter, *Capitalism, Socialism and Democracy*. A very compelling exploratory analysis. My brother sent it to me for Christmas and I'm just now getting into it."

"Noted. I don't get much time to read for my own pleasure. I'll look into that though."

"What do you have there, a rough?" asked Daly.

"Two roughs. I would like you to read these two draft messages. Cables as you diplomats call them. One is a two part message. First part is my initial analysis on the feasibility of establishing a DF activity here. The second part is a proposed message to Lisbon, proposing the DF operation. The shorter message is a report on the German presence here, including Major Ziegler. Feel free to make any comments or criticisms you wish."

Daly leafed through the paper clipped pages of the two drafts, "This one on DF is really quite long. I'll read the Ziegler cable first." He spent several minutes reviewing the draft. "Tony, I have to say, I thought it was odd that you took no notes during our conversation. I even thought that you were, perhaps, just letting me talk. Humoring me, as it were. But it seems you have something of an exceptional memory. I have no corrections, comments or criticism of this Ziegler report. You reorganized my ramblings superbly. I would like to have this go to State, in addition to who you wish, of course."

"Alright, Leonard, agreed."

"Excellent! Now to plunge into this tome of yours," Daly said jokingly.

Tony watched Daly's body language. The eyebrow movements, facial muscle twitches, leg shifts, breathing. Tony could see there were areas of concern to be discussed.

After several minutes of reading, Daly laid the draft on the coffee table between him and Tony. "I'll probably have to read that again. As I said, you've got one hell of a memory and a unique skill in organizing facts and making points succinctly. Part one is mainly technical in nature, so I have no comments on that at all. Part two, the proposal for Lisbon, uh, it tends to read as if I have no concerns. That we need to work on."

"Of course," Tony said. "Let's go through it, line by line, and make it something you can agree with, or support with specific concerns stated."

"How about we go get a bite to eat and think about it?" asked Daly

That Afternoon, Washington Time
4:30 p.m., Thursday, January 14, 1943
Commander Jerry Webber's Office
OP-20-GB, Main Navy Building
Washington, DC

The intercom announced the arrival of Lieutenant Commander Paul Archer. Webber nodded at Archer and pointed at the chair beside his desk, "I have something for you to read Paul. It's a limited distribution message from Commander Romella in the Azores." He handed the multi-page message to Archer.

Archer looked up after a thorough reading. "What do you want me to do?"

"Short version is that putting a temporary DF system in there is feasible, not ideal, but impossible without the OK from the Portuguese Prime Minister, which has yet to be proposed. He made a strong case though. So, we need to be ready to act if Lisbon makes a deal. I want you to start thinking about a plan. The steps and all details necessary to get that site into operation. If you have any questions, get them to me. If I don't have the answers, I'll send a message to Romella. He needs to get back to Casablanca on other matters, but he can still answer anything we need to know. I'd like to see your draft plan on, let's see," he referred to his calendar, "make it Friday after next, the 22ʳᵈ."

The Next Day, London Time
8:30 a.m., Friday, January 15, 1943
Owen Langsdale's Office
Special Operations Executive S02 Branch,
Mansion Office Building, Greater London

"Sorry I couldn't meet with you last eve, Bill. I had a dinner meeting in London I could not reschedule," Langsdale said, then took a sip of tea. "By the way, chaps at Bletchley told me the documents from Casablanca were brilliant. The MI6 analysts in London are thrilled with the boxes from Casablanca as well. Be sure to pass the Crown's appreciation for his efforts."

"I am glad to know that, Ed. I'll let Tony know when he returns."

"Let's get to it, Captain. What brings you here today?"

Captain Taylor drank the last of his tea and put his cup down, "Jayne makes a fine pot of tea Ed. Alright. I doubt you've seen the Commander's message I forwarded to you about the Germans in the Azores."

"Right. Do tell," Langsdale said with interest.

"It probably won't clear our system and get to you for several hours, but I brought a copy you can read." Taylor reached into his attaché case for the message and handed it to Langsdale.

Langsdale read each page carefully and handed it back to Taylor. "Right. That's a great deal more than I knew. As you well know, the Crown has quite the interest in the Azores, as do you lot."

"Exactly, Ed. I spoke with our OSS boys and they do not have an officer there and none are expected anytime soon. They have an informant, however. It sounds like you don't have an agent there either."

"We do not. But I am more interested in having someone in there now than I was yesterday," said Langsdale, beginning to twist the ends of his mustache. "What is Commander Romella doing there?"

Taylor laughed, "Oh no you don't, Ed. Tony is not available. He'll soon be back in Casablanca. I was hoping you had more about the Germans there than we do."

Langsdale cracked a sly grin, "Right. Thanks to the Commander, we each have equal information."

Taylor sat forward and clasped his hands on the table. "In any case, our countries have high hopes for a successful joint agreement with Lisbon on allowing air operations from the Azores. If Major Ziegler or any of the Germans on the island get wind of those plans and alert Hitler, that would have very damaging results. Let's think about how our Consulates in the Azores can collaborate on getting a firm handle on whether Ziegler, or any of the others, are up to no good."

11 - News

9:20 a.m., Friday, January 15, 1943
Leonard Daly's Office
U.S. Consulate, Ponta Delgada, Azores

Tony came to Daly's open doorway, "I suppose, Leonard, this is what you would say is a typical rainy, windy, Azorean winter day!"

"Indeed it is, Tony," Daly replied from his comfortable chair by the window.

"Any news from DC?" asked Tony.

"None. Oh, that's not true. They are dedicating the Pentagon today. I can't imagine the confusion in moving the entire War Department there. Have a seat."

"The good news there, is that we are not any part of that," Tony said.

"Thank God, huh? Tony, I have a visa applicant to interview at 10, but we can chat until then," said Daly.

"Thanks, by the way, for putting umbrellas in the apartment," Tony said. "I'm glad I brought my boondockers. It's a wet and muddy day for dress shoes. Still reading Schumpeter?"

"Oh, that reminds me, I should also put some galoshes in the apartment too. I'll include those on my wish list for Lisbon. Schumpeter, yes, I just started the last chapter. Quite a thought provoking book. What's on your mind?"

"I'm just curious about what kind of reception those messages got at Navy and State," said Tony. "No response from anyone at all, huh?"

"Nothing. No news is good news, right?" replied Daly.

Tony laughed, "Maybe. Time will tell. Anyway, I know it may not be a great day for it, but can I ask you to give me a tour of Lagoa das Furnas, and show me Ziegler's local apartment, sometime?

"Sure! There will be a break in the rain, or at least a let up, soon. The rains usually don't last," replied Daly. "The lake is only about 20 miles from here. Ziegler's place is right on the way, not far."

"Yes, according to the map in your file, he's about a mile down the road, east from here," said Tony.

"That's right. Nothing very special, either," said Daly. "Definitely a lower standard of living than his house at the lake would have been."

Tony was sitting in Daly's favorite reading chair by the window, watching the harbor activity. Nearly an hour had passed before the rain squall slowly moved away.

Daly left the conference room and came to his office doorway, "C'mon Tony, my interview is over. Let's get in the car. We'll have a quick sandwich downstairs, then get on the road.

Daly's Packard was parked in the back yard of the consulate. They headed east down the back alley, turned right and then made a left onto Avenida Infante Dom Henrique.

"You know, Leonard, when you think about it, cobblestones are probably quite an economic option for a road surface." The rumble of the tires on the cobblestone road was something Tony had not experienced before his first ride to the consulate. It was a curiously pleasant rumbling sound, but the ride was bumpy.

"I suppose you're right," said Daly. "They manage to keep it surprisingly well maintained. I'm told that one of the options citizens have to pay their taxes, is to work them off maintaining the roadway. That includes the cobblestones and roadside flower beds."

They passed the apartment where Tony was staying. "Maria taking good care of you?"

"She certainly is. She scolded me for trying to clean up after myself in the kitchen. The place is spotless," replied Tony.

"Good! Oh, here's Ziegler's place coming up. The one with the door coming open. I'll pull over."

They watched from three doors down. "Is that him?" asked Tony, as he watched a stalwart man in a navy blue business suit and Stetson-like hat. He was locking the door with a key."

"Yes, that's him," said Daly.

"Look at that car in front! What is that thing?" asked Tony, pointing at the long, elegant, black roadster in front of Ziegler's house, puffing grayish-white exhaust from the tail pipe.

"A Hispano-Suiza K6 Cabriolet, from Spain. Don't ask how I know that," said Daly, grinning.

"I hope that convertible top is sealed well, with the weather you have here," said Tony. "Damn thing is kind of large for most of the roads here. Interesting that he has a driver, too. He's clearly a man of means and influence."

"I think I mentioned it, but he's high on the police watch list, too, allegedly," said Daly. "He's probably off to work at the pineapple farm, har de har," Daly said, smiling.

"Certainly not in the fields dressed like that. After all, he's a principal in the business," Tony said sarcastically.

When Ziegler's car pulled away and turned north, Daly continued along the coastal highway. Leaving the Ponta Delgada area, the cobblestone roadway ended and became a very narrow dirt road. The more densely populated villages along the road were cobblestoned. The road width was so narrow in some places that two vehicles could barely pass. They slowed to a creep and passed within a few inches on either side. Stretches of two story whitewashed row homes were separated by farmland, becoming more rural the further east they traveled. Kids playing in the street smiled and waved. The adults looked briefly at the car but paid no mind to them. Draft animals pulling carts plodded along unimpressed, fearless of the car's presence. Daly concentrated on defensive driving while Tony absorbed the sights.

After riding for a while, Daly announced, "Ponta Garcia," as the road became cobblestone. "I'd say we're about 10 minutes from the lake."

How I wish Petra could be here to see all this, Tony's mind rambled. I don't regret choosing the Navy over a math professorship. I would never have met Petra. I would probably never have gone where I've been in the last year. I want this war to be over so I can show her and her son more of this world.

Daly made a left turn onto a dirt road, leaving Ponta Garcia, for the interior. They meandered through farmland, stopping for, and navigating through, animals and carts. Daly made his way through farmland and forested areas. The road meandered erratically, narrowing sometimes to just a single car width and became densely forested on both sides of the road. After a hairpin turn back toward the east, the road seemed to become mainly straight but more inclined, often with steep rocks on one or both sides. The dirt road became cobblestoned, even though still rural in appearance, to Tony's surprise.

"Home stretch Tony. It's right up ahead."

"A beautiful ride, Leonard. I'm enjoying this to no end."

In a few moments, the south end of Lagoa das Furnas came into view on the left. It was clearly an ancient caldera filled with water. Its color was a light tan, especially at the edges, from silt drainage from the rains. The road soon was running just yards from the water's edge in some places, providing a splendid view. Some of the shoreline was shallow, with small trees and brush jutting out of the water. The extensive network of floating logs the Portuguese military anchored in the middle to counter seaplane landings, were now visible.

"As I recall," Tony said, "Ziegler's former home should be up here, just a bit further, on this side of the lake."

"Yes, it is, I'll point it out," said Daly.

As they neared a point a little more than halfway to the north end of the lake, Daly slowed to a stop and pointed.

Sitting perhaps twenty yards up the side of the hill from the road, sat a forty-foot wide, one story flat-roofed home. The façade was made of gray volcanic rock with whitewashed mortar. A large picture window was to the right of the centered doorway and two standard sized windows to the left. A slate stepped path led up to a portico, from a gate in a low rock wall that ran along the road, the width of the property.

"So that is the alarming Ziegler mansion," said Tony. "Well, it damn sure has a commanding view of the lake. It looks occupied, too. I suppose some wealthy, trustworthy Portuguese person was allowed to take it."

"Probably. I don't have any info on who got it, or how," said Daly.

"There's no garage," said Tony. "So, just like Ziegler, he gets picked up and dropped off."

"Interesting, isn't it?" asked Daly. "We'll go to the end of the lake and double back. It will be a lot faster ride back to the consulate than it would be if we went around, the way the roads are laid out. I know, I tried it."

That Afternoon
Leonard Daly's Office

"Cables are on your desk, and here's a note," Daly's secretary said when he and Tony entered the consulate. "Senhor Tinto stopped by while you were out."

"Let's go up and see what these two cables are about Tony," said Daly. "Make yourself comfortable in my office while I decipher them."

"I can't wait," Tony said, following Daly up the stairs.

"But you will, indeed," Daly said with a chuckle. "I'm not a fast typist or cipher clerk, especially with this strip cipher contraption."

Tony sat down in the chair by the window and watched the boats moving around the port.

Daly returned to his office a half hour later, "One is for me and one is for you." He handed Tony his message and went to his desk. "Mine has nothing to do with the cables we sent. Your cable was interesting, was it not?" asked Daly. "I couldn't help but skim read it as I deciphered it."

"Yes! A C-47 aircraft is coming to San Miguel to take me back to Casablanca. It's flying into the Portuguese Air Force Base Number 4 tomorrow around 1500 hours. It will depart the next day, Sunday morning, at 0900. I'm surprised they got clearance to land there. Is that the base on the other side of the island?" asked Tony.

"Yes, it is," Daly replied. "It's a relatively new base, near the port of Robo de Peixe, in Santa Ana, northeast of here, on the north side of the island. I'm going to miss having you around, Tony. Let's plan on a farewell dinner tonight. Pinto wants to meet for dinner tomorrow night."

"Sounds fine to me, Leonard."

"I'll drive you across the island to the airport Sunday morning. Probably take at least an hour to get there due to slow going on the roads. How's an 0700 pickup sound?"

"Great, thanks. And please don't make Maria come make breakfast. I'll set the alarm clock. I'll scramble some eggs, have a couple slices of buttered Portuguese bread and some coffee. I'll be just fine."

"Alright. If you insist," Daly said with a grin. "But don't try to clean up, otherwise she'll be pissed when she gets there."

Tony laughed, "I'm sure that's true."

"For your info, State has decided to send me a Vice Consul. He is expected to arrive sometime in the last two weeks of February. Flight arrangements haven't been completed yet. So, I will tell Pinto that I want the apartment next door. I'll begin making arrangements with State to complete the contract."

"I see a smile, Leonard, continue," Tony said.

"My plan is to put him in the VIP apartment and stall on furnishing the one next door until it's clear that your proposal is either approved or not."

"I really like that plan," Tony said grinning.

"I'd appreciate it if you would keep that between us," said Daly.

8:40 a.m., Sunday, January 17, 1943
Portuguese Base Aérea No. 4
Santa Ana, San Miguel Island, Azores

It took over a half-hour to get through the gate. Were it not for the Consul General being present, they would have been summarily denied entry. However, a runner was dispatched from the gate to the base commander's office to get clarification. Once, cleared, a soldier on a bicycle led them to a parking spot near the flight line.

Tony lifted his sea bag out of the trunk of Daly's car. "They're pre-flighting the aircraft, Leonard. You don't need to stay."

"It was a pleasure to meet you, Tony, perhaps we'll cross paths again, sometime," said Daly, shaking Tony's hand emphatically.

The soldier escort opened the passenger gate to the flight line. Tony proceeded to the aircraft. It looked familiar. He recognized Sheila Malden, exiting the cabin. She was now standing by the boarding steps, smiling at him. Major Jim Morris, just finishing his pre-flight, waved at him. He was glad to see the same crew that flew him to Casablanca. "Good morning, Captain Malden," said Tony, as he dropped his bag by the stairs. "Those Captain's bars look good on you, Congratulations."

"Thank you, Commander. It's just you this morning, drop your seabag. We'll load it in the cargo hold." They shook hands.

Morris was just finishing his preflight inspection of the port wing and wheel, then came over and greeted Tony with a strong handshake. "Mornin' Commander. You sure get around. It took an act of congress to get her refueled here, but we managed. We had to sleep on board the plane last night. No arrangements for quarters had been made."

Tony laughed. "It wasn't easy getting through the gate, either. What are you doing here, besides giving me a ride?"

"Just giving you a ride. We took a plane full of VIPs from London to Casablanca last Wednesday and were standing by, to stand by. You know how it goes. Then we got the orders to come get you. The flight will be about seven hours or so. We'll be landing at Medouina Airport. We'll stow your bag. Get aboard and make yourself comfortable. We're ready to go."

12 – Star Struck

Combined (U.S. and British) Chiefs of Staff, Anfa Hotel

ASSIGNMENT: CASABLANCA

3:25 p.m., Sunday, January 17, 1943
Anfa Hotel, Casablanca, Morocco

Security measures for entry into Anfa Camp and the hotel had been doubled. The lobby was hectic. The conference of the top military minds in the U.S. and Great Britain were meeting in, what had been, the main floor dining room. It had been secured as the main conference room for the duration of SYMBOL. Several armed guards stood at the entrance to the conference room and several more were dispersed in the lobby.

Tony stopped at the front desk for his room key. The corporal at the desk handed him his key and an envelope containing phone messages that had been taken for him. He put the envelope in his pocket, slung his bag over his shoulder and hiked up to Room 210.

He put his sea bag at the foot of his bed, took the envelope out of his pocket and sat at the desk to read the messages. One was from Lieutenant Junior Grade Roy Hall, saying not urgent, but to call. Another was from Chuck Rossi, saying welcome back, call if you need anything. The last one was a handwritten note on the tri-folded letterhead of Captain Lattim, USN, Aide to Admiral King. It said simply, to call him, Room 200.

He picked up the phone and asked the switchboard to connect him. "Good afternoon, Captain, this is Commander Romella. I just got back a few minutes ago."

"Good afternoon, Commander. Please come and visit."

"I'm still in khaki's that I've been wearing since oh dark thirty. Can I have a few minutes to change?" asked Tony.

"No need for that, just come see me before I get commandeered," replied Lattim.

Tony removed his shoulder holster and went to Room 200.

"Come in," Lattim called out when Tony knocked. "Glad to meet you. I've heard some good things about you. Tony is it?"

"My pleasure, sir, yes, Tony is fine," replied Tony.

They shook hands. Lattim turned the desk chair toward the stuffed chair which Tony settled into. "Steve is fine with me, Tony. OK, Admiral King wanted me to pass his apologies for the behavior of Captain Milz. He's back in DC, reassigned to a photo reconnaissance interpretation unit."

Tony wanted to smile. "Let the Admiral know that an apology is not necessary. I just considered him to be one of the 10% that we all know exists."

Lattim nodded. "My background includes some work in intelligence, so the Admiral wanted me to be your point of contact on those appendices. Before he left DC, he and I had a chance to review them with Commander Webber. They are impressive and I agreed in principle, not knowing how SYMBOL will go. The first meeting of the Combined Chiefs of Staff laid out the agenda for the remainder of the conference. A side meeting of select flag officers from the U.S. and U.K., including Admiral King, discussed all forms of intelligence to support future operations, including communications intelligence. They agreed, primarily for security reasons, no appendices would be included in the planning documents, but approved the proposed activities of U.S. and U.K. intelligence agencies to support whatever operations may ensue."

"Makes perfect sense to me," said Tony. "I should have my copies of those appendices destroyed."

"Where are the draft appendices you brought?" asked Lattim.

"I have them stowed in secure storage down below, in Conference Room D."

"Based on the Admiral's comments of the SYMBOL agenda meeting, I think it would be prudent to destroy them. If anything referring to COMINT operations comes up again, Admiral King or I will call you. Tell you what, until I say otherwise, be in the lobby or your room, between 0800 and 1700. Be in uniform, because you may only have five minutes notice."

"Aye, aye, sir. I'll get those destroyed right away."

Lattim smiled, "I think you'll have to put that off until later this evening. Give me a moment." He turned his chair around toward the desk and picked up his phone. "Villa #3 Anfa Camp please... this is Captain Lattim... May I speak with Mr. Hopkins, please?...Good afternoon, Harry, Steve Lattim. I have Commander Romella here...Oh, 45 minutes would be perfect. See you then." He turned to Tony, "Go get cleaned up and into dress blues. We're taking a walk in 30 minutes."

"Where are we going?" asked Tony.

"Just meet me in the lobby in 30 minutes," replied Lattim with a sly grin.

45 Minutes Later
Villa #3, Anfa Camp, Casablanca

National Museum of the U.S. Navy

Villa #3, Anfa Camp, Casablanca, Residence of U.S. President Franklin D. Roosevelt

Lattim avoided revealing to Tony who they were going to visit during the 200 yard walk around the circular road to a freshly whitewashed two-story villa. A makeshift sign at the side of the entrance gate, hanging from a rope looped over a bush branch, identified it as, Villa #3. The grounds in the front and sides were well tended gardens with various flowers and fruit trees. They provided a complex but pleasing aroma of sweetness and citrus. Tony noted snipers on the rooftop and also those nearby. He also noted, on the way to the villa, several anti-aircraft batteries, camouflaged in a way to be less obtrusive. There were other batteries distributed throughout Anfa Camp, and Casablanca in general. Several Army guards were maintaining a perimeter around the villa. Two of them, along with two men in civilian clothes, were checking IDs and Anfa Camp badges at the villa's entrance gate.

After successfully passing through the security gauntlet, Lattim and Tony approached the front door and knocked. A butler answered the knock and invited them into the foyer. A man in wrinkled suit trousers and open collar white shirt promptly appeared and said, "Hello Steve, thanks for coming by." They shook hands.

"I'd like you to meet Commander Anthony Romella," said Lattim. "Commander, please meet Harry Hopkins, Special Assistant to the President."

"What do your friends call you Commander?" asked Hopkins, as they shook hands.

"Tony, sir, pleased to meet you." Tony's heart rate was accelerating at the prospect of what may come.

"Please call me Harry. Come in. There's someone I want you to meet. I saw your name on the SYMBOL attendee list and it rang a bell. I checked and found out you are indeed the Project CIGAR man from London. I learned a few other things about you from Captain Taylor. You've been busy."

Tony turned red. "Yes, sir, that I have. I'm sure you've been as well."

Hopkins laughed, "That I have, Tony, that I have. This way, please." He escorted Tony and Lattim into a large open room that served as both living and dining room. It was busily furnished with an eclectic assortment of leather and printed cloth stuffed chairs, a couch, and an oversized dark mahogany dinner table, with three sections added. The bare glistening surface of it was spotless. One wall had a tall window, that extended from the baseboard to at least seven feet high, with garish red curtains that had large white prints of swans and flowers. A butler stood attentively by the stairs in a tuxedo and white gloves. It was all of extravagant, modern, unique taste, and simplicity. Tony thought, I'd like to meet the people who normally live here. I wonder where they've gone.

National Museum of the U.S. Navy

Villa #3, Living Room, Facing Rear

National Museum of the U.S. Navy
Villa #3 Living Room, Facing Front

"Steve, make yourself comfortable," Hopkins said to Lattim. "The butler can take your drink order. I'm going to take Tony down the hall."

Down the hall? Tony mused. Who's down the hall? If it's the President, it will be difficult to control myself.

Hopkins led Tony down a short hallway, nodded to the Secret Service Agent standing next to a door, knocked and opened it. "Mr. President, this is Commander Anthony Romella. Go on in Tony." The door closed. Holy shit, I am alone with the President of the United States. In his bedroom. In Casablanca. This just isn't real. Don't be nervous. How do I do that?

"Good afternoon, Mr. President, it's an honor to meet you, sir," said Tony.

"Commander, it's my honor as well," said FDR. He removed his spectacles, laid them on a small side table next to his wheelchair, then reached up to shake Tony's hand. It was a surprisingly firm and sincere handshake. The President was sitting, in front of a full length mirror, facing a bed.

National Museum of the U.S. Navy

Villa #3, FDR Bedroom

Tony's eyes made a rapid scan of the room. It reflected strong décor preferences of a woman. To the right of FDR was a corner desk that was snug against tufted panels adorned with family photos displayed on them. In front of the desk, was a stuffed chair with wooden arms, facing FDR.

National Museum of the U.S. Navy

Villa #3, FDR Bedroom

The pink tinted wall opposite the doorway had a blonde wood dresser in the center of it, with a mural above that. A window with sheer pink curtains was next to the dresser. A few of FDR's personal items were on the top of the dresser, where there surely was, prior to FDR's arrival, a collection of things feminine, such as colognes, perfumes, hairbrushes, combs, hand mirrors, and the like. Opposite the window was the bed, sitting on a six-inch earth tone print fabric platform. The bed had a shiny red satin duvet with a pink tufted satin headboard. Pink and red satin pillows were piled against the headboard. The wall behind the bed was wallpapered with a repeating print of large non-descript shapes with pink, red, maroon, and tan on an eggshell background. Between the bed and the corner of the room was a large, dark oak, clothes closet with a full length mirror on the door. The room visually screamed femininity, which was confirmed by the subtle fragrance of her perfume that still lingered.

"What do you think of my bedroom?" FDR asked with a nifty grin.

"It's uh, it has the touch of a woman," Tony said.

FDR let out a laugh, and with a playful smile, said, "You mean, like a madam's house?"

Tony's restrained his response to only a wide grin and a nod.

"Please, Commander, have a seat there. I'd like to spend a few minutes with you. As for the villa, the Secret Service leased this place and installed the steel shutters. I try to keep them open as much as I can. It's too damn dark otherwise. Please excuse my slippers, shorts and t-shirt. I'm relaxing after a morning of meetings, a working lunch and a meeting after that. The reason you're here is, you see, when Harry told me you were in Casablanca with SYMBOL, I told him to arrange for us to meet at the first opportunity. Right now was as good a time as I might get to tell you, personally, that the CIGAR project you completed at Bletchley was more valuable to me than you can know. Do you want to talk about it?"

"No," Tony replied without thinking, embarrassed with his curt answer, still red as a beet, and adrenalin raging.

FDR laughed, "Relax, Tony. Would you like a drink?"

"No, thank you, Mr. President," Tony said with a smile. He looks tired, thought Tony. Time difference, long trip, busy schedule, all taking their toll. Just the same, Tony was unable to ignore the calming effect of FDR's welcoming manner.

"You can consider this villa a Top Secret facility. I've been meeting with my Chiefs of Staff in this room and in the great room. Now, about CIGAR. Did you think you'd find a different result?" FDR asked.

"No sir, I didn't. I hadn't been at Bletchley long before I realized that they were dedicated to the efficient and timely production of communication intelligence. But more than that, they were genuinely free of the influence of government politics in their reporting, which went directly to operational commands as well as others. There was no political filtering. What their political consumers did with their reports seemed none of BP's concern."

FDR nodded, with a thoughtful gaze. "Ambassador Winant told me the delay in getting the CIGAR information was due to their close supervision of you."

"That's a good summary of the situation, Mr. President. They had their marching orders on my access, as did I. The main problem was that the intercepts and decryptions of Japanese messages showing intent to attack Pearl Harbor were stowed in an archive room inside the work area that I was assigned. I was not authorized to go into that archive. They brought me what I needed. At least one British person was present in the office at all times. Except just once, that is."

FDR flashed a broad smile. "Carpe diem!"

"Exactly, sir. That one time was probably the only opportunity I would ever have had, and I knew it."

"Harry also briefed me on your activities in London, France, and Norway. He got the information from a friend of mine, Captain Taylor, who thinks a great deal of you, by the way. Give him my regards when you get back. I haven't seen him since he went to London. He's a fine man. He and Evelyn are great dinner company."

"Yes, sir, I agree. He's been a great mentor. I'll certainly pass your regards to him." Bill never mentioned he knew FDR personally, Tony thought, he's always holding something back.

"Tony, that Norway operation may only be known to a few, and may remain that way for a long time, but it is a critical one. I know you understand that. Your work was very significant toward the planning for its success. Winston personally expressed his appreciation for our help, your help. It's still in progress, you know."

"I am aware that it's not complete. You may not know, Mr. President, but I lost two men getting out of there. I hope the mission is ultimately successful," said Tony.

FDR sipped the last of an Old Fashioned that was on his side table. Condensation dripped from the bottom of the glass onto his t-shirt. "The British are doing all they can to make it a success. We just cannot allow the Germans to beat us to an atomic bomb. The threat of such a weapon can win these wars, Commander."

"Their SOE leadership is exemplary, Mr. President. The Germans won't get that heavy water out of Norway."

"Sure you wouldn't like something?" FDR asked after studying Tony's face a moment.

"Yes, sir, I'm sure."

"I rarely get the chance to talk with bright military people that don't have big titles and stars on their shoulders, Commander. I'm enjoying this. I hope you are as well."

"You've been very generous with your time. It's an honor to have had the chance to meet you, Mr. President." He felt uncomfortably calm.

"I'm not dismissing you, Commander," FDR said with an infectious smile. "Tell me a little about your background."

"I grew up in Maine. Doctorate in Math from Harvard. I couldn't find a job that interested me. I looked into what the Navy had to offer and joined in 1937."

"Joined in '37 and already a Commander. That's impressive. How did you get into the intelligence business?" FDR asked.

"I went to the battleship *Maryland* out of OCS. During the year in the Communications Department, I completed a correspondence course in basic cryptanalysis. They touched on codes and ciphers in Harvard, but not enough to satisfy my curiosity. It made that Navy course fun and I flew through it. Shortly after that, I got orders to DC for cryptanalysis training at Arlington Hall. From there, I went to OP-20-G in the Main Navy building on Constitution Avenue. Right after Pearl Harbor, I went to London. The rest is history."

"I see you're married. Where's your wife?"

"London, sir. She's a WREN in MI5," Tony replied.

FDR smiled. "Keeping it in the business! Any children?"

"A step-son, Ives, 10 years old. We're newly married, sir. She was a war widow; he was a British fighter pilot."

"This war certainly is changing many lives, some for the good, many not so good." FDR said thoughtfully.

"So very true, sir," Tony said.

A nod and a smile by FDR preceded a segue, "How long have you been in London? What would you like to do next? Where would you like to go?" asked FDR.

Tony's mind stumbled. He paused to collect his wits. "Frankly, sir, uh, no pun intended, I'm quite happy and challenged as Naval Attaché, London. I got there just before Christmas of 41."

FDR smiled. His face then became serious. "I was just curious. Tell me, Commander, and you can decline to give an opinion. Captain Taylor certainly appreciates your thinking. Getting unbiased thoughts on just about anything is difficult to find and it is valuable to me. I'm wondering what your thoughts are on a political matter to be decided in this conference. There are three proposals for France's future after the war. One is for General de Gaulle to lead France. Another is for General Noguès to lead. The third is for a coalition government with de Gaulle and Noguès having joint responsibilities, pending a free election. Any thoughts about that come to mind?"

Oh my God, thought Tony, dare I? Should I even try to offer an opinion. His mind sorted through the range of possible replies. "Mr. President, this is a hot potato. Each option one settles upon leaves very unhappy people. But without question, the powerful egos and vastly different intentions of both men would be best held in check. An Allied flag officer or foreign service officer that would function as an interim governor, pending national elections, may be prudent. Some sort of French political coalition is another, as hairy a political foray that would be. But choosing between de Gaulle and Noguès, I would be hard pressed to accept that." Stop there, said Tony's guardian angel.

Tony watched FDR soaking up his comments. His serious face relaxed, and his head nodded slightly.

"Thank you," FDR said softly. "You obviously are keeping up with international politics. On a lighter note, did you know all four of my sons are military officers on active duty? Elliott is Army Air Force, came in from London to be with me for SYMBOL. He is over at Winston's Villa at the moment. It's just a short walk, which is handy for the PM and me. Franklin is on a Destroyer in port and hopes to break loose and visit tomorrow. James is a Marine Colonel, and CO of the Fourth Marine Raider Battalion in the New Hebrides. My youngest, John is a Navy Lieutenant Commander on the USS *Wasp* in the Pacific. Would you please come have lunch or dinner with me tomorrow, if I can shake loose of all the flag officers? I'd like you to meet Franklin and Elliott."

"I'm at your service, Mr. President. It would be an honor and a pleasure, sir."

"Purely social. I think you boys will find each other interesting. For now, I have some reading to do before dinner tonight. Prime Minister Churchill, Lord Leathers, British Admiral Cunningham, your Admiral King, General Somervell and Averell Harriman are coming over. See what I mean about stars and titles? We hope to come to an agreement about what war resources get shipped to whom at what priority. I need to do my homework before they arrive. Do you know any of those gentlemen? Have you had any involvement in London with Allied shipping requirements?"

"I've met Admiral King, I have not had the pleasure of meeting the others, sir. Negative on having much involvement with Allied shipping," Tony replied. "But I have a good understanding of the Lend Lease Program. I have gotten a number of questions from other Allied and neutral country Attaché's about it."

FDR fussed with his left eye, clearing a hair or particle from it. "Commander Tony Romella, I wish I had more time to spend with you. You're quite an interesting man. I do want you to meet my sons before we all leave Casablanca. I would also like to talk with you again." FDR extended his hand.

Tony stood and shook FDR's hand, "Honored, Mr. President. I hope SYMBOL goes your way." Exiting FDR's room he thought, I would have given my right arm if I could have had Petra and Ives with me just now.

13 - Military Brotherhood

7:55 a.m., Monday, January 18, 1943
Conference Room C
Anfa Hotel, Casablanca, Morocco

Two smaller conference rooms in the hotel, labeled B and C, were inspected by the Army's security personnel and were kept secure, around the clock, for classified side meetings by the SYMBOL participants. Admiral King arranged for Captain Lattim and Tony to meet with him in Conference Room C at 8 a.m.

Tony arrived early and selected a rear corner table for the meeting. He stood when the Admiral and Captain arrived.

"Good to see you again, Commander," greeted Admiral King. "Last we talked was in Main Navy, back before Pearl Harbor."

"Good morning, Admiral. Affirmative, I left Main Navy right after Pearl. Good morning, Captain," Tony said, shaking their hands.

"Did you know your 20-G offices are moving to Nebraska Avenue next month?" King asked.

"Yes, Admiral, I know about that. It will give them much needed additional space. But I'm thankful I'm not there for that move."

"Moves of any sort are not fun," King said. "Commander, let me get right to my concern. The SYMBOL group will be forming up in the main conference room shortly," said King. "Yesterday, the conferees agreed that the top priority for our respective operational forces was anti-submarine warfare. ASW is the linchpin for successful operations in both theatres. The threat from an ever increasing population of U-boats in the Atlantic appears to be critical at the moment. They are launching 30 new U-boats a month now. The ratio of what we destroy to their launchings is in their favor. The losses being seen in merchant ship convoys are close to intolerable. The amount of shipping that will be required to support Allied operations this year in the Mediterranean and Europe will be tremendous. Better radar and sonar systems on combatant escort vessels will help. But when Admiral Dönitz implemented the new Enigma system for his submarine forces, he put blinders on us. We need to know where those U-boats are patrolling. Captain Lattim has given me a good briefing on the content of the COMINT proposals for Allied operations. But what is missing, for my background information, is what we are doing to take those blinders off?"

Tony leaned forward and put both arms on the table, palms down, which provided a few moments to respond. He began in a soft voice, "Gentlemen, you cannot repeat what I will tell you. I am giving you the benefit of my personal knowledge, integrated from several sources. It is for your personal background information only." He paused for their acknowledgement. They nodded affirmatively. "At the end of last October the Royal Navy captured U-559. Before the German efforts to scuttle her succeeded, we recovered two critical code books that the U-boats use for the weather and current location elements of their status messages. Those elements, and others, comprise the whole status message, which is then encrypted in their new Enigma system. Those code books provide valuable insight for decrypting the Enigma messages. Those books arrived at Bletchley Park at the end of November. It is now a matter of brute force decryption processes by machines. They will work on current intercepts first, then work backwards on the backlog. They are building more of those machines to help with productivity."

"The so-called, bombe machines, with an e?" asked Lattim.

"Affirmative. Also, OP-20-G contracted with NCR Corporation, in Dayton, for building a couple dozen of those machines on an accelerated basis for our use. Funds are being pursued for many more of them. As they are built, they'll be installed at the new HQ at Nebraska Avenue. Personnel for operating them have already been identified, mainly WAVEs. We will coordinate with Bletchley for processing the current Enigma intercepts and backlog, eliminating duplication. So, you see, blinders are coming off as fast as humanly possible. By the time the Allies start sending massively more convoy tonnage, we'll have a current plot of all U-boats and their orders from Admiral Dönitz.

King smiled as he absorbed the briefing. "The last time we spoke, you addressed issues with direction finding, and thus, locating U-boats. You made a good point that DF data, although imprecise, is useful due to the timeliness of the intelligence reporting from the moment of the U-boat's transmission, compared to ULTRA reports after decryption of U-boat transmissions. Do you have anything to add?" asked King.

Tony nodded, "We're designing better DF equipment on a priority basis and replacing some of the older equipment that is deployed, worldwide. We're also using an experimental fix calculation system, in an effort to expedite and improve DF fix validity. As you recall, sir, one of the problems in the eastern side of the Atlantic is the lack of U.S. Navy DF stations. The geometry necessary for high quality DF fixes just isn't there for many areas of the eastern Atlantic. But coordination with British DF networks, particularly on U-boat targets, has improved. Also, responding to the need for geometry improvement, we are working on getting an experimental DF system into the Azores. That would significantly improve fix validity because of it being able to provide a more perpendicular line of bearing to use in conjunction with bearings from other sites that are generally looking east to west and vice versa. It's not easy to simplify that. Suffice to say, it should help, significantly. We are negotiating with Lisbon now, regarding the Azores. I cannot venture a probability of success on those negotiations, but we are hopeful and almost optimistic."

King swatted at a fly hovering near him. "Flies here in Casablanca look just like the ones in DC and just as big of a pain in the ass. Alright. Change of subject. Tell me, is it realistic to expect 20-G to put a COMINT team on a carrier or flagship going into the Med, as the draft appendices mentioned? I'm told by the task force commanders in the Pacific that those teams have been valuable in warning of incoming air attacks, well beyond the radar range."

"Aye, sir. If it has not been requested, I would suggest that you do so when the planning sessions are concluded, and war plans are better defined," said Tony. King looked at Lattim.

"I'll take that for action," Lattim said.

Tony sat back, "Gentlemen, I realize I've given you a ton of technical information that's not native to your backgrounds. But I thought it necessary to demonstrate that my optimism is not without sound basis. Boiling it all down, the merchant convoys in 1943 should have a decreasing loss rate due to greater COMINT successes alone, across the board."

"That last sentence, Commander, with the background you have provided, gives me the confidence I sought. Thank you. It's time for me to move into the main conference room. Just be reachable during the remainder of the day."

"Roger, sir. I'll be in my room, the lobby, the NOB comm center, or possibly at the U.S. Consulate."

That Evening
Villa #3, Anfa Camp, Casablanca

Tony became a little more excited with each step he took from the hotel toward FDR's villa. Once again, he survived the security gauntlet, passed through the front gate of the villa, and knocked on the front door.

"Commander Anthony Romella, I presume," Lieutenant Colonel Elliott Roosevelt said when he opened the door. "I'm Elliott. I saw you getting the business at the gate. Come in, come in. Glad you could make it."

"Tony, sir, pleased to meet you."

Elliott ushered Tony into the great room. Domestic staff were preparing a white linen covered rectangular table for dinner. "We hoped to dine outside on the patio, but it's too breezy and chilly. My brother is in with Pop. I'll let them know you're here. Have a seat. We'll be out shortly."

A butler in a dark suit and tie came promptly to get Tony's drink request. His scotch and water took just a few moments to arrive from the bar at the end of the room by the stairs. The final details of the place settings for four were made and the first course, tossed salad, was placed on the table. Tony was in awe of his situation. The adrenalin began to flow. A private dinner with the President, how in the world could I have imagined this? Just then, he heard FDR laughing as he was being wheeled down the hallway by Lieutenant Franklin Roosevelt, Junior. Lieutenant Colonel Elliott Roosevelt was right behind them. Both of FDR's sons were in uniform. The President was in Navy blue slacks, white shirt, and a dark blue tie with a gold anchor print.

"Commander Tony Romella," FDR called out, "Nice to see you again. I want you to meet my son, Franklin, at the wheel here."

Tony stood, "Good seeing you, Mr. President. My honor and pleasure to meet you Franklin."

Franklin nodded, "Likewise Tony," as he pushed FDR to the head of the dining table. The butler staff came forward and filled their glasses with white wine.

"Sit boys, I'm hungry," said FDR. "This is yours, Tony." He pointed at the place setting to his right. The other two place settings were on the other side of the table. Once the men had taken their seats, FDR bowed his head and said softly, "God bless the men and women in the armed services. Fair winds and following seas to those who have given their lives, and to those who will give them in the months to come. Amen."

Tony crossed himself and uttered, Amen, in unison with the Roosevelt sons.

As soon as FDR picked up his wine glass, the other three did the same. "To success with SYMBOL, our operations in 1943, and the downfall of Hitler." The tinkling of glasses and cheers filled the air briefly.

"Three Navy to one Army Air Force. Elliott, you're outnumbered," FDR said with a big grin and picked up his salad fork. After taking his first taste of the salad, he leaned toward Tony, "I counted myself as Navy because I was Assistant Secretary of the Navy, from 1913 to 20. Did you know that?"

"Affirmative, Mr. President, I did know that," Tony replied. "What an exciting and challenging time. That period covered World War One."

"Yes, the war began in July of 14 and ended in November of 18," said FDR. "The exciting and challenging part was when the war was on. The frustrating and sad part was the politics involved with keeping the fools in Washington from all but scuttling the Navy. These tomato slices are the cat's whiskers. Tony, tell them what you've been up to in London."

Tony laughed. The Roosevelt men made him feel very much at ease. "Mr. President, you know that if I told them, I'd go to jail." FDR laughed, as did his two sons. "The short version is," Tony continued, "I'm the Naval Attaché in the London Embassy."

"Boys, so far in London, Tony took on a very sensitive mission for me in Bletchley Park. He brought me a fine cigar," he said, winking at Tony. "One day, I'll tell you about that cigar. He also has been on missions with the underground in France and Norway. He's not just sitting behind a desk in London, pushing papers. You boys remember Captain Bill Taylor? Well, Bill pulled him out of DC to London with him. Bill is the Defense Attaché there. Bill just can't say enough good things about Tony." Tony felt his face turning red. "Elliott, tell Tony what you're doing."

Tony was following the example of the Roosevelts, taking a bite, or sip of wine, between a sentence or two. The lively banter at this table would make this a long, enjoyable dining experience.

"I'll say one thing, first off. If Bill Taylor likes Tony, then so should we. That said, I'm an air recon guy, Tony. I'm currently the Commander of the 3rd Air Reconnaissance Group with the 12th Air Force in the Med. My HQ is in Algiers right now."

FDR swallowed quickly to insert, "And when he was flying out of England, he and his group did the recon photos to support the final planning for Operation TORCH. He gave us a current view of French forces in Casablanca and the other landing locations." He put his fork down on his plate and looked up at the butler. The staff removed all the salad plates at that point, without regard to the amounts that might be left on any of them.

"Where in England?" asked Tony.

"Membury for a couple months, then Steeple Morden for a couple months, then when TORCH was over, on to Algiers."

"I can guess where you were flying recon missions to, out of Steeple Morden," said Tony.

Elliott smiled, "You'd be right, too."

The main course was a seafood platter with a dome of yellow rice, shrimp, broiled mackerel stuffed with crab meat, and buttered cut carrots.

Once FDR had sampled each of the food items, he looked at Franklin, "Your turn son."

Franklin had a slice of carrot halfway to his mouth and put it down, with a chuckle. "OK. I'm the Executive Officer, and Gunnery Officer, on the USS *Mayrant*, DD-402. We were part of the TORCH task group that provided covering fire support for the Casablanca landings. We leave port tomorrow for the U.S. We'll be running east coast convoy protection ops."

Throughout the main course, two bottles of chardonnay and finally, chocolate cake, they talked about their families, college days, duty stories, books and movies. When FDR finished his meal, they retired from the table. FDR's sons took the couch, and Tony sank into a stuffed chair. FDR positioned his wheelchair in the middle, opposite them. A butler brought FDR a cigarette in a long holder and a lighter with a ceramic Presidential Seal on the face. FDR flipped the cover on the lighter, spun the flint wheel to light it, and puffed the cigarette to life. The other butler delivered drinks.

FDR looked squarely at Tony, "I'm interested in hearing your input on something. Cordell Hull, my Secretary of State, sent me a brief this morning. It was about the submission of a proposed anti-submarine project at the Ponta Delgada Legation. It was, ostensibly, to be a separate issue to be discussed with Prime Minister Salazar of Portugal. That is, purposely not consolidated with the talks regarding Allied use of the Azores. Your name was given as the proposing agent for that project. Secretary Hull fears this project could be the straw that breaks Dr. Salazar's back on Allied use of the Azores, in general. You have your fingers in a lot of pies. What is this particular pie all about?"

Tony blushed slightly, "I'm waiting to hear Dr. Salazar's response. No way of knowing when that might come. But it's a very critical item for passively locating U-boats."

Franklin, Jr. sat forward, "Pop, that's important. Can you help there?"

FDR took a small drag on his cigarette. "As I understand the brief of this project, I support the goal of it. But I worry about killing the negotiations for Allied use of the Azores. I indicated my personal interest, though, merely by asking for more details from State and the Lisbon Legation. I'll see how that develops. Salazar has been very stubborn. Winston is working on him too. Between the two of us, we'll find a way. The Azores is too important, strategically, to let slip from our fingers."

"I can make a query on that, next time I'm over at Winston's villa on other stuff, if you want, Pop," offered Elliott.

"That's not necessary, son," FDR said, waving his cigarette holder. Winston and I are keeping each other appraised on the Azores. We're finalizing the joint plans for going in there peacefully, and also plans for taking the Azores by force, if that's what it comes to. We'd rather be going in with Salazar's blessing, naturally. The crux of the matter is, the Allies need the Azores and we don't want Germany in there, so one way or the other…"

"Having Allied naval and air bases there would be incredibly useful," said Franklin Jr.

FDR nodded in agreement. "More than useful. Critical, for supporting Allied operations in the Med and Europe." He gazed at the embers of his cigarette a moment, then looked up at Tony. "Yesterday I asked you about France's future government.

Churchill is stubbornly behind de Gaulle! How can I convince him to change his mind? I've already talked with them about it," he motioned at his sons.

Tony didn't hesitate, "The Prime Minister is just dead wrong, if I may say so. There's obviously something political that is preeminent."

"I just think they've bonded on a personal basis after de Gaulle arrived in London, in exile," Elliott interjected.

Tony shook his head in wonder, "Maybe my military background keeps me from seeing the logic in remaining stubborn in the face of contradictory facts. But I can't imagine liking someone so much that I would be blinded to a position that would have a negative impact on my, or any, country's future."

Elliott sat forward, "Politics can be a powerful force, Tony. A person's vision can be filtered to see only what will pass through. But I agree with you. There has to be more than what's on the surface."

FDR was listening intently to the discussion that ensued. "Gentlemen, I see the overarching fact of them both being colonialists. Birds of a feather. They see colonies as the measure of greatness. Colonialism has been a failure, at the very least, for the colonies themselves. They've been raped of their resources without reimbursement or investment. Look at colonies like India, Indo-China. I visited Bathurst, Gambia on the way here. It's just sinful what France has done to that country. I told the Gambians that I'd help them get independence when the war is over. I'll tell the Sultan of Morocco the same thing when we meet. I'll tell any colony, for that matter. Colonialism is clearly not the way for the future. The question I put to you boys was, how do I convince Winston to back a coalition government for France? I can't even get him to convince de Gaulle to come here and take part in this conference. Actually, I think that might be Winston's doing. But no matter."

After a few moments of silence, Tony piped up, "Mr. President, you're the one closest to all the issues surrounding this one. You've been communicating with Winston on a personal basis. Only you know the answer to that question. Stick to your guns and use your keen intuition. There has to be some incentive for Winston to change his mind. Maybe that would simply be your clear statement of unwillingness to budge."

FDR smiled at Tony and puffed the last inch of his cigarette a few times. He inspected the cigarette holder as if he hadn't seen it before. He squinted at his watch. "Gentlemen, I'm going to bed. I have more questions for you, Commander. I appreciate your thinking and candor. But I'm just too damn tired. I hope we'll get a chance to talk again. You boys are getting along so well, don't make the Commander go home on my account. Play some poker or something."

The next morning, FDR, Elliott, and Franklin Jr., were chatting over pre-breakfast coffee in FDR's bedroom.

"Well, boys, what do you think of Commander Romella?" asked FDR.

"Don't get in a poker game with him," said Elliott, jokingly.

"That's for sure," said Franklin Jr., grinning, "I think he's a card counter. He'd be a great Pinochle partner."

"Aside from that?" asked FDR, grinning.

"Interviewing him for a job, Pop?" asked Elliott.

"You know how I am always looking for talent, in general. When a need comes up, it's nice to have someone in your back pocket."

"I think he's going to be good at any challenge he gets. He's an intellectual in hiding," said Franklin Jr.

"I can't add to that, Pop. He's great company. If I get back to London, I'll look him up," said Elliott.

"Me too! I like him," said Franklin Jr.

14 – Detour Ahead

Two Days Later
8:50 a.m., Wednesday, January 20, 1943
Crypto Room
Naval Operating Base, Casablanca

Tony spent yesterday sitting in the background of the SYMBOL conference in the hotel, providing inputs to Admiral King on the U-boat threat. Today, and for the remainder of the SYMBOL Conference, Tony was on-call.

Lieutenant Junior Grade Hall responded to knocking on the Crypto Room Door. "Good morning, sir," said Hall. "Welcome back, boss. How was the Azores?"

"Good morning, troops," Tony replied. He motioned for Chief Johnson to sit back down and continue working. "The Azores was pretty damn nice."

Hall smiled, "SYMBOL has kept you busy since you got back, huh?"

Tony smiled, "Has it ever." He was slightly tempted to tell Hall about his visits with the Roosevelts, but he saw no reason to gloat or name drop.

"Well boss, we received more messages on the mid-watch for you. I didn't call you this morning to tell you, since you mentioned last night that you'd be here early. The Eyes Only for you I processed, as you directed, when I got in this morning. Good stuff in the folder, sir."

A reading folder was waiting for Tony at Hall's desk. Tony read the four messages in the folder carefully. He couldn't help but smile. Things were happening much faster than he dreamed possible.

Hall was helping Johnson sort decrypted incoming messages for the NOB into date and time order. He looked over when Tony pushed away from the desk and crossed his legs, thinking.

"I told ya it was good stuff," Hall said. "I'll get you a pad of blank message forms for your replies."

"You two stop what you're doing. Bring chairs over," said Tony. When Hall and Johnson were seated by the desk, Tony said, "As you know, the SYMBOL Conference ends on the 23rd. The special intelligence communications services we are providing for it terminates at midnight on the 23rd. But we're not going home right away. We're going to the Azores sometime afterwards. When, is still up in the air."

"Holy s...smokes, sir," Johnson reacted. "Hamill too? Should I get him in here?"

Hall chuckled, "When I saw that question in the Eyes Only message asking you who you wanted to take with you, I just knew it would be us."

Tony nodded. "I'll tell you what I know right now. You can tell Hamill when he comes on watch this evening. We're going to set up an experimental DF system on San Miguel Island in the Azores. The project is classified Top Secret. Everyone that needs to know where we are going is aware. Tell nobody else. It's going to be temporary duty. OP-20-G will bring in men on permanent assignments, depending on how this experiment goes. They're still figuring out how to get the equipment to us, as well as our transportation. In the meantime, you will all need civilian clothes to wear to the Azores. You will be in civvies for the entire time you're there. Your cover story is that you're diplomatic staff. I've already been there in uniform, so they want me to stay in uniform. You'll be wearing suits whenever you are outside the facility, which includes our departure from here. What you wear inside the Azores facility can be casual. I'll give you more francs to cover the civvies. Go buy the civvies right away. We may not get much notice to leave. Bring all your gear and weapons with you, since we may not return here again. Mr. Hall and I will be the only ones wearing weapons. Chief, you and Hamill stow your weapons and ammo in your seabags. I suggest you get a second sea bag or suitcase for the civvies. Remember, keep track of your expenditures down to the franc. That's all I have for you right now. I'll keep you informed as things progress. Questions?"

Their replies were simply nods and smiles.

Tony waved them away, "Back to work. I have replies to messages I need to work on."

That Afternoon
5:20 p.m., Wednesday, January 20, 1943
Captain Taylor's Office
U.S. Embassy, London

"Good afternoon, Captain. I expected to hear from you about now. News about Tony?" Petra asked, hanging her hat and bag on the clothes tree.

"Good afternoon, Petra. Yes. Come sit. I do have some news to share," Taylor replied, moving to the sitting area.

"I anxious for SYMBOL to end. When will he be back?" she asked with anticipation.

Taylor hated to see her optimism disappear. "Not right away, I'm sorry to say."

Her smile turned to a serious frown, as though a switch was thrown. "Right. Tell me."

"He and his team are getting orders for a short term task at another location. He will be in friendly territory, so don't worry. I can't tell you more about it."

"How long will he be there?" she asked.

"Until they can get men transferred there to relieve them. Hard to say exactly, at this point, but I would guess a month or so."

She sighed deeply, clearly disappointed. "Well, we must keep our peckers up. One day the war will be over. We'll look back at what we've been through and smile."

"Atta girl! Chins up, smiles on our faces, as best we can," he said. "How about I treat you to supper?"

"Smashing idea!" she said.

The Next Morning
9:30 a.m., Thursday, January 21, 1943
Major Rossi's Office
U.S. Consulate Annex

"Thanks for making time to come talk," said Major Rossi. "I needed a safe place to discuss classified subjects, which is why I asked you to come here."

"Understood. Thanks for the buggy ride," Tony said. "So, what's on your mind, Chuck?"

Rossi had the grin of the proverbial cat that ate the canary. "You're just not going to believe the coincidence of this. I'll just say that I'm aware of your visit to San Miguel and the proposal you made to Lisbon. I've seen several diplomatic cables forwarded after the fact by General Donovan, in DC. The cable you sent, that summarized the German presence there, provided new intel which peaked Donovan's curiosity. Long story short, he is dispatching Mike Nelson to this Consulate to lead a couple missions. He's arriving tomorrow. One of those missions involves us hitching a ride with you to San Miguel. Mike and I will be out of your hair while we're there."

"Well now ain't that something," Tony said laughing. "It will be good to see him. I have to advise you that my orders do not provide for me to be involved in your little OSS caper."

"Just riding with you, that's all," Rossi said. "It's not all that easy to get inconspicuous transportation into there. You will have diplomatic sanctioned entry.

Can't beat that. We'll probably come back with you as well, for the same reason. We're flying, I assume."

"Aircraft is the current thinking, anyway. Surface ship is just too risky. Just thinking, the Consulate has limited visitor quarters. It will be pretty cramped."

"Oh, we have our own arrangements, Tony. We'll get picked up by a contact we have there. You probably won't see us again until we leave. I'll keep in touch somehow to coordinate the return ride."

"Figure out when the three of us can have supper after Mike gets here," said Tony.

"I'm afraid Mike and I will be out of out of the area until we meet you at the plane. We have some business to take care of," Rossi said with a wink. "When you have an ETD, just call the Consulate and leave a message for me. Just state the date, time and phonetic first letter of the airport name."

Two Days Later
9:10 a.m., Saturday, January 23, 1943
Crypto Room
Naval Operating Base, Casablanca

Tony spent most of the last two days in the NOB Crypto Room, reading and replying to 22 classified messages that straggled in from OP-20-G and the Consulate in Ponta Delgada. They were close to nailing down the transportation of the experimental DF system and his team to the Azores.

"I scrounged a bag of pastries from the galley," Hall said as he came through the door into the Crypto Room.

"Excellent, Roy! I'm ready for one of those and a coffee refill," Tony said.

"Me too," said Johnson as he grabbed Tony's and Hall's mugs and headed for the coffee mess in the Communications Center.

"Nothing heard from anyone about transportation and equipment since last evening, Roy?" asked Tony.

"Not a peep," replied Hall. "It's not because they lack information, though. Right down to the width of the door in the Azores Consulate."

Tony smiled, "I damn sure didn't want to be unpacking crates outside the Consulate." He wolfed down a cinnamon bun and mug of coffee, then looked at his watch. "I have a jeep and driver waiting. I'm going back to the hotel. I'm still on call with the conference. With the time difference, it will be a while before the DC wheels get in their offices and accomplish anything. Call me if something comes in."

An Hour Later

Front Desk, Anfa Hotel

"Yes, Commander, I just put a phone message in your box," said the sergeant at the front desk.

Tony's face flushed when he read it. "Call me as soon as you get this. Lieutenant Colonel Roosevelt." He hurried to his room, sat down at the desk, took a deep breath, and picked up the phone. The switchboard connected him with the number on the note.

"Elliott speaking."

"Commander Romella, sir."

"Ah, Tony, glad I caught up with you. Can you come over for lunch at 1330? Pop has some questions about something in your purview. He wants your personal explanation."

"I'll see you then, Elliott."

That Afternoon
1:30 p.m.
Villa #3, Anfa Camp, Casablanca

Tony made his way through a gaggle of suits and uniforms outside the villa and knocked on the door.

"Come in, Commander," said the butler, recognizing him.

Elliott came around the corner as the butler was taking Tony's hat. "Pop and Winston are in the living room. They have been discussing the Azores. They want more info before they agree to let your project go forward. Winston thinks it could put the rest of the Azores plans at risk. I mentioned you were still here in Casablanca. Talking to you will save a lot of time trying to get answers by diplomatic cables. That's what I know about it all. Ready?"

"Affirmative," replied Tony, feeling guardedly relaxed.

"OK. Let's go in," Elliott said, leading Tony into the living room. FDR was in his wheelchair facing the couch, where Winston Churchill was sitting.

FDR waved at Tony, "Commander Tony Romella! Come meet my good friend Prime Minister Winston Churchill. Winston, please meet Commander Anthony Romella."

"I'm honored, Mr. Prime Minister," Tony said as he approached Churchill and shook his hand. FDR put his hand out to shake Tony's hand as well. Elliott disappeared up the stairs to the second floor.

The President of the United States and the Prime Minister of the United Kingdom at the same time. Lord, give me wisdom.

"Sit, Commander, easier for me to see you both," said FDR pointing at the couch. "Winston, this is, by the way, the man who lead the U.S. Navy radio intercept team on one of the early Operation GROUSE missions."

Churchill was expressionless for a second as his brain sorted information, then a grin appeared when it clicked. "Right. The cabin affair. Jolly good show, that. My personal appreciation for a valuable contribution. You lot all back in London?"

"No, Prime Minister, two are MIA. They were lost coming back out," Tony replied.

Churchill tapped his cigar ashes into an ash tray on the couch arm, while shaking his head slowly, "Very sorry Commander. We lost several in there earlier. But we press on with that one."

FDR broke a short silence. "Commander, I wanted you to come give us the details which the State Department and Foreign Office haven't provided on this Azores project you proposed. We're not sure we want it to go forward. As we read between the lines, Dr. Salazar gave a very reluctant go ahead but with a number of strings attached. We are concerned that this small project could jeopardize the larger negotiations we are deep into. I'm speaking of establishing Allied airfields in the Azores. You're familiar with all that, as I recall."

"Yes, I am, Mr. President."

"Alright. Tell us what this project is really about. What value would it bring?" FDR asked.

Churchill was impatiently manipulating his cigar between his teeth.

Tony turned in his seat to more directly face the two leaders and inhaled deeply. "The point of it comes down to more rapid and accurate geographic location of U-boats, through direction finding of their transmissions on the short-wave radio band." He paused, recognizing the faces of both FDR and Churchill indicated their minds were processing that sentence.

Churchill's cigar tip became bright red as he drew air through it. He put it down in the ash tray on the side table beside him. "Right. We already have that ability. Why the Azores?"

"Briefly, Mr. Prime Minister, it provides a unique geometric line of bearing that will produce smaller areas of probable inclusion of the sub's location," Tony replied.

Tony could see their brains were on fire digesting that sentence. "Please indulge me while I break that down. Essentially, lines of bearing to U-boats from the UK run westerly into the Atlantic. Lines of bearing from the east coast of the US on them run easterly into the Atlantic. They don't make refined, intersections, cross-hairs, if you will, being somewhat parallel. The lines of bearing on them from the site in Keflavik run somewhat southerly, making something of a cross-hair. But they can't always hear the U-boat signals, when the Azores possibly can, and vice versa. Often, both will. The precision of the fix area for the location of the sub is therefore increased by the

Azores contribution." The brain fires seemed extinguished, and Tony could see light bulbs coming on.

"Right. But Bletchley's ULTRA on U-boat locations is spot on, now that we have that problem solved again," Churchill offered proudly. FDR looked at Tony expectantly.

"Absolutely, the Bletchley Park intelligence on those transmissions are indeed, spot on. However, DF fixes, although they involve search areas, not actual locations, they are available in minutes. BP takes hours, sometimes many. Minutes can make the difference for a convoy's defense. Make no mistake, BP's ULTRA validates and refines location data and provides many other intel details. It's just that a DF fix provides a quick snapshot that is tactically useful, sometimes critical."

FDR smiled, "That insight, Commander, is what I was missing."

"Right," Churchill uttered emphatically through teeth still holding a cigar.

"My only other question for you, Commander," FDR continued, "is can you actually meet Dr. Salazar's limitations, his conditions?"

"Yes, Mr. President. The equipment will have no external appearance, that is, no visible antennas and such. The men will be in civilian clothes and under diplomatic cover as attaché personnel. They will be in a building alongside the existing Consulate, marked as the Consulate Annex. There will only be one junior officer and two enlisted personnel there, to start. At this point, this is only a feasibility program. In fact, it may be terminated and removed within a month or so, if its usefulness does not pan out. But if effective, the enlisted complement will rise to eight. A junior officer, six operators and one electronic maintenance technician."

FDR and Churchill sat looking at each other, as if they were communicating telepathically. Both nodded.

"Right," uttered Churchill, tapping his cigar out in the ash tray. "We must not lose merchant ships to the deep at the hands of the wolfpacks. Those merchant ships, laden with troops, petrol, tanks, planes, machines, and supplies are the dominant factor for the success of all else we do in the European war. Mr. President, I say we let the Commander give it a go."

"I agree, wholeheartedly," said FDR.

"Thank you, Commander," said Churchill. "Now I must go lunch with my Chiefs of Staff." He stood, as did Tony. Churchill shook hands with Tony and FDR before departing.

"Can you stay for lunch, Commander?" asked FDR. He motioned to the butler, putting two fingers to his lips. "It will just be Elliott and Harry Hopkins." The butler promptly brought FDR's cigarette holder, a cigarette, and a lighter. "Call it compensation for consultation services," FDR said with a grin. "Elliott and Harry will be down shortly. Meanwhile, tell me about your Navy career before London."

Petra's face filled Tony's mental imagery. He could see her expressions if she were to know his stories of Villa #3.

15 – New Adventure

Four Days Later
7:10 a.m., Wednesday, January 27, 1943
Port of Casablanca

The SYMBOL conference ended on schedule, which gave Tony and his men a chance to sightsee Casablanca. Messages arrived two days prior containing unclassified orders for them. Today was the day they had been anticipating, their departure for the Azores.

An Army sedan delivered Tony to the pier where the PanAm Clipper was waiting at the far end. The morning was cool, humid and breezy, with rain forecasted. It was nearly dark, with sunrise being hidden by dense low lying clouds and light fog. He could see Hall, Johnson and Hamill walking a third of the way down the pier, seabags over each shoulder. Hall also had a small case in his left hand that contained the mission's crypto rotors and key lists. As Tony was about to put his sea bag over his shoulder, a Consulate vehicle pulled up nearby.

"Tony!" yelled Mike Nelson. "How the hell are ya?"

"Damn good to see you, Mike," Tony said as they shook hands vigorously and slapped each other's shoulder.

Rossi was grinning as he watched Tony and Nelson. "You guys must know each other pretty damn good," he said jokingly.

"Oh hell yes, we do," said Nelson. "You have no idea."

Nelson and Rossi each pulled two large aluminum sided suitcases from the car, one in each of their hands and joined Tony on the walk toward the end of the pier.

Those guys are traveling loaded for bear, thought Tony, I'd love to see inside those four cases.

Once they all were down on the floating platform, next to the Clipper, Tony introduced Hall to Nelson. The Radiomen were surprised and glad to see Nelson. The last time they saw him was in Norway.

The steward opened the Clipper's entrance door. First Officer Cliff Harkin appeared at the doorway. "Commander! Looks like you get to fly with us again. Brought along some company, this time, huh?"

"I sure did, Cliff," Tony said, and introduced the rest of the men.

"Let's get all your luggage aboard before we board you," Harkin said, stepping onto the floating platform to make way for the luggage transfer.

"Still doing your, uh, southern route?" asked Tony, while two pier workers handed the seabags and suitcases to the Clipper's steward.

"Affirmative. By the way, before we departed the states, we detoured to the Potomac River, landed and docked at the Naval Research Laboratory. We picked up several crates for you."

"Great. That was going to be my next question," Tony said.

"Are we expecting anyone else, Commander?" asked Harkin.

"Negative. This is the whole party," Tony replied.

"Alright. Looks like the luggage is stowed. Time for you all to come aboard," Harkin said. "I'll need to see everyone's ID cards as you come through the door. Just follow the Commander forward and make yourselves comfortable."

That Afternoon
3:10 p.m., Wednesday, January 27, 1943
Port of Ponta Delgada, San Miguel, Azores, Portugal

The Clipper was secured to an anchorage buoy, just inside the breakwater. Two Portuguese Air Force seaplanes were tied up to buoys nearby. The water was fairly calm inside the breakwater, with just enough wave action from the cool on-shore breeze to rock the plane perceptively. There was a pleasant, rhythmic sound of water lapping against the hull. The wake of each fishing boat that passed by caused the plane to bob more notably. The passengers put their jackets on and made their way to the compartment with the entrance door. The steward was bringing their luggage from the compartment aft of the entrance compartment.

Harkin came down from the flight deck and entered the compartment where they had gathered. "You can open her up, Greg," he said to the steward. "Gentlemen, the Captain of the Port advised that a boat is just leaving to come get you and the crates. They prefer passengers on the first run, then they'll return for the crates. We'll need one of you to stay behind to help offload those crates. None of them can be handled by one man. They aren't all that heavy. Just unwieldy, and we don't want to lose any over the side."

"I'll stay behind," said Tony. "Mike, I could use your help."

"Roger, Tony, can do."

It took an hour to shuttle the passengers to the dock, and to get the crates transported, cargo netted and hoisted out of the boat onto the dock as well. The sun was being blocked by low level clouds that hurried across the sky. By the time Tony and Nelson got onto the dock, Leonard Daly, U.S. Consul General, had introduced himself to everyone else.

"Good to see you again, Tony. I think we have everything covered," said Daly, as they shook hands.

"Good to be here again. Consul General Leonard Daly, I'd like you to meet Mike Nelson. He and Major Charles Rossi are not part of my group. They just hitched a ride."

"Understood. I received a cable about Mr. Nelson and Major Rossi. Pleased to meet you, Mike," Daly said.

"Great meeting you also, Leonard," said Nelson.

"Tony, I have managed to preclear the entire party with the port authorities. Don't ask. All we have to do is get you all, your luggage, and the crates to the Consulate. I hired an ox cart. That's it down there, making its way to us. It's big enough to haul the luggage and all the crates. We can walk along with the cart. I didn't drive. I figured you'd want to accompany the crates all the way."

"Good plan, Leonard, it's just a few blocks," Tony said. "You have gone the extra mile to get everything taken care of. I very much appreciate that."

Nelson put his hand on Tony's shoulder. "Tony, if you don't need us to help with the crates, our ride has just arrived."

"No, Mike, my guys can take care of everything. Go catch your ride." Tony exchanged a wave with Rossi, who was standing by an old, probably 1920s, black two-door coupe.

U.S. Consulate Annex
Avenida Infante Dom Henrique
Ponta Delgada, San Miguel Island, Azores

The Portuguese policeman outside the Consulate had the most curious of looks as the men escorted the cart to the front of the building next to the Consulate. It was dusk, darkened by the gray clouds overhead. The light fixture above the door glowed a bright pale yellow. The wooden sign on the door indicated that it, too, was the U.S. Consulate. A second sign, in Portuguese, indicated that the Consulate business entrance was next door. Daly showed Tony the floor plan drawings on his last trip to Ponta Delgada, so there were no surprises. It was close to the same floor plan as the Consulate, just not as expansive.

Daly unlocked the front door to the Annex and handed two keys to Tony. "I changed the lock. There are three keys, I have the third in my pocket. It will be kept in my safe. I couldn't get my hands on a large refrigerator, but there's two smaller ones in the kitchen. I'll come up with a larger one at some point. They are well stocked for at least dinner, breakfast and lunch. Maria will deliver food stock each day. Let me know of anything you guys need."

"Thanks, Leonard," said Tony.

"My deputy isn't due in for a few weeks, so I have the VIP apartment ready for you, Tony," said Daly.

"Excellent."

"We'll talk later about what you want to do about Maria and Jorge helping you with housekeeping, and so on," said Daly. "They do not have keys and will stay away until I tell them otherwise. Oh, and Jorge loaned me a claw hammer and big chisel. I thought you'd need those for the crates. They are just inside, on the floor next to the door."

"We'll need them," Tony said. "Once we get settled, I can think about custodial services. Otherwise, we'll manage."

"I'll be next door if you need me," said Daly. "When you're ready, stop over and we'll go to dinner."

Tony opened the door, "Come on in men, let's see what we have here."

"Living room is unfurnished," said Hall.

"Affirmative, Roy. Here's a key for you to hang onto. Yes, I told Daly to furnish the kitchen, but not to provide anything else but the minimum for topside, such as four floor lamps, three cots, two armoires, a table, a desk, a locking file cabinet, six folding chairs, and so on. We can add what's needed once you get settled. That's the kitchen through that door."

"Still better than the cabin, sir," said Hamill, referring to the Norwegian cabin.

"Sure as hell is," agreed Johnson.

Hall had a puzzled look on his face.

"Inside joke, Mr. Hall," Tony said laughing. Hall did not have the need to know what took place in Norway. "Put the crates in the living room. Biggest crates along the far wall. Once everything is moved in, lock the door, go topside and change into your working civvies. The big room on the right up there will be the operations room. The smallest room is Mr. Hall's. The other one is for you two. Put my sea bag by the door, here."

"Aye, aye, sir," said Johnson.

"Once everything is inside, make yourself some chow," said Tony. "You can tackle the crates after you get something to eat. I'm going next door."

Tony sent his encrypted arrival report to OP-20-G via Daly's Western Union channel. Then Daly took him to the village of Sao Roque, just east of Ponta Delgada, for dinner in one of Daly's favorite little holes in the wall.

"It's a pot-luck kind of place," Daly said. "Mama's meal of the day, but always wonderful. They don't speak English, but I know enough Portuguese to get the job done."

They waited in unfinished wood rocking chairs in front of the building, just off the cobblestoned street. If there was a moon, it was obscured by clouds. Subdued light from inside shown through a small plate glass window, providing a false warmth to the cool evening. It was not long before two people left, and one of the four tables inside became available. Shortly after being seated, they were served a large bowl of seafood stew with clams, mussels, chunks of fish, cubed potatoes, and tomatoes, accented with a tantalizing mix of spices. Portuguese sweet bread and local red wine topped off the main meal. Dessert was a rich caramel custard that made their taste buds sing. They argued congenially over payment, but Daly insisted.

On the dark ride back to the Consulate, among small talk, Tony mentally ran through the steps that needed to be taken to become a functional direction finding site. The ability to communicate directly with the Atlantic DF net control station, across the ocean in Cheltenham, Maryland, or at least the Embassy in London, was critical. Western Union telegrams would be unsatisfactory. The ability to hear and accurately measure the direction of target signals, given the much less than desired physical characteristics of the Annex, was uncertain. All the uncertainties bothered him. Just one of them could be prohibitive. He shook off the fact that he could potentially be spending the next few days repacking the equipment and coordinating transportation back to London. We've got to make this work, he thought. Those damn U-boats have to be outsmarted.

Daly stopped in front of the Consulate Annex, dropped Tony off, then parked his car in the rear of the Consulate. Tony exchanged nods with the policeman stationed outside the Consulate, unlocked the door to the Annex and stepped inside.

Hamill was just coming out of the kitchen with a glass of milk, "Good evening, sir."

"Good evening Hamill. Smells like you had a seafood dinner too," said Tony.

"Affirmative, fish filets, bread, butter, and some local peas that were kind of tough. I cooked and they didn't complain," said Hamill with a grin.

Hall was kneeling next to a crate in the middle of the floor, holding a claw hammer and chisel. Two floor lamps were casting light up to the white ceiling, providing ample work light for the room. The shades on the front window were pulled down. "Almost have this one open. We've opened several already. So far, we have DC to AC power converters, a transceiver, two batteries for it, a battery charger and an antenna. Also a bunch of clerical supplies, some tools, like screw drivers, pliers, hand drill and bits, wire stripper, extension cords, and stuff like that. We discovered there's a basement, so we're stowing the empty crates down there. The unpacked equipment is topside in the ops room. We're organizing things as we go."

"Very well, Mr. Hall, carry on!" said Tony with a smile.

Johnson held the crate steady as Hall pried off the top. After packing material was removed, Johnson said, "Oh, that's the ECM, our crypto machine. There's a one-time pad booklet in here also."

"Before I forget to tell you, the Consulate in Casablanca had a great idea for a covert radio antenna. They put a screw eye into the brick on the inside of the chimney, at the top, secured the antenna to it and dropped it down to the hearth. Totally invisible from outside. Let's try that. Do that tonight, under cover of darkness. There should be an access hatch to the roof in the hallway up there. You should be able to run the shielded transmission line from the antenna up through the floor into the ops room topside. Hide it as best you can from obvious visibility down here."

"Roger. I'll figure something out, boss," Hall said.

"I'm going topside and see what you've done so far," Tony said.

16 – Smoke Test

7:55 a.m., Thursday, January 28, 1943
U.S. Consulate Annex
Ponta Delgada, Azores

Tony's men worked until midnight the previous night, unpacking crates of equipment and unique supplies, and assembling the prototype DF system, known as the DX. They awoke at 5 a.m., anxious to finish the setup. A quick breakfast of scrambled eggs, bacon, bread and butter and whole milk, and back to work they went.

Tony left dishes in the VIP apartment sink to keep peace with Maria, put on his wash-khaki uniform and ventured out into the drizzle, under an umbrella, and wearing galoshes. The walk was a conveniently short one from the VIP apartment to the Annex.

"Ahoy!" Tony called out after closing and locking the front door of the Annex.

"Good morning, sir" Hall and the others called out.

"How's it going up there?" Tony asked as he got out of the galoshes and started up the stairs.

"Just finishing up a few final preparations," Hall replied. "We haven't plugged anything in yet. We thought we'd wait for you to do the honors."

Tony laughed, "Roger! Well, let me think about the smoke test priorities. Most critical thing is communications."

"We put the transceiver battery on slow charge all night, should be ready to go," Johnson said.

"OK. Connect the battery and turn the transceiver on. Let's see if we can hear the NSS DF net. Then we'll listen for London. We'll only be using the DF net to report line bearings. The London Embassy will be used for sending and receiving encrypted messages, and as a backup channel for DF reporting." Tony said.

Hamill connected the battery to the transceiver. Johnson put on the headphones and flipped the radio power switch on. He referred to a 3-ring binder of instructions and information, found the frequency plan for the Cheltenham DF Net Control and searched for signals in the range most likely to be heard at their location. "Bingo," Johnson called out. "I hear NSS and some of the outstations. NSS is fairly strong, most of the outstations are weak, but copiable."

"Outstanding!" Tony exclaimed. "Alright, try to make contact with NSS. I'm crossing my fingers."

Johnson waited for a lull in net activity and tapped out the callup on the hand key. He repeated it a second time. "Sure is a whacky alpha-numeric callsign they gave us. I think it took them by surprise. Anyway, they said QSA2, they hear us strength 2."

"I'm amazed it's 2," said Hamill. "Damn antenna hanging in a chimney and a piss ant transceiver, reaching across the Atlantic. I owe Johnson 20 dollars."

"OK, check the Embassy station," said Tony.

Johnson changed frequencies and made contact with London. "Strength 3 with London, sir."

"Very well. DX system next," Tony said.

Hamill put the DX power cord plug into the DC-to-AC converter receptacle. Lights and dials of the experimental direction finder system came to life. The DX was a large, clumsy-looking contraption, typical of experimental models of electronic systems. The Naval Research Lab modified the configuration for compatibility with the Annex room where it was to be installed. After removing the light fixture from the ceiling, there were just a few inches of clearance. A standard R-series shipboard receiver sat on a low table in the center of the room, 1.5 feet off the floor. Bolted on top of the receiver case, was a 2.5 foot square, 1" thick wood plate. Bolted onto the wooden plate was a structure that included a 4 foot diameter loop antenna, with a crank and gear mechanism to turn the loop. A bearing readout gage near the crank indicated the calibrated azimuth of the loop's direction, to one-half degree resolution. The line of bearing of a signal was determined by the operator finding a null in the signal strength, while carefully turning the loop.

Johnson moved to the DX console, sat on the low stool in front of the receiver and put headphones on. "Lots of signals, sir," he reported as he tuned the receiver, while reaching up to rotate the loop. He referred to his list of known shore stations to be used for check bearings. After a few minutes of tuning the receiver, rotating the loop antenna, and reading the azimuth gage, he reported, "Norfolk fleet broadcast and a London Western Union station are both right on the money."

"Very well. Baker Zebra on the calibration and site setup, men. I see you made calibration marks on the table. Since a bump or just normal use could move the antenna out of physical calibration, I want you all to check that every hour and take check bearings in each quadrant. Johnson, make up an hourly calibration log for that. It's very important.

"Aye, aye, sir," said Johnson.

Men, this is really promising. Alright, the three of you take turns taking the check bearings on known stations we need to report to get operational certification. You need to log at least 500 of them so I can calculate the interim systematic error and standard deviation. Once we report that data, and they approve, we can join the DF net."

"Aye, aye, sir," Hall said. "I'll go through the list first, then Johnson, then Hamill, and we'll keep doing that until we log the 500."

"Roger," said Tony. "I'm going to draft the initial operational report for encryption. Test the ECM crypto machine next, to complete the startup system tests. Looks like we're going to be in the Azores for a while."

Late that evening all check bearings had been accomplished, system performance data and readiness was reported and orders to join and participate in the Navy Atlantic DF network was received. The first line of bearing on a U-boat signal was reported to the network that night at 10:49. The watch bill was simple. Hall was bolstering the busy day watches and part of the evenings. Johnson and Hamill were doing eight on, eight off shifts.

17 - Stuff Happens

Three Days Later
9:45 a.m., Sunday, January 31, 1943
U.S. Consulate Annex
Ponta Delgada, Azores

An efficient routine in DF net operations was well established by Hall and the Radiomen. Most of the U-boat signals that were flashed to the Atlantic DF network by the net control station were heard and their line of bearing reported. Their morale was high, knowing that they were contributing to critical intelligence on threats to convoys.

Tony was in the kitchen, pouring himself a mug of coffee, when he heard a knock at the front door. He took a look through the peep hole. Mike Nelson was smiling back at him.

"It's a decent day, Tony, can you take a walk with me?" asked Nelson when Tony opened the door.

"I'll get my hat," Tony said. Oh boy, this isn't going to be a social call. What's he up to now?

"I need to discuss something with you," said Nelson as Tony locked the door.

Tony smiled, "Before you get too far into this conversation, I'm not going back to London any time soon, Mike."

"Good! That's not why I'm here," Nelson said as they strolled slowly toward the waterfront. "I have an interesting development," he said in a soft voice.

"Oh brother!" said Tony in an equally low voice.

Nelson grinned, "Oh, it's not that bad. But yes, I have a request. As I mentioned, Chuck and I are checking on German citizens on the island. We are focused on Ziegler, Major Bruno Ziegler. We knew he was a kingpin here. But somehow, we missed the fact that he was a retired German Army Major. We found that out when we read the report you sent to the Navy. Things just aren't adding up with him."

"I'm not surprised at that, Mike."

"Yeah. My gut says he's up to no good, but we're running into dead ends. So, how's your experiment coming along?"

"OK," Tony said.

Nelson lowered his voice to a whisper, "Any chance you can see if anyone on the island is on short-wave and where they are at? Like you did in London?"

"I recall you saying that the only involvement I would have with you is that you were just hitching a ride," Tony said sarcastically.

"Yeah, well, the situation we're dealing with has changed. I didn't know what I know now," Mike said.

"Sounds like it's what you don't know now," Tony chided.

"That too. Well? Can you help us?" asked Mike.

"Damn it, Mike, we don't exist. Understand?"

"Neither do we!" Mike replied.

Tony nodded with a smile. "I would have to clear this with DC, Mike. I just can't do it otherwise. I'd have to tell them who is asking."

"It's really important, Tony. Give them my name and title. Make the message INFO to OSS Washington too."

"Alright. I'll pass on your request with my support for it. You need to understand that it would have to be on a low priority, not to interfere, basis. And I won't be able to tell you where the transmitter is located, just where it appears to be coming from, somewhere along a line from my building. I won't have any cross-bearings."

"Tony, just that, would be a great help. I'll drop by Tuesday afternoon."

"I'm pretty sure they won't be able to react that fast," Tony said. "Come by Wednesday, soonest."

The Next Day
9:30 a.m., Monday, February 1, 1943
Commander Jerry Webber's Office
OP-20-GB, Main Navy Building
Washington, DC

"I know you're busy with the move to Nebraska Avenue, Paul, but did you see the message from Commander Romella about OSS support?" asked Commander Webber.

Lieutenant Commander Paul Archer didn't hesitate, "No, sir, I'm sorry, but I haven't seen today's message board yet. In fact, I just got back from Nebraska Avenue and saw the note to come see you. It's been hectic all weekend and today's no different. It will be long, crazy days until we're moved over there completely."

"Then you haven't seen where 90-some thousand German 6th Army troops surrendered at Stalingrad yesterday. The commanding general and his entire army. That's a blow that Hitler cannot afford," said Webber.

"Damn, that's good news for the Allies!" exclaimed Archer. "Adolph's great Russian campaign is essentially over, a massive failure. I did see where 50 American planes bombed the crap out of Wilhelmshaven naval base last week. Things are going sour for the Germans."

"RAF bombing raids on Berlin are shaking things up too," said Webber. "I would think Hitler's military staff will soon start wondering whether they are on the winning side of this war."

"I have a lot of intel and theatre action summaries to catch up on," said Archer.

"Lots going on in the Pacific too. Alright, here's a copy of Commander Romella's message for you," said Webber. "Drop what you're doing and staff this request through OSS, specifically Brigadier General Donovan's office. Here's his number. Make sure he personally concurs. Let me know when you get a reply. I won't take the request up the chain here until I confirm Donovan's chop on it. Let them know we have no objection at this point."

"Aye, aye, sir," Archer said.

"While you're here, do you have any results on the Azores' DX accuracy study?" asked Webber.

"I did some number crunching last night. I just haven't finished the report. I'm surprised at their results. Azores heard 82% of the eastern Atlantic signals of all types flashed to the net. I only analyzed their line bearing value on those targets. In summary, it appears they are reducing the fix areas by an average of 58%. That's a reduction of a hell of a lot of square miles of ocean to search for U-boats. Really outstanding. I'm totally amazed."

Webber began scribbling some notes and paused to think a moment. "Very well. Talk to the personnel detailers. Tell them to identify a permanent staff for Ponta Delgada. We'll need a Junior Officer, six DF operators and a qualified receiver repair tech. Oh, and tell them we want the tours to be staggered. This time make the officer and half the enlisteds to be 12 month tours and the rest to be 24 month tours. I have no objection to Romella's initial staff recommendations, either."

"Aye, sir. When are they needed? Yesterday?" asked Archer.

"Affirmative. As soon as they can round them up and arrange transportation," said Webber. "In the meantime, if things go sideways in the Azores, for any reason, we can always cancel the orders."

Three Days Later
1:10 p.m., Thursday, February 4, 1943
U.S. Consulate Annex
Ponta Delgada, Azores

Tony returned to the Annex after a bologna, cheese and mustard sandwich lunch, with coffee, of course, in Leonard Daly's office.

"I'm just finishing up the decryption of a message from OP-20-G, sir," Hall called out when he heard Tony's footsteps in the upstairs hallway.

"Subject line?" asked Tony.

"OSS support."

"That was fast. Let me read it before you put it onto a message form."

When Hall typed the last encrypted character on the ECM keyboard, he tore the long tape of printed decrypted text off the ECM machine and handed it to Tony.

Slowly pulling the narrow tape through his fingers, Tony, read the text and handed it back to Hall. "OK, finish processing it and give Chief Johnson his instructions. Take note, this task is on a not-to-interfere basis but consider it a high second priority. Search for ground-wave Morse signals during all slack time. Make a special task log for me. I'll need date, time, call signs, text and line of bearing."

Two Days Later
5:30 p.m., Saturday, February 6, 1943
U.S. Consulate Annex

"Come in, Mike," Tony said. "DC certified your clearance yesterday, with limited access. Go get some coffee in the kitchen and have a seat. I'll be right back. Clear the table. I have a map to show you."

"Roger! What's limited access mean to me?" asked Nelson.

Tony smiled, "You can't go up the stairs, and I can tell you only what you specifically need to know."

"Telling me what I need to know is exciting," said Nelson.

"One exciting thing for the Allies is that they have control of Libya now, which doesn't make Rommel happy. Anyway, I need to get something you'll also find exciting."

Tony went upstairs and returned with a rolled detailed map of the middle third of the island, which included the Ponta Delgada area. Rolled inside the map was a large sheet of onionskin paper. He cleared the table, unrolled the map and aligned the onionskin overlay to alignment marks on the map. He used knives and spoons from the utensil drawer to hold down the corners of the map and overlay. "OK, Mike, here's what we have so far. We've heard two transmissions, each starting at 0300 hours. One, two days ago and one, last night. These two lines of bearing are so close they look like one line drawn twice. The signal is somewhere on that line from here at the Annex, along the right side of the town of Faja de Cima, on into the Saint Vicente area here, and onward to the north shoreline."

"Tony, that's nowhere near the Major's house or plantation. Way off. Are you sure of these measurements?" asked Nelson.

"Affirmative. No question," replied Tony.

"Are the messages in open text?" asked Nelson.

"No. Both are ciphers. Which means this is unquestionably an illicit transmitter. Both times they sent messages containing five-letter cipher groups. Also typical of illicit activity is that they used alpha-numeric callsigns. The station that answered the local transmitter was distant from this island, on a line that points toward Berlin. Again, it could be anywhere along that line and accuracy degrades as the distance increases. My guess, based on the frequency they used, it would be Europe though, probably eastern Europe. I'm working on the ciphers, in hopes they are using something relatively simple. But it could take a while. The messages aren't very long, in fact, the second one is very short, which doesn't give me much to work with. However, I sent them to DC to work on also."

"Holy shit," Nelson blurted out, running his finger along the pencil line. He paused, slowly scratching his bald head. "This means the Major isn't working alone. OK Tony, give me the dates and times of those transmissions. I'll check with Rossi and see where the Major was at those times."

Tony showed Nelson the intercept logs.

Nelson took cryptic notes in a pocket notepad. "Is there any possible way, at all, that we can get a cross-bearing to narrow down the location of this transmitter?"

Tony chuckled, "Nope."

Nelson referred to the map scale and finger measured the line's distance, "Easily 10,000 yards across the island. This is good intel on one hand, and useless on the other. What the hell am I supposed to do with it?"

"Remember how you told me one time that shit just happens? Well, my friend, shit just happened," Tony said. They both laughed. "If we can break the plain text out of the messages, we might get some location clues. Give me a few days to work on this stuff and maybe get more intercepts."

Three Days Later
3:50 p.m., Tuesday, February 9, 1943
U.S. Consulate Annex
Ponta Delgada, Azores

Nelson sat down across from Tony at the kitchen table, dark brown eyes twinkling and a grin on his chicken pox cratered face, "I can tell you have some news for me, Tony."

"And I can tell that you are anticipating more than I have," Tony said. "We haven't heard any more from the transmitter. However, DC decrypted the first message. Interestingly, it reported the opening of this Consulate Annex, with a Navy officer and three civilians. The message signature was, quote, *Affenpinscher.*"

"Damn, your cover is blown with the Germans already," Nelson said as he took notes in his notebook. "*Affenpinscher.* Well, we know the agent's codename now."

"Roger. One piece of the puzzle," Tony agreed.

"Will they pull you out of here now that you're blown?" asked Nelson

"After thinking about it, as long as they don't know about the DF system, we're fine. Berlin would more likely assume this to be the establishment of a Naval Attaché, which makes perfect sense for this port. That's how State is billing it, also."

"OK. Good. I hope they don't pull you before Rossi and I finish here. How about the other message?" asked Nelson.

"The second message was very short, which makes it more difficult to decrypt. They are still working on it in DC. So, tell me, was the Major somewhere else when the transmissions took place?"

"Affirm. He sure was. Definitely at home asleep."

"Any hints of the Major being associated with anyone besides his driver and the pineapple plantation employees?" asked Tony.

"Negative. That appears to be a very real business. He's making a lot of money from exports to neutral European countries. There are significant profits, and he is using the Portuguese bank here in town for everything. There's no evidence of transfers of funds to or from German banks since he's been here. He's smart and represents all the Germans on the island with the authorities. Son of a bitch is not hiding, like you'd expect of an agent. He's a puzzle."

"Does he have a dog? An *Affenpinscher*?" asked Tony, humorously but also seriously. "There is such a breed, by the way. I checked, on a hunch."

Nelson chuckled, "That's actually a good question, Tony. I'll pass that on to Rossi. I personally have not seen him with a dog, though. That would be something. Well, I need to get going. I'll be back on Friday."

Peter J. Azzole

18 - Shield

Three Days Later
8:15 a.m., Friday, February 12, 1943
U.S. Consulate Annex
Ponta Delgada, Azores

Lieutenant Junior Grade Hall heard Tony coming through the front door. He hurried down the stairs to meet him with incoming messages in his hand. "Good morning, sir. We have message orders."

"Let's go to the kitchen. I haven't had my morning coffee. I'll pour myself a cup and read them there," said Tony.

"We're all excited, but we have a little problem," said Hall.

Tony poured a mug of vaporing black coffee and sat down at the table. "OK, let's see what we have here, then we'll discuss the problems."

He sipped the hot coffee carefully while reading. The first message contained orders for Hall to be the Naval Observer of the Consulate for one year, effective immediately. Johnson and Hamill were to remain in Ponta Delgada as Assistant Naval Observers for one year, effective immediately. A second message contained one-year orders for a receiver maintenance technician and four more DF operators, and all as Assistant Naval Observers.

Tony looked up at Hall, "And the problems are?"

"What the hell is a Naval Observer, and does that change our jobs?"

"Roy, think of the Observer being one click under an Attaché in pecking order. Technical differences between the two are irrelevant in your case. No it doesn't change your job. It's just a way of changing your chain of command to hide your purpose here. For clarification, I'm no longer in your chain of command. You report to the Consul Daly now. Anything else?"

"Yeah, boss, we still have stuff in our quarters and lockers back in London, and no place for these additional personnel to sleep when they get here," replied Hall.

138

Tony laughed, "No problems at all. Just give me the quarters info and locker numbers and keys and I'll see that your gear is forwarded to you by diplomatic pouch when I get back to London. As for the new men, they won't start arriving until a few weeks or so. Just make enlisted quarters for everyone in the basement. I checked it out. It's dry and free from mold. Finish it out enough so it's decent. Help Mr. Daly with the budget necessary to make that happen. The room the men are sleeping in topside can then be your office. Move the crypto out of the DF room into the office, it's too crowded in there anyway. Use your imagination, discretion and authority. Anything else?"

Hall smiled. "Aside from that, the guys like their orders, but they won't like not working for you. For me, it's a terrific career move, thank you, very much."

"Thanking me is not necessary. You earned it," said Tony.

"But there's no orders for you," Hall said.

"Affirmative. Because my open-ended orders to Casablanca, and such other locations as deemed necessary, were to return to London at my discretion. Which I will do when the OSS support is completed, or when I decide otherwise, whichever soonest."

"Roger that, sir," Hall said with a grin. "Also, the items in today's theatre action summary you might be interested in reading about are that we took Guadalcanal, which kills their ability to expand further into the Pacific, and that General Eisenhower has been named Commander, Allied forces Europe.

"Keep that summary out for me to read later on. For now, Naval Observer Hall, Ponta Delgada, get your suit on, we're going next door and formally introduce you to your new boss, Consul General Leonard Daly. By the way, your first official act will be to relieve him as Crypto Clerk and get the Consulate's classified traffic delivery means changed to your ECM system, so you don't have to use that damn strip cipher. That will make him very happy. Until then, do the strip cipher work for him."

That Afternoon

"Since you let me in, I take it you have something for me," Nelson said as Tony secured the dead bolt on the Consulate Annex door.

"Affirmative. Make yourself comfortable in the kitchen. I'll be right back," said Tony.

"No map?" asked Nelson when Tony returned to the kitchen with documents in hand.

"Negative." Tony took a seat across the table from Nelson. "We heard him one more time, 0300 hours last Wednesday morning, and the DF results are not any different."

"What do you have, then?"

"Decryptions from DC, interesting ones," said Tony. He referred to the documents he laid on the table. "That second message we intercepted, the really short one, well, even though we know the plain text, it's still a puzzle. The text is, quote, the beer is warm, unquote. It's a code phrase, but we have no idea what it means."

"Damn, Tony, that could mean something is good, or something isn't good, depending on whether you like beer warm or cold."

Tony nodded. "You can't read anything into that. Code phrases usually don't carry a logical external meaning. The Japanese Winds Messages, sent in the clear, on a weather broadcast, are examples. On the surface, you wouldn't think, quote, east wind rain, unquote, would indicate to all Japanese diplomatic offices that war was being declared on the United States, destroy all your classified material. But it did."

"We may never know what the beer message means, then," said Nelson.

"Not unless we get the code book that contains the meanings," said Tony.

"If we can figure out who this is, we'll go through his trash," Nelson said smiling. "Anything else?"

"Yes, the last message, the one intercepted Wednesday, has been decrypted," Tony said. "This one is very interesting. The plain text translation is, quote, "Mission update. Have volunteered as a janitor and yard worker for a nearby church. *Schild* is stalling. Believe *Schild* more interested in money and pineapples. Will continue attempts to recruit, unquote."

"Who the hell is *Schild?* Major Bruno?" asked Nelson.

"Good question and good guess. All we know in fact, is that *Schild* is an apparent codename for a contact or target. That word in German translates to shield, by the way.

"Holy shit, Tony. That's great intel. Sure sounds like the Major is Shield," Nelson said excitedly.

"That's just one conclusion, Mike. Be careful. There are other pineapple plantations or farms on the island."

"Roger, but… alright, did you check for churches on the map, along the DF line?" asked Nelson.

"Sure did. My guess is that it narrows the location down to the towns of Faja de Baixo, Faja de Cima, and Saint Vicente, in that order going outward. Logic says the one closer to the line of bearing, Faja de Cima, is the most probable."

"Damn, Tony, this is good stuff. What's your gut tell you?"

"You're going to love this, Mike. Bear with me. My gut is saying the Major is Shield also. Here's why. Daly has a decent library. I borrowed his German-English dictionary to just mess with the code words in that second message. I also, God knows why, looked up the Major's first name, Bruno. Turns out, the derivation of Bruno is

Germanic, from the word *brun*. Now, *brun*, has two meanings, brown and, get this, armor!"

"Shield!" exclaimed Nelson.

"Exactly, Mike. Now, the fact that there's logic involved with this, tells me that it's just a coincidence. So, let's be careful with conclusions. Let's keep our thoughts open to other solutions."

"OK. Let's just go with that solution, for right now, Tony. Bear with me. The Major, Bruno, or yes, whomever, is apparently not thrilled with the idea of spying for Germany. Maybe even thinks Germany is going to lose the war. They have a good life here and don't want to get deported. We can assume he's also afraid to turn the spy in to the authorities, for many reasons. We have two options, contact Bruno to see if he'll help us or the authorities, to see if he can ID them or set up a sting. Or second, just watch the Major closely to see who he talks to and follow them. What's your thinking?"

"Talking to Bruno, or the Portuguese, is out," Tony said, waving his finger back and forth. "I think it would reveal our intelligence capability. You must remain covert. Watch Bruno. Follow his visitors or those who contact him elsewhere. Sooner or later, you'll find one who lives near a church, reasonably close to that line on the map. Then you can decide how you're going to neutralize him, without getting caught, and without involving the Portuguese."

They sat there looking at each other for a moment now and then, sipping coffee and thinking.

Nelson broke the hush, "I might need your help with this op, Tony."

"Damn it, Mike!" Tony laughed.

"I know, I know, we're just hitching a ride," said Mike. "But there's only two of us and I know how you operate, firsthand. I can trust you, your abilities, and your judgement. You're as good as either one of us. This is going to get sticky at some point, and Rossi and I just may not be enough."

Tony clasped his fingers, stared at them and rolled his thumbs. "Were you once a used car salesman? That's a good line of bullshit, my friend."

"Oh, it's not bullshit, and you know it. Don't say you can't, because I saw your orders to Casablanca. They are so wide open, you can do anything you want, well, you know what I mean. I'll only need you for a takedown, or a house search. Things like that. Not every day. Just you, none of your guys here. What do you say?"

"Mike, even for my blanket orders, neutralizing an agent is a hell of a stretch. I've been down that slippery slope already in Casablanca, but they gave me specific authority to do it. Clear this with General Donovan. I know he'll coordinate with Captain Taylor and OP-20-G. Use Daly's diplomatic comm channel."

19 – Doghouse

Three Days Later
2:45 p.m., Monday, February 15, 1943
U.S. Consulate Annex
Ponta Delgada, Azores

Tony was sitting in the kitchen, peeling an orange. The strong citrus fragrance that came from tearing the skin always pleased him. He looked up when the front door opened. Hall and Nelson came in together and headed for the kitchen. Both had big smiles.

"What are you two so happy about?" asked Tony, as he split off a section of the orange, put it in his mouth and ejected two seeds onto a saucer with the skins.

"I just decrypted a message from State, advising that I'm on the promotion list for Lieutenant, effective the first of March," Hall said.

"Congratulations Roy, glad to hear it," Tony said. He stood, wiped his hand with a towel and shook Hall's hand. "I'll send you Lieutenant devices and gold stripes when I get back to London."

"Thanks, Tony. No hurry. They also advised that, as Naval Observer, I could remain in civvies unless attending ceremonies or meetings of military personnel. There's not much of that going on here."

"Let me tell you, Roy, as a Naval Observer, you'll have no idea what the next moment brings," Tony said with a grin.

Hall nodded, "Mike, you can tell him the other news. I have to go topside."

"Alright Mike, what's your smile about? I think I can guess."

"Roy was just finishing up with a classified message for me from DC when I knocked on their door over there. Basically, General Donovan, Captain Taylor and OP-20-G gave us, including you, the go ahead with neutralization of *Affenpinscher*. But there's a hitch. We have to interrogate him extensively. Then we have to do all we can to convince him to double up. If he refuses to be a double agent, we can neutralize.

He also advised that new intel on *Affenpinscher* shows that he's been sent to sniff out what's going on with Allied interest in the Azores. Additionally, he was given a recruitment target of a former German military officer, referred to as *Schild*."

Tony smiled, "That confirms what we learned. Wait a minute. How are we going to interrogate? Neither of us speak German. Does Rossi?"

"He sure does," said Nelson. "OK, where was I? OK, that's the summary version of the message. Go over and read the entire message when you get a chance. I left out some details. Plus, I want you to see that you were specifically authorized to participate, by name."

"Roger. Have anything else you can share?"

"Now that Donovan pulled you into this, I have plenty. We've been busy, Tony. I shadowed Major Ziegler and got lucky. Two days ago, just before lunch, the Major visited Fort Sao Bras. Been there?"

"Sure! West end of the harbor, right down the street."

"Affirm. OK, so he's touring the Fort, like a tourist, taking pictures with his camera. Then he lingered near the area where the old canons are pointing at the harbor. A tall thin guy with a full beard, dark brown trousers, brown dress shoes, tan wool sweater, leather jacket and cap, wanders over by him and strikes up a conversation. I was too far away to understand any of it. Although I am pretty sure they were speaking German. Anyhow, Major Ziegler's gestures made it clear that he was not agreeing with the conversation. I was sitting on a bench, reading a Portuguese paper, at a location where both of them had to pass by within ten feet. They left several minutes apart, *Affenpinscher* first."

"You don't know Portuguese, I hope the newspaper wasn't upside down," joked Tony.

"Ha! Not funny," said Nelson, grinning.

"Yes, it is. Anyway, you're going to tell me how you know it was him in a bit, aren't you?"

"Affirm, be patient. So, *Affen*... oh hell, let's just call him, Dog, left in what I would characterize as an angry mood. When the Major went past, he looked shaken, scared, pale. My guess is that the Dog gave him an ultimatum. Rossi picked up the tail on the Dog, not literally, and I followed the Major. The Major walked home and didn't leave his house the rest of the day or evening. I watched until midnight and went to bed. Here's the good part. Rossi followed the Dog to a farmhouse that sits back about 50 yards from a narrow dirt road, more like a path that comes off a dirt road. Get this, 500 yards east of the church in Faja de Cima. Your data was accurate."

"Well, I'll be damned," exclaimed Tony. "Go on. Have you seen this place?"

"Yes, we both reconned it from a distance late yesterday, and again after dark, closely, thanks to a little moonlight."

"Good. Hang on, I'll go get the map, so I can fully understand the location."

"And burn it into your steel trap memory too," joked Nelson.

"That too," said Tony with a laugh. He returned a couple minutes later and spread the map out on the kitchen table. "OK, my friend, show me."

The tip of Nelson's index finger pressed down on the location of the Dog's farmhouse. "Right there. It's small, about 15' by 20', in disrepair, but has electricity. The powerline to it is kind of a jerry rig affair. It's draped along little 8' poles spaced across this field. There's a little barn, half the size of the house, with an inoperable windmill near it, that used to pump water into a cistern. Of interest to you, near the windmill, there's a little flat roof shack, maybe eight foot square. There's a wire running out of it, across the ground to the base of the windmill, then up the side of the windmill tower to the top."

"Vertical long-wire antenna!" said Tony.

"Affirm," Nelson said, nodding. "The shack had a padlocked door. We didn't get inside. There are no livestock, just maybe a dozen chickens running around the property during the day. Roosts for them are in the barn. The fields are overgrown. They're not being tended. Xavier, my local contact, said the original owner passed away about a year ago, and the farm was abandoned because there are no relatives on the island. We learned that the Dog bought it for back taxes and moved in about two months ago. Nobody seems to know where he came from. The Dog has no neighboring houses within a maybe 400 yard radius. An ideal isolation."

"Anybody else in the house?" asked Tony.

"Negative, as far as we can tell."

Tony passed his palm over his bristly GI haircut, "The fact that the Dog bought that property strikes me odd. An agent would be expected to rent. He must be planning to be here for a long time. Possibly even taking on some... farm hands, to help out with the, uh, pigs and cows. Getting agents in here from submarines and German merchant ships would be simple."

Nelson grinned, "That's an interesting thought. A cell headquarters, basically."

"All part of the German plan to gather intel prior to taking the island at some point. But none of that matters right now, Mike. Time is of the essence, since he threatened the Major. We need to act, the sooner the better."

"Affirm. Let's come up with a plan."

Tony fidgeted, head down a few moments, thinking. "How much do you trust Xavier? I mean, really trust. Where does he live? Tell me about him."

"He was born and raised on this island. He has his late father's farm near Faja de Baixo, about a thousand yards east southeast of the Dog's farm. Damn guy was right under our nose. Which I think is very handy," said Nelson.

"Handy, if there's no problem with me going to Xavier's farm after dark."

"Negative, none at all," Nelson said. "Rossi and I have been sleeping there since we got here. Xavier's wife passed away a couple years ago and his two sons are grown and married, both of them living in Ribeira Secca, farming tobacco, on the other side of the island. Xavier has a sister and brother in law that moved to Rhode Island ten years ago. Everyone in the family is very pro-American. I trust him totally."

"Does he know who you're targeting? Does he know the Dog?"

"Negatory on both," replied Nelson.

"Don't bring him in on any part the operation, Mike. He needs only to be hosting us, OK? Letting us stage out of his location, no questions asked, would be a tremendous asset."

"Should be no problem at all, Tony."

"Can we walk to the Dog's house from Xavier's and remain undetected?" asked Tony.

"Affirm. We can avoid roads and paths, and just go through farmland and lightly forested hills, but yeah, completely. That's what Chuck and I did."

"Mike, I want to be clear about my role. I only have a shoulder holstered 38, which I intend to use only in defense. My only interest is in getting into that shack by the windmill and the farmhouse to find code books and to document the radio equipment. I'd like to be part of the interrogation from the viewpoint of his communications procedures, communications training and the like."

"Roger. Understood."

"Alright, Mike, let's talk about the operation, step by step. What's your plan?"

That Night

Xavier turned his coupe onto a rutted path that led up to the side of his farmhouse. Mike Nelson was in the front seat, Tony in the back. Charles Rossi heard them approaching and exited the back doorway on the side of the house to greet them.

"We meet again," Rossi said as Tony followed Xavier and Nelson to the door. "First I've seen you in civvies. Where'd you get that outfit?"

"Borrowed 'em," Tony said with a chuckle.

"Hey Chuck, come take a walk in the moonlight with Tony and me, while Xavier puts the kettle on," said Nelson.

Xavier's English was very good. He picked up the hint and went inside.

"Chuck, anything change since we went to pick up Tony?" whispered Nelson.

"Negative," replied Rossi quietly.

"Good. Tony, I reviewed the plan with Chuck when I got back this afternoon. There are no changes to what we discussed."

"Roger. What's Xavier know about it?" asked Tony.

"Nothing, other than we're going out with Sten submachine guns for a while tonight," said Nelson. "He doesn't ask questions. He's happy just knowing he's helping us do something important."

"Yes, Tony. This guy has really been a valuable, informant," Rossi whispered.

"OK, Mike, when's zero hour?" asked Tony.

"Right after we finish our coffee," replied Nelson.

They trudged a good mile on an indirect route, designed to avoid neighbors. They walked through rows of crops, and a small forested hill, until finally, they had gotten within sight of the Dog's farmhouse. Then they began walking crouched through the overgrowth of the Dog's fields. When they got within a hundred yards, they stopped and watched. The house was dark. Aside from a distant hound barking now and then, it was eerily quiet. Nelson and Rossi, Stens strapped over their shoulders, got binoculars out of their back packs. They scanned the farmhouse, barn, and the shack by the windmill. An unobstructed half-moon provided enough light for them to see.

"The chickens are quiet and not visible," whispered Nelson. "They should be in their barn roosts. Let's hope they stay there and don't start squawking. We wait 45 minutes to make sure it's quiet in the house before we move out." They all checked their luminous dial watches.

They sat down to wait out the countdown, rising intermittently to check the farmhouse for activity. They could hear each other's breathing rates increase as the final minutes approached.

"Holy shit," whispered Nelson. "I just realized that his car isn't there. Maybe it's on the far side of the house."

"Damn!" whispered Rossi. "It was there yesterday afternoon when we passed by and again last night. It's usually parked right in front. I'll circle around and check out the other side of the house."

"Roger, we'll wait here," whispered Nelson.

Twenty-five minutes later, Rossi returned. "Negative. The car's not there. Barn maybe?"

"If we check the barn for it, we wake the chickens and that won't be good," Nelson whispered. "So, that's out. If he wasn't using the barn before, it's not likely he started now." He paused to think about their options. "OK, we go inside and wait for him to return. We have more control of the situation by going in now and surprising him when he comes back, than going in when he's there."

"Affirm," whispered Rossi.

"Roger that," whispered Tony.

"Move out!" said Nelson.

They moved quietly to the back door of the farmhouse as planned, weapons ready, alert for sounds of an approaching vehicle. The skeleton key lock was an easy pick. They systematically cleared each room and confirmed it was uninhabited.

"Let's wait by the front door for him. Tony, stay on that side of the door and cover us," said Nelson, pointing. "The opened door will hide you. Rossi and I will be on this side and will take him down and restrain him as soon as he enters."

"Roger," said Tony. "I'm wondering what the hell he's doing out at this time of night. Let's hope he's not taking out the Major."

"That thought crossed my mind," said Nelson, putting his backpack in the corner. Rossi did the same.

They ran out of patience in an hour--still no Dog. It was impossible to keep from checking watches. They paced, did pushups, squats, sit-ups and grumbled.

"Quiet!" said Tony. He detected the distant sound of a vehicle approaching. Was the wait over? His watch said 1:30 a.m. Eventually, they heard a car driving up to the front of the house. The headlights illuminated the front windows then went out. The engine shut down. A car door slammed shut. Then a second car door slammed shut. Tony gave Nelson a curious look and saw the same on the faces of Nelson and Rossi. Nelson whispered planned actions into Rossi's ear. Rossi nodded. They put their Sten gun straps over their shoulders to free both of their hands. Tony took the safety off of his 38 and was ready to shoot anyone who got away from Nelson and Rossi. Two voices, speaking German, approached the house. Two sets of footsteps were heard coming up three noisy wooden steps onto the front porch.

The sound of a key in the door lock released an additional rush of adrenalin into Tony's bloodstream, making his heart race faster, breathing increase and a million butterflies take flight in his stomach. Here we go, he thought. These two are going to get the surprise of their life.

The Dog opened the door a third of the way and reached to the left for the light switch. Nelson grabbed his hand, threw him to floor, face down, with both arms painfully pulled to his back and then cuffed. An unlit flashlight fell to the floor from Dog's right hand. Before the Dog even hit the floor, Rossi jumped into the doorway and grabbed the second man, throwing him to the porch deck, face down, and attached hand cuffs. The Dog and his guest were angrily spouting German, between sounds of pain.

"Good!" reported Nelson.

"Good!" reported Rossi. He then barked orders to the two Germans to be quiet, in their native language.

Nelson looked at Tony. "Go get some of that clothesline I saw around back so we can immobilize these two goons," said Nelson.

Tony got a knife from the kitchen and went out the back door. He returned with four long lengths of clothesline and cut them into shorter lengths. By then, both

Germans had been taken to the living room. They were lying on their stomachs in the center of the room.

Nelson handed Tony his Sten submachine gun. "Keep an eye on these two while we bind their feet. If they try anything, shoot to kill."

Rossi repeated the warning in German. Every time they tried to speak, he ordered them to be quiet.

Tony watched as the Germans' feet were bound, then another line was attached, taught, between their hand cuffs and the bindings on their feet.

Once the prisoners were blindfolded and secured, Rossi motioned to Tony and Nelson to come outside the living room door, but with the prisoners still in view. "You need to know what I learned from what these guys said as they walked from the car," he whispered softly. "Did you notice the muddy shoes and water stains on the pants legs of the guy Dog brought home? He was put ashore by a U-boat. Dog's flashlight was used to signal the U-boat. I didn't hear where the landing took place."

"Son of a bitch," whispered Nelson. "OK. Interrogate and make the final offer."

Tony nodded, "Better interrogate them separately," he whispered. "Let's do Dog first." Nelson and Rossi nodded.

Tony guarded the other German while Nelson and Rossi dragged the Dog into the bedroom and left him on the floor.

Nelson returned to the living room. "Go do the honors."

"Roger," said Tony, returning the Sten.

Rossi removed the gag from the Dog when Tony came into the bedroom.

"Do you speak English?" Tony asked the Dog.

"Yes, and Portuguese," the Dog replied in excellent English with a German accent.

"Good. What's your date of birth, full name at birth and where were you born?"

Perspiration began to form on the Dog's forehead. He shook his head from side to side, "I don't remember, I lost memory when my head hit the floor."

"Oh, that's not going to work. Here's the deal. You have a choice to make. I represent the United States. You can cooperate with the United States, become a double agent, or you can die. It's a simple choice. What's your decision?"

Tony watched fear set in and the color drain from the Dog's face. "What do you mean, cooperate?"

"It means that you answer any question the United States asks you, at any time, and truthfully," Tony said. "If we determine that you have lied, you will die. You will follow all orders we give you. Also, any orders you receive from anyone else you will report to us and act on them only as we direct you to."

"If I do this, will you protect me? Will you get me out of the Azores?" asked the Dog.

"Yes, of course we will protect you. We will take all reasonable and possible measures to protect you. But we want you to remain here."

"How do I know you won't get all you want to know from me, then kill me anyway?"

"You only have my word. But you also have my word that, in less than ten minutes, if you don't agree to cooperate and be a double agent, and start talking, you are going to die," Tony said sternly.

The Dog swallowed hard. His body was shaking constantly. "OK, OK, I'll do it."

Tony realized that in the current state, the Dog was not useful. "Your new U.S. name is Fernando. Only use it with us. You're safe now. I'll give you some time to calm down. Remain here until we talk with the man you brought here. I'll free you when I come back. And Fernando, if you call out to the man in the other room, you will die." Fernando nodded agreement.

Once Tony returned to the living room, Nelson relieved Rossi in the bedroom so that he could go translate for Tony.'

Rossi came to the living room and ordered the German not to yell, then removed his gag.

"Do you speak English?" Tony asked.

The reply was a negative head shake, "*Nein!*"

"Give him the deal," Tony said to Rossi, who translated.

The German glared up at Tony from the floor, then uttered an angry reply under his breath.

"I don't think you want to hear what he said," Rossi said.

"Just in case he thinks I'm not serious, tell him he has five minutes to change his mind," said Tony, watching the man's sullen face.

Rossi translated. The man spit at Tony's feet.

"That's it. He's done," said Tony.

Rossi smiled and nodded, "Keep your gun on him, I'll be right back. We're not going to make any noise with gunfire to wake the neighborhood, if we can help it. I have just the thing for this situation."

Tony suspected the German might know English, but it didn't matter. He leaned toward the man and whispered, "If you have any last thoughts or prayers, now is a good time for them."

Rossi returned with his backpack. In full view of the German, he took out a small aluminum box, put it on the floor, unlatched and opened it. Inside was a syringe, three injection needles and three vials of lethal doses of potassium chloride. He attached a needle to the syringe and drew a dose of solution into the needle from a vial. Rossi whispered to the man in German that this was his last chance to change his mind.

"*Heil Hitler!*" the man replied.

"Hell is waiting for you," Tony said, and returned to the bedroom.

Rossi ripped the sleeve off of the German's left arm. He kneeled on his cuffed hands, painfully immobilizing the man. The dose was quickly injected into the exposed median cubital vein inside the bend of the man's left arm. "Go straight to hell, you Nazi bastard," Rossi said slowly and softly. The man's squirming and yelling quickly stopped.

"That was a fast interrogation," said Nelson when Tony entered the bedroom. "I guess he didn't have much to say."

"Nothing I wanted to hear. He made his choice. His last one," replied Tony. "Remove Fernando's cuffs and ropes."

"Thank you," said Fernando.

Tony looked at Nelson, "you need to stay and witness."

"Roger," Nelson said, crossed his arms on his chest and leaned back against the wall.

"What did you do with Heinrich?" asked Fernando.

"He had the same offer you did," Tony said. "His choice wasn't the same as yours." Fernando displayed surprise.

"It was quiet, fast and painless," said Tony firmly. "Get up and sit on the bed. What is Heinrich's full name?"

"That's all I know about him, only his first name," said Fernando nervously. "I don't think it's his real name."

"Where did he come ashore?"

"An isolated shoreline about a kilometer south of Mosteiros," replied Fernando.

"Where is that?"

"Uh, northwest end of the island."

"How did they know that would be a good place?"

"They asked me to find a place that would be safe, undetected. I radioed it to them."

"He came ashore in a rubber raft, right? What did you do with it?"

"Yes. He told me that he let the air out, dug a hole with the paddle and buried it. I can show you the spot," replied Fernando. Sweat was forming on his brow. "I waited and watched, by my car on the side of the road, while he buried it."

"Where did you learn such good English? Have you been to America?"

"No I haven't been to America. I studied English at University, Berlin, a second major, you would say. Then I moved to Rostock and worked for a merchant ship company where I worked with English speaking customers, until the war started."

"And then you went into the Army?"

"Not my choice. I was conscripted. After new army officer's school, they sent me to Gestapo training, then special training for agents. After that, they sent me here, on a merchant ship."

"Why did you buy a farm?"

"My orders were to find a remote building, to provide a temporary place for new agents, build a network, and find places for them to live near ports and military bases."

"How did you find this farm?"

"Berlin told me to contact a well-established local businessman, a German, Heir Bruno Ziegler, to help find a place. He knew about this farm."

"Is Ziegler an agent also?"

"No. And he didn't know I was an agent, until they wanted me to recruit him. But he is stubborn. He thinks Hitler is insane and the Nazis are dangerous for the country. I think maybe both are true. But I know if I don't follow orders, they'll send someone to kill me. That's why I need your protection. It would be more safe in America."

"OK, Fernando, about Herr Bruno Ziegler. You will not contact him again unless we tell you to. If you do, you know what happens. If anything bad happens to him, you will die. Understand?"

"Yes, sir."

"Do you have orders to pick up, or knowledge of, other agents coming in by any means? Or knowledge of any other agents that are already on this island?"

Fernando shook his head from side to side, "None."

"If you learn of another agent coming in, or one that's already here, you must report that to us immediately."

"Yes, OK."

"Now, I want to know who you are communicating with on the wireless?" asked Tony. It was important for Fernando to know that they knew about his radio and what was being sent and received.

Fernando's eyes snapped from his clasped hands to Tony. Surprise was evident on his face. "Uh. I don't know who it is. I don't know the person. I only know that it's a Gestapo office in Hamburg."

"At 0300 hours, you're going to report the successful arrival of Heinrich. You're going to keep him alive, as far as Hamburg is concerned. On tomorrow's communications schedule, you're going to report that Herr Bruno Ziegler has agreed to help you. After that, we will tell you exactly what to report and when. You will not report anything we don't tell you. You will make all your required contact schedules. You will give us exact copies of everything Hamburg or any German contact sends you on wireless or by any other means. Do you understand?

"Yes, sir," Fernando replied genuinely.

Tony stepped close and put his hand on Fernando's shoulder. "You're going to be very valuable to the Allies here in the Azores and you will be rewarded. You're more valuable to us than you are to Germany. OK. Let's talk about your communications equipment and procedures and prepare the report about Heinrich for you to send on your 0300 scheduled contact with Hamburg."

"Yes, sir."

"After that, you will dig a grave and help us bury Heinrich before the sun comes up," said Nelson.

That Morning

Contact was made with Hamburg, on schedule, at 0300 hours. The encrypted report about Heinrich's arrival was transmitted. Then they buried Heinrich several feet under the empty pig sty, where fresh digging or sod disturbance would not be evident. Tony hand copied the secret key list from Hamburg for the rest of the year's daily settings for Fernando's cipher machine.

"We need to get a move on," said Nelson. "There's only three hours of darkness left."

"Roger," said Tony. "I just finished the key list. Now I'm copying the code book of phrases and their meanings. I should be done in twenty minutes at most."

Nelson nodded, "We can't wait any longer than that. It's a long walk."

Tony, Nelson and Rossi made the trek back to Xavier's farmhouse without incident. Exhaustion from overdue sleep and the energy surges from adrenalin made the trip mostly without any discussion. They craved sleep. Those moments spent in quiet thought while they walked were focused on reviewing the evening's events and ideas for next actions.

Xavier was awakened by the sound of the men coming back into the house. "Want some breakfast?" he called down into the basement, where the men were getting ready for the rest their bodies could no longer postpone.

"All we want is sleep, go back to bed," replied Nelson.

All three went to sleep on the basement floor, on and under blankets.

12:50 p.m., Tuesday, February 16, 1943
U.S. Consulate VIP Apartment
Ponta Delgada, Azores

Tony, Nelson and Rossi woke up, had a late breakfast and borrowed Xavier's rattle-trap of a car to bring Tony back to Ponta Delgada. Nelson and Rossi had cleaned up a bit and changed into clean clothes. However, the Portuguese police officer that focused his patrol on the Consulate apartment gave the disheveled Tony a suspicious and inquisitive look. Once Tony unlocked the door, the officer continued on his beat.

"Make yourselves comfortable in the living room while I go shower and change," Tony said. On the way up the stairs, Tony pondered whether or not it was advisable to burn the soiled clothes. *Oh what the hell, Maria may as well wash them. They don't divulge anything, and I might need the damn things again before I leave.*

"OK, guys, let's go sit at the kitchen table and talk," said Tony.

"You look a lot different all cleaned up and in your khaki uniform," said Rossi with a grin.

"Alright," Nelson said softly as he sat. "Let's get our heads together on this one. This isn't exactly a classified space, so keep it down. What are you thinking, Chuck?"

"Well, first order of business is a handler for Fernando," replied Rossi. "He speaks English, but I think it should be me since he's dealing with Germans, and I speak the language. So, I will stay here and do that until General Donovan gets somebody in here permanently or reassigns me."

Nelson nodded, "Absolutely. But let's not put Xavier into more jeopardy. Get yourself a place to flop, preferably in walking distance to Fernando. I'll give you enough escudos to rent a place somewhere for a few months and get a junker or something to get around. You'll need to get to the Consulate for communications and diplomatic mail."

"Roger," Rossi said.

"Chuck, I'll need to spend some time with you on the communications procedures," Tony said.

"You can do that when I go to the Consulate to file my report to DC," said Nelson. "Anything else we need to think about, Tony?"

"Nothing that shouldn't be second nature to both of you," Tony said with a grin. "I'll have my men continue the monitoring and DF task until ordered otherwise. Hall will be sending all intercepted encrypted message to DC. Chuck, you can pick up results from Hall in the Annex when you visit the Consulate. You can compare the activity and decrypts of messages he intercepts with what Fernando is saying and showing you. It would be great to trust him completely. But we can't."

"Affirmative," said Rossi.

Tony raised his index finger to his forehead as an idea struck his conscious thinking. "What you guys need to work on, is a good disinformation plan. That is, what you're going to tell Fernando to report to Hamburg and when. It's got to be a steady, reasonably timed stream of real facts you can afford to send to them. Believable but usefully fake facts. Maybe that's something General Donovan's office should originate so it supports and contributes to General Eisenhower's deception plans."

"I'll handle that. I'll include that in my report today," Nelson said.

"Excellent," Tony said. "When I get back to London, if I get any intel on a U-boat heading to the Azores, or agents going there, or already there, of course, I'll let Mike know. And guys, if I can help with anything downstream, don't hesitate to ask."

"More thoughts?" Nelson asked, looking back and forth between Tony and Rossi. "OK then. Tony, I'm ready to go back to London when you are. Is there a second bedroom upstairs I can use until we leave? The less people at Xavier's the better."

"Sure, Mike, let Leonard know when you go over to file your report. He'll let the housekeepers know to stock more food."

"I'll head back to Xavier's place after Tony briefs me on comms," Rossi said.

Nelson stood up and gave Rossi a friendly punch in the shoulder, "Roger that, Chuck. Visit Fernando every damn night, at least for a while. Tony's right, we'll never be able to let his leash get too long. I'm sure I'll see you again before we leave."

"Mike, I'll head over to the Consulate when Chuck leaves. I have reports to file too. I also need to brief Roy Hall about continuing the program for detecting illicit transmissions and Chuck's role in all that. I'll see you over there."

20 - Back in the Saddle

5:25 p.m., Saturday, February 27, 1943
Flight Line
High Wycombe Airfield
28 Miles NW of London

The previous two weeks had been many things, from interesting, to boring and sometimes anxious for Tony. However, his time in Ponta Delgada certainly was productive. Waiting for travel arrangements was tedious. He was anxious to be back in London with Petra, functioning in his primary assignment. But monitoring the progress of the new double agent was interesting. As far as Rossi could tell, Fernando was doing everything he was told, no more, no less. The Morse intercepts of Fernando's communications with Hamburg, were reflecting that the plan was working flawlessly. All that behind them, Tony and Nelson rode the PanAm Clipper again, this time to Casablanca. Nelson went off on his own. Tony spent two restless nights at the Anfa Hotel awaiting a ride to London.

This morning, at long last, a C-54 cargo aircraft crew let him ride to High Wycombe. As it taxied to a parking spot on the flight line apron, he could not keep from smiling. In a couple hours, he would be surprising Petra at The Dorchester Hotel. The anxiety to be back in London grew during the four days it took to travel from Ponta Delgada to London. He was out of his seat the moment the engines shut down. He was on the tarmac as soon as the passenger door opened. It was cooler than he expected, about 35F, but with a clear sky. The air smelled clean and dry. With the sounds of aircraft taking off and landing in the background, he took a deep breath and exhaled in a sigh of relief. When the ground crew offloaded his seabag, he threw it over his shoulder and walked toward the flight line office building to arrange a ride to London. A black British government coupe came through the gate of the flight line fence and was moving slowly in his direction. As it neared, he saw Captain Taylor's smiling face in the left front seat. Ten yards away, it stopped, and Taylor got out and

155

pushed his seatback forward. Petra hurriedly squeezed out of the sedan and ran to him. He dropped his seabag. They hugged and kissed, muttered softly to each other, repeatedly dried their eyes, and continued clinging and swaying.

Captain Taylor caught up with Tony and shook his hand. "Welcome back, sailor!"

"Oh my God, what a surprise," said Tony, still hugging her. "How did you know?"

Taylor grinned, "I got a message from the State Department saying you were on your way back to Casablanca. I called Petra and told her you were on your way back home."

Petra smiled brightly, "It was easy to figure out from there. All I had to do was watch the incoming flight manifests." Tony recalled that MI5 knew who was arriving and departing on all ships and aircraft.

"Where's Nelson?" asked Taylor.

"He's in Morocco. He said he would be there about a week," replied Tony.

"Let's get you and your gear in the sedan so that young lady in the Auxiliary Territorial Service can drive us home and get herself home for supper," said Taylor.

8:10 p.m., Saturday, February 27, 1943
The Dorchester Hotel, London

Captain Taylor chatted with the driver, purposely leaving Tony and Petra alone to catch up. They cuddled and whispered to each other in the back seat of the coupe during the trip from High Wycombe to The Dorchester. The ride home was excruciatingly long for the two lovebirds. But arrive they did.

"Stay out of the office tomorrow. See you Monday, Tony," said Taylor.

They wasted no time getting up to their suite, shedding their clothes onto the floor and getting under the sheets of the four-poster. An hour of passion left them breathless. Their two bodies clung together as their hearts and breathing returned to normal level.

"Darling, I missed you so much," she said softly. "I would just lay here looking at your imaginary face until I fell asleep. Lovely having you back."

"You were in my mind before going to sleep, and when I awoke," he said. "That's when you really commandeered my senses." He sighed. "It seemed longer than a couple months."

"Precisely two months, if you please. And listen to me. 27 is an important number for us. It all came to me earlier this afternoon. I first laid eyes on you on Saturday, 27 December, two years ago. You left for Casablanca on the 27th, December. Then today, Saturday the 27th, you returned from Casablanca. Odd, don't you think, love?"

"That's an interesting set of coincidences," he replied.

She poked him in the side, "Crazy yank. Shall I call the kitchen?"

"Absolutely. Whatever you order will be fine," he said.

They put on their fleece robes. She went to the writing desk and picked up the phone. He rooted into his seabag for two boxes, put them on the side table by the stuffed chair and sank into it.

She ordered supper, then settled into his lap, one arm around his neck and shoulder, the other hand inside his robe, on his chest. "Right, Commander Romella, tell me all about Casablanca."

"Well, Mrs. Romella, first, open the boxes on the table. They have traveled all the way from Morocco and their contents cannot wait any longer to see you."

She untied the twine that secured the wrapping of the smallest box. The lid was laid aside and crumpled Moroccan newspaper was carefully removed, unraveled and anxiously tossed onto the floor. Inside was two little boxes containing bottles of French perfume. "I don't speak French, but I understand *violette* and *jasmin*," she said as she read the words on the boxes. She removed the bottles from their boxes with care. Her sparkling eyes went from hand to hand, admiring each bottle. Her smile told him this gift was making her happy.

He patted her shoulder and said, "They smelled wonderful in the shop in Casablanca."

"We shall see," she said, and opened the square white ceramic bottle with a detailed relief of a flower bloom on each side. Placing her finger over the small hole in the top, she tilted the bottle for an instant, and wiped her fingertip on her wrist. "Heavenly," she said after waving her wrist by her nose. She passed her wrist under his nose.

"Oh, jasmine. It smells better on you than it did in the store."

She did the same with the round translucent purple glass bottle, applying the sample to her other wrist. "Oh, Tony, I don't know which I like best." It too was drifted by his nose.

"They have taken the aroma of violets to a wonderful place," he said. "Either one will be deadly to me."

"Then I need not choose. Just alternate."

"At your peril, dear."

"Threatening, are we?" she asked softly.

"Promising!"

Knocking on the door interrupted their flirting. "That's our filet of sole knocking us up," she said. "Please get the door whilst I visit the loo."

They resumed their cuddling on the stuffed chair after dining on white wine, broiled sole, potatoes, butter simmered carrots and chocolate mousse.

"What's in this box?" she asked picking up the one still wrapped. She shook it gently by her ear.

"Nothing that will rattle, or break."

She quickly untied the string, removed the brown wrapping paper and opened the box. She pulled out a floor length, sheer, cream silk and lace negligee, that tied in the front with a silk satin bow. "Bloody brilliant, Tony!" Off his lap in an instant, she took off her robe and put on the negligee. She modeled it, turning, posing, keeping her smiling face focused on him. "*C'est magnifique?*"

"Very!"

"Right. But too chilly for now," she said laughingly. Her robe went back on and the negligee was folded and put back in the box. She sat back in his lap, held his chin in her hand, looked deep into his eyes, gave him a kiss and said, "Thank you, sweet Yank. Now…Casablanca, darling. I must know. Did you get to see Winston Churchill?"

He nodded, smiling, "Yes, I did."

"How close, tell me!"

"Oh, maybe, uh, one meter. I was wishing you were there beside me, honey, believe me."

Her surprise and envy was visible in her expression. "Blimey, I do too. Tell me you didn't get to talk with him or shake his hand!"

"I cannot lie. I did both, indeed. He was quite congenial."

"Bloody hell. Right. Quite congenial. You're putting me on."

"I swear, honey, I'm not." He was enjoying this.

"Right. I suppose you saw your President too?" she said with one eyebrow cocked.

"Affirmative. I did," he said, grinning widely.

"Rubbish! A meter? Shook hands? Congenial?"

He laughed, "Yes, yes and yes. I wished you were there beside me then as well."

"Crazy Yank! Bollocks!"

"I swear that's true. I saw them both at the same time in a small side conference. I would share more if I could." If I told her that I visited FDR in his bedroom, and dined with him and his sons, she would surely reject that and anything else I said.

She looked into his eyes for a few moments and sensed he was telling the truth. "I so wish I had been there. Tell me about Casablanca, itself."

"First, tell me how Ives and your folks are doing," he said. "Have you talked with my sister? Hopefully, we can get our Sunday calls in to them tomorrow."

They spent the next hour catching up with each other's lives and talking about Casablanca. Their yawning became distracting and they got back into bed. They went to sleep curled up with each other.

Their lazy Sunday was spent having a late breakfast. Then they took a taxi to Piccadilly Circus. They walked hand in hand along the streets that spoked off of the roundabout. It was a sunny, low 40s F day and the streets were crowded. Uniformed men and women from neutral and Allied countries added to the many Londoners enjoying the fair Sunday. Taxis, horse drawn carriages, double-deck buses, military vehicles, bicycles, and people filled the streets. They window shopped in clothing stores and stopped at book and newspaper stands. After lunch at a Chinese restaurant, they sat in a nearby park until it was time to go see Irving Berlin's musical film, *Holiday Inn*, with Bing Crosby, Fred Astaire and Marjorie Reynolds. That evening they were able to call Petra's parents' home and spoke for an hour with them and her son. The attempts to get a line to the U.S. to call Tony's sister were unsuccessful.

The Next Morning
5:10 a.m., Monday, March 1, 1943
Naval Attaché's Office
U.S. Embassy, London

Tony awoke an hour before sunrise. Petra stirred when he tried to leave the bed carefully. "I'm wide awake, dear. I'm going to work. Go back to sleep, you have another hour before the alarm goes off."

Petra mumbled something, as he kissed her cheek. She rolled onto her side and pulled the duvet over her head.

He was anxious to get to work and dive into a fast catch up. A quick shave and shower, then into a fresh uniform and down the elevator he went. A waiting taxi sped off into another clear, 40-something day.

The Embassy was quiet at this hour, aside from the Marine guards and a few shift workers going about their business. The Naval Attaché office suite was dark. He turned on the lights in the administrative staff area, then entered his office and turned those lights on. His desk was polished and made orderly. Captain Taylor informed everyone on Friday of his return, so his in-basket was full. He looked at his sparkling clean coffee mug and yearned for it to get filled soon. Tony sat down and attacked his in-basket. The various summaries that he quickly read through brought him up to date on intelligence, war activity and collateral information. One surprising item was that shoe rationing went into effect in the U.S. on the 9th of February.

Noises outside his door meant his staff was arriving.

Chief Yeoman Alise Haydin knocked on his door and opened it. "Good morning, sir. Welcome back. I thought I was going to beat you in. The coffee pot will be perking shortly. Anything else you need?"

"Good morning, Chief. Yes. When the mess opens, bring me some scrambled eggs and buttered toast, please."

"Aye, aye, sir. Anything else?"

"That's it so far."

"Your schedule is open all day, sir, aside from a 1500 appointment with Captain Taylor, topside. If you rough out what you wish for the rest of the week, I'll get it typed up."

"If anyone has need for a one on one, schedule them after 1630. I'll be in all day. Oh, you did get notice that Lieutenant Hall has been transferred, right?"

"Aye, sir, there were no details, just that he's been transferred. Everything OK with him?"

"Absolutely, Chief. A mission popped up and he was assigned to it. He probably won't be back. Which reminds me, I need to have his personal effects boxed." He reached into his pocket and pulled out three keys. "Here's his BOQ locker key. These other two keys are for the lockers of Chief Johnson and Radioman Hamill. They were transferred with Lieutenant Hall also. Send someone to the Knockholt Y-Station to box their personal effects. Get all their belongings sent via State channels to the Consulate in Ponta Delgada. If you run into any snags, let me know. I'd like to see this completed quickly."

That Afternoon
Captain Taylor's Office
U.S. Embassy, London

"Good afternoon, Commander. Welcome back," said Sharon Freedman, Captain Taylor's Admin Officer. "Go on in, he's got company, but you're invited."

Tony knocked on Taylor's door and entered. He was surprised to see Ed Langsdale in the sitting area with Taylor. "Good afternoon, Captain, and to you, Ed."

"Welcome back! Come join us, Tony, Ed has news," Taylor said.

After smiles and handshakes were exchanged, Tony sat in a stuffed chair near the couch where Taylor and Langsdale were sitting.

"Good or bad news Ed?" asked Tony.

"Quite good indeed, Tony. Getting right to it, the four British commandos of the Operation GROUSE reconnaissance party, which you were initially expecting at your cabin, successfully parachuted into a remote location in the Telemark area on 18 October. The intelligence you provided on your mission forced a bit of a change in their drop location, which may have saved their lives. They landed in the area of Fjarifet, a wilderness free of Germans. They had a tough go of it, and had to ski for 15 days, nearly starving, but finally met up with Swallow Blue's brother, somewhat near the Møsvatn Lake dam. After months of delays, mainly weather, we were able to press on with Operation GUNNERSIDE. Six SOE commandos were put in by glider, landing a few miles southwest of Møsvatn dam on 16 February. Twelve days later, they successfully disabled the heavy water production system of the hyrdro plant."

Tony was on the edge of his chair during the briefing. "Any killed or wounded?"

"None, Tony. Bloody amazing success. All got away," Langsdale said smiling.

"Do you know how much damage there was? How long until they resume production?" Tony asked.

"Right. Based on their report, it may be a year, or more. We have intel that says they have some heavy water stored in tanks elsewhere in the plant, however," Langsdale explained.

"Moving those tanks should be easy to spot, if you have constant eyes on the rail system from the plant to the ferry," Tony said, recalling the communications intelligence he gleaned on his mission.

"Aye, indeed. Swallow Blue is still in place, and they are watching," said Langsdale.

"I'm just curious, do you know if they have discovered the cabin?" asked Tony.

"We don't know. Iceberg was ordered to stay away from the Lake, in any case."

Tony smiled. "Congratulations to you and SOE on GUNNERSIDE. Denying Germany of that much heavy water will have a huge impact on their atomic energy research progress."

"Right, and congratulations to you and your team. I got the word this morning that all men that set foot in Norway on these operations are being written up for awards. That includes your team, Tony, including the two men that were captured and killed. I visited Captain Taylor today to obtain proper names of all involved. It was his decision to let you know about it now."

"Thank you, Ed, and Bill also," Tony said.

"Such things as award recommendations travel through many hands and suffer many delays. It may take a long time before they see light of day. On this one, due to the classification, it could be after the war. I'm sure such processes are suffer the same delays in your country," said Langsdale.

"I'm afraid so," said Taylor. "We won't hold our breath."

"Oh, by the by, the material you sent back from that German site in Casablanca was of very high value," said Langsdale. "Those were important captures of Enigma settings for German Navy B-Dienst intelligence stations. They yielded many significant decrypted messages and continue to do so. The Germans that vacated the site must have reported them as destroyed, to cover their arses. Thus, Berlin considered them safe to keep using."

"Yes, DC said it was a good haul for us as well," said Taylor. "This is the first chance I've had to talk with Tony since he got back. It made Washington very happy."

Langsdale took a deep breath and turned to Tony, "On a sad note, I think you knew Dilly Knox, Chief Cryptanalyst at Bletchley. He passed away last Wednesday. He succumbed to consumption. Many of us in MI6 and BP are quite saddened."

"I did meet him a few times, briefly. That's a terrible loss to the effort there," said Tony.

"Gentlemen! I would stay for tea, but I must get back to the mansion. It was good to see you both," said Langsdale.

Handshakes and pleasantries were exchanged and Langsdale departed.

"Sit back down, Tony. I have some things to pass on," Taylor said and returned to the couch. "Reading your reports and messages related to you in Casablanca is like reading an action novel. My God man, you turned an easy trip to Casablanca into things I don't even know about, I'm sure."

Tony laughed. "Not my doing. I was just following orders and dealing with situations, boss."

Taylor laughed. "Roger that. Alright. Like I say, I'm sure I don't know exactly what all you've been up to. Must have been interesting to get summoned to General Patton. I didn't see the details behind that. But to change the subject, how in the world did you…" he paused and smiled, "I got a handwritten note in the priority diplomatic mail Friday, telling me what a fine man I had on my staff, and so on, and asked me what my plans are for you."

Tony took the inquiring look from Taylor as an invitation to comment. "Wouldn't be Leonard Daly, would it?"

"No, damn it," Taylor said grinning. "It was the President of the United States. What the hell is that all about?"

Tony could feel his face and ears get hot. "It started with Harry Hopkins. He told me he saw my name on the SYMBOL attendee list and recalled my involvement in Project CIGAR."

"Uh huh. You realize that I know Harry, the Roosevelt family and Lattim?"

"I didn't before, but I do now."

Taylor grinned, "Harry asked Captain Lattim to confirm you were one and the same guy for CIGAR. Lattim got a call thru to me, asking for more info. I sent him an Eyes Only message with a few personal and professional details."

"Hall and Johnson are sure trustworthy. They never even hinted about that Eyes Only message about me. Lattim had to get it from my guys," Tony said.

"As it should be, it wasn't for your eyes," said Taylor, grinning.

"Affirmative. Well, apparently Harry thought the President should get to meet me. Boss, I wound up talking with the President, just the two of us, in his bedroom. He was in his damn slippers, Bermuda shorts and skivvy shirt. He thanked me for the CIGAR info, asked me loaded questions, like who should run France after the war. Then he wanted me to meet his sons for supper the next day. That wound up in a poker game with his sons after the President went to bed."

"Tony, I hope you let them win."

"Oh, hell no, only when they earned it."

"Then I hope you didn't clean them out!"

"Nah. Only about a hundred from each."

"That wasn't politically smart, ya know!" Taylor said, laughing

"I'm not a politician, boss. I don't play by politician's rules," he laughed. "Don't worry, they had a hell of a good time and they said so."

"The Roosevelt boys probably gave FDR an earful!"

"I don't think so, not a negative earful, anyway. We got along great all night. After I came back from the Azores the first time, I got summoned to FDR's villa again. I briefed Churchill and FDR on why the Azores DF project was important to the war effort, then had a simply dandy lunch with Elliott, Harry and FDR. That's how the project got approved."

"How'd you and Harry get along?"

"Absolutely fine. They were all very welcoming and congenial. I was pinching myself."

"I know the feeling," said Taylor with a smile. "By the way, Ambassador Winant is in Washington for a few weeks of consultation. In fact, he was on FDR's calendar this morning and a few other dates coming up. He didn't say why he was going. Not that he was obligated to do so. Any idea what that's about?"

"I saw where the TRIDENT conference with Churchill and the combined Joint Chiefs is coming up next month in DC. Looks like planning for what comes next after the decisions made at the SYMBOL conference in Casablanca. He's been heavily involved in getting messages back and forth between the PM and the President. Aside from that, I damn sure don't know what that, or any of this stuff, is about."

Taylor took a deep breath. "All I know is, the President has an uncanny way of identifying talent and cultivating it. The fact that your meeting with him lasted more than five minutes is very significant. I know from personal experience, going back to when I was a young junior officer on his staff when he was Under Secretary of the Navy. I know how he operates."

"Well, sir, all I know, is the President became very chatty. What stands out is that he asked about my Navy career before London, where I wanted to go next, and what my career plans were. I told him I liked it here in London."

"Something strange is going on, Tony," Taylor said, laughing. "For example, before you came into the office, Ed Langsdale told me, for the second time now, that he'd like to have you on his staff. And he was dead serious. Interested?"

"I want you to know, Bill, I'm not out fishing for a transfer. As far as SOE goes, if Petra wasn't in my life, I might consider it. But a full diet of SOE missions is not where I see myself going now."

Taylor sat back with his hands behind his head. "Don't get me wrong. I sure don't want to lose you. But I'll be the first to help you get a career enhancing opportunity. It's one of the reasons you're here. Anyway, Tony, I'm going to have to answer the

President's question, you do realize that, I hope. What do you want me to say? Petra would probably love DC, assuming that's what's at hand. Plus you could take Ives."

"Boss, tell him you don't have any plans for me. Wait. No. Tell him… damn. I don't know what you should tell him. Tell him I'm relatively new in this job and we've been too busy to discuss career goals. I think he's just curious, is all."

"Just curious, huh? That, my friend, may be the first patently wrong thing I've ever heard you say. I'll just say one thing, Tony. It's a damn good thing to have friends in high places. It can be life changing, and a lot of difficult things can be accomplished, but it's only possible through a symbiotic relationship." Taylor went to his desk, picked up a pipe that was sitting in his ash tray, tapped the ashes from the bowl, refilled it and lit it. The pipes bowl was a carving of a lion's head. "About the Azores," he said, walking back to the couch. "From what I read, it's a clumsy rig, but seems to be working well. Are they going to replace it with an updated model?"

"Ah, that's the same great smelling tobacco blend that you had before I left. I don't know what they plan to do about updating the DX. But clumsy is being kind. They have to operate it sitting on a stool eight inches off the floor," Tony replied.

Taylor blew a smoke ring toward the ceiling. That was something he just loved doing, especially when he was mentally exploring something or choosing words. "How did you get roped into that op with Mike Nelson?"

"It just happened. Nelson stumbled into a surprising development, and he asked if there was any way I could help. It just had to be done. German agents in the Azores just can't happen. I got G20's, and General Donovan's chop on it," Tony explained.

"Yes, I read the messages to and from G20 and the OSS. I'm not objecting one damn bit, mind you. As I understand the summary, two German agents were identified, and one converted to a double?" asked Taylor.

"Affirmative."

"What about the other guy?" asked Taylor.

Tony looked into Taylor's blue eyes for a few moments. He didn't know what Nelson reported, so he just shrugged his shoulders and said, "Mike's action report should have covered the disposition of number two."

Taylor smirked. He caught on that Tony wasn't going to address that. "I apparently missed that. OK, moving on. How was your weekend?"

"Terrific! We made good use of the fine weather. Spent the day in Piccadilly," Tony said.

"Ah, very nice. We've had great weather the last couple weeks. Before I forget it, I spoke with Lady Inga Watson on Friday. You and Petra are invited to a social this Friday evening. I declined due to other commitments. She said she would put an invitation in the post to you. It will be service dress blues. She asked that you RSVP by Thursday noon."

The day had been a fleeting one. He didn't realize that it was beginning to get dark until Chief Haydin came in to close the blackout curtains of his windows. He continued reading the backlog of documents. He kept working while waiting for a call from Petra, before leaving the office to hail a taxi.

She was standing outside her office building on St. James Street when the taxi stopped to let her in. "Ello, Yank," she said smiling brightly, cheeks red from the chilly air. She slid into the back seat with Tony, put a peck on his cheek and snuggled close to him.

"Ello, bird," he mocked, putting his arm around her. "Busy day?"

"Quite. Your first day back, so, you as well?"

"Took all day to work my way to the bottom of my in-basket."

"Right. I rarely see the bottom of mine."

"Oh, I know you'll be happy about this, we're invited to Lady Inga's on Friday evening for a social. 1900 to 2100. Shall I RSVP for us?"

"Yes, brilliant. Can't wait."

"Good. I'll do that tomorrow. I don't enjoy the trips to her mansion after dark, but it's never a dull time."

"Right, be glad you don't have to do the driving. They are used to it."

"Roger that. New subject. I have a surprise for you."

"Should I be happy?" she asked teasingly.

"I received an interesting call from The Dorchester this afternoon."

"Oh, no! That sounds ominous."

"No, no. We can stay where we are or choose another larger suite that has come open. It will be available to occupy tomorrow afternoon. We can look at it tonight, though. The key is waiting at the lobby desk for me. I didn't want to commit until you saw it."

"You sound excited about this," she said. "Have you seen it already?"

"I certainly am excited and yes, I dashed over and took a look earlier."

"Straight away then, darling."

Tony stopped at The Dorchester Hotel's front desk for the key and slipped it into his pocket. They walked briskly to the elevators, arm in arm. "7th floor," Tony said as they approached the operator. One of the three formally dressed elevator operators motioned for them to enter, "This way, sir."

They watched the brass pointer in the elevator rise up from L to 7. He took her arm and lead her to the suite door, number 701. He put the key into the lock. "They said it's ready except for towels, soaps and the like."

"For the love of God, love, open it!" she said excitedly.

A floor lamp near the door, and two others in the room, had marble bases that glowed from small bulbs in them. It was enough for him to see that the blackout curtains in the room were drawn. He flipped the light switch, which turned on the chandelier over a four-place dinner table on the left. To the right was a large sitting area, desk and floor to ceiling window shrouded in dark brown print pulled-back drapes and light brown curtains.

"Oh, darling, this is… just… gorgeous," she said in awe.

"That's a door to a balcony, big enough to sit out. There's a view of the park."

"This parquet flooring is beautiful, Tony. Look at that oversized couch in front of the fireplace. That must be a console radio and record player over there. Oh, you are off your trolley now, my darling."

That's the bedroom through that door, I'll turn on the light."

She stepped through the doorway and slowly scanned the room. She turned to him with tears in her eyes. "Bloody lovely." She threw her arms around him and looked up into his eyes. "You don't need to do this for me! I'm happy where we are. It's only a large bedroom and a bath, yes, but…"

"I took what I could get at the time, honey, and it is very nice, I know. But I'm used to having more space. I feel cramped. Not enough room for our clothes. We eat from our laps on that little side table with extension flaps. Now we can sit at a table. Even entertain, if we wish."

"But this must be…"

"Expensive? Is that what you're going to say? Sure. But it's incredibly more convenient for us. It's more tolerable for a long stay. Plus, I made a very good deal with them."

"Yes, but…" she hugged him, lost for words.

He laughed, "You've been keeping my checkbooks while I've been gone. You know this is easily within my means. It's not a great deal more per month, since I made a one year deal with them, which, by the way, includes four meals a day."

She wrapped her arms around his waist. "Is that a door to a patio as well?"

"Sure is."

"Very soft carpet for my bare feet. There's another desk. I'll decide which desk is yours," she giggled. "Two large armoires too, another decision to be made. That chest of drawers is huge. So is the bed."

"Yes, I'm disappointed it's not a four-poster," he said.

She laughed, "How much more is there to this castle?"

"Just the bathroom, all white marble, like the one we have now."

She opened the door to the bathroom, "Arranged quite different, but just as magnificent."

"So, Mrs. Romella, shall we do this? I told them I needed your approval. As I said before, we can live high while the war is with us, then we will deal with the reality of peace."

Back into his arms she went, "I know you want this. You spoil me, Yank. When do we move?"

"They will start moving our things in the chest and armoire tomorrow afternoon. The rest of our things we move tomorrow evening. Let's go down, make the final arrangements and have dinner in the restaurant."

"Is your sister as posh as you?" she asked with a smirk.

"Oh yes, Maria is posh. She's doing quite well for herself."

"Why doesn't she marry?" she asked.

"She works a lot. A hell of a lot. She's a hell of a lot more interested in building her career as a DC lawyer than dating. One fine day I might have the time, she always says."

21 - Champagne

Three Days Later
11:10 a.m., Thursday, March 4, 1943
Tony's Office
U.S. Embassy, London

The Soviet Naval Attaché, Captain Valentine Pankov, had swagger and determination in his walk. Tony rose to greet Pankov, ushered into the office by Chief Haydin. A few inches shorter than Tony with broad shoulders and a stocky body, he was the consummate Russian.

"Good morning, Commander Romella, I learned you returned from travel. The United States I hear. Was the trip a good one?"

"Yes, Captain Pankov, it was a good trip, but too long in the air."

"I hope you didn't have to buy shoes, Tony. I read that shoes are rationed now. Making boots for soldiers, dah?"

"Yes, we are, Val. Many of them will be shipped to Murmansk for Soviet soldiers to fight the Germans," Tony said.

Pankov roared and shook Tony's hand firmly. "Good humor! But some truth, dah?"

"Make yourself comfortable, Val," Tony said, motioning at the couch. "Can I get you something? Coffee? Tea? Coke?" He mentioned Coke because the bio on Pankov said it was something he craved.

"Nothing, thank you. Maybe a Coke, if you might have it," said Pankov. "I recently read that Coca-Cola charges soldiers only five cents a bottle since the war started. A good patriot company."

"That is true." Tony nodded at Haydin, who was waiting to see what might be needed.

"While the Chief brings us our sodas, what did you have on your mind when you called to schedule a meeting?"

Pankov moved to the edge of the couch toward Tony's chair, "I said to you, before you went to America, that in London, we understand more of the war problems than the people across the Atlantic. We are concerned of the Casablanca decisions to reduce convoy shipments to Murmansk, and put priority on supplies for a Mediterranean war…"

"Val, please understand," Tony interrupted, "the decisions they made in Casablanca have not gotten to me, yet. Did your leaders not voice concerns at the conference?" Tony knew that answer but wanted to appear distinctly out of the loop.

"Comrade Stalin could not go to Casablanca because of the attack on our cities by the Germans," explained Pankov. "They sent Comrade Stalin their decisions by diplomatic cable."

"I can tell our Secretary of State that some explanations are requested for any Casablanca decisions relating to your country," said Tony. "But I am not the proper contact. It should be Moscow to Washington." Why is he putting these questions to me? thought Tony. What's the underlying scheme in this?

Chief Haydin knocked on the door and entered with two bottles of Coke and paper coasters.

"Thank you," said Pankov and drank a third of the bottle before sitting it down on the coffee table.

"Anything else on your mind, Val? Are you still free for lunch?" asked Tony.

"One more thing before we lunch. Moscow has requested from Washington, to consult with the man from your office that you charged as a spy, Mr. Harry Zykin. They have heard nothing from Washington. Moscow has directed me to confirm that you sent him to Washington after you arrested him."

Tony muffled a soda burp, put his Coke bottle down and said, "I only know that I put Mr. Zykin on a plane they sent for him. Where exactly they took him, I don't really know. They told me he was going to the U.S."

Pankov's expression was initially one of frustration, then a slight smile. "One more thing to ask."

"Of course, Val."

"We learn from Casablanca decisions of Allied interest in the Azores Islands. Our intelligence says the German Navy also is interested." Pankov paused for a response.

Tony showed his best poker face, despite his surprise. He shrugged his shoulders, "That sounds logical for long range planning. I have no more information than you on that. Why do you ask?"

The last of Pankov's Coke was polished off, then he said, "It would involve the American Navy and I wonder if attention to the Azores would use ships now protecting convoys to Murmansk. You are the Naval Attaché, so you might know some answers on that."

That, my Russian friend, was your real question, thought Tony. "Aye, Val, about me, that is true. About answers, I have none," Tony said with a smile.

"I am hungry for lunch," Pankov declared.

Late That Afternoon
Captain Taylor's Office
U.S. Embassy, London

"Good afternoon, Captain. I hate it when you call me up here unexpectedly," Tony jested, as he entered the office.

"Have a seat here, we have a few things to discuss," said Taylor, pointing at the chair next to his desk. "Don't worry, you're not being loaned to SOE." He took a drag on a large black cigar.

"You're supply of special cigars arrived, I see," said Tony.

"These things cost an arm and leg, so I ration them to one a day. How's your new hacienda?"

"Glad you asked. Are you free for a good old Sunday lunch at our place?" asked Tony. "I sent a note up about it an hour ago. Probably in your in-basket."

"I just got back from the Admiralty about twenty minutes ago and have been on the phone with DC. But I am absolutely free. I am anxious to see how the rich and famous live," Taylor said, laughing. "What's Petra think about it?"

"She tolerates me so well, but she loves it, of course," Tony said with a chuckle.

"Say, where were you last Wednesday night when the air raid sirens went off?" asked Taylor.

"We were having a late dinner at home. When alarms go off, we just go into the hallway to escape flying glass. The reason I chose the Dorchester is that it's construction is the next best thing to a bunker. They did create something of a bomb shelter in the kitchen area. I just don't use it."

"Have you been reading the articles in the newspapers about the disaster Wednesday night at the Bethnal Green tube station? I just skimmed the headlines."

"Yes, it's awful," Tony said. "No bombs, according to the papers. But 173 trampled to death when several hundred were trying to get into the tube station. Panic set in when they got spooked by the sounds of a new rocket battery nearby. What was so upsetting is that 62 of the casualties were children. Many others were injured."

Taylor blew one of his signature smoke rings up at the ceiling. "I guess the bombers aborted since it was raining and low visibility. Hitler was probably sending a response to the massive bombing of Berlin Monday night. I guess you read that, on the first of the month, the rest of the German Navy implemented the same four-rotor Enigma that the U-boat force was using."

"Affirmative. I was sorry to see that. It raises the processing time for decrypting the rest of the Navy's messages. Not a good thing to happen before we, and the British, have been able to build enough additional bombe machines to process them. Especially when we're about to really push into the Mediterranean for a landing in Sicily. Good thing that the progress on building more bombes is going well."

"Aye. The Admiralty is concerned about it. But that's not why I called you up here."

"Good news or bad news, boss?" asked Tony.

"Good, in my estimation. I venture to say, you will agree. When I returned from the Admiralty, Sharon called my attention to a few important incoming messages and got me a connection to DC. I'll skip the details. You can read all that for yourself. Sharon made copies and has them in an envelope for you to take back to your office." He paused and took a couple slow savoring drags on his cigar.

"The way you're enjoying the suspense building, I know it's good news," Tony said.

Taylor laughed heartily. "Yes indeed, I am. OK. First of all, you're out of uniform. As a Captain in this man's Navy, you should not be wearing a Commander's uniform."

"That's a sick joke, Bill. I'm not falling for it. I've only been an O-5 since last July. You can't shit me. That's impossible."

"There's two things wrong with that assessment," Taylor said, using his cigar as a pointer. "Rule number one is, during wartime, nothing is impossible. Rule number two, and I told you once before, and now you suffer the benefit. Number two is, it's good to have friends in high places."

"Oh my God... Bill... You're dead serious. I don't know what to say. Whatever you had to do with it, thank you! But I know a lot of commanders that, including some at OP-20-G, that are going to be scratching their heads. Probably going to be pissed off, too."

"That is their issue, not yours. Naval Attaché is a Captain's position in this Embassy and rank comes into play in military politics. That's why I took measures to try and make it happen. Just a matter of diplomatic equality. When you read your promotion message, you'll see that there's a catch. It says, in so many words, you can wear the insignia and enjoy the privileges and seniority of a captain until such time as you are advanced to captain through normal processes for pay purposes. Heaven knows, you don't need the money. And, you won't be reverted when you leave this position."

"This is just... incredible," Tony said.

"Rule number one! By the way, Ambassador Winant sent his congratulations from DC. That's in your envelope too." They both laughed, stood and shook hands. Taylor slapped Tony's shoulder a few times. "That extra stripe is a just reward, my friend. I'm not done with good news."

"Now you have me worried, Bill."

"Nothing to worry about. My phone call to DC was with Harry Hopkins. He called while I was out of the office. The President is going to huddle again with Churchill, and the Combined Joint Chiefs again, in DC, mid-May. The meeting is codenamed, TRIDENT. The purpose will be planning for military activities where the SYMBOL plans ended. That's all in the envelope too. What Harry called to tell me is that there's a message coming in later today with details. The President has requested your attendance at the TRIDENT conference. They also thought you would carry more weight with four stripes on your sleeve. Harry said to tell you to plan on coming as early as you like, but no later than the first of May. He also suggested that you find a way to bring your wife. I didn't ask why. Looks like the Roosevelt boys didn't take offense to getting their asses beat at poker."

Tony laughed hard. "I could have taken more, but I held back."

Taylor laughed just as heartily. "Ah, there's a politician hiding in there somewhere. OK, don't leave the building until we get that last message in hand." He crushed the lit end of the small cigar stump in his ash tray and looked up. "Rule number two, Tony."

"Aye," said Tony. "Boss, I have one thing to pass on to you. I reported it up the chain already. You'll see it in your message read file. Summary is, Captain Pankov called on me today. He brought up Harry Zykin again. They really want at him. Plus, they are curious about Azores planning. Yes, they are an Ally. But, as far as I know, they've been given limited information on those plans. If they learn more somehow, that's not good. If it leaks to the Germans, it could upset the apple cart."

"Alright. I'll keep my ear to the ground. Just give him nothing on those subjects. They need to be handled only by DC. Speaking of the Azores, when you read the messages in that envelope, you'll find out that your experience there is why you're going to DC. Meanwhile, get to the tailor shop tomorrow morning. I don't want to see you in this building until you're in uniform. The staff won't be told until tomorrow. You're excused, Captain Romella!"

While Tony walked back to his office, he thought of all the options for when and how he would break the news to Petra. By the time he sat down at his desk, he had it figured out. He sat there, dumbfounded, looking around. Then his discipline kicked in. He smiled. OK Tony, get your shit together, you have work to do.

That Evening

"Tony, I must say, I am appreciating this suite," she said, as they entered it, returning from a long day at work. "It's a pleasure to eat at a proper table. Then relax on the couch, listening to the radio, in front of dancing flames in the fireplace. Just lovely, darling. It takes me back to our days in your cottage at Bletchley."

"Mmhhmm, and I don't even have to get firewood. There's always eight logs in the buckets when we come home." He turned on the light in the bedroom. "Glad you're coming around to my way of thinking, honey."

She giggled, "Right. I must try and not think of the money. I'll get into my PJs and robe, then call for our supper straight away."

"Roger. Oh, Captain Taylor will be here for Sunday lunch," Tony said.

"Brilliant. Your best mate will be our first guest!"

"He said he's anxious to see how the rich and famous live," he said with a chuckle.

"Cheeky man, he is. It will be lovely to see him."

"When you order supper, have them bring a bottle of champagne, if it's available," he said casually. He turned away from her purposely, afraid his facial expression would give himself away. As he hung his jacket and trousers in the armoire, he felt her tap on his shoulder. He turned and saw her standing there in her Royal Navy regulation undies, with a sly grin on her face.

"Tony, the last time you ordered champagne for us, you proposed. Pray tell us what mischief you're up to."

"Oh, nothing much. By the way, I'm going to Washington in about two months."

Her expression went blank. "For how long?"

"I'll be back around the end of May," he said with a straight face.

"Washington. Like the last time?" she asked in disbelieving tones.

"Oh, definitely Washington. Not a cover story. One more thing you need to know about it. You're invited to go with me. We have a month or so to figure out how to make that happen."

Tears welled up in her eyes, "Are we having a laugh?"

"No, honey, I'm quite serious, Petra. Do you think they'll let you get away?"

She hugged and kissed him. "I do hope so," she said. "I never dreamed that I would see America." They stood, hugging, her head snuggled into his chest. "So that's what the champagne is about."

"Partly," he said softly.

She leaned back and looked into his eyes, "Partly? What else?"

"Tomorrow I have to go to the uniform tailor shop when they open."

"Right. And?" she asked, suspiciously.

"I just have to get another stripe sewed onto my sleeves, that's all," he said, as if a matter of routine.

"What are you saying, Yank?"

"I also have to buy some eagles for my collars and raincoat, also new shoulder boards…"

She was back into his arms, having a joyful cry. "How is that possible? Brilliant darling, congratulations. Champagne, indeed!" They hugged and swayed while they both recouped their emotions. "Captain Romella! Bloody hell!"

22 – 30th Street

Over the course of the previous seven weeks and five days, Tony and Petra pursued their normal routines. In addition, they attempted, unsuccessfully, to find a way to get Petra orders to the U.S. as a courier of classified material, or as part of the TRIDENT support team. But MI5 saved the day by agreeing to grant her leave so she could visit the U.S. in tourist status. Workloads were juggled and bureaucracy was fought until they obtained an expedited passport and visa for Petra. In parallel, Tony arranged air transportation, a straightforward task due to his high priority orders and diplomatic status.

At long last, Tony's and Petra's two day trek of many boring hours in a C-54 troop and cargo aircraft was over. They hopscotched across the northern Atlantic Ocean's seaboard, including an overnight in Greenland. Their feet were now on U.S. soil.

Library of Congress, Jack Delano [Public domain]
Washington National Airport, Terminal A, 1941

6:25 p.m., Tuesday April 27, 1943
Terminal A, Washington National Airport

Tony spotted Maria's smiling face as soon as he and Petra pushed open the door to exit the Customs area. He dropped his two large suitcases as Maria ran toward him. "I'm so damn glad to see you! How's my little sister?" They hugged tightly for a few moments.

Petra put her suitcases down and watched the two happy siblings. Despite the fact that she was more than congenial on the phone, she didn't know what to expect of Maria. But there was Maria, tall, slender, curly dark brown hair, and the face of a model. Consummate Yank barrister, she thought, admiring the pin-stripe navy suit jacket and skirt, and black and white spectator pumps.

"I was thrilled when you told me you were coming back on business," Maria said to Tony. "Petra is gorgeous, just like you told me. Welcome to America, Petra. I'm Maria."

Petra felt blush come to her cheeks, "Lovely meeting you, Maria. This puts a face to a friendly voice on the phone. You're too kind. I'm sure I look dreadful. I'm knackered from lack of sleep and the time difference." They hugged like best of friends.

"I hope you two can wait another half hour before you eat, but dinner will be ready shortly after we get home," said Maria.

He looked at Petra, "She has a wonderful Italian cook and a maid."

"Right. We have staff as well," Petra said to Maria. They all had a good laugh.

"Your suite sounds terrific," said Maria. "I'm glad to hear that Tony is taking good care of you. We can't have a Romella living in a barracks."

Petra smiled, "Right. I'm living the proper life of a Captain's wife."

"Congratulations once again on the promotion, Tony. You and the Navy must like each other," Maria said.

"Thanks, sis. How did you know when we were arriving? Or have you been here for hours?"

"I phoned the Military Liaison Desk here in the terminal. They were getting updates on your flight," said Maria. "Your plane was just pulling up to the terminal when I got here. I saw you two walking across the tarmac to the Customs entrance."

"I'm anxious to see how your new house turned out," said Tony, picking up his bags.

"You'll love the third floor guest suite, Tony. It's all primped and pretty for you." Maria took one of Petra's bags and headed for the exit. "Come on, boys and girls, spaghetti and meat sauce awaits."

"Petra, the last time I saw Maria's house was the day after she closed on it, just before I left for London. She already had work crews in there remodeling it," Tony said. "I'm sure we're in for a treat."

"Lovely weather you arranged for us, Maria," said Petra.

"You're welcome, but it was nothing," Maria said with a chuckle. "It's been very nice lately, 40s at night, 70s during the day and fairly dry," Maria said.

"How's the law practice doing, Maria? Has the war hurt your business?" Tony asked as they walked to the car.

"I'm the corporate law part of Acton, Ryan and Romella," replied Maria. "I've got as much work as I have time to pursue, mainly defense contractors. Steve Acton, our founder, does criminal prosecution. Dave Ryan does patent, copyright and trademark litigation. They are both are up to their ears. We moved to a larger office in Georgetown last January and hired three more legal assistants. We've all been working 60 or more hours a week, so we're going to bring in a new law grad to help us out. It's been great."

"Sounds like our schedule," said Petra. "Full days and half days on weekends."

As they approached Maria's black 1940 Cadillac four-door sedan, Tony said, "I see you took my advice about the convertible."

Maria laughed, "Petra, before he left, I was looking at this car and a convertible Cadillac. I wanted that convertible. But brother here, kept talking about the woes of snow and rain. Especially since there was no garage at the new house. So, I got this one. I trust his judgement completely. I even let him manage my investments. When the estates were settled, I told him, whatever you do for yourself, do the same for me. As you know, we've done very well, thanks to him."

He smiled, "She only listens to me when she chooses. We rolled the dice a couple times on investments, and we were incredibly lucky," Tony said.

"Don't listen to him, Petra, the math wizard knew just what he was doing."

They stowed their suitcases in the trunk and got settled in the car. "Alright, I'll save the scenic tour for another day, Petra," said Maria. "I'm going to take the most direct route home. I have some afternoons planned to show you Washington, while Tony is working."

"Brilliant. No worries," said Petra.

Maria turned from M Street onto 30th Street in Georgetown. After driving several blocks, she made a U-turn at an intersection and parked in front of a three-story house. "Home, sweet home," she said. "Carmella will fetch the suitcases later. We'll just go in and have a drink while Alicia gets the water boiling for the pasta."

Petra got out of the car onto a red brick sidewalk. She counted 17 white trimmed windows on the pale moss green painted brick front. Each of the windows had lace curtains and dark green shutters. Shiny black painted wrought iron railings bracketed four gray marble steps up to a white four-column portico. "Maria, this is simply beautiful."

"Absolutely!" said Tony. "It looks nothing like it did when I saw it last."

"Thank you, both!" said Maria, leading the way to the door.

"Quite a contrast with this cardinal red door, sis. I like it," said Tony.

Carmella and Alicia were waiting in the foyer. Maria made the introductions. Petra noted thick Italian accents. Alicia returned to the kitchen, while Carmella took drink orders, jackets and hats.

"Come to the living room, make yourselves comfortable," said Maria.

"I'm glad you went with the colonial décor, sis," said Tony. "What do you think, Petra?"

"Rebellious colonists you lot, but, alas, we tolerate you Yanks," Petra said teasingly when she saw the large painting over the couch. It showed General Washington battling the British in New York.

"All you red coats wanted from us was our taxes," said Tony, grinning.

"A spat between two warriors, how entertaining," joked Maria.

Carmella returned with a tray full of drinks. "Cheers!" said Maria, holding her glass up toward Tony and Petra on the couch.

"Cheers!"

"I'll give you the house tour after dinner," said Maria. "The dining room table can seat 12 with all the slats in. The second floor is my home office and bedroom suite. The third floor is the guest suite. It includes a second smaller bedroom with full bath on one end for third members, kids, and the like."

"Did you decide to keep the coal furnace?" asked Tony.

"No. Too much trouble. I converted it to kerosene," said Maria.

"I just couldn't see you shoveling coal and clinkers," said Tony.

Maria laughed, "That was an easy decision. I remembered what Dad went through with the coal furnace we had."

"And I remember what my chores with it were like," Tony said with a laugh. "Any trouble getting kerosene now?"

"I keep the thermostat pretty low in the cold months," explained Maria. "We just layer up and use the fireplaces. During the winter months, Carmella's husband, a local carpenter, keeps a supply of firewood in the shed in back and stocks the fireplaces every day. I managed to stay close to my fuel ration. I ran out of fuel for a day, during a bitter cold snap last winter. Otherwise, fine. What's your schedule, Tony?" asked Maria.

"I have two numbers to call tomorrow to give them the phone and street address here. Also tomorrow, I have a meeting at Nebraska Avenue at 1:30. On the 13th I'm at the Federal Reserve Building at 10:30 for the day. That's what I'm aware of right now, anyway. At some point during this visit, I'd like to visit with Bill Taylor's family in Baltimore. Aside from that, I am on-call until otherwise directed, seven days a week."

"Ah, so your daytimes are tied up. You won't be free to tour the city and shop with us," said Maria with a joyful tone. "What a pity, just us girls to ourselves."

"Sounds dangerous to my wallet. Which reminds me, I need to visit the bank. But, yes, my days are taken," said Tony. "Seeing anyone special, Maria?"

"My brother seems to want to attend my wedding. No, Tony, I still have no time for someone special. I'm happy with my independence and busy work schedule."

"That's what I thought too! Then I met Petra," he said, smiling.

"Sorry to change the subject, Tony, dear, but can you take care of your own transportation?" asked Maria. "It's all I can do to keep gas in my car as it is. Ration coupons are only good for three gallons and I can barely keep my tank at a quarter full. The station nearby limits us to three gallons per day. Clients have the same problem, so they want me to come to them. Thus, dear brother, between touring Petra and the clients…"

Tony interrupted her, "Say no more, dear sister, I'm authorized to use all forms of public transportation as is necessary, and I'm happy to do so."

"Good! Now Petra, I am going to make sure you go home with some good memories of America. I've blocked out most of my schedule in the afternoons so we can galivant. I've arranged for us to be at the dedication of the Jefferson Memorial on the 13th. I'll let Tony explain who Thomas Jefferson was."

"I'm a bit familiar with that colonist and his rebellious Declaration of Independence," Petra said grinning. But I'm sure Tony can educate me more thoroughly."

"Then, best of all," continued Maria, "I cashed in some favors and arranged for us to be in the gallery on the 19th for Winston Churchill's address to the joint session of Congress."

"Brilliant!" exclaimed Petra. "Tony's already met him, formally, in Casablanca. At least I'll be able to say I've seen the PM in person."

"I'm not surprised that Tony has met him. I figured if he was in London long enough, that would happen. Strange that we've talked twice on the phone since he got back from Morocco, and he didn't mention it." She gave Tony the side eye. "You keep everything close to the chest. Tell me all about it before you leave," Maria said.

"I can't tell you much more about, it. If I told you all about it, they would arrest me," Tony said humorously.

"At any rate, Petra, on other afternoons that I can break away, we'll visit the Washington Memorial, Lincoln Memorial, Smithsonian Institute, and so on. Tony can explain those too. By the time you leave, you'll be proud of what your old colony has become."

"You're most kind, Maria. I don't know how to thank you for such grand hospitality," said Petra.

"You're family now, Petra. You made my brother a happy man. That, dear lady, is thanks enough. Oh, Alicia is here. She's ready for us to take our seats at the dinner table."

23 - Prelude

U.S.
Navy

Naval Security Station, OP-20-G Complex (Circa 1943-1950)
3801 Nebraska Avenue NW, Washington, DC

1:30 p.m., Wednesday, April 28, 1943
Captain Jerry Webber's Office
OP-20-G Headquarters Building
3801 Nebraska Avenue, Washington, DC

Tony knocked on Webber's office door and entered. "Good afternoon, Jerry! Congrats on your selection to captain."

"Good afternoon, Tony, likewise."

"You survived the move from Main Navy, I see. What a great facility this is."

"That it is. Have a seat, Tony. Now that we're completely in and organized, we're elated, but it was a stressful move for all of us. Thanks for coming in. I wanted to talk with you before the TRIDENT Conference began. The last time I saw you a couple years ago, in our old office at Main Navy, you were a Lieutenant Commander. How in hell did you manage Commander and Captain in that timeframe? For your sake, I sure hope it was legal. Was it Bill Taylor's sway with the White House?"

Tony couldn't tell if Webber was angry or not. He certainly was bothered. "I'm still drawing Commander's pay. It's all diplomatic smoke and mirrors. Frankly, I am not sure how it happened. I didn't know anything about either until I got message notification. Ostensibly it's all about rank equality among the Allied Naval Attachés."

Webber paused, looked at a lined pad full of notes, and looked back up, "I am also puzzled about why you're representing Navy COMINT at the TRIDENT Conference. They never asked us for a representative. What's that all about?"

"It's a long story…"

Webber interjected, "I'll make time. Go ahead with it."

"Jerry, I'm not representing Navy COMINT. I'm there because of the Azores. It all goes back to the SYMBOL Conference. Harry Hopkins saw my name on a list and inquired if I was the same person that was involved in a special op that had White House attention."

He continued on with a description of the evolution of conversations with Hopkins and FDR leading up to the briefing for Churchill and FDR on the Azores. He also related the conversation he had with Admiral King and Captain Lattim."

"Quite a story of right place, right time," Webber said. "You've managed to parlay that attaché job into strange areas. France, Norway, the Azores…" Webber paused, sat back and crossed his leg. "What's your career plan, Tony?"

Unable to hold back a chuckle, Tony replied, "Jerry, you're not the first person to ask me that question lately. I told Bill Taylor that I'm not looking for another job. I like what I'm doing and where I'm at. The special ops have all been rooted in the COMINT mission. I might add, all have been signed off by 20-G, by Captain Stone, personally."

"Yes, they have. OK, the Azores is on the list of topics for TRIDENT and the White House asked for you by name?"

"Affirmative."

"Do you have any idea why Captain Stone wasn't invited?" asked Webber.

"Negative. The subject of any other Navy participation has never been discussed with me, nor have I heard any scuttlebutt. It's my understanding that the White House and 10 Downing Street determined the attendee lists," replied Tony.

Webber nodded, "I suppose our best representative at the table is Admiral King. He visited us several times a week when we were over at Main Navy. As busy as he was as Chief of Naval Operations, he made the time. He has a great appreciation for communications intelligence. It's down to once a week or so since we moved."

"Yes, sir, I briefed him several times when I was in 20-GI, before London. He was keenly interested in DF on U-boats."

"On that subject, what's your take on the performance of the DX in Ponta Delgada?" asked Webber.

"Jerry, for the life of me, I'm amazed that it's as good as it is. There's no electronic ground plane, it's closer to other metal objects than we'd like, it's clumsy and crude, but damn, it works."

"You know Lieutenant Commander Paul Archer, right?" asked Webber.

"We've met, briefly, yes."

"He's in 20-GI now. He did an analysis for me on the DX performance. It showed better than expected performance. That's why I decided to keep it going for an unspecified period of time. If it becomes an impediment to the negotiations in Portugal on Allied use of the Azores, or becomes controversial in some way, or the performance goes down, we'll shut it down. If anybody asks, you can tell them that, too."

"Understood, Jerry. Rest assured that I'll contact you if questions are best handled by you. I'll make sure any contributions I make are documented and delivered to you."

"Alright, Tony. I suppose it's good that we have a seat in the conference. I don't want you to fail for lack of information. Go find Paul Archer. Spend as much time with him as you need to get fully briefed on all the intelligence they have on U-boats, Azores and Portugal in general. Talk to whomever is necessary to make sure you know what our COMINT obligations are to support anti-submarine warfare in the Pacific and the Atlantic. Also, get briefed thoroughly on our specific roles in supporting Operations HUSKY and OVERLORD."

"Aye, aye, sir."

"That should keep you busy for the rest of the day. And Tony, I absolutely want to be appraised of anything that is discussed at the conference that involves Navy COMINT operations," said Webber.

That Evening
Maria Romella's Home, Georgetown

"We're in the living room, Tony," Petra called out as he came through the front door. He put his hat and jacket on the clothes hooks in the foyer.

Tony walked into the living room. Petra stood to greet him. He gave her a big hug. "How did you day go, ladies?" he asked.

"Smashing, love," Petra said.

"Good evening Tony," said Maria. "Yes, it was a really nice day. We have only been home about 45 minutes, ourselves. I gave her the deluxe car tour of DC and stopped at the Smithsonian. She chose the natural history part. We spent the rest of the afternoon there."

"I saw the White House and Parliament, excuse me, Capitol," Petra gushed. "It felt incredible that I was seeing them firsthand. How was your day, love?"

"Lots of talking, reading, certainly not as pleasant and leisurely a day as you ladies had," he replied. He sat on the couch next to Petra.

Carmella came in and took Tony's request for red wine, same as the ladies were nursing.

"I'm sure you're hungry, Tony," said Maria. "When I heard your taxi pull up, I told Alicia to finish preparing the chicken cacciatore. For dessert, Alicia made cannoli. I'm ashamed of you, Tony. Petra's never had a cannoli!"

"We live in London, not Rome," he joked.

"By the way, Tony, I put a message on the desk in your sitting area upstairs," said Maria. "Mr. Harry Hopkins called while we were out. He requests your presence, if I recall it accurately, in the White House East Wing at 12:30 p.m. on the 30th. My goodness Tony, the White House?"

"Maria, you might as well save your breath," said Petra. "Whilst he was in Casablanca he spoke with the President and my PM. But he won't talk about it."

"One day, ladies, maybe," said Tony. "It's just conference preparation."

Maria looked at Tony with a grin and a lifted eyebrow. "Is that so? Well, he's my brother, and I love him to bits, but just so you know, Petra, none of us were able to control him. You've probably come the closest." The ladies laughed at Tony's expense.

"Also, love," injected Petra, "we're all having dinner at the Taylor's in Baltimore tomorrow evening. Maria arranged it with Evelyn before we went out today."

ASSIGNMENT: CASABLANCA

Two Days Later
12:20 p.m., Friday, April 30, 1943
White House, Washington, D.C.

The normal 20 minute taxi ride was doubled, as he expected, with noon hour pedestrians and noisy traffic. A chatty driver kept Tony from exhaustively pondering the possible reasons for Hopkins' request to meet. The taxi finally turned onto East Executive Avenue and stopped in front of the gate at the north entrance of the East Wing of the White House.

When Tony walked to the gate, a White House policeman approached and asked, "Do you have an appointment, Captain?"

"Yes, officer, with Mr. Harry Hopkins," said Tony, offering his Navy ID card through the bars in the gate.

The policeman reached for Tony's ID and took it to the guard house. Tony could see him searching a list, with a secret service agent. The agent made a phone call. A bright, 65 degree day, with a light breeze, made the wait pleasant. The officer and a secret service agent returned to the gate.

"Captain, are you carrying any weapons with you?" asked the agent, while studying his face and referring to Tony's ID picture.

"No sir."

"Mr. Hopkins is expecting you," said the agent, nodding to the police officer. When the officer opened the gate, the agent handed Tony his ID, pointed and said, "Doorway in the portico."

It was a short walk up the curved driveway to the portico. The Marines at the door saluted. One of them opened the door. A receptionist, a Secret Service Agent and a White House Police officer were just inside the door of the wood paneled foyer. As he was presenting his ID to the receptionist, Hopkins came around the corner into the foyer.

"Good afternoon, Captain," said Harry Hopkins, and approached to shake Tony's hand.

"Good afternoon Mr. Hopkins. Good to see you again," said Tony. He noted that Hopkins still looked as tired as he did in Casablanca.

"Glad your schedule allowed us to meet today, Tony,"

"My pleasure, Harry, I was wide open today."

The receptionist completed her log entries, and Tony signed the visitor log. She handed him a visitor badge, which he clipped to his lapel.

"My office is around the corner to the right, at the end of the hall," said Hopkins, taking the lead. "Admiral Leahy, who I believe you met, is down the hall to the left."

"I haven't formally met him," said Tony. "But I've been in the conference room with him."

"Oh, well, he's out of the office this afternoon, or I'd take you down there after our meeting to introduce you," said Hopkins.

A man was hurrying down the hallway toward them. He was wearing a suit, with his collar unbuttoned, and a red, white and blue striped tie that was loosened. Tony recognized him, but before he could say anything, the man looked up briefly and did a double take, "Anthony Romella, right? Formerly Commander?"

"Yes, Mike, one and the same. I see you survived the Casablanca trip," Tony said, grinning, and stopped to exchange a handshake with Mike Reilly, the Supervising Agent of the White House Secret Service Detail.

Reilly grimaced, "I couldn't wait to get him safely back here. Don't let me hold you up, Harry. Nice to see you, Captain."

At the end of the paneled hallway was a waiting room, which had doors to Hopkins' office and that of his secretary. Hers was open. She looked up, smiled and continued with her work.

Harry went to his cluttered desk and sat down, "Make yourself comfortable, Tony. We have an appointment in the Oval Office at 1, with Secretary Hull. But I wanted to talk with you first, so you wouldn't be caught cold. This just popped up yesterday when the President mentioned to Hull that you were in town. They were arranging a discussion about the Azores. Hull, as best as I can tell, wants to discuss the Azores. He also wants to update the President on his project to create a United Nations organization. The President offered to have you discuss the Azores here, rather than over at State," said Hopkins. "Be aware that Secretary Hull is put out that he's not been part of the Allied war planning meetings. The Secretary also hates the idea of taking the Azores by force. Let's not say anything to instigate discussion of those items with Hull, if at all possible. He's a long-time personal friend of the President, but they have their differences."

"Understood, Harry" said Tony.

"The Secretary will probably have a personal chat with the President first. They'll call for us," said Hopkins.

"OK," said Tony.

"Don't let the Oval Office unnerve you. It tends to intimidate people, although it seems you are not easily taken off balance," said Hopkins with a smile.

Tony nodded. "Harry, I've had my share of threatening situations," he said with a smile. Just the same, his heartbeat was elevated at the awe of the situation. I'm not sure my opinion of anything is worth being heard in the Oval Office, Tony thought.

"So I've heard," said Hopkins with a smile. "I understand your wife accompanied you on this trip."

"Correct. It took some doing, but I'm glad she got to see DC. I'm staying with my sister, in Georgetown. She is giving Petra the grand tour of the city."

Hopkins paused, rubbing his chin, "Mike Reilly hates unofficial visitors, but, since he knows you, maybe we can work something out for your wife and sister to get a decent tour of the White House," said Hopkins, "if you're interested, of course."

"Harry, I would be absolutely indebted if that was possible."

"No promises, and I can't venture to guess the possibility. But here, write down your sister's and Petra's full name and dates of birth, and a phone number where you are staying."

"Harry, I thank you a million times over for just thinking about this." As he wrote the information on the pad, he thought, I just wonder what the price will be for all the high level kindness in Casablanca and now the White House. I'll find out soon enough.

"Alright, we'll see how it goes. But for now, we need to stroll over to the West Wing waiting room, outside the Oval Office. It's a nice day, and I would normally walk outside, but, since it's your first visit, I'd like to take you straight through the White House corridors."

"Terrific, Harry!"

The walk through the East, Central and West Corridors was exhilarating. Hopkins described the significance of certain items and identified the rooms behind some of the dark oak doors. Just walking the halls, that so many of historical significance have walked, was awe inspiring. He passed marble pedestals spaced along the walls with exquisite busts and sculptures mounted on them. The many pieces of priceless artwork on the walls begged for close scrutiny. Beautiful wooden cases displayed a selection of china used by prior presidents. He passed the impressive central staircase to the first floor, opposite the Entrance Hall. At least a hundred feet of corridors later, they came to the entrance to the West Wing. Hopkins navigated the maze with aplomb to one of two waiting rooms, the one used by lower ranking visitors.

"We're a bit early, but they may call for us ahead of schedule. His time is heavily booked, getting a jump on time is useful," said Hopkins, taking a seat.

Tony admired the waiting room furnishings, a mix of comfortable antique and modern formal. There were several exquisite paintings on the walls, which he walked around to examine and read the posted descriptions.

It was 1:04, by Tony's watch, when a secretary appeared in a side doorway and nodded at Hopkins, "Miss Tully said to go in, Mr. Hopkins."

"Thank you, Miss McIntyre," said Hopkins. He led Tony through a doorway, across a hallway, and into the Oval Office. FDR was in a wheelchair in front of his desk. This time, unlike Casablanca, he was wearing a tan stripe seersucker suit, brown and white shoes, a white shirt with gold cufflinks, and a navy blue tie with gold embroidered anchors. FDR swung around to take a drink of water from a glass on his desk. As was the case in Casablanca, Tony could see a gas mask bag was attached on the back of the wheelchair. One of Mike Reilly's nonnegotiable Secret Service security rules, he learned. Hull was sitting in one of the three chairs set in a semicircle facing FDR.

Harris & Ewing [Public domain]
President Franklin D. Roosevelt, Oval Office, The White House

"Good afternoon, Mr. President, Mr. Secretary," said Tony.

"Cordell, I want you to meet Captain Anthony Romella," said FDR, swinging back around to face them all. "Captain, this is Secretary of State, Cordell Hull."

"Pleased to meet you, Captain. I've been reading a lot of cables about you regarding the Azores," said Hull in a serious tone.

Tony noted a lack of appreciation in Hull's tone of voice. His eyes were both bright and penetrating and his handshake was politely firm. Hull's silver hair, dark blue three piece business suit, and general demeanor was the epitome of a statesman. "Honored, Mr. Secretary."

FDR raised his hand up toward Tony, "By the way, congratulations, Captain," he said with a wink. "Please sit, gentlemen. I have the Vice President at 1:45 and the Cabinet at 2, so let's get into it."

The Oval Office was impressive. It conveyed a formal feel, but with surprising simplicity and functionality. Tony's eyes were trying to take it all in without being obvious. Shiny brass sconce lights complimented the light provided by lamps behind the cornices around the office. The bright indirect light from the white ceiling, devoid of a chandelier, was ingenious and very effective. FDR's surprisingly plain oak desk had numerous desktop items, evidence of a practical man. Hopkins previously indicated that FDR had insisted on using the desk of his predecessor, President Hoover. There were many personal items on the desk, such as figurines, small framed pictures and knickknacks. Directly in back of the desk were three, floor to ceiling windows. Each of them had a large box valance of navy blue material, trimmed with gold striping, and a white federal eagle in the center. Solid navy blue curtains were tied back, with shades drawn on the bottom half, blocking the view to and from the garden. On one side of the center window was the U.S. flag, and on the other side, the flag of the U.S. Navy. The cream walls either side of the desk had paintings that were clearly of FDR's choosing. A dark blue rug covered the floor. The rear area of the room, opposite the desk, had map stands for the many briefings on war progress and planning. A 3' x 5' world map was displayed with layers of several other maps folded over the back of the stand.

"Cordell, let's address the Azores first. If we're going to run out of time, we'll at least have finished this topic," said FDR.

"Will we need the map for this?" Hopkins asked.

"I don't believe so, sir," said Tony.

Hull shook his head, "No, thank you, Harry."

"Alright, go ahead, Cordell," said FDR.

"Mr. President, thank you for the opportunity to discuss this," Hull began. "Captain, I won't deny the fact that I was displeased with the pursuit of putting that intelligence operation in Ponta Delgada. The President is well aware of my objection to it."

FDR interceded, "At the time, Cordell, you didn't have the benefit of the Captain's briefing to me and the Prime Minister on the value of that project. We saw no need for further deliberation on the merits."

Hull took a deep breath, "Nonetheless, it complicated already difficult negotiations with Dr. Salazar on Allied use of the islands. My team in Lisbon had a royal fit. I believe we are very fortunate that Dr. Salazar considered it to be an issue separate from the preexisting negotiations."

FDR nodded, "Tony, please brief the Secretary as you did me and the PM in Casablanca."

Tony proceeded to give Hull the same briefing on the Azores he presented in Casablanca.

"Thank you, Tony. Cordell, if that wasn't a verbatim, it's terribly close. Tony, what results, to date, can you report?" asked FDR.

Tony sat forward in his chair and looked intermittently between Hull and FDR as he spoke. "The intelligence contributions of Ponta Delgada have been beyond our expectations." He described statistics on U-boat DF fixes that Ponta Delgada contributed to, and the quality improvements of those fixes that resulted from their information. "On top of all that, the system discovered two recently deposited German agents on the island. One of them has become a valuable double-agent. As I'm sure you are aware, through combined intelligence sources, we know that the German High Command has plans for putting U-boat bases in the Azores. Ponta Delgada has been specifically mentioned. I might add, we haven't seen any indication on when that plan will be set in motion, but we know they do not intend to negotiate first. Thus, our tipoff on that plan will most likely come from German instructions to our double-agent, if COMINT doesn't pick it up elsewhere first. Pardon my enthusiasm, Mr. Secretary, but that project is worth its weight in gold, and then some. At the very least, from an intelligence viewpoint."

Hull sat with one leg over the other, shifting legs a few times, but focused on Tony as he spoke, without expression.

FDR slapped his knee when Tony paused, "I'm more convinced now than ever. See what I mean about him, Cordell?"

Tony fought off the inclination to smile. Clever, thought Tony, he put his support in there before Hull could comment.

"Thank you, Captain," Hull said. "Very enlightening. I'll take that information and your earnest evaluation under advisement. I pray your project doesn't negatively impact the negotiations for Allied use of the island."

"I think we are finished with the Azores," said FDR. "Do either of you have anything more for Captain Romella?" asked FDR.

"I'm satisfied, Mr. President," said Hull.

"I have nothing, Mr. President," said Hopkins

"Gentleman, I am running out of time. I need a few moments with Cordell. Good to see you, Captain. I expect I'll see you again with TRIDENT before you return to London. If not, my regards to Petra."

Tony was impressed that FDR remembered her name. "It's been a pleasure Mr. President, Mr. Secretary," he said, and exited with Hopkins.

Later, After the Cabinet Meeting
The Oval Office

FDR wheeled himself for the short trip from the Cabinet Room of the West Wing into the Oval Office, with Hopkins leading the way, opening doors. FDR pointed at a chair alongside the desk. "Harry, sit a moment. I would like five minutes of your time."

"That was a lively meeting, Mr. President."

"They work hard, get little credit and take lot of criticism from the Republicans and press, even some Democrats. They all want more personal time with me than I have to give them. So they unload in cabinet meetings. But that's not what I want to discuss. What's your opinion of Captain Romella?"

"Oh, I think he's a really good man," said Hopkins.

"OK, but why?" asked FDR

"Very bright. Very wealthy, apparently from parent's estates and the stock market. But he doesn't go out of his way to convince you of either his IQ or his money. He's honest. Unshakeable. Very sociable. Totally professional. Tactful. No hidden political agenda. I could go on," replied Hopkins.

"Franklin Jr. and Elliott had essentially the same opinion of him in Casablanca. So do I. He strikes me as a man of great potential. Do you know if he's a Democrat?" asked FDR.

Hopkins didn't hesitate, "I already checked. He's not registered to vote in any of the states that he has lived, gone to school, or been stationed. He doesn't show up on significant donor rolls for either party. I can't tell which side he favors either."

"Well damn it, let's make him want to be a Democrat, or at least support us," said FDR laughing. "I just like him a lot."

"Making him a Democrat could be a tall order," said Hopkins, with a smile. He took a few moments to frame his thoughts. "Don't you think he's getting an awful lot of attention for an attaché? And a brand new Captain? I know you had a hand in that with Secretary Knox. But you know how jealousy creeps into things with the eagles and stars. They don't like line jumpers."

"I don't care about that. Bill Taylor thinks the absolute world of him, and you know what Bill's opinion is worth," said FDR. "Bill says he's a loyal, skilled warrior with superior leadership skills, and is an administrative whiz. I really think we need to cultivate Romella…Tony. I'm not exactly sure where he fits right now, but when I figure that out, I want him to say yes. He's going to be worth our attention, one day."

"Alright. One thing for sure, Cordell isn't a big fan of the Captain. But… that aside, I have an idea about something we can do right now, along that line," said Hopkins. "He brought his wife, Petra, to DC with him. She's a British citizen, a WREN, on leave. She works in MI-5. Maybe we can twist Mike Reilly's arm to allow Petra and Tony's sister Maria, to get a special tour of the White House."

FDR pondered the idea for a moment, "I think he told me that Maria was single, and a lawyer in Georgetown, is that right?" asked FDR.

"Correct. The Romellas are staying with Maria in her Georgetown home," said Hopkins.

"Mike shouldn't have any security issues whatsoever with any of the Romellas. Get Mike on my calendar today for ten minutes. I want to get them all in for a tour before they go back to London. Also, Harry, check on his sister's politics."

24 - Cultivation

Three Days Later
12:40 p.m., Monday, May 3, 1943
Maria's Home, Georgetown

The three musketeers spent the morning visiting the Washington Monument. Maria brought her Kodak Brownie along. It was the first opportunity for Tony to join them on a tour. Everywhere the ladies went, Maria made a point of taking pictures for Petra to take back to London. They worked up a big appetite at the monument and walking the surrounding grounds. One of Alicia's splendid lunches was served when they returned. They devoured calzones and were enjoying coffee, tea and conversation.

"Alicia, lunch was brilliant!" exclaimed Petra, when the cook came into the dining room to finish clearing the table. Alicia beamed and nodded.

Tony smiled, "We grew up on food made with old Italian food recipes my Mom got from her grandmother. Alicia's cooking reminds me of Mom's."

The phone on the table in the hall began ringing. Maria answered it, then returned to the dining room and announced, playfully, "Paging Captain Romella."

"This is Captain Romella," Tony answered.

"Tony, this is Harry. Can you and the ladies be here at three today for a tour?" asked Hopkins.

"Absolutely," Tony said, holding back excitement. "Thank you, very much, sir."

"And Tony, have them bring their passports. I'll have your party registered at the gate to expedite things. Same one you used," said Hopkins.

"Are you leaving us," Petra asked when he returned to the table.

"Nope," he said, with forced calm, "I arranged a tour of a museum I thought you'd both be interested in seeing. They called to confirm a time of 1500. That's 3 p.m. for you, sis. I hope you two didn't have other plans."

"Nothing we can't change, Tony," Maria said. "A surprise, apparently. Are you going to tell us which museum?"

"Nope. It's a special guided tour, though, and you'll enjoy it, I'm sure. They said for you to bring your passports."

"Passports?" asked Maria. When she saw Tony's expression, she realized she needed to go along with a ruse. "I know just where mine is."

"Lovely!" said Petra, with a bright smile. "I fancy Tony's surprises!"

That Afternoon
2:50 p.m., Monday, May 3, 1943
Pennsylvania Avenue, Washington

The taxi proceeded past the White House on Pennsylvania Avenue. Petra was transfixed, gazing at the structure out of the right rear window. "Majestic, but less grand than Buckingham Palace."

"We don't have a king, dear, we have a President, elected by the people," teased Maria.

"Quite. The colonist's disdain for their rightful king, it seems," Petra said with a chuckle.

When the taxi made a right turn onto East Executive Avenue, Maria, sitting on Tony's left, poked him in the ribs. Petra was still oblivious, as the taxi stopped at the north gate of the East Wing of the White House.

"This is it, ladies," announced Tony.

"What museum is this," asked Petra. The view of the White House was blocked by the East Wing and she had not made the connection.

"It's known simply as the East Wing," Tony said. "They will want to see your passports for identification, ladies. Just some wartime security measures."

Security hurdles were cleared with ease. Tony walked up the driveway to the portico with a lady on each arm.

Inside the door, Petra spotted the arm patch of the White House Police officer as Tony presented his ID and their passports to the receptionist. She squeezed his hand really hard. The proverbial cat was out of the bag. They all signed the clearly marked White House Visitor Log.

"Ladies, I would like you to meet someone," as he lead them toward Hopkins, who was waiting at the end of the foyer, by the hall. "Mr. Hopkins, I would like to introduce my wife, Petra, and my sister, Maria. Ladies, please meet Mr. Harry Hopkins, Special Assistant to the President." God help me, Tony thought, the price for this favor is going to be steep.

Formalities completed, Hopkins said, "This way, ladies. Tony has already had this tour. So this one is for you. Feel free to ask any questions you might have. I just might have an answer," he said with a smile.

They proceeded directly into the East Corridor, Maria alongside Hopkins and Petra on Tony's arm. Hopkins was congenial, and chatty. Ladies, gushing in awe, with many questions, stopped to admire certain pieces of art and sculpture. The squeezes on Tony's arm told him she was nervous and amazed.

"Passing through this doorway, we enter the East Corridor of the White House," Hopkins said.

Tony felt Petra shiver and squeeze his arm tightly. He squeezed back.

"On the right is the Library and on the left is the Social Room. If you need to stop to powder your nose, we can do that."

The ladies shook their heads, indicating otherwise.

"Very good," Hopkins said, "opposite the staircase is the China Room. I know you'll enjoy a look at the china cabinets displaying the tableware of previous Presidents." He held the door open for them to enter. Tony and Hopkins stood in the center of the room, as the ladies went from cabinet to cabinet, whispering to each other, admiring the historic pieces.

"Tony, did you know Army Lieutenant General Frank Andrews?" asked Hopkins softly.

"No, Harry, I never met him. But I know he was instrumental in the creation of the Army Air Force. Why do you ask?" replied Tony.

"He was killed in an airplane crash in Iceland today. He was flying back from England to be named Supreme Allied Commander in Europe and get his fourth star. A terrible loss," said Hopkins.

"Oh my God. May he rest in peace. Such a tragic end to a wonderful career," said Tony.

"The President had great admiration for him and is very sad about it," said Hopkins.

The ladies completed their round of the cabinets and came to the men.

"Alright, let's proceed," said Hopkins, leading them out the door. "On the left is the Diplomatic Reception Room, opposite the North Portico Entrance Hall." He held the doors open to each so they could take a quick look. "Next on the left, the door with the Marine in front of it, is the entrance to the Map Room. That's our information center, where war related cables, files and maps are filed. The President visits it frequently, impromptu sometimes, for war progress updates. Next on the left is the Clinic and Admiral McIntire's office, the President's personal physician. The next door on the right is the Kitchen. I would offer to take you in there, but we're a little short on time. I suspect you could spend an hour in there. They have the latest food service equipment."

"My cook would probably enjoy it more than I would," joked Maria.

Hopkins smiled, "Alright. Through the next door, we'll take the outdoor colonnade, a shortcut to the West Wing of the White House. The most important office in this wing is the Oval Office." When they all were through the door, he continued. "The garden on the left is the Rose Garden, which you've no doubt heard and read about."

The walk along the left-angled colonnade was pleasant, being a sunny and breezy day. Hopkins stopped near the end, opened a door, and motioned for them to take seats in the rear of the office inside. It was the office of the Personal Secretary to the President, Grace Tully.

The ladies had no clue who the secretary behind the desk in this office was, but Tony did. They are really pouring on the syrup, he thought. Even I didn't get this treatment. So, I'm guessing the Oval Office isn't empty.

"Grace, this is Captain Romella and his party," said Hopkins.

"Good afternoon, Captain and ladies," said Tully. "Harry, we just need a few minutes."

Hopkins winked at Tony and took a seat next to the ladies. "Ladies, we're going to get a look inside the Oval Office when it's free."

Petra took Tony's hand and squeezed it really hard. He squeezed back twice, but more gently. Maria gave Tony the charming grin of an adoring sister.

Admiral William Leahy came through the door from the Oval Office. He gave a note to Tully and looked over toward the guests. "Captain Romella, I saw your name on the schedule for today. I'll see you in the TRIDENT meetings. I'm late for an appointment at the Pentagon. Enjoy the tour, ladies." He exited to the colonnade.

Tony whispered to the ladies, "Admiral Leahy is serving both as the President's Chief of Staff and the Chairman of the Joint Chiefs of Staff."

Tully nodded at Hopkins.

"Alright let's go take a look at the seat of power," said Hopkins. He went to the door the Admiral just exited and opened it.

When they all entered, he announced, "Mr. President, may I present Captain and Mrs. Petra Romella and the Captain's sister, Maria Romella. Ladies, the President of the United States, Franklin D. Roosevelt."

"Come over ladies, I want to shake your hands," said FDR with a happy grin. He joked, "I've shaken yours, Tony, stand at ease. Oh, come on over too. Ladies, it's a pleasure to meet you. Mrs. Romella, the next time I see your PM, I'll thank him for sparing you. I hope you're enjoying your visit."

Petra felt her face flush, "You're too kind, Mr. President."

After ten minutes of amiable social banter with FDR, Hopkins escorted them from the Oval Office, through the West Wing maze to the wing's West Executive Avenue entrance.

"Harry, I very much appreciate your precious time," Tony said.

"My pleasure, Tony. I hope you enjoyed yourselves," Hopkins said.

"Indeed! You are most kind, Mr. Hopkins," Petra said.

"Wonderful, Mr. Hopkins. Tony must have been a good boy, for a change," said Maria.

"Miss Romella, you have no idea," Hopkins said with a sly smile. "Do you have a card?"

"Certainly," Maria said, getting her gold plated business card case from her pocketbook.

Tony and the ladies walked the curved pathway from the wing toward West Executive Avenue. When out of earshot of the guards, Petra whispered, "Tony! No messing about, tell me what is going on?"

"Exactly, dear brother," Maria said softly.

"Just high level planning that I happen to be privy to, is all."

"Rubbish, yeah?" exclaimed Petra, as Tony hailed a taxi.

"The American word for that is bullshit," said Maria, laughing.

"Beyond what I have told you, I have no idea, ladies," said Tony, blushing.

"A special tour of the White House, a visit to the Oval Office, introduction to the President of the United States, and that's all you offer us? Oh Tony, you have a lot of explaining to do," said Maria.

"Just get in the cab, ladies, and stop the jibber-jabber," said Tony.

That Evening
Maria's Home

Alicia served tossed salads and filled their glasses with red wine. Maria said grace. They touched their glasses together, took first sips and started into their salads.

"Tony, seriously now, is there something you can share with us? It's all so bizarre to me," said Maria.

"Spot on," agreed Petra.

"It is rather odd to me as well, but I promise you, I don't think there is anything sinister going on," Tony said, knowing he chose that word carefully. He took another sip of wine. "It's just that, well, I've done some things which received White House attention. I attribute all that to be the reason. There's also the fact that Bill Taylor is a personal friend of the President, which I only recently learned about. I suspect I'm pulled into the circle through that connection."

Maria looked across the table at Petra, and with a skeptical look, asked "Shall we buy that?"

Petra looked at Tony, then back to Maria, "Bollocks!" she said, grinning. The ladies laughed. Tony feigned insult.

Two Days Later
2:30 p.m., Wednesday, May 5, 1943
The Oval Office

"Good afternoon gentlemen," said FDR. "I want to discuss a staffing idea. Please have a seat."

Admiral Leahy and Harry Hopkins sat down in chairs near the side of the desk.

"I want to groom Captain Romella for higher service," FDR began. "His considerable talents can contribute more to this country here, than in London. Your concerns for placing him in a position over senior military officers is valid. But I came up with an idea that brings him into the White House with due respect for that issue. We've had some turmoil the last couple months resulting from Admiral McCrea's departure to command the battleship USS *Iowa* and Admiral Brown coming in as his replacement as my Naval Aide. I would like to discuss creating a position with the primary responsibility of Map Room operations, and the daily theatre intelligence and progress summaries. There are other things he can participate in, once he's here and settled. Admiral Brown has had a very full plate with Lend-Lease and a plethora of things. He doesn't have time to be in charge of the damn Map Room, which needs attention."

Leahy and Hopkins looked at each other.

Hopkins sat forward, "His scope of knowledge, intellect and potential do seem exceptional. This would give us a close look at him. Once he has the Map Room figured out, he'd be right under our nose, available for anything we need, special projects, and the like. I have to agree with the President, the idea has merit. Bill, would there be any thorny issues with more senior captains in the intelligence specialty? Or perhaps with Admiral Brown?"

"Interesting proposal. Unfortunately, Wilson Brown is out of town, or we could ask him directly. I'll get a call in to him. As for thorny issues with others, in this circumstance, they can't argue with the President's wishes," said Leahy.

FDR waited for more from Leahy but detected hesitance. "Bill, we both know there's progress to be made in the Map Room. The Pentagon has its intelligence directorate to support the Chiefs, but all I have to assist with making the final decisions, is a sitting room made into a Map Room, which we're trying to make a prime intelligence and combat information center. Captain Romella has the skills to improve it, quickly, and with ease."

"I don't disagree with you, in principle," said Leahy. "I just haven't had direct exposure to Romella's abilities. When you brought up his name after Casablanca, I had Wilson pull reports on what he's done in London, France, Norway and Casablanca. I know for a fact that Admiral King likes him a great deal. As for seniority issues in the Map Room, Colonel Hammond is transferring out soon, and will surely be amenable. Otherwise, there are only O-5s and below, Army and Navy, in the Map Room right now. I would like to sit down with Romella and Wilson to see how our personalities fit. If it doesn't seem to be going well, we can end the interview. If we feel positive, we could tour the Map Room, and see what his reaction is. Depending on how all that goes, we have the option to continue and more seriously discuss the position with him."

"Excellent idea," said FDR. "Try to get that done before TRIDENT starts."

"Yes, Mr. President. Wilson will be back from Groton tomorrow. We have plenty of time."

"Good. New subject. Any news on the return of the bodies of General Andrews' and the others?" asked FDR.

"An aircraft departed the U.K. early this morning for Iceland. The bodies should be arriving here tomorrow or the next day," said Leahy. "General Arnold's investigating team is on-scene in Iceland. They have already interviewed the sole survivor."

"Alright. Make sure there are full honors on their arrival and for their funerals. On that subject, is there deliberation among the Chiefs of Staff regarding who we might appoint Supreme Allied Commander, Europe, in place of General Andrews?" asked FDR. "Any, shall we say, suggestions, from anyone in Congress?"

Leahy took a long breath, "As you might expect, there are several volunteers. So far, Congress has been quiet, with me at least. We have all been busy with our normally hectic routines as well as preparations for TRIDENT. We would like to hold discussions on that until after TRIDENT."

"I see. Well, I've already heard from a few on the hill. Is General Eisenhower one of the volunteers?" asked FDR.

"Not that I'm aware," said Leahy. "He is a bit junior to others available and doesn't have any combat experience. It would be presumptuous of him to put his own name forward. However, General George Marshall did offer up his name."

"General Marshall says Eisenhower has a superior intellect, is one hell of a planner, and is an excellent organizer and administrator," said FDR. "All of those things may just make the difference in this war, rather than just brute strength and attrition. George Marshall and I would like his name on the list for consideration," said FDR. "Unless either of you have something further, thank you, gentlemen."

10:30 a.m., Saturday, May 8, 1943
Admiral Leahy's Office
East Wing, White House

"Welcome back, Wilson," Leahy said. "How did the speech go at the submarine base in Groton?" asked Leahy.

"Excellent, Bill. It was my first visit there. They were very gracious," said Brown.

"I'm sorry you weren't here for a discussion we had with the President last Wednesday, Wilson. The subject was the creation of a new staff position to lead Map Room operations," said Leahy.

"Oh, thank God," said Brown. "I am stretched too thin to give it more than passing attention, and that bothers me a great deal."

"The President has a candidate, Navy Captain Anthony Romella, out of OP-20-G, currently Naval Attaché, London. Do you know him?" asked Hopkins.

Brown shook his head, "That name is not familiar to me."

Leahy laughed, "Well that's good, you have no preconceived ideas then. He's coming in at 1100 hours for an interview with the three of us. We're authorized to tender an offer today, if we all are in agreement. As for the structure of the interview, I'll get it started and we'll go from there. Harry, have you come up with ideas on structure for the position? Maybe we can nail that down before he gets here."

"Yes, I have. I have two separate thoughts. First, of course is the Map Room. But second, is Wilson's workload, which is unduly heavy, as he said, due to Lend Lease and the tempo of the war. In a response to those two items, I'm thinking about a position encompassing Director, White House Intelligence and Deputy, Naval Aide. The position would fall directly under Wilson."

"Your thoughts, Wilson?" asked Leahy.

"That idea has promise," said Brown. "As a Deputy, rather than Assistant, he'll have more authority to take on some of my tasks and do so on my behalf. However, that will only work if he proves that he has what it takes to do so."

"I think you need not worry about capability, Wilson. The President and I have direct experience in that regard. As do other reliable references," said Hopkins. He handed a file folder to Brown. Take a look at his file, while we wait for him to arrive."

Leahy's phone rang at 10:52. "Admiral Leahy…I'm expecting him. Send him in."

"I'll go fetch," said Hopkins.

"I have the conference room blocked out. Take him in there," said Leahy.

Leahy and Brown were standing behind their chairs in the conference room when Hopkins brought Tony in.

"Admiral Brown, please meet Captain Anthony Romella. Captain, this is Admiral Wilson Brown, Naval Aide to the President," said Hopkins.

"Admiral, my honor, sir," said Tony, shaking Brown's hand, then Leahy's and Hopkins'.

Leahy sat at the head of the table, with Brown on his right. Hopkins pointed at the chair on Leahy's left for Tony and sat next to Brown.

Tony looked across the table at Brown and Hopkins, wondering which of them was assigned as the bad cop. Probably Brown, he thought.

"As Harry mentioned on the phone, Tony, we wanted to discuss an opportunity with you," said Leahy. "Thank you for making yourself available on this sultry, overcast Saturday afternoon. Please know that there will be no negative impact on your career should you decide to remove yourself from consideration."

"Understood," Tony said.

"Captain, for the benefit of Admiral Wilson Brown, please review your education and Navy experience," said Leahy. "There are no classification limits, aside from that involving information controlled by the British Government. Share what is permissible."

Tony spent forty minutes summarizing his life to the present, with congenial questions from Brown interspersed.

"Harry, do you have any questions for Tony?" asked Leahy.

"No, sir, I do not. He covered everything very well," said Hopkins.

Leahy looked at Brown inquiringly.

"I have nothing further at the moment. Thank you, Tony," said Brown.

"We owe you a full explanation of the position, Tony. Harry, run it down for him please," said Leahy.

Hopkins spent ten minutes describing, in detail, the position they had created. As he spoke, he observed Tony maintaining a calm demeanor, with an attentive and receptive attitude. "Any questions or thoughts?" Hopkins asked when he finished.

"I understand the position as described," said Tony, concealing his absolute excitement with being in the running. "I am honored that you are considering me for this interesting and challenging job. What will be the length of the tour of duty?"

Hopkins and Brown looked at Leahy, who replied, "The length of the war, like the rest of us at this table, circumstances notwithstanding. When would you be able to report for duty?"

Tony thought for a moment, "Given personal, professional, diplomatic, and transportation complications that have to be resolved, I would estimate the first of July. Is that prohibitive?"

"I believe that would be acceptable," said Leahy, after noting Hopkins' and Brown's deferring glances.

"Before we get further into this, is there any chance I could get a look at the Map Room?" asked Tony.

"It belongs to you, Wilson. Is it available for Tony to see right now?" asked Leahy, giving Brown a gentleman's way out, should there be hesitance.

"Of course. Let's take a walk over there," said Brown.

"You take him over, Wilson. Come get us in my office when you are through," said Leahy.

Brown and Tony returned to the East Wing, after a thorough tour of the White House Map Room, and an overview of its operations. They reconvened in Leahy's office.

"Impressions, Tony?" asked Hopkins.

Without hesitation, Tony asked, "Could I hire and fire? Could I make operational changes?"

Hopkins gave Brown a little grin, "Wilson? Could he? It's your baby."

"You would be the Director, Tony, with full responsibility and accountability," said Brown.

"Gentlemen, I would be honored to serve in that position. I assume you are interviewing others. When will you be announcing your decision?" asked Tony.

"We'll let you know fairly quickly, Tony. Do you have time to lunch with us?" asked Leahy.

"Affirmative," Tony said.

"We have a 1300 lunch appointment in the West Wing, so we need to get over there now," said Hopkins. "We'll come back here to fill out personnel and security papers required of all White House job applicants."

They transited the White House corridors, now familiar to Tony. His excitement built when they entered the west colonnade. It was clear they were headed for Grace Tully's office, not the Navy run mess hall in the West Wing.

"Go right in," said Tully, when they entered her office.

"Captain Tony Romella! Glad you could break bread with us today," said FDR. A butler was helping him out of his desk chair into his wheelchair. A round table had been placed in the center of the Oval Office, with place settings for five. Salads were already in place.

"Good afternoon, Mr. President," said Tony and the others.

"Come over, Tony, I want to shake your hand," said FDR. "The reason you're here for lunch is that these gentlemen have selected you for the job."

Tony felt the effects of a large adrenalin dump. Lord, help me, he thought. I have changed the lives of everyone in my life. "I am both honored and without words," he said.

Flashing a bright smile, FDR said, "I asked them to give me the pleasure of telling you. Congratulations. When are you coming aboard?"

That Afternoon
Maria's Home

"We're in here, Tony," Maria called out from the living room.

He hung his hat and jacket on the pegs in the foyer.

"Tony, what is it?" Petra said cheerfully when she saw his smiling face. She got up to greet him with a hug. "Give us the news, it must be brilliant. Look at that face, Maria. Come on love, don't be daft and try to tell us porkies."

"Looks like the cat that ate the canary," Maria said.

"Oh I have news, alright. I had to make a decision without the luxury of talking with you about it first." He sat down on the couch with Petra. "I'm getting a new duty assignment…"

Petra interrupted him, "It's the White House, yes?" She quickly repositioned to kneel on the couch beside him.

"Yes, the White House," he said.

"Bloody hell," said Petra, teary eyed. "What will you be doing? How long will I be on my own this time?"

"It's not publicly announced yet, but it is Deputy Naval Aide to the President. You won't be on your own, honey, you and Ives can come live in Washington. We'll be a whole family," said Tony.

Maria got up from her chair, came to the couch and leaned down to kiss Tony on the forehead, "My brother working in the White House, and living in Washington. Wonderful news! I'm sure this is a very important career move."

He pulled his handkerchief from his pocket for Petra. "Happy tears, I hope, honey."

She dried her eyes. "Such a drastic change. It's just overwhelming, love, but yes, being all together would be quite wonderful," said Petra. "This is just incredible. When does it happen?"

"The plan is for me to start on the first of July," he said. "We'll be busy getting things all squared away when we get back to London," he said. "Maria, I should start looking for a house while I'm here. I am sure that you can suggest a real estate agent."

"How long is this posting?" asked Petra.

"When I asked that question, their answer was, until the end of the war," Tony said.

"Oh, an idea just popped into my head," Maria said, returning to her seat. "You are welcome to buy this house. It will be perfect for you. It's really too big for me, but it was a great buy. There are some stately brick houses here in Georgetown that I have had my eye on. We can all live right here until I find a place and get settled. A perfect transition for us all."

"Great idea, I love this place," said Tony.

"That would be quite lovely," said Petra. "Blow me down with a feather. I'll be a nutter by July. There's so many things to think about, and sort. What if Ives doesn't want to come? What if my government won't let me come?"

"Petra, it will be on my shoulders to do most of the thinking and arranging. Once here, it won't be necessary for you to work. You can concentrate on your son, getting him a fine education, and keeping our nest feathered. I can't imagine Ives won't want to be with you. You know how much he misses you. Just don't conjure problems before they rear their head. Whatever comes up, we can work out, just fine."

"You're right, Tony, I'm off my trolley with it all," said Petra. "I know how long it takes to get long term residential permission in the U.S. for citizens of other countries, even the U.K."

"Petra, I hesitate to say this, but you have no idea how easy that will be for me to arrange. I'll share Captain Taylor's rule number two with you. That is, it pays to have friends in high places."

Maria laughed aloud, "Oh, Petra, my brother sure as hell has those friends now. This calls a celebration tonight. I have two bottles of really, really fine French champagne in the wine cellar that I have been saving for a special occasion. It's been down there since before the French occupation. Tonight, we will find out just how fine it is, or if it has become vinegar."

25 - TRIDENT

10:00 a.m., Monday, May 10, 1943
Captain Jerry Webber's Office
OP-20-GB, 3801 Nebraska Avenue, Washington, DC

T he walk from the taxi drop at the compound gate to the Navy's communications intelligence headquarters building was not enjoyable. Grass, blacktop and cement each have their unique, and unpleasant, smell when wet. Even though it was just drizzling, his shoeshine got ruined. Despite a raincoat and umbrella, the legs of his uniform trousers were spotted.

Captain Webber settled back into his chair. "It was raining when I came in. Your raincoat is wet and you're carrying an umbrella, so it must still be foul."

"Aye, that it is. Intermittent all morning, but raining lightly now," said Tony.

"Sit down, Tony, and tell me, what brings you to this neck of the woods today?"

"Last Saturday I was offered a job at the White House, effective the first of July," said Tony modestly. "I felt you should find out from me before the scuttlebutt got to you."

"That explains why we received a message from the White House this morning requesting your security status, and date of your latest background investigation. This is going to be very interesting. A cryptologist in the White House. That could be very valuable to us. What's the position?"

"Deputy Naval Aide to the President, and Director, White House Intelligence," said Tony.

"My, my, my, Tony. I don't know what all you've got, but if you can bottle it and sell it, you'll be a millionaire. Of course, riding Bill Taylor's coat tails didn't hurt. He's always been able to get anything he wants. I assume he knows about this."

Tony detected an attitude of either jealousy, or sarcasm in Webber's demeanor. Possibly a combination. I better make this meeting short and to the point. "Yes. I got a line through to him yesterday morning, our time…"

"What was his reaction?" Webber interjected.

"Congratulatory. He said they consulted him prior to making their decision," said Tony. "You mentioned possible value to 20-G. That goes both ways. I may need some help in reorganizing the intel feeds to the White House. I was hoping I would have your support. I might ask for an analyst or two as well."

"I'm sure Bill's fingerprints are on your selection for that job. Be damn sure you thank him when you get back to London. All that aside, if you find yourself in a position to help in our funding, or otherwise supporting our operations, it would not go without appreciation," said Webber.

Tony wondered how he would solve this chicken or egg quandary. Which of us would have to do what, first, in order to get something? That's silly, I'll have to deliver, something, first, no doubt. "I would be pleased to help in any way I can, Jerry."

"TRIDENT kicks off in a couple days," said Webber. "Will you need support from us? Your focus in those meetings is still the Azores, correct?" asked Webber.

"Affirmative," said Tony. "Anything you might see in COMINT that relates in any way to the Azores, or Portugal in general, I'd like to know about promptly. They'll no doubt run a phone message board outside the conference room. I'll check it, and the reception desk, after each meeting. Just leave a message for me. I can run over here after they adjourn. I don't need to have copies of anything. I just need to read whatever you come up with."

Webber nodded slightly, "And you would, or course, let me know if you pick up any comments or issues regarding COMINT operations to support the plans they discuss. Also let me know about holes in existing Navy COMINT support, and any ideas you might have in that regard."

"Affirmative, Jerry." There's the quid pro quo, he thought, but it's reasonable.

"Do you know your schedule yet?"

"I know that Admiral Leahy will propose that the general meetings be from 1030 to 1245, followed by a luncheon. I plan to pass on some of the luncheons, if I can. The meetings are still scheduled to be held in the Federal Reserve Building's Board Room. There will be a few meetings at the White House with the heavies. I'm not sure when those are scheduled yet. I am not expecting to be invited to those."

"Weekdays, or?" asked Webber.

"Oh no, daily, including Saturday and Sunday. By the 23rd, it will have settled down to nitpicking the final positions, agreements and reports, so I won't need intel support after the 22nd. I'm scheduled to depart by air for London on the 27th."

"Alright, Tony. We can do that for you. If I don't see you again before you go back, have a safe trip. Come and visit after you get ensconced in the new job. I'll arrange a lunch with Captain Stone. You missed him again. He's over at the Pentagon."

"Thank you. If I may, before I leave the building, I'd like to visit with Paul Archer to see if there's been any developments with the double agent in Ponta Delgada," said Tony.

"I'll call down and let Paul know you're on the way," said Webber.

Three Days Later
9:40 a.m., Thursday, May 13, 1943
Board Room
Marriner S. Eccles Federal Reserve Building
20th Street and Constitution Avenue
Washington, DC

Federal Reserve
Marriner S. Eccles Federal Reserve Building, Washington, DC

Tony showed his Navy ID card to one of the four armed Marines at the second floor lobby. They were checking everyone coming up the stairs or getting off the elevators. The foyer outside the Board Room was at the end of the corridor, where two armed Marines, and a secretary with a clipboard were clearing people for entry into the Board Room. Waiting rooms on each side of the entry foyer were now guarded clerical areas to support the meetings. One side was for Pentagon clerks, the other side was for British Embassy clerks. The Pentagon clerks were removing copies of documents from boxes. Those documents were then carried into the Board Room and placed on the table at each seat.

"Good morning, Captain. ID please," said a civilian woman with a Pentagon ID badge clipped to her jacket.

"Good morning, Miss Montgomery," Tony said, reading her name from the badge.

She took Tony's ID and checked for facial likeness. Then she flipped pages of a listing until she found his name and put a check next to it. "Thank you, sir," she said with a smile, returned his ID, and motioned toward the doors.

Marines saluted as he approached, then opened the two heavy oak doors. Tony proceeded through into the large white-walled rectangular Board Room.

Federal Reserve

Federal Reserve Boardroom, Washington, DC

The pine scent of rug cleaning fluid lingered in the air from last night's final round of room cleaning and preparation. A mural size map of the United States caught his eye first. It filled most of the end wall on his left. The locations of the Federal Reserve Banks were marked. The other walls were adorned with a couple dozen large graphs of various economic factors. The center of the room was occupied by the longest conference table Tony had ever seen, with seating for 26. A huge bright chandelier hung above it. A growing pile of documents, lined pad and three pencils were carefully placed on the mirror shined table in front of each chair. There was side seating on the far wall for the lesser lights attending. A British Brigadier General, seated at the map end of the table, looked up briefly, nodded and continued concentrating on a document he was reading. His index finger traced his progress down the page.

The second to arrive, Tony had his choice of the wall seats. He chose one nearer to the head of the table, put his hat under his chair and his leather attaché case alongside his chair. The case contained a copy of his orders, an unclassified information guide for TRIDENT attendees, a pocket calendar planner, a lined pad, a spare mechanical pencil, a paper tube of extra leads, and a gum eraser.

When each seat at the table had gotten its copy of the document from the Pentagon, the clerks began putting a copy on each of the wall seats. Tony was given his copy of the document -- *C.C.S. 215, INVASION OF THE EUROPEAN CONTINENT FROM THE UNITED KINGDOM IN 1943 – 1944, Memorandum by the U. S. Chiefs of Staff.* He speed read it and placed it on the floor between his feet.

Admiral Leahy told him that he expected this meeting to be relatively short. Leahy planned to present the groundwork for the daily routine of the meetings, disseminate *C.C.S. 215* for overnight consideration by the principles, and make a general strategy statement. Just the same, the Admiral made it clear that Tony should attend this and all subsequent meetings.

Attendees began streaming in. Admirals Leahy and King acknowledged Tony and took their seats. By 10:10, all were in place and were reading *C.C.S. 215*. Tony counted 15 other men in the room, 13 of which were seated at the conference table. The four members of the Secretariat were seated at the far end of the table. They constituted the U.S. and U.K. joint keepers and publishers of the minutes of the meetings.

Admiral Leahy, being the host, was chairing the meetings. When his watch indicated 10:30, he announced, "The 83rd meeting of the Combined Chiefs of Staff shall come to order."

Aside from Leahy, the other principles at the table were, for the U.S., General G. Marshall, Admiral E. King and Lieutenant General J. McNarney. For the U.K., were General Sir Alan Brooke, Admiral of the Fleet Sir Dudley Pound, Air Chief Marshal Sir Charles Portal, Field Marshall Sir John Dill, and Lieutenant General Sir Hastings Ismay. This tableful of the most senior military leaders of the two most powerful free world countries was an impressive sight. It produced feelings of awe and pride.

Leahy continued, "I would like to thank the British members for leaving their duties and traveling the distance, in recognition of the great importance of personal joint planning. Getting right into it, I would like to take this early opportunity to clarify our position regarding the use of massive air power, to answer some inquiries I have received. The United States believes that air power alone will not win this war. Air bombardment will reduce German military power to such a degree that German forces could not succeed against Allied ground forces and will facilitate the ability of Allied forces to defeat Germany."

As with the meetings in Casablanca, each of the other principles addressed burning issues they wished to get off their chests at the outset. Tony soaked it all in.

General Brooke commented that obtaining the use of the Azores would provide very valuable advantages. That peaked Tony's interest, and explained why Leahy wanted him present. The Azores had become a high interest item. Brooke continued with an explanation of a British staff analysis on potential reactions by Germany to Allied use of the Azores. "A German advance into Portugal would require fighting through Spain, and would require 15 to 20 divisions, with attrition from resistance. The economic and logistic issues involved in such an undertaking, due to poor communications by road and rail, would surely be recognized by Germany as prohibitive. Portugal is asking for guarantees of defense in exchange for use of the Azores. Keeping sufficient forces and ships in place to meet such a commitment would be prohibitive to the Allies. The only option we have in these negotiations," he continued, "is to offer no guarantees. Rather, convince Portugal that Germany was in no position to invade them."

The principles then began discussing options, in the event that Portugal denied the Allied use of the Azores. The British felt that they were not in a position to be part of an invasion of the Azores, due to their negotiations with Portugal regarding assisting them in the defense of their islands.

General Marshall broke the silence of churning minds with a suggestion that plans for the acquisition of the Azores, by force, be postponed until after Operation HUSKY, if it became necessary to exercise that option. He indicated that ships returning from HUSKY operations in the Mediterranean would be available to support the acquisition of the Azores.

Just then, a British clerk came into the room, gave General Ismay a note, then departed. Ismay read it, looked up and announced, "Gentlemen, a telegram has just been received from the British Cabinet stating that the Foreign Secretary believes that Portugal is close to agreeing to a British occupation of their islands. I will circulate further details when available."

Leahy took the opportunity of a pause in the conversation to declare adjournment until the next day at 1030, barring no objection. None was raised. "Captain, a moment, please," he said to Tony.

Tony collected his things and took a seat next to Leahy. The table, at that point, was empty. Clerks were collecting unclaimed copies of the Pentagon document.

"You'll need a place to review and stow the numerous documents this conference will generate. Admiral Brown and I have identified the former Military Aide's office as your office, down in our end of the building, effective immediately. It's been cleared and cleaned and ready for you. You're on the permanent staff list with the Secret Service. When you drop that document off today, just ask a secretary in our area to show you which office is yours. You can come and go as you please, independently, any time of the day or night. The secretary in the adjoining office is available to you for any support you require. If we have any notes, messages or correspondence for you, we'll leave them in your in-basket."

"Thank you, Admiral, that's very gracious," Tony said, holding back excitement. "That answers my question about a place to study classified material and their stowage."

Four Days Later
10:30 a.m., Monday, May 17, 1943
Federal Reserve Board Room

Admiral Leahy called the 86th meeting of the Combined Chiefs of Staff to order. The table was filled with generals and admirals. Present were the seven principles, 18 additional military officers, nine each U.S. and U.K., plus two guests from China, General Chu and Dr. Soong. Four members of the Secretariat, two from each country, were also present.

The three previous meetings had involved the Azores only peripherally. Today Tony knew would be different. A thorough study, titled, *Use of Portuguese Atlantic Islands*, developed by the British War Cabinet Chiefs of Staff, was distributed the prior Friday as *C.C.S. 226*. It was agreed at that time to be discussed today. Tony was anxious to hear this discussion. The agenda showed it as item four.

The first item on the agenda was Admiral King's invitation of the Combined Chiefs to visit the Naval Academy, in Annapolis, the following Sunday. The second item was the approval of the minutes of the last meeting. The third item was a lengthy discussion of the situation in China.

Finally, after a brief intermission, Admiral Leahy introduced item four. Use of the Portuguese Islands was on the table.

Tony could sense the sleeves being rolled up, mentally, around the table. Body language of expected professional disagreement was evident. It was clear to him, knowing the U.S. position on these islands and having studied the British paper, there was sure to be lively discussion.

Admiral Pound presented a chart showing the vital role of the islands in sea route security.

Admiral Leahy suggested a delay in further discussion with the Portuguese Government until U.S. and British forces were available to seize the islands, if negotiations were unsuccessful.

211

General Brooke voiced the great value of the islands' role in the projected operations in the European Theatre.

Tony became frustrated that they seemed to be arguing while being in agreement, at least in principle. It also bothered him that, although Admiral Pound addressed sea route security, the discussion had not pointed out the criticality of the Azores in facilitating several aspects anti-submarine warfare. He wrote a brief note on his lined pad...*ASW VALUE OF AZORES!* He looked at it for a moment, wondering if he dared give this to Admiral King. He walked over and gave the note to King, who read it and passed it to Leahy, sitting next to him.

Admiral King interrupted the din of several whispering consultations among those around the table by offering his agreement with the importance of the Islands, particularly with respect to the protection of convoys from U-boats sailing the routes to the Mediterranean Sea from the States. He pointed out that his opinion had changed. That it was apparent that time was of the essence and delaying negotiations, which were already in progress by both countries, did not seem prudent.

Several of those at the table then voiced their opinion of delaying or not, and why.

Admiral Leahy, noted that all those at the table who wished to make their points on this topic, had done so. He decided to go with his gut on his next move. "Gentlemen. I believe we have consensus. Coordinated diplomatic discussions shall continue without delay. Before we deliberate on the timing, strength and source countries of the forces we may need, in event of diplomatic failure, I would like to introduce Captain Anthony Romella. He will provide a concise briefing on the importance of the Azores as a U-boat intelligence node."

God give me wisdom, Tony thought. He walked to the corner of the head table. His mind was churning at high speed, putting together a briefing he was not expecting to present. "Good morning, gentlemen. First let me preface my words by saying that the value, to the Allies, of the Azores as an intelligence node and operational location, is equal or greater to the German Navy. We know for a fact that they recently attempted to place an agent into San Miguel Island. We also have reliable intel that Admiral Dönitz has a plan for the establishment of U-boat bases and U-boat supply stations, without warning, on at least two islands of the Azores. Although the intel sources do not reveal a D-Day for this assault, the tone was that of sooner, rather than later, which is unsettling. Also, for your info, Ponta Delgada recently became a covert Allied intelligence node, a vital link in the U.S. Navy's high frequency direction finding network. As an aside, but relevant, this project was approved by Dr. Salazar in recognition of the value of ASW in Allied operations, planned and in progress. This node is providing significantly improved and critically rapid U-boat location data, preliminary to other sources. This data, in conjunction with high quality data provided by British sources, is resulting in ever greater success against the U-boats." Tony continued with essentially the same briefing given to FDR and Churchill, shaved and reshaped for this audience. After several questions were asked of Tony, he took his seat.

Admiral Leahy thanked Tony for his briefing, then skillfully guided conversations that produced a consensus paper on the Portuguese Islands for presentation to FDR and Churchill.

Following another short intermission discussion ensued on Item 5, Agreed Essentials in the Conduct of the War. The document, *C.C.S 232*, on this subject, previously distributed at the 85th meeting, was the basis for the discussion. The level of detail on this item, developed by each side, was impressive. Bringing the positions of each side into consensus took considerable deliberation.

Item 6, Agenda for the Remainder of the Conference, was dispatched with ease. At this point, 17 people left the conference, including Tony. Admiral Leahy wanted to discuss Item 7, Operation HUSKY, and Item 8, Operation UPKEEP, with only the principles present.

That Afternoon
Admiral Leahy's Office
The West Wing of the White House

Leahy's secretary summoned Tony to the Admiral's office. "Captain, come in," said Leahy. "I just returned from lunch and hoped to be able to speak with you before you left your office for the day."

"I was studying the documents regarding the Portuguese Islands," Tony said. "I'm trying to formulate a firm opinion about a best strategy, in my own mind. Like the other conferees, I see the quandary between peaceful and forceful occupation. They agree in principle about the absolute need for the Azores. But nobody wants to commit to taking the Azores by force."

"Correct,' said Leahy.

"Aside from the need to divert valuable forces for an assault and occupation, I don't think we want bad relations with the locals, or the Portuguese government, by using force."

"Agreed," said Leahy. "And?"

"The answer for successful negotiation lies solely in developing an incontrovertible assessment for Dr. Salazar regarding the reality of Germany's inability to commit forces to occupy Portugal," said Tony. "The intelligence summaries that Admiral Brown has been routing to me, had two items that are pertinent to the discussion. One is the surrender, four days ago, of the remaining 250,000 German and Italian troops in North Africa. That is very convincing evidence of the wisdom and success of our war plans. The second item, which may be difficult to share, but can be sanitized to hide the means, was yesterday's Operation UPKEEP dam busting raids by the RAF. The flooding they created put the Ruhr valley military and industrial factories out of business, probably for years. Those two items, in conjunction with the successes in bombing raids in Germany, should convince Dr. Salazar that Hitler is unable to mount a campaign into Spain and Portugal.

Leahy smiled, "I'll make sure those points are passed to the Pentagon J-2 staff. They are working on a point paper for Dr. Salazar, in conjunction with the State Department. Alright, Tony, I won't keep you from your pursuits any longer. I wanted to just say that, I wouldn't have put you in that position today if I didn't have confidence that you would be able to perform. It struck me that, at that point in time, certain things needed to be said, and you were the right person to say them. I received several complimentary comments during lunch."

"Thank you, Admiral. I appreciate those kind words. I didn't see anyone nod off," Tony said.

"Quite the contrary," said Leahy. "It helped to reinforce the importance of the broad strategic value of the Azores. You managed to change my mind from delaying negotiations to expeditious action so that operations are in place there, well before we begin the major thrust into the Mediterranean. We can't afford to lose any combatants or supply ships heading into the Med."

The meetings of the Combined Chiefs of Staff in the Federal Reserve Building adjourned for the final time on Monday, May 24th. The final of six TRIDENT meetings of the conference principals with the President and British Prime Minister, in the White House, occurred the following day. Tony attended all of those meetings. All that was behind him now. The task at hand was packing for the return to London.

26 – Lame Duck

6:55 a.m., Monday, May 31, 1943
Captain Taylor's Office
U.S. Embassy, London

C aptain Taylor left his desk to greet Tony, "Congratulations, let's sit over here where it's more comfortable."

"Thank you, Bill, I owe you," said Tony.

They shook hands vigorously then sat on the couch in the sitting area. A fresh carafe of coffee, cinnamon buns, napkins, cups and saucers were already in place.

"You owe me nothing, Tony. How's the time lag?"

"We spent all day yesterday napping and snacking. I feel fresh now. We were both anxious to get back to work today. We have a lot to do and the time will fly by, I'm sure," Tony said, pouring two cups of coffee.

"How are things in DC?" asked Taylor, then took a bite of pastry. Tony did the same. "How's Maria, by the way?"

"DC is no different these days. Lots of spoiled people there. They need a taste of London these days."

"No kidding! Sounds like you made a hit at the White House."

"Affirmative. Although I think Secretary Hull is lukewarm at best. But I'm sure you already know that," Tony said. They both laughed. "Maria is doing very well. She and Petra got along like blood sisters. They had a great time together. Maria showed her everything worth seeing in DC. I managed to get them a tour of the White House. Hopkins went a step further and got us into the Oval Office to meet FDR. They were ecstatic."

Taylor smiled. "That must have been a real treat for the girls. Oh, Evelyn told me you all came over for dinner. They had a terrific visit. Evelyn thinks Petra is the cat's whiskers, by the way. How was TRIDENT?"

"I learned so much my head hurts. I haven't had to pay much attention to the Pacific Theatre, until now. I certainly didn't need to concern myself with a high degree of detail about the entire European theatre, either. But Bill, I'm damn sure up to full speed on all of it now. It will come in handy back in DC."

Taylor topped off their cups, "I spoke with the President, Admiral Leahy and Harry Hopkins about what they planned to do with you. You're really well suited for that job. That elephant's mind of yours will amaze them. And Tony, that's a career move people would kill for."

"I know that. But the reason I took it was for the fun and challenge of it. Everything else about it is gravy," Tony said. "If I didn't think it was intellectually worth doing, I would have declined."

"I left my family in Baltimore for this job for the same reason, Tony. Oh, speaking of changes in jobs, your good friend Mike Nelson has been transferred from the Embassy staff and has gone to the OSS London headquarters on Grosvenor Street. I have a note on my desk for you. He left his phone number and asked me to have you call him."

"I'll sure do that. Any idea what he's up to?" asked Tony.

"He didn't say. By the way, I haven't told a single soul about your departure, aside from Ambassador Winant and Sharon Freedman. I told her ten minutes ago. Winant already knew. The President mentioned it to him the last meeting they had in DC. I asked him to keep a lid on it until we announced it. Which brings me to yet another change for you. Since you are a lame duck Naval Attaché, I'm reassigning you to my staff, effective immediately. That new man, Commander Clark Benning, made Captain last Friday. He doesn't know it yet, but I will move him into the Naval Attaché slot. You'll have a lot to arrange and you'll need some time to get it all squared away. Spend today getting moved to another office. After you tell your staff, let Sharon know. Sharon will then coordinate with your Admin Chief to get you relocated. The reason you didn't see Sharon out there when you arrived, is because she's checking out a vacant office we have across the hall. It's a really decent one, you won't be disappointed."

"Bill, I really thank you. I will need a lot of time to arrange things, instead of a big office and a big workload. Clark only came aboard two days before I left, so I don't know much about him. I'll spend a couple days with him, getting him up to speed. Somewhere downstream, Petra and I are going to take leave and go up to Ticknall, to visit her parents and her son. We are planning to take Ives to DC with us. We're also thinking about doing that formal affirmation of vows I mentioned a while back. Hopefully, we can get that done before we leave for the States."

"I will certainly want an invitation, Tony. So will Lady Watson, as you recall."

"Of course. By the way, do we have anything on paper, or a message, with my orders?" Tony asked. "I tried to arrange a household goods shipment of Petra's and her son's things from Ticknall. The Supply Officer told me that my wonderful diplomatic blanket orders cover just about everything, but not household goods."

"Negative. I haven't seen anything. Are you sure it was definite when you left?" asked Taylor.

"Affirmative. The President told me personally," Tony said. "But that was on the 8th of May. The call from the Supply Officer has me suspicious now. I have always had the policy that it's not official until there's ink on paper."

"I understand your angst, Tony. But I haven't heard anything about it from DC, one way or the other. Remember, that's DC and the level of bureaucracy is incredible. Good point though, about being over three weeks, given the short fuse involved. Want me to make some calls?"

"I don't know, Bill. I don't want to appear to doubt their word. But damn, there's only a month before reporting for work there. Without orders, I can't arrange for Petra's and Ives' travel either. I also don't want to make any arrangements, like The Dorchester, and Petra's job, for example, that can't be pulled back gracefully."

Taylor leaned back on the couch and closed his eyes for a few moments. "Alright, you have valid concerns. I will call the White House personnel office for an orders reference number that Supply can use for shipping household goods. That is absolutely not an insulting inquiry. I'll do it at 0830 their time today. OK?"

"Affirmative, thank you," replied Tony.

That Evening
Suite 701, The Dorchester Hotel

Tony left work earlier than usual. When Petra arrived, he was relaxing on the couch, in his skivvies, sipping red wine, listening to Mozart's "Violin Sonata No. 6," playing on the radio.

"Lovely piece, darling," she said, closing the door behind her. "I was unable to break free when you were ready to come home at half-four."

"I took advantage of a rare opportunity to get out of there early," he said, enjoying some hugs and kisses. "Go get comfortable and call the kitchen, pretty please. I'll pour you some wine."

"Brilliant, love. Give us a few minutes. Please open the windows, it's a tad stuffy." She returned later in a white cotton robe and handed him one. "I ordered for eight o'clock. I have news to discuss." She snuggled up to him on the couch and reached for her glass of wine on the coffee table. "Cheerio, love."

"Cheers! Tell me the news," he said.

"Right. First, my resignation won't be accepted, due to wartime freezes. But Sir David was appreciative. He said he was sure he could arrange to have me reassigned to our Washington Embassy. My duties would be determined by the Ambassador."

"Well that sounds like a reasonable solution."

She gave him a quizzical look, "But, love, Ives would be left alone with us both working."

"My guess is that working hours in the DC Embassy would be nothing like you've been seeing here. It would very likely be eight or nine to five. Or even part-time. But no matter, we can hire a nanny to bring him home from school and take care of him until we get home."

She looked at him for a moment, perplexed, "A nanny? Don't be daft."

"Petra, it's damn sure better than leaving him thousands of miles away in Ticknall, losing out on the love and influences of his mother," he said, emphatically.

She put her empty wine glass on the side table and hugged him. "Quite. I just, well, leaving the care of my son with a stranger..."

"Honey, in DC, we can find a highly qualified nanny with references. It will be fine. Plus, I expect to have a maid and a cook, as well, since we'll be busy during the day. It worked so well at Maria's. They will also be able to keep an eye on Ives, and the nanny, until we get home. Plus, if he doesn't like the nanny, we'll get another."

"It would be smashing to have him with us. OK, love, your turn. Give us your day."

The Next Day
10:45 a.m., Tuesday, June 1, 1943
Grosvenor Street, London

Tony left the Embassy on foot. He walked around the corner onto Grosvenor Street, eastbound, into a 55 F. breeze on a dreary overcast day. He thought about going back to get his bridge coat, but with only two and half blocks to walk, he kept going. A half block from 70 Grosvenor Street, he saw Mike Nelson exit a door and look in his direction. Nelson waved and waited.

"Welcome back, Tony," said Nelson as they shook hands.

"Likewise! I'm anxious to hear how things went with Fernando after we left the island," said Tony.

"Come in. We can talk. I also have somebody I want you to meet in a bit," said Nelson.

The entrance marked merely "70" was right off the sidewalk. Nelson faced the peep-hole in one of the two plain, but sturdy, windowless wooden doors. One was opened by a security officer. Inside was a reception area with a female Army corporal behind a counter. Also in the room, were three heavily armed Army soldiers. One tending the locked entrance door, the others on each side of the counter.

"Let's get you logged in for a visitor's badge, then we'll go upstairs to my office. She'll need to see your ID," Nelson said.

They took the stairs to the second floor and entered a door that was unlocked by Nelson pressing a sequence of numbers on a keypad mounted on the wall. Inside was an office with a secretary, that led to an inner office. Nelson made introductions and said to her, "Let 109 know we're in, please."

Nelson's office was modest and decorated with austerity and practicality in mind. It was very much Nelson. The walls were covered with maps of European countries. The end wall, opposite his desk, had a black roll-up screen that was pulled down to cover something sensitive. Nelson's large wooden L-desk had a clutter of classified documents, an in-basket, a lamp, a phone and a typewriter sitting on the L.

"Plant it, Tony. Pardon the low budget furnishings. I raided an Army warehouse for a few things I needed. OK, you said you were interested in an update on Ponta Delgada. Well, first, let me tell you how much Rossi and I appreciate your help there. I told Captain Taylor as much as I could about it and bragged you up. Fernando really is working out to be a great double. He's been doing everything to the T. He's a real gold mine. Oh, we decided to put Bruno's mind at ease. He's cooperating now also. That's about all I can tell you."

"Roger. Glad that worked out, Mike. So, my friend, you obviously have something to discuss, or we would have just met somewhere for lunch."

"Affirmative. Bill Taylor told me you took Petra to DC. How'd she like it?"

Just then a man came into Nelson's office in a sharp khaki Army uniform. Tony recognized "Wild Bill's" face from pictures he had seen.

"General, I'd like you to meet Captain Anthony Romella. Tony, this is Brigadier General William J. Donovan," said Nelson. "Let's move to the conference table, Tony."

Donovan and Tony shook hands with a strong, pumping grip and sat down at the conference table. Tony took note that the General was wearing only his four most senior decorations. The Medal of Honor ribbon sat conspicuously on top of the other three. The round wooden conference table clearly had prior heavy use, evidenced by a badly scratched surface. The barely padded wooden chairs looked likewise.

"Tony, I have read a lot about you," Donovan began. "It's a pleasure to meet you. Mike's, and Major Rossi's, reports on your work in London, France, Norway, Morocco and Azores made some good reading."

"Thank you, General. They were all jobs that fell into my lap," Tony said.

"Don't be so modest. I know natural operators when I see them, and you certainly are one of those. You got them because people knew who to give them to. Which is why I wanted to talk with you. As you are no doubt aware, OSS is expanding in DC,

London, Lisbon, Cairo, Lagos, Chungking, and elsewhere in the world. Finding grunts for field work isn't too difficult. But finding seasoned, capable leaders to manage operations is very difficult. I want you to be part of things here in London or DC, in particular, but anywhere else you choose. Not for field work, but at a higher level. We're embarking on some really interesting work. Would you like to be part of that?"

"I sure would, but there's a development that precludes it," Tony said. "I am being transferred in a few weeks to the White House. Otherwise, I'd have high interest in the OSS and many questions for you."

"Damn, Tony, I'm going to miss you here," Nelson said. "Petra going with you?"

"Yes, she is, and so is her son," Tony said.

"I got the word about that," said Donovan. "It created a little stir in the military intelligence organizations. Is that something you really want? I can talk to the President and possibly get that changed. You could come to work at my HQ in Washington, if that's where you want to go."

"I appreciate your offer, General. I really do. But I agreed to take that job because I was excited about it," Tony said.

"Congratulations, Tony," Nelson said.

"Donovan nodded sharply; his blue eyes locked with Tony's. "If at any time you want to make a change, just let me know. I will stay in touch with you in DC. Your intel role with the Map Room will involve working with my Research and Analysis Division. You'll be receiving unique intel products from us for the President. Once you're settled in DC, let's get together periodically."

"Roger that, sir" said Tony.

Donovan looked at his watch. "I have to go take care of something, but both of you please meet me in the lobby at noon for lunch."

"Damn, Tony, I was looking forward to having you as my boss," Nelson said, when Donovan departed. "That is what I am pretty sure was in store for you, running the Operations Division here. I've been kind of functioning in that role, but I hate it. I just want to operate, and we are cranking up here."

Tony laughed, "Sorry to disappoint you, Mike. It's too bad the timing was off."

That Afternoon
Tony's Office
U.S. Embassy, London

Tony sat down at his desk, picked up his phone and dialed. "I'm back in the office, Sharon," Tony said.

"We just took a phone message for you, Captain. Hold on, I'll get it and read it to you... OK, the message says, Mrs. Gertrude Parker of St. George's Church said that the only available date this month is Saturday, the 12th, and she would like you to return her call."

"Very well, thank you, Sharon."

He dialed Petra. "And this is Captain Anthony Romella," he said, smiling.

"Captain Romella, sir, how may I be of service?" she said cheerfully. He heard the Wren sitting nearby chuckle.

"Well, First Officer Romella, the church has the 12th available. Any reason we can't reserve it?"

"Perfect," she said. "I'll sort the days prior and post for leave. Ta, love, we'll talk tonight."

Tony immediately returned Mrs. Parker's call and reserved the Church for the 12th. He pulled a document from the top of his in-basket. It was a report on British Operation MINCEMEAT. A note attached to the front cover indicated Captain Taylor wanted all attachés to be aware of it, in case anything related to it, in any way, were to arise in conversations with Spanish military or political personnel. He flipped the cover over and began reading about this clever deception operation. The summary stated that the operation was designed to provide evidence that the Allies planned to invade Greece and Sardinia, and that leaked plans for invading Sicily were a deception. The summary stated that a British submarine dumped the unclaimed body of a derelict man, in Royal Marine uniform, off the Spanish coast on April 30th. The body was carrying bogus identification and a sealed pouch of bogus messages between two British generals. The body was discovered by a Spanish fisherman. Spanish officials shared the contents of the pouch with a German agent, who forwarded them to Abwehr officials in Berlin. On May 13th, Spanish officials advised the British that they had buried Royal Marine Major William Martin in the Cemetery of Solitude in Huelva, Spain. They also returned the seemingly untampered document pouch. However, decrypted German messages confirmed that the Abwehr had indeed received copies of the documents, and declared the information valid.

I have to file this away as a good idea for the future, he mused.

That Evening
Suite 701, The Dorchester Hotel

"Are we calling the kitchen, love?" Petra asked when they entered the suite.

"Yes, I think so. Let's get out of these uniforms."

"Right. When you called and said the church was available the 12th, I wanted to chat more, but I had someone waiting." She dialed the kitchen and ordered dinner in an hour.

"They only do them on a Saturday, and they only had one available, for several reasons," he said as they began to shed their clothes. "Maybe we should try and call your folks sooner than this Sunday."

"Yes, they will think it's a rush, as it is. Be right out, love, I need to sort some things. I'll meet you in the living room. Pour me a brandy," she said.

She brought their robes out to the living room and put them on the end of the couch, handy to get into when the waiter arrived with dinner. It was too warm for them to be worn until needed. They got settled into a snuggle on the couch, in their skivvies, big band music playing on the radio. They sipped their pre-dinner brandies while they caught up on the day.

"I visited Mike Nelson today at the OSS office on Grosvenor Street. I was surprised to find out that he had moved out of the Embassy," said Tony.

"If I didn't know you have to be in DC the first of the month, I'd be worried about him whisking you off to some lovely holiday," she said sarcastically.

Tony laughed. "Nothing like that. I met General Donovan over there."

"I knew he was in town. He always calls on Menzies and Hambro. Mind yourself, we think of him as a schemer, if I may say so," she said.

"Of course he is, honey. OSS is a mirror image of SOE. So there's going to be a lot of covert deals being made."

"How's Mike getting on?"

"Just fine. He's not happy managing operations, he wants to be in the field."

She looked at him with a raised eyebrow.

He smiled, "The General did offer me a job, essentially anywhere I wanted. But London and DC were his preference. I told him I was spoken for."

"Tempted, were we?"

"Can't say I wasn't. But I'm committed. He even said he could whisper in the President's ear and possibly get the orders changed to the OSS. I declined."

"Quite! Schemer, you see? What's his nickname? Wild man?" she asked.

"Wild Bill, from his World War One days."

"Right. Well I hope he doesn't mess about with your orders."

"Staying in London wouldn't be all that bad, would it?" he asked with a chuckle.

"Winding me up now, are we?"

"Just a bit, honey. No, we're going to DC and I'm going to the White House."

"Good! Back to the church ceremony. Mum will be thrilled. Dad, will too, yes, but he hates putting on a suit more than once a week for Sunday services."

Tony laughed. "He'll tough it out for this occasion, I'm sure."

"Did you talk with Reverend Williams?"

"No, Mrs. Parker. The Reverend is on holiday."

"Gertrude is a lovely lady. I've known her for years," she said. "We need to get cracking on invitations and a list." She looked at him with slight evidence of tears, "It will be wonderful for Ives to be with us. They must have wonderful schools there."

"We'll get him into a private school, where he'll get a damn good education. Speaking of Ives, do you think we should bring him back to London with us, or wait until closer to our departure?"

"He would be daft from boredom by the time one of us got home from work. He's used to being up early and doing chores. It would be lovely for me, but not for him, I fear."

"I suppose you're right. OK. We wait."

"Oh, Tony. Bloody hell, I can't imagine me running a household with a cook, maid and nanny. It will be such a vastly different life for me, and for Ives."

"You wouldn't be alone, honey. We'll be doing it all together, though. We'll interview help together. The main thing, as I have said before, is that Ives needs the love, influence and attention of his mother. We'll do what we must for his benefit."

She hugged him tightly. "My darling, crazy, Yank, you have turned my life topsy-turvy."

"For the better," he quickly added.

She giggled, "Quite! Yes, Tony, you're right. Just pray I won't go off my trolley."

27 – Home on the Farm

James Allan / Courancehill farm

11:30 a.m., Thursday, June 10, 1943
Western Outskirts of Ticknall
South Derbyshire, U.K.

Four hours of driving under a sky of thick gray clouds, and over 100 miles northwest of The Dorchester Hotel, the destination was in sight. Tony turned the Embassy sedan onto a long volcanic-gray dirt driveway to Petra's childhood home. At the far end of the driveway, the home and barns stood against a gentle green slope, rising to a stretch of forest, with a ridge beyond that. Sheep were scattered about, grazing in emerald green pastures on either side of the driveway. Tony looked over at Petra.

She was focused on the view ahead, tearing and smiling. "There's Dad leaving the barn. He's waving…and going to the house to tell Mum and Ives," Petra said.

The sedan was 30 yards from the house when Ives came bounding out of the house, off the porch and toward the car. Tony stopped when Ives neared. Petra got out and held her arms open and caught him up in a long swaying hug. Her mother and father waited patiently on the porch. Tony set the parking brake and walked around to Petra and Ives.

"Ives, this is Mr. Tony Romella," she said.

Ives raised his hand for a shake, "Finally I get to see you!" Then he hugged Tony.

"Yes, Ives, finally," said Tony, patting him on the back. "We get to talk eye to eye instead of by telephone. How are you, young man?"

"Good, sir," said Ives.

"Don't sir me, Ives," Tony said laughing, "why don't you just call me Tony."

"Right, Tony," Ives said with a big smile.

"Get in the car with us and show us where to park," Tony said.

Ives kneeled on the seat between Tony and Petra, with his hands on the dashboard. "Papa moved a tractor from the equipment barn for your car. That's the barn with no doors." He was pointing.

The farmhouse had a smaller cottage right behind it. Both had brightly whitewashed sides and thatched roofs. The driveway angled to the left to nearby barns.

"That's Grammy and Papa on the porch," said Ives. They waved as the sedan made a turn by the house and parked in the tractor barn.

"Come, let's go see Mum and Dad, the suitcases can wait," she said.

Ives walked to the porch between Tony and Petra, holding both their hands.

"Grammy, look who I have," Ives called out.

It was only a 15 yard walk to the porch. "Mum, Dad, I want you to meet Captain Anthony Romella. Tony, this is my Mum and Dad, Hazel and Nicholas Graham."

Tony hugged Hazel and then shook Nicholas's hand while giving him an upper arm grip. "I am so pleased to meet you both."

"Just call me Mum," she said, warmly.

She's five foot seven, I'd guess, and not more than five pounds too many, late 40s, he thought. I can see where Petra got her good looks. Hazel had red, but graying, curly hair and lively blue eyes.

"Prefer ya call me Nick," he said.

Five nine, trim and strong, about fifty, thought Tony. Nicholas had a full head of brown and gray curly hair, and a full trimmed beard. There were strong vibes of old school and hard knocks coming from Nick. Tony also was aware that, in Nicholas' mind, his suitability for his daughter had not been decided.

"Tony is fine for me."

"I don't have a funny name, just call me Ives." They all chuckled.

"OK, Ives, I will do that," said Tony. "Do you want a funny name?"

"Not right now, maybe when I'm older." They chuckled again.

"Come through," said Hazel. "I've got the kettle on for a cuppa and sandwiches."

"I want to sit between Mummy and Tony," said Ives excitedly.

"Get the stool then, Ives, too tight for a chair between," said Hazel.

The Graham's one-story farmhouse was everything Tony imagined. Plain, practical, comfortable. Wood floors, plaster walls, exposed beams in the ceiling. The kitchen was large. It had a big wood fired, four-burner stove for the winter, and an electric range with an oven. The focus of the room was a sturdily built dining table that could sit six comfortably. It was Nicholas' own hands that crafted the table and chairs, Tony learned from Ives. There was no need for a dining room. There was a small living room, but it probably got little use.

"Mummy," Ives said excitedly, tugging on Petra's sleeve, "Grammy opened up our house and cleaned it. She said I can sleep in my old room while you're here."

"Of course, Ives, that will be lovely," said Petra.

"Ives helped me, didn't you?" asked Hazel.

"Yes, and it was hard work, too," said Ives.

"Tony the cottage in back is where I lived before the war," explained Petra. "Two bedrooms, a bath, kitchen and living room."

"Grammy is going to make an early 10 years birthday cake for me, while you're here. Because I won't be here next month," Ives said. "You can help her, Mummy."

"Right. We'll have jolly good time, Ives," said Petra.

Lunch consisted of cucumber, cheese and dill sandwiches, also butter, tomato and sliced onion sandwiches. The latter was Nicholas' favorite, which Tony liked as well. There was tea too, of course, and plenty of chatter between Petra, Hazel and Ives. Questions about life in America dominated most of the conversation. Petra did her best to bring her father into the banter, but he was content to listen and observe.

"Hazel…Mum, I hope you're not offended or disappointed that I arranged for the Wheel Inn on Main Street to do the reception after the ceremony," said Tony.

"Don't give it a thought, Tony, it will be brilliant. Relieves me of all the troubles," said Hazel. "People can't come all the way out here for that anyway. How many do you expect to come up from London?"

"Just two or three. But we thought that with the short notice, rationing, and all…" said Tony.

Hazel interrupted him, "Quite so, no worries."

"Will cost ye some pounds," said Nicholas.

"Yes, but I'm happy to do it for this special occasion," Tony said.

Nicholas nodded. "Shall we lug the cases, Tony?" he asked, rising from the table.

"Sure," said Tony, and followed Nicholas out the door.

"Ye seem a fine and able bloke, Yank that ye may be," said Nicholas with what Tony took to be a congenial tone as they walked to the barn. "Taking me only child and grandson across the big pond, yeah? What will ye do about it if she wants to come back?"

"If she wants to come back, then I'll see that she does. But when the war is over, we expect to settle here in the area, somewhere. Nick, she's the most wonderful woman I've ever known, except for my mother. I thank you and Hazel for her. Rest assured, I'll take good care of her."

Nicholas was quiet for a few moments. "Mum cleaned the cottage and aired it out. Been empty since Petra left for the service."

"I'm sure it will be just fine, Nick. Listen, I brought some old work uniform shirts, trousers and boondockers. If I can help you with anything while I'm here, let me know. I'm happy to give you a hand."

"Right. Always plenty of work, every day. I have 213 sheep, pastures, and patches of vegetables," said Nicholas. "Ever do any farm work?"

"A little farming, horses, lumberjacking, sawmill…plenty of hard work in my early days," Tony said.

"Right. Mum gives the kettle a go at five. Then she makes me two fried eggs and plenty buttered bread to get me day off. Just come through. I'll feed ye, then put ye to work. If you're not in the kitchen by 10 past, ye might just as well stay in bed."

"Five it is then, Nick. I look forward to it. Hard work is good for the soul," Tony said.

"Aye, lad, aye," said Nicholas.

28 – Amen

Saint George Church, Ticknall, South Derbyshire

2:00 p.m., Saturday, June 12, 1943
Church of Saint George
Ticknall, South Derbyshire, UK

Nicholas did as he promised. He gave Tony plenty of hard work, which they accomplished side by side. Ives tagged along often, doing what he could as well. Tony and Nicholas sat on rocking chairs on the porch after the evening meals, talking about farming, the war, and the future. They were now very fond of each other. Today, Nicholas had no reservations about his daughter's choice of a husband.

Saint George's, of the Church of England, was consecrated in 1842. A magnificent sight, it was constructed in Perpendicular Gothic style with sandstone ashlar and had slate roofs. They arrived early enough for Petra to show Tony the remnants of the old chapel that dated back to circa 1200.

Tony and Petra were sitting in the front row, in their dress blues, with her mother, father and son. A bright blue sky day made the several surrounding tall stained glass windows glow majestically. The chiming of the church bells brought villagers in to observe the ceremony as well. Each time Tony turned to look back through the 100 year old pews, there were more people filling the bride's side. Petra and her parents were well known, having lived on Church Lane with her parents until she was six. The Grahams then purchased the sheep farm and moved. But they remained parishioners here. Thus, the word of today's ceremony had spread through the village. On the groom's side of the pews there was Captain Taylor, Lady Inga Watson and Mike Nelson. Behind them, half of the groom's side was filled with overflow from the bride's side. The village eagerly turned out to witness this celebration.

The magnificent 1869 pipe organ stopped playing at 2:05. Reverend Percy Williams came to the center aisle at the front row of pews. "Good afternoon!" he bellowed. When the chatter and whispering stopped, he continued, "I want to welcome the Graham family here today. Nicholas and Hazel Graham have been parishioners since their marriage in this church. They bring us their daughter, Petra, who was baptized here, and her husband Captain Anthony Romella, for a Thanksgiving for Marriage ceremony. This is a modified form of the marriage ceremony, which you may not have witnessed previously. You see, Captain Anthony Romella and First Officer Petra Wilkinson nee Graham were married last December 13th, in a private ceremony in the American Embassy chapel in London, by military chaplains. They wish now to reaffirm those vows in this church which has great meaning to the Graham family." He took a deep breath, opened a book in his hands and began to read from it. "The grace of our Lord Jesus Christ, the love of God, and the fellowship of the Holy Spirit be with you…"

Prayers were read, hymns were sung, and bible passages were read. Tony and Petra now stood in front of the congregation, facing each other, smiling joyfully. Nicholas, Hazel and Ives were standing with them, facing the Reverend.

Reverend Williams' deep voice carried throughout the nave as he read with great feeling. "We have come together in the presence of God to give thanks with Anthony and Petra for these months of married life, to rejoice together and to ask for God's blessing…" When he completed the ceremonial passages, they reaffirmed their vows. The rings were presented by Ives to the Reverend for blessing. Tony and Petra slipped them back onto each other's fingers and the ceremonial kisses were exchanged. After the Lord's Prayer was recited by all, the Reverend proclaimed, "God, the Holy Trinity, make you strong in faith and love, defend you on every side, and guide you in truth and peace; and the blessing of God almighty, the Father, the Son, and the Holy Spirit, be among you and remain with you always. Amen!"

A resounding "Amen," from the congregation ended the ceremony. Villagers formed in the center aisle for their turn to congratulate the Romellas and Grahams. Many hugs and handshakes ensued, as well as plenty of joyous tears. When the last of the villagers departed the church, Taylor, Nelson, and Lady Watson approached the couple to congratulate them and meet Petra's family.

"Absolutely lovely. It was brilliant," Lady Watson said to Petra. "I was quite pleased when your invitation arrived."

"This was nice. But where's the beer and food?" asked Nelson jokingly. Tony poked him in the shoulder.

"All the very, very best to you both," said Taylor.

"Thank you all for coming the distance. I really mean it," said Tony. "Now let's go see what the Inn has to offer."

They all departed St. George's and walked up Church Lane to the Wheel Inn on Main Street.

Stuart Woodward Esq. Collection, Ticknall

The Wheel Inn, Ticknall

The Romellas graciously hosted not merely those on their guest list, but a good many of the Ticknall villagers. They formed a line outside after the pub in the inn filled to capacity. It was an orderly, albeit raucous, affair. People came in, greeted the Captain and Petra, had a pint and a sandwich, and departed to make room for those waiting outside. The beer, sandwiches, villagers and joyful noises flowed freely until the proprietor yelled, "Half four! Knees up is over. Thanks be to the Captain."

Tony settled his bill with the proprietor, then escorted his party to the sedan which he had parked on a nearby side street.

As Tony pulled away for the drive back to the farm, Nicholas leaned forward from the back seat and tapped Tony on the shoulder. "Ye a mint Yank man, feeding and watering the whole of Ticknall." He laughed and sat back.

Petra and Hazel joined in the laugh. "Aye, Dad, that he is!" said Petra.

"I'm a hell of a lot lighter now than I was when I walked into that inn," Tony jested.

29 – Change in Plans

7:45 a.m., Monday, June 14, 1943
Tony's Office, U.S. Embassy

Tony entered his office and sat down at his desk. The delight of the previous weekend in Ticknall still meandered through his mind. He and Petra talked about it again during the taxi ride from the hotel to her office door on St. James Street. About the emotions they experienced during the ceremony. About the warm feelings of a cohesive family. About Ives' obvious joy with their presence and sadness with their departure. But it was time to knuckle down and get back to work. He glanced at the full in-basket, sipped on a mug of coffee, just delivered by his Yeoman, and scanned his calendar. The 14th! Good grief! Do I have orders in this basket? A thorough search of the basket and the morning message folder found none. Checking with his Admin Chief was also negative. Damn it, I shouldn't have let this go so long. He dialed Captain Taylor's number.

"Good morning, Sharon...Please pass a message to Captain Taylor...OK, when he returns, just tell him I said that I don't see any orders in my basket...Thank you."

That Afternoon
1:45 p.m.

"Go straight in, Captain. I'm glad I caught you in your office." Sharon said to Tony. "He's on the phone but wants you to go in and sit by his desk."

"Tony just came into the office," said Taylor. "Harry, I understand... OK...alright, here he is."

"It's Harry Hopkins," said Taylor, as he handed the phone to Tony.

"Hello Harry, this is Tony."

"Good afternoon, Tony," said Hopkins. After a deep breath, he continued, "I wish there was a better way to tell you this, but there's been a change in plans. The short version is that the President had to make a tough decision, not 15 minutes ago. The word of the new position spread like wildfire. The House Armed Services Committee Chairman called on the President and offered an alternative candidate that happens to be his son in law. He's a senior Navy Captain in the intelligence community. His selection for the job will be announced this afternoon. We so regret this, Tony."

"I appreciate your call, Harry. I am honored that I was considered for the job," said Tony with a calm voice, but a churning gut.

"The President, Admiral Leahy and Admiral Brown wanted me to express their sincere apologies," said Hopkins. "The politics were just too powerful. We have to pick our fights. But you will not be forgotten, Tony."

"Thank you for those kind words. Please give the President and the Admirals my very best regards. Again, Harry, thank you for telling me personally." He put the phone back on the cradle.

"Let's talk," said Taylor.

"Politics are a son of a bitch, Bill. They have a way of creeping into things that have any type of value, especially money, power and status."

"I know. Harry explained the situation and apologized to me as well."

"Damn it, Bill. I really wanted that job. I suppose it was just not to be. What a dog's dinner, to borrow a local phrase."

"Wish we could have found out before I had Captain Benning relieve you," Taylor said. He leaned back, then rotated his chair around to pick a pipe from the rotating rack and fired it up. It gave him time to think.

"Ah, the Kodiak bear head pipe, good choice, boss. I think the face on that thing is so ferocious. We're dealing with a bear of a situation, which I'm finding hard to bear."

"You had to do that, didn't you," Taylor said with a groan.

"Sorry. Couldn't resist. Well, relatively on this subject. I had an interesting lunch a couple of weeks ago. I was going to tell you about it next time we talked. This is that time." Tony gave Taylor the substance of the conversation with General Donovan.

"What's your feeling about all that right now?" asked Taylor.

"I have to say, just being truthful, I'd be hard pressed to turn it down."

"You do know General Donovan probably has only one friend in the White House, the President, right, Tony?"

"I've heard there's some consternation among the military and State Department intel organizations with the creation of OSS. Major rice bowl issues. The old story," said Tony.

"Yep. Secretary Hull has no time for him, either," Taylor said.

"I think Wild Bill and I have that in common," Tony said, smiling.

"J. Edgar Hoover hates him. He's suspicious of him. Allegedly he's got the FBI watching Donovan like a hawk. There's a funny story about all that. The FBI was routinely entering the DC Spanish Embassy, in the dead of night, copying documents. One night, some FBI agents caught some of Donovan's men doing the same thing. Hoover and Donovan got into a damn big pissing contest on who can operate on U.S. soil."

"Let me guess, Bill, Donovan didn't back down."

"Not at all. It went downhill from there. All that aside, what I was about to say is, when they put the OSS under the Joint Chiefs of Staff, it was at the objection of the Pentagon in general, and the military intelligence organizations, specifically. Even OP-20-G is fearful of the OSS robbing War Department money they sorely need."

"Are you trying to say something, Bill?"

"I just want you to know the politics involved with the OSS, Tony."

"Well, I wouldn't volunteer for the OSS HQ in DC. I'd choose London. All that crap would most likely never seep down to me here."

"Oh, I don't know. Even though you would be here in London, it would probably put you in somebody's crosshairs by reason of association. I have to say, though, Donovan's got some really high level friends here in London. All the way up from the MIs, to 10 Downing Street, my God, even to Buckingham Palace."

"I'll have to think hard about this situation," Tony said. "Really hard."

"Don't forget that SOE put in a bid for you."

"Oh I haven't forgotten that, Bill."

"While we're talking about MI6, Tony, a little bird told me that their Chief, Sir Stewart Menzies, told Donovan not to conduct operations anywhere in the United Kingdom."

"I guess the term, operations, begs definition. My guess is that he meant, with British citizens as targets. But if Sir Stewart feels that way, I'd have to take a careful approach to talk with SOE about joint ops with OSS," said Tony. "Maybe I should have a chat with Langsdale. He would be honest about the situation."

"I have to ask. What's your inclination right now, Tony?"

"I think I'd like to hear your plan for me, before I answer."

"Right now, unless something comes up to change my mind, I'm happy to keep you right where you're at. My right hand man," said Taylor. "I would formally establish the position of Deputy, Defense Attaché. That way you could take on some of my responsibilities and workload. I'm just not going to jerk Benning out of your old chair. Wouldn't be right."

"Concur with that, boss. That sounds like a great proposal."

"If you'd like to take Petra and Ives to DC, you could always go back to OP-20-G."

"That's crossed my mind," Tony said.

"Look, Tony, my good friend, I would love to have you on staff. But your situation being what it is, whatever you decide to do, I will happily respect and support."

Tony returned to his office, slumped into his chair, crossed himself and closed his eyes. God, I hope you've given me the wisdom I need for this one. He sat forward, put his forehead down on his arms. One thing's for sure, I know Petra would want to stay in London. Who do I call, Bill Taylor, Ed Langsdale, or Mike Nelson? Minutes passed. Damn it, I never had such a difficult time making a decision.

Several moments of deep thought were interrupted when his phone rang.

***

Peter J. Azzole

GLOSSARY

Abwehr German military intelligence organization: espionage, human intelligence, counterespionage, etc.

Admiralty British Royal Naval Headquarters

Auxiliary Territorial Service (ATS) The women's branch of the British Army during the Second World War. It was formed on 9 September 1938, initially as a women's voluntary service, and existed until 1 February 1949, when it was merged into the Women's Royal Army Corps.

B-Dienst (German: Beobachtungs dienst) (English: observation service) A department of the German Navy Intelligence Service. Primarily tasked with radio intelligence (COMINT) operations.

Biggin Hill RAF Station: one of the principal fighter bases protecting London and South East England from attack by German Luftwaffe bombers.

Bimble a leisurely walk (British slang)

Bletchley Park aka cover name Government Code and Cypher School (GC&CS); British center for communications intelligence operations, famous for deciphering German Enigma messages, et al.

BP Frequently used acronym for Bletchley Park.

BZ Also referred to as "Baker Zebra" (in WWII phonetics). In naval signaling, typically conveyed by flag hoist aboard ship or other communications, meaning "Well Done"

C-47 The Douglas C-47 Skytrain is a twin-engine military transport aircraft developed from the civilian Douglas DC-3 airliner.

Callsign Sequence of alpha-numeric characters that identify the sending or receiving station in telecommunications of various methodology.

CBs (See SeaBees)

ASSIGNMENT: CASABLANCA

CI   (see Counter-Intelligence)

Cipher/Cypher   Generally, a character for character encrypted plain text. Ci/Cy variants are U.S./U.K. differences in spelling.

Code   Generally, a group of 1 to n alpha-numeric characters which has a specific plain text meaning each time it is used, e.g. A27 might mean, "commence firing" usually derived from a code book or other reference material.

COMINT   Communications Intelligence; the exploitation of communications systems.

Combined Operations HQ A department of the British War Office set up during WWII to harass the Germans on the European continent by means of raids carried out by use of combined naval and army forces.

Counter-intelligence   Information or activities related to the protection of a country against an opposition's total range of intelligence activities.

CRM   Abbreviation for U.S. Navy Chief (Petty Officer) Radioman.

Cryptology   Broad field of operations that produce communications intelligence (COMINT) and electronic intelligence (ELINT). This involves, but is not limited to, generating strategic and tactical top secret intelligence through analysis and exploitation of all forms of electronic signals.

Cumshaw   Slang Navy term alleged to originate in the British Navy, possibly as early as 1839, during their visits to Chinese ports. It is derived from the Chinese Xiamen dialect word for grateful thanks.

Darlan   French Admiral of the Fleet Jean Louis Xavier François Darlan was a military and political figure. He was Admiral of the Fleet and Chief of Staff of the French Navy in 1939 at the beginning of World War II. After the French armistice with Nazi Germany in 1940, Darlan served in the pro-German Vichy regime. When the Allies invaded French North Africa in 1942, he was the highest-ranking officer there, and a deal was made, giving him control of North African French forces in exchange for joining their side. Less than two months later he was assassinated.

D-Day   Military plans are developed often without the benefit of knowing the exact year(Y), month(M), day(D), hour(H), minute(M) or second(S) that the plan and its elements will be implemented. All elements of the plan's timeline are thus easily scaled from the establishment of the base moment. For example, an attack on an objective would be assigned the base timeline position of zero for YMDHMS. A preparatory activity scheduled 24 hours prior would be assigned, D-1. A post-attack activity planned one hour after attack commencement would be assigned the timeline position of D0, H+1.

DF	Direction finding/finder; measurement of a single line of magnetic bearing from a known location (DF site); intersection of lines of bearing from different DF sites determine the location of the signal transmitter.
DF Fix	Geographic location determined by multiple intersecting DF bearings. Consists of a latitude and longitude, plus a radius about it, in which 90% probability of actual location is calculated.
DG	Director General (MI-5, but not limited thereto)
Donovan	William Joseph Donovan was an American soldier, lawyer, intelligence officer and diplomat, best known for serving as the head of the Office of Strategic Services (OSS), the precursor to the Central Intelligence Agency, during World War II.
ECM	The Electric Code Machine (ECM) Mark II was a rotor machine used by the United States from WWII until the 1950s. The machine was also known as the SIGABA or Converter M-134 by the Army, or CSP-888/889 by the Navy, and a modified Navy version was termed the CSP-2900.
Eddy	William Alfred "Bill" Eddy, Ph.D., Col., USMC, was a university professor and college president (1936–1942); U.S. Marine Corps officer, serving in World War II; as a U.S. intelligence officer.
Enigma	Electromechanical rotor-based enciphering machine adapted and modified for military use by the Germans from a commercial version of the era.
ETA, ETD	Estimated Time of Arrival/Departure
Eyes Only	A category of message restricted for viewing only by the person(s) specified
Field Day	U.S. Navy term for extensive cleanup of an area.
General Service	A general categorization of all Navy persons, organizations or activities other than those of Navy Signal Intelligence.
Gestapo	An abbreviation of Geheime Staatspolizei, or the Secret State Police, was the official secret police of Nazi Germany and German-occupied Europe. During WWII, the Gestapo played a key role in the Nazi plan to exterminate the Jews of Europe.
Giraud	French General Henri Honoré Giraud was a leader of the Free French Forces during the Second World War. From within Vichy France he worked with the Allies in secret and assumed command of French troops in North Africa after Operation Torch (November 1942) following the assassination of François Darlan. In January 1943, he took part in the Casablanca Conference along with Charles de Gaulle, Winston Churchill

and Franklin D. Roosevelt. Later in the same year, Giraud and de Gaulle became co-presidents of the French Committee of National Liberation, but their continual disagreements forced his retirement in 1944.

Hambro   British Air Commodore Sir Charles Jocelyn Hambro worked in various positions in the SOE (Special Operations Executive) during WWII and became head of the SOE in 1942. In 1943 through the rest of the war he acted as head of the "British raw materials mission" in Washington; a cover for exchanging information and technology between Britain and the United States which led to the detonation of the first Atomic Bomb as part of the Manhattan Project.

Heavy Water   Deuterium oxide is the isotopic compound of hydrogen of mass 2 with oxygen. It is was valued by the early atomic bomb experimenters for researching reactions.

HF Band   High frequency (HF) is the ITU designation for the range of radio frequency electromagnetic waves (radio waves) between 3 and 30 megahertz (MHz). Its wavelengths range from one to ten decameters (ten to one hundred meters).

HFDF   High frequency (aka short-wave) direction finding/finder

Hopkins   Harry Lloyd Hopkins, the 8th Secretary of Commerce, and President Franklin Delano Roosevelt's closest advisor on foreign policy during World War II. He was one of the architects of the New Deal, especially the relief programs of the Works Progress Administration (WPA), which he directed and built into the largest employer in the country. In World War II, he was Roosevelt's chief diplomatic troubleshooter and liaison with Winston Churchill and Joseph Stalin. He supervised the $50 billion Lend Lease program of military aid to the Allies.

HUMINT   Human Intelligence; information obtained from human sources (spy, interrogation, etc.).

HUSKY   (See Operation HUSKY)

Illicit Communications   In this context, communication between entities engaged in activities considered spying or espionage.

Kilometer   One mile = 1.6 kilometers.
One kilometer = 1,094 yards or 0.6 miles.
One meter = 0.9 yards.

MAIN NAVY   The building that housed the Navy's high command until after WWII, located off Constitution Avenue, in Washington DC, with a primary entrance facing 18th Street. Notable among the occupants were the offices of the Secretary of the Navy, the Chief of Naval Operations and their staffs, and pertinent to this novel, OP-20-G.

MI5	British domestic counter-intelligence agency
MI6	British agency that collects foreign intelligence aka SIS (Secret Intelligence Service)
Minox©	Minox is a trade name of cameras, known especially for subminiature design. The first product to carry the Minox name was a subminiature camera, conceived in 1922, and finally invented and produced in 1936, by Baltic German Walter Zapp. The Latvian factory VEF (Valsts elektrotehniskā fabrika) manufactured the camera from 1937 to 1943.
MOD	British Ministry of Defense, London
NKGB	(Russian: Народный комиссариат государственной безопасности) Peoples Commissariat for State Security; conducted a wide range of intelligence and espionage activities, both offensive and counter. AKA "KGB."
NOB	Naval Operating Base
Noguès	French General Charles Noguès served as Resident-General in Morocco and Commander-in-Chief in French North Africa during WWII.
O-1,2,3,4…	U.S. military commissioned officer paygrades, 1 being lowest.
OCS	Officer's Candidate School, primarily for college graduates entering the Navy as officers.
OP-20-G	Office of Chief of Naval Operations (OPNAV), 20th Division, the Office of Naval Communications, G Section/Communications Security; the unclassified title of the U.S. Navy's signals intelligence and cryptanalysis headquarters during World War II. It was located on the top floor of the Main Navy Building, Constitution Avenue, Washington, DC, until it moved to 3801 Nebraska Avenue, NW, DC in February 1943.
One-time-pad	An encryption technique that cannot be cracked but requires the use of a one-time pre-shared key the same size as, or longer than, the message being sent. In this technique, a plaintext is paired with a random secret key (also referred to as a one-time pad). Then, each bit or character of the plaintext is encrypted by combining it with the corresponding bit or character from the pad using modular addition. If the key is truly random, is at least as long as the plaintext, is never reused in whole or in part, and is kept completely secret, then the resulting ciphertext will be impossible to decrypt.
OpCen	British Admiralty Operations Center, London
Operation HUSKY	The Allied invasion of Sicily, codenamed Operation HUSKY, was a major campaign of World War II, in which the Allies took the island of Sicily from the Axis powers. It began with a large amphibious

and airborne operation, followed by a six-week land campaign, and initiated the Italian Campaign.

Operation TORCH — Operation Torch (8–16 November 1942) was an Anglo–American invasion of French North Africa during the Second World War. It was aimed at reducing pressure on Allied forces in Egypt and enabling an invasion of Southern Europe. It also provided the 'second front' which the Soviet Union had been requesting since it was invaded by the Germans in 1941. The region was dominated by the Vichy French, officially in collaboration with Germany, but with mixed loyalties, and reports indicated that they might support the Allied initiative. General Dwight D. Eisenhower planned a three-pronged attack, aimed at Casablanca (Western), Oran (Center) and Algiers (Eastern), in advance of a rapid move on Tunis.

OSS — Office of Strategic Services (forerunner of the CIA)

PHOTINT — Photographic Intelligence

QSL — Morse communications signal meaning "I receipt for..."

Quarterdeck — The main ceremonial and reception area on board a ship or station. The term is derived from the raised deck behind the main mast of a sailing ship. Traditionally it was where the captain commanded his vessel and where the ship's colors were kept. This led to its use as the main ceremonial and reception area on board.

RI, Radio Intercept — The term for copying/intercepting radio communications between two entities, without their knowledge.

RM(1,2,3) — Navy Rating abbreviation for Radiomen, followed by a number indicating their Petty Officer rate (paygrade).

Roosevelt, Elliott — American aviation official and wartime officer in the United States Army Air Forces. He was a son of President Franklin D. Roosevelt and First Lady Eleanor Roosevelt.

Roosevelt, Franklin Jr. — Served as an officer in the United States Navy during World War. He was the son of President Franklin D. Roosevelt and First Lady Eleanor Roosevelt.

H. Earle Russel — Joined the State Department in 1916 and worked with them until his retirement in 1950. He served in various capacities in several countries, especially as Consul General in Morocco during World War II, and received the Medal of Freedom from the War Department.

Salazar, Dr. — António de Oliveira Salazar GCTE GCSE GColIH GCIC was a Portuguese statesman who served as Prime Minister of Portugal from 1932 to 1968. A trained economist, Salazar entered public life with the support of President Óscar Carmona after the Portuguese coup d'état of 28 May 1926, initially as finance minister and later as prime minister. Opposed to democracy, communism, socialism, anarchism and liberalism, Salazar's rule was conservative and nationalist in nature. Salazar distanced himself from fascism and Nazism, which he criticized as a "pagan Caesarism" that recognized neither legal nor moral limits. [https://en.wikipedia.org/wiki/António_de_Oliveira_Salazar]

Scuttlebutt	A common Navy slang meaning gossip, idle chatter.
SeaBees	Popularized term for CBs (Navy Construction Battalions)
SHAEF	Supreme Headquarters Allied Expeditionary Force was the headquarters of the Commander of Allied forces in north west Europe, from (officially) late 1943 until the end of World War II. U.S. General Dwight D. Eisenhower was the commander of SHAEF throughout its existence.
Ship's Company	Those personnel permanently assigned to a ship or shore station.
SIGABA	(See ECM)
SIS	(see MI-6)
Skinny	Slang for information.
Smoke Test	Navy humorous jargon; plug it in and see if it smokes.
SOE	(Special Operations Executive) A British World War II organization. Following Cabinet approval, it was officially formed on 22 July 1940, to conduct espionage, sabotage and reconnaissance against the Axis powers, and to aid local resistance movements.
SOL Militia	The Service d'ordre légionnaire (SOL, "Legionary Order Service") was a collaborationist militia created by Joseph Darnand, a far right veteran from the First World War. Too radical even for other supporters of the Vichy regime, it was granted its independence in January 1943, after Operation Torch and the German occupation of the South Zone, until then dubbed "Free Zone" and controlled by Vichy. Pierre Laval himself (supported by Marshal Philippe Pétain) passed the law which accorded the SOL its independence and transformed it into the Milice, which participated in battles alongside the Nazis against the Resistance and committed numerous war crimes against civilians. After the Liberation, some members of the Milice escaped to Germany, where they joined the ranks of the SS. Those who stayed behind in France faced either drumhead courts-martial, generally followed by summary execution, or simple lynching at the hands of résistants and enraged civilians.
SS	The Schutzstaffel (SS), also stylized as "ᛋᛋ," translated literally to "Protection Squadron," was a major paramilitary organization under Adolf

Hitler and the Nazi Party (NSDAP) in Nazi Germany, and later throughout German-occupied Europe during World War II. From 1929 until the regime's collapse in 1945, the SS was the foremost agency of security, surveillance, and terror within Germany and German-occupied Europe.

STEN (gun) The STEN (or Sten gun) was a family of British submachine guns, used extensively by British and Commonwealth forces throughout World War II.

Strip Cipher The U.S. Armed forces made extensive use of the strip ciphers from the 1930's through WWII. The true strip cipher device used was the M-138, which used alphabet paper strips. This consisted of an aluminum frame (or later wooden/plastic) with room for 25 or 30 paper strips. Each strip had a random alphabet. The daily key specified the strips to be inserted and the order that they were to be inserted in. The plaintext was written vertically at the first column by rearranging the strips. Then another column was selected to provide the ciphertext.

SYMBOL The Casablanca Conference (codenamed SYMBOL) was held at the Anfa Hotel in Casablanca, Morocco, from January 14 to 24, 1943, to plan the Allied European strategy for the next phase of World War II. In attendance were United States President Franklin D. Roosevelt and British prime minister Winston Churchill. Also attending and representing the Free French forces were Generals Charles de Gaulle and Henri Giraud, though they played minor roles and were not part of the military planning. Premier Joseph Stalin had declined to attend, citing the ongoing Battle of Stalingrad as requiring his presence in the Soviet Union. The conference agenda addressed the specifics of tactical procedure, allocation of resources, and the broader issues of diplomatic policy. The debate and negotiations produced what was known as the Casablanca Declaration, and perhaps its most historically provocative statement of purpose, "unconditional surrender". The doctrine of "unconditional surrender" came to represent the unified voice of implacable Allied will—the determination that the Axis powers would be fought to their ultimate defeat.

TAD Temporary Additional Duty

TORCH (See Operation TORCH)

Transceiver Radio equipment designed to both transmit and receive.

TRIDENT The Third Washington Conference (codenamed TRIDENT) was held in Washington, D.C from May 12 to May 25, 1943. It was a World War II strategic meeting between the heads of government of the United Kingdom and the United States. It was the third conference of the 20th century (1941, 1942, 1943), but the second conference that took place during the US involvement in the Second World War. The delegations were headed by Winston Churchill and Franklin D. Roosevelt, respectively. The plans for the Allied invasion of Sicily, extent of military force, the date for invading Normandy, and the progress of The Pacific War were discussed.

ULTRA   A Top Secret (U.K. Most Secret) information classification compartment originally created by the U.K. and subsequently shared with and adopted by the U.S. This was used to identify information gleaned from decrypted enemy communications considered operationally or strategically important. It was reported to a very restricted list of high level tactical, strategic or policy officials pertinent to the specific information.

WAVE   (Women Accepted for Volunteer Emergency Service), was the women's branch of the United States Naval Reserve during World War II. It was established on July 21, 1942 by the U.S. Congress and signed into law by President Franklin D. Roosevelt on July 30.

Very Well   U.S. Navy phrase, used by a senior to acknowledge a statement, advisory or report from a junior.

Vichy   Vichy France is the common name of the French State headed by Marshal Philippe Pétain during World War II. Evacuated from Paris to the city of Vichy in the unoccupied "Free Zone" in the southern part of metropolitan France which included French Algeria, it remained responsible for the civil administration of France as well as the French colonial empire. From 1940 to 1942, while the Vichy regime was the nominal government of all of France except for Alsace-Lorraine, the Germans and Italians militarily occupied northern and south-eastern France. While Paris remained the de jure capital of France, the government chose to relocate to the town of Vichy, 360 km (220 mi) to the south in the zone libre, which thus became the de facto capital of the French State. Following the Allied landings in French North Africa in November 1942, southern France was also militarily occupied by Germany and Italy to protect the Mediterranean coastline. Petain's government remained in Vichy as the nominal government of France, albeit one that collaborated with Nazi Germany from November 1942 onwards. The government at Vichy remained there until late 1944, when it lost its de facto authority due to the Allied invasion of France and the government was compelled to relocate to the Sigmaringen enclave in Germany, where it continued to exist on paper until the end of hostilities in Europe.

Winant   John Gilbert Winant served, among other places, as the U.S. Ambassador to the United Kingdom, in London, from March 1941 through April 1946.

Wolfpack   German U-boat force tactic of operating a group of two or more submarines as a coordinated force to inflict more massive damage to assigned targets and to both confuse and disperse responding antisubmarine efforts.

Wren   Nickname for WRNS (Women in the Royal Navy Service). The WRNS was the women's branch of the United Kingdom's Royal Navy. First formed in 1917 for the First World War, it was disbanded in 1919, then revived in 1939 at the beginning of the Second World War, remaining active until integrated into the Royal Navy in 1993.

Yeoman   An enlisted clerical rating in the U.S. Navy.

Y Station   British communications intercept station.

- - -

ABOUT THE AUTHOR

Peter J. Azzole, a retired US Navy Officer, served 20 years of active duty as a cryptology specialist. His career encompassed many aspects of communications intelligence abroad, afloat and in the United Sates. Peter currently resides in New Bern, NC.